THE

EARTH HUMS IN B FLAT

THE

EARTH HUMS IN B FLAT

MARI STRACHAN

CANONGATE

Edinburgh · London · New York · Melbourne

First published in Great Britain in 2009 by
Canongate Books Ltd., Edinburgh, Scotland

Printed in the United States of America

FIRST AMERICAN EDITION

ISBN-13: 978-1-84767-192-9

Canongate
841 Broadway
New York, NY 10003
Distributed by Publishers Group West
www.groveatlantic.com

09 10 11 12   10 9 8 7 6 5 4 3 2 1

I

Tirion Gwyn, Sawel Hedd, Betsi Branwen a Twm Caradog.
Caru chi!

PART ONE

1

I fly in my sleep every night. When I was little I could fly without being asleep; now I can't, even though I practise and practise. And after what I saw last night I want more than ever to fly wide-awake. Mam always says: I want never gets. Is that true?

Last night began like every other night. I went to bed and changed under the bedclothes so Buddy Holly couldn't see me, and I laid my pink polka-dot hair ribbon down the middle of the mattress to show which side was whose, and Bethan said, like she always does: I don't want to sleep on your old side, anyway. Then, as soon as she was snoring she flung her arm across my face, and when I pinched her she swung her leg across my stomach.

So, it was hard to fall asleep. But when I did I left Bethan to spread herself across the whole bed and I soared into a sky that wrapped me in air as light and warm as an eiderdown. I listened to the town below breathe its shallow night-time breaths, in and out, in and out, and all around me the Earth sang.

For a while I hovered above the town's higgledy-piggledy houses. They cling to their streets as if they might roll all the way down to the sea and fall in if they let go. But last night, as usual, none of them let go and I didn't have to save anybody. I swerved away and rose high to avoid the Red Dragon flapping against its pole above the castle gatehouse, and swooped low over the council houses and across the sands to the sea where the air is always thick with salt that crusts on my lips as if I'd that minute undone a blue twist from a bag of crisps and licked it.

The sea, too, breathed in and out, its breast swelling with each breath until I was half afraid that the Leviathan from the Bible would burst from its depths and shower me with spume. Whales, porpoises, mermaids and mermen, dead sailors, fishes, crabs, tiny shrimps; the sea is forever full of eyes that watch me. I never fly far beyond the shore. If my town were a map the bay would have *Here be Monsters* written on it in golden ink.

Like every other night, I sped from the sea to drift along the road that winds its way beyond the Baptism Pool and the Reservoir high into the hills behind the town. As I passed above the Pool I saw a man floating in it with his arms outstretched and the moon drowning in his eyes. That was not like every other night and the fright plummeted me back to my bed, right on top of Bethan. I couldn't push her to her own side to make room to lie down so I got up early to practise wide-awake flying.

It's cold down here in the living room so I fasten up all the buttons on my cardigan. I need to be high up and Tada's armchair has the highest seat, but the cushion is old and saggy and it's difficult to balance on it. When I glimpse my reflection in the looking glass above the fireplace I see a scarecrow frowning at me, a skinny arm sticking out each side and red hair erupting from her head. Tada says it's the family hair, but Mam always says: Pity you have that old family nose to go with it. It's best not to look in the mirror too long in case the Devil appears in it so I scrunch my eyes closed until I feel the freckles pop on my cheeks. The tick-tock of the brown clock on the mantelpiece is loud and the tap that Tada has mended three times drip-drips in the scullery. Fly, I tell myself. Fly, fly, fly. Slowly, the sounds fade and I feel warm and weightless. I'm just about to rise from Tada's chair, light as an angel, when Mam's slippers go slap on the stairs and I fall off the seat.

John Morris opens an eye and squints at me from the other armchair.

'I nearly did it,' I whisper to him. 'Really.'

He purrs, then wraps his tail around his face and goes back to sleep.

I pull *The Tiger in the Smoke* that Aunty Lol lent me from beneath the saggy cushion, blow some Marie biscuit crumbs from the pages, and curl up tight as a fist in Tada's armchair to read it.

As soon as Mam comes through the living room door she sniffs so hard I can hear the hair clips on her yellow pincurls chatter against each other.

'It smells sooty in here,' she says, 'and it's chilly. You could have made the fire instead of sitting there with your beak in a book.'

'I don't like lighting the matches. You know that.'

'Don't be silly, Gwenni.' She kneels down and begins to riddle the half burnt lumps of wood. Clouds of fine ash billow around her. 'A girl of thirteen,' she says, and sighs.

I uncurl and push my book back under the cushion. 'Twelve and a half,' I say.

Mam rams the half full ash pan back into place and crumples newspaper into the grate over which she lays a grid of kindling and three logs. The matches sputter and die but at last the paper catches light and the wood begins to crackle. Mam stands up and shakes the folds of her blue satin dressing gown. The stale scent of Evening in Paris drifts from them with the ash. I try to hold my breath but I feel a throb above my eyebrows, like the ghost of the dripping tap, and the back of my neck stiffens. I rub it with a cold hand, and remember what I saw in the scullery when I got up.

'There's a mouse caught in the trap,' I say.

'Dead?'

'I think so.'

'A dead mouse won't hurt you.'

'I'm not afraid of it. I just don't like touching it.'

Mam takes the empty wood box into the scullery. Through the door I watch her as she crouches by the trap. John Morris follows her and she pushes him away with her elbow, then eases the spring from the mouse's broken back and picks up the body.

'Nain said she pulled a mouse out of a trap by its tail like that once. It was only pretending to be dead and it swung right round and bit her thumb,' I tell her.

Mam carries the corpse out through the back door and throws it into the bin. 'Nasty, dirty thing,' she says and slams the bin lid over it.

She washes her hands under the dripping tap and says, 'Bring in the kettle to fill, Gwenni. The fire'll be hot enough. Your father'll be wondering where his cup of tea's got to.'

I take the kettle into the scullery. The green distemper on the walls is beginning to peel and flake, shaping faces with sly eyes and mouths tight with secrets. There are new faces there every day. I try not to see them watching me.

'Mam,' I say, 'when I was flying last night I saw something that scared me.'

Mam fills the kettle and puts it on the fire in the living room.

6

Her hands shake and some of the water slops over onto the logs, making them hiss.

'In the Baptism Pool,' I say.

'Don't talk rubbish,' says Mam. 'And I thought I told you I didn't want to hear about that flying nonsense again. You haven't been telling anyone else about it, have you?'

'I asked Aunty Lol if she could remember me flying when I was little.'

'How many times do I have to say it, Gwenni? People can't fly.'

'But I can remember it. I can, really. You and Aunty Lol were holding my hands and swinging me and then you let go and I just flew along the ground without touching it. Like this.' I crouch and fold my arms around my legs.

Mam grasps my arm and yanks me up. 'Stop that. Stop that,' she shouts. Her dressing gown slithers open and she pulls it tight around her and takes a shaky breath.

'Listen to me, Gwenni. It never happened; that was a dream, too. Don't you dare say anything to anyone about it again.'

'Why not?' I rub my arm where Mam has squeezed it.

'You don't want people to think you're odd, do you?'

'Odd?'

'Yes, odd. Touched. Funny in the head. Like Guto'r Wern.'

The kettle lets out a gentle steam, blinding the window, shutting out the rest of the world.

'People won't think I'm like Guto just because I can fly in my sleep,' I say.

'Dreaming is one thing. Saying you really do it is another. What did Aunty Lol say?'

'She said perhaps I was a witch.'

'You see what I mean?' says Mam. Her knuckles turn white as she tightens the dressing gown's sash around her waist.

7

The kettle belches steam in great snorts.

'Fetch the tea tray,' says Mam and takes it from me when I bring it into the living room. The cups and saucers rattle on the tray. It's early for Mam's nerves to be so bad. She sets the tray down on the table, then picks up the milk bottle from it and pushes it in front of my face.

'You've given John Morris the top of the milk again,' she says.

'He likes it,' I say.

'So does everyone else,' says Mam. 'I've told you before not to waste it on the cat. I may as well talk to the man in the moon.'

She bangs the bottle down on the tray and scoops tea into the teapot. Two scoops. She lifts the kettle from the fire, holding it away from her to keep the soot from her dressing gown, and pours the water into the pot.

'So, promise me you won't say anything to anyone about it,' she says.

'About what?' I say.

Mam's hand shakes again as she puts the lid back on the teapot. 'This flying nonsense.'

'Not even to Alwenna?'

'Certainly not,' says Mam.

'But she's my Kindred Spirit. I want to show her how to fly, once I remember.'

'Not Alwenna. It would be all round the council houses in no time. Cross your heart.'

I make a big cross over my heart. But I cross my fingers at the same time. Alwenna already knows about the flying I do at night. 'Cross my heart,' I say. 'And hope to die.' I drop down into Tada's armchair and pull out my book.

Mam slips the knitted cosy over the teapot. 'Don't start reading now. You've got to get cracking this morning.'

'Why? I can't change the beds if Tada and Bethan are still in them.'

'Bethan can do that today. I've promised you to Mrs Evans Brwyn Coch this morning to look after the two girls.'

'I hate going to Brwyn Coch.'

'Don't be silly. You like the children.'

'But I don't like Mr Evans.'

'Don't like Ifan Evans?' Mam stops pouring milk into the cups. 'He's a wonderful man. Well respected. I only promised you to Elin as a favour to him.'

'His face is too red.'

'He can't help his red face, Gwenni. It's because he's out in the fields all day.'

'He's just like those Toby jugs.'

Mam looks up at the three jugs on their shelf above the looking glass. Straightaway, the Toby jugs pretend they're not staring at the china woman that Mam and Tada were given as a wedding present by their best man who died in the war. The china woman stands on the sideboard and doesn't wear any clothes at all, not even knickers. When the Toby jugs watch her they forget to smoke their pipes or drink from the tankards in their hands and their fat cheeks turn redder and redder and their eyes grow darker and darker.

'Mr Evans doesn't smoke or drink,' Mam says. 'Chapel deacons aren't allowed to.'

'Do I have to go?' I say.

'I said you'd be there by half past nine,' says Mam. 'Mrs Evans has to go to Price the Dentist. He's in town this morning, but only for a couple of hours. So hurry yourself.'

'Don't make me go, Mam.'

Mam lifts the teapot and pours a steaming brown stream into each cup.

'Don't be silly,' she says. 'Now, have your cup of tea, brush that hair and get your Wellingtons on.'

'But it's not raining.'

'The fields will still be wet after the snow. I'll take this tea up to your father and wake Bethan. I want you in your Wellingtons ready to go when I come down.'

Mam picks up the biggest cup and saucer, the ones with *A Present from Llandudno* written on them in gold, and opens the living room door. The cup trembles on the saucer. She looks back at me. 'You have to go,' she says.

The door closes behind her and I listen to her slippers slap-slapping all the way up to the bedroom.

2

When I fly above the town at night, all is still and the windows in the houses and shops are blank with sleep. As I walk through the street this morning, crows from the castle squabble over crumbs outside the bakehouse and a ginger cat sits on Jones the Butcher's windowsill and twitches his nose at the reek of hundreds of faggots cooking; Mam says everyone has faggots for their dinner on Saturday. Shop signs swing and squeak in the breeze and in the houses lace curtains twitch aside behind the windows as I pass by.

My fingers are sticky from Mam's blackberry jam, which is runny and pippy unlike Nain's jam. Mam says that eating in the street is common as dirt, but I escaped with my bread and jam before she came downstairs again.

Just as I lick my fingers Mr Pugh waves at me from behind his wide counter in Pugh's Stores, where he's framed by pyramids of tins full of food from faraway countries. Mr Pugh won't tell Mam I'm being common as dirt. He often gives me chocolate biscuits from the broken-biscuit tin to eat in the street when I fetch the messages for Mam or Nain. But Mrs Llywelyn Pugh would probably tell her. Mrs Llywelyn Pugh never, ever serves in the shop and she wears a dead fox around her neck to go to Chapel. Whenever I mention the dead fox Mam says: Don't be silly, Gwenni; it's not a dead fox, it's a fox-fur. Mrs Llywelyn Pugh sits two pews in front of us in Chapel and the dead fox's paws and head loll on her back and its glass eyes stare and stare at me.

As I walk up the hill I see the glint of spectacles above the cream lace in Kitty Hawk's parlour window. Alwenna always says: Let's give her something to look at. So on Sundays, when she wears stockings, she lifts her skirt and fiddles with her suspenders. Every Monday morning Kitty Hawk hovers above her front step and squawks at Mam on her way to clean the Police House: That Alwenna has no shame.

In my sleep I fly from the bottom of the hill up over the Baptism Pool in no time at all; it takes me longer to walk here. Alwenna says the Scotch Baptists from Rehoboth Chapel dress in white sheets and their minister throws them into the water of the Baptism Pool, and then they're baptised.

Last night the Pool was full of water, the way it is in winter, when I saw the man floating on it. His arms and legs were spread out like a cross and his white shirt ballooned on the surface. But it was his moonshiny eyes that scared me into falling. Was it a drowned Baptist? Or a Baptist's spirit? Do spirits float?

I make my eyes into slits to look into the Baptism Pool. There's no one in there. Maybe there are things I can see only when I'm flying. The railings around the Pool's edges are rough with rust that rubs off on my mackintosh when I lean over them. The Pool has lost its winter water and looks like the swamp in a film that Alwenna and I went to see in the picture house. I had nightmares afterwards that woke everyone, even Bethan, and Mam said: I must have my beauty sleep, Gwenni. The water in the Pool smells worse than Jones the Butcher's faggots. It's lucky I'm a Methodist and not a Scotch Baptist.

The sun sneaks from behind a cloud; I close my eyes and lift my face to it. Its big yellow eye looks right through me. What does the sun see? Does it see the same things as I do when I'm flying?

I wonder what time it is. If I were a castaway like Robinson Crusoe I would be able to tell the time by the sun.

Robinson Crusoe could have escaped from his desert island if he'd been able to fly. When I was little and wanted to fly I would crouch down and wrap my arms around my knees, like this, and then I would lift above the ground and skim over it. Fly, I say to myself now. Fly, fly, fly. But it won't happen. All I do is fall over. If I were a lizard on Robinson Crusoe's island I could stay here all day basking in the sun's warmth; I wouldn't have to go to Brwyn Coch and see Ifan Evans with his raw face and his eyes that are dark and sour as sloes. When I told Mam and Tada that Alwenna calls him Paleface, Tada laughed until Mam frowned at him. That Alwenna has no shame, she said.

Look, the primroses on the bank at the side of the road are open and tiny violets hide their heads in the grass beside them. I'll pick some primroses for Mam on the way back and I'll pick a posy of violets now to take to Mrs Evans. Mrs Evans likes violets; she read a poem to us in an English lesson at primary school about a girl as shy as a violet, and once she made fairy cakes for a chapel supper that had pretty sugared violets on the icing. I can taste them now, sweet and scented and fizzy on my tongue. A posy of violets will cheer her up before she goes to Price the Dentist.

Mr Price took out all Mam's bottom teeth when I was five. She came home and sat on the step at the foot of the stairs and whimpered with pain, a handkerchief of Tada's pressed to her mouth and soaked with blood. Alwenna says that Mr Price has to have a glass of whisky to steady his hands before he takes your teeth out; that's why his breath smells so sweet. Tada says it's worth the pain, he says his false teeth are much better than the real thing.

Deep down where the stems of the violets leave the ground the grass is cool and wet. I tease several of the flowers from the bank and some of their true-hearted leaves to put about them, and then tie the stems around and around with a long blade of grass to make a posy.

When I look up the Reservoir walls loom at me from the other side of the road. Last summer a dead sheep lay in the Reservoir for weeks before anyone found it. Alwenna says that maggots came through the taps in her house. My stomach shifts at the thought of it.

There's Mrs Williams talking to Guto'r Wern at the house gate to Penrhiw farm. Alwenna says everyone knows that Guto's mother dropped him on his head when he was a baby so that he grew up strange. And now his mother's dead and he can't look after himself although he's a grown man. Once, Guto told me he could fly, and he tried to show me how, but it didn't work. Mam says I'm not to encourage him but Tada always says: There's no harm in him, he's innocent as a child. Mrs Williams waves me over to her; Guto waves, too, the torn sleeve of his coat flapping up and down, up and down, like a crow's wing. Mrs Williams gives him a little push and he moves away, eating the bread and butter she's given him. We both watch him hop and skip down the road to the town.

'That poor boy,' says Mrs Williams. 'I don't know what'll become of him.' She turns back to me. 'So, Gwenni, are you off to Brwyn Coch this morning? Elin mentioned that she was having a tooth out. And how's your nain? I haven't seen her for weeks. Don't tell me, I know what she'd say: Mustn't grumble, Bessie. That's what your nain always says, bless her: Mustn't grumble. Tell her I've been churning butter and I've got plenty of buttermilk. She likes her buttermilk, I know. You look more like her every time I see you. How time flies. Last time I saw your Aunty Olwen was when the Silver Band came round playing at Christmas. Must be a bit noisy for your nain to live with that trumpet. Are those flowers for Elin? Don't stand there with your mouth open, Gwenni. You're probably late already. You'd better run the rest of the way.'

Alwenna says that Mr Williams winds his wife up every morning; she says you can tell by the way Mrs Williams talks more slowly in the afternoons and has nothing at all to say by evening. When I told Mam she said: Don't be silly, Gwenni.

The gate to Brwyn Coch's field opens with a groan, as if it doesn't want to let me by. When I step into the long grass, I feel the wet seeping in through the sides of my shoes. I've forgotten to put my Wellington boots on. The lambs run away, bleating for their mothers, and their silly tails wobble behind them. Tada says Ifan Evans is good at his job, he says that Twm Edwards is lucky to have a man so useful with the sheep. Alwenna says that's because Paleface likes anything female. When I told Mam her hands shook so much she dropped her *Woman's Weekly*. That Alwenna has no shame, she said.

The sun has vanished again but it's not raining, so I'll take the children outside to play. Why is there no smoke coming from Brwyn Coch's chimney? Has Mrs Evans left already and taken Angharad and Catrin with her? Mam will be cross with me.

I knock on the heavy front door. Mot starts barking around the side of the house; he doesn't run at me so he must be tied up. Does that mean Ifan Evans hasn't gone to see to the lambs yet?

I can hear the geese honking in their pen behind the house but I can't hear the sound of people. As I lift my arm to knock again the door swings open. Mrs Evans stands in the doorway with her apron held up over her mouth. Blood seeps through the apron onto her hands. She looks like Mam looked when she sat, all blood and tears, at the bottom of the stairs. Mrs Evans's eyes are full of pain and her hair is coming loose from its silver combs.

'Oh, Mrs Evans,' I say, 'you've been to Mr Price already, I'm sorry I'm late, Mam'll be so cross with me.' I hold the posy of violets out towards her bloodied hands. 'I stopped to pick these for you.'

3

Mrs Evans's hand trembles as she takes the posy from me. I try not to look at my own hand; I don't want to see her blood on it. She mumbles something that I don't understand and stands aside for me to walk into the narrow passageway. As I pass her she sways and her eyes flare open, the way John Morris's eyes do when he's frightened, and there's a whiff of blood that makes my stomach tighten. I hold my breath as long as I can.

Once we're in the kitchen I say, 'You ought to sit down, Mrs Evans. You're bleeding more than Mam was when she had her teeth taken out. Did Mr Price forget to have his whisky?'

She slumps into the high-backed chair by the range; my posy of violets drops to the floor. The room is cold without its fire. Mrs Evans shivers; her head shivers, her hands shiver, her legs shiver, until she shimmers. The fire is laid; it only needs lighting. But I don't like to strike the matches.

'I know a good thing to stop the bleeding,' I tell Mrs Evans.

I take a cup with a pattern of forget-me-nots on it from the dresser and carry it over to the cupboard beside the range where the salt box sits. Tada says salt water cures everything; if I have a scraped knee or a sore throat or a cut that won't stop bleeding, he says: Use some salt water on it. I'm not sure how much salt to use for Mrs Evans so I put a handful into the cup.

As I cross to the big stone sink I trip and have to catch hold of the edge of the table to stop myself falling. The poker with the brass phoenix on its handle is lying across the flagstones and when I push it aside with my foot I tread in something tacky. The left-overs from breakfast are scattered across the table with a jar of blackcurrant jam on its side staining the tablecloth; someone must have spilt some of the jam on the floor. And there's a plate that matches the cup from the dresser in pieces on the floor between the table and the door. The children will have to be careful not to tread on the bits. What a mess everywhere. My stomach clenches. Tada says I have the family stomach. Whenever anything makes me feel queasy he says: It's that old family stomach, Gwenni.

'Where are Angharad and Catrin?' I ask. 'Are they with Mr Evans?' But Mrs Evans rocks herself backwards and forwards on the chair and a high-pitched hum comes from her throat and she doesn't answer.

I hold the cup under the tap and fill it with water. I can't see a clean spoon anywhere so I give it a good stir with my finger until the salt has dissolved. The water is icy and my finger turns white. Then I wash my hands under the tap; there won't be any blood on them now. I pick up a blue bowl that's drying on the draining board and take that and the cup of salt water to Mrs Evans.

'Here you are, Mrs Evans,' I say. 'If you rinse your mouth with the salt water it'll stop the bleeding and clean out the old blood. You can spit it out into the bowl.'

Mrs Evans lowers the apron from her mouth and takes the bowl from me and rests it on her lap. She trembles as she holds the cup and puts it to her lips. The skin on the back of her hand is scraped into little curls, and her mouth is swollen and purple.

'Nain always says that Mr Price is brutal. Alwenna says it's when he's run out of whisky,' I say.

Mrs Evans sips the water and I try not to hear her spitting it into the bowl. I look at the photographs hanging above her on the wall next to the range. Here's one of Mrs Evans when she was younger, holding two babies, one on each arm. They're alike as twins. I wonder who they are. Mrs Evans's dark hair is loose and reaches down to her waist. Beneath is a picture of Ifan Evans; with one hand he holds a long gun over his shoulder and from the other hand he dangles a fox by its tail. It looks just like Mrs Llywelyn Pugh's dead fox. I look away, but not before I notice the hole in the fox's head and have that old family stomach again.

Mrs Evans holds her empty cup out to me and I take it and put it in the sink. She drapes her apron over the bowl and waves away my hand when I offer to take it from her. Then, she pushes herself up from the chair as if she's worn out and takes the bowl to the sink and empties it. When she turns on the tap the water whooshes down into the bowl and then up again in a fountain and sprays me and her and the window behind the sink so that the whole world looks as if it's crying. Mrs Evans doesn't notice; she bends down, holding on to the sink, and starts to pick up the pieces of broken plate. I lean across and turn off the tap, then wipe my face with the sleeve of my mackintosh.

'I'll do that if you like,' I say to Mrs Evans. 'Shall I use a broom?'

She nods at me. 'In there, Gwenni,' she mumbles, and points to the cupboard under the stairs in the back hall. As I unlatch the cupboard door I glance into the parlour and see Angharad and Catrin huddled together on the back window-seat sharing a large picture book that's open on their laps.

'Hello, you two,' I say. 'You've been very quiet. Have you been sitting in here reading? Don't worry about your mam, she'll be fine in a little while. My mam bled a lot, and cried a lot too, when Mr Price took her teeth out.' They both look up at me and Catrin leans a little closer to Angharad and reaches up to whisper in her ear.

I pull the broom and dustpan out of the cupboard and go back into the kitchen to sweep up the broken china. I try not to tread on the sticky jam. But what if it's not jam? What if it's Mrs Evans's blood? I hadn't thought of that. I don't look at the stickiness as I sweep the pieces into a pile and push them onto the dustpan.

As I take the china out through the back door to put it in the dustbin Mot barks again, and appears round the corner of the house, straining on his rope, lowering his belly to the ground and wagging his tail. 'Be quiet, Mot,' I say in a stern voice, and he stops barking. I lift the lid from the dustbin and disturb a wasp that drones sleepily around some broken bottles in the bottom of the bin. I wrinkle my nose at the sweet, sharp smell that drifts up. 'You'd better move out of the way,' I say to the wasp, and empty the dustpan over the bottles. The wasp makes an angry noise and I throw the lid onto the bin.

When I go back indoors I put away the broom and dustpan. Mrs Evans is leaning on the sink looking out through the window. I try not to look at the dark stickiness on the floor, but I say, 'Would you like me to wash the floor, Mrs Evans?'

'Thank you, Gwenni, but no,' she says, and I understand her better now. 'D'you think you could take Angharad and Catrin out to play for a while so that I can put a cold compress on this?' She points to her swollen mouth.

'You have to be careful not to get a draught in it, Mrs Evans,'
I say. 'Nain says you have to cover your mouth before you set a
foot out through Mr Price's door if you have a tooth out; he leaves
such a big hole.'

'I'll be fine, Gwenni,' she says. 'Will you take the girls?'

She starts to run the tap, holding a cloth under the cold
water. I go through into the parlour to fetch the girls. The parlour
has shelves full of books. Mrs Evans once said I could borrow as
many as I wanted. When I told Mam she said: Neither a borrower
nor a lender be. Angharad and Catrin are still huddled together
on the window-seat.

'What are you reading?' I ask them.

'*Alice in Wonderland*,' says Angharad. 'But I have to read it
to Catrin, she can't read yet. She's a baby, she's afraid of falling
down a rabbit hole and never getting out again.'

'I borrowed *Alice in Wonderland* from the library, a long time
ago,' I say. Mam says I'm allowed to borrow books from the town
library, that's what we pay the rates for. 'Is yours from the library?'

'Aunty Meg sent it to us,' says Angharad. 'Look at the lovely
pictures in it, Gwenni. Isn't Alice pretty? She looks like your
Bethan.'

'She's a bit stupid, that Alice, isn't she?' I say.

'She's stupid to go down a rabbit hole. What if she can't get
out?' says Catrin.

'Come on,' I say, and hold out a hand each to them. 'Let's
go and see if we can find Alice's rabbit hole and I'll hold your
hand tight, Catrin, so you won't fall in.'

'Perhaps we'll see the White Rabbit,' says Angharad.

'There're lots of rabbit holes by the stream,' says Catrin. 'Are
you sure I won't fall in one, Gwenni?'

Angharad slides from the window seat and helps Catrin down.

They hold my hands and we go through into the back hall for them to put their coats on. I fetch their Wellington boots from the kitchen where Mrs Evans is pressing the cold compress to her lips. The girls stand in the doorway and watch her.

'Better already,' she says to them. 'Now, you go out with Gwenni for a while and I'll be fine when you come back. And remember what I told you.'

The children catch hold of my hands again and Angharad's hand tightens on mine as she nods at her mother.

'I'll ring the bell when it's time for you to come in,' says Mrs Evans.

Catrin points to the big brass bell by the back door. 'That's Mami's old school bell,' she says.

'I know,' I say. 'We'll be down by the stream, Mrs Evans.'

'We're going to look for the White Rabbit,' says Catrin.

4

'White Rabbit, White Rabbit, we're going to look for the White Rabbit.' Catrin sings as she pulls at my hand, and we round the corner of the house and skip down the field towards the stream. Mot follows as far as his rope will let him, leaping into the air and barking at us.

'Is your father coming back for Mot?' I ask.

'Don't know,' says Catrin. 'He's got the black dog today. Sometimes he forgets all about Mot when he's got the black dog.'

'Look, Gwenni,' says Angharad. She lets go of my hand and points to a shed hidden in a dip in the field. 'Have you seen Tada's fox hut? Look at all the tails he's got nailed to the door.' She runs towards the shed. I look away, but not fast enough to stop myself seeing the tails.

'Come on, Gwenni,' Angharad calls. 'Tada's got lots more tails inside.'

Catrin's hand is as weightless and warm as the baby blackbird Aunty Lol and I found fallen from its nest last spring, but her fingers clutch mine now. 'I don't like them, Gwenni,' she says.

'Don't look,' I say. Catrin and I gaze down the field and out to the sea until Angharad comes back to us.

'Why does your father kill the foxes?' I ask.

'Because they go after the lambs and the geese, silly,' says Angharad.

'Tada likes killing them,' says Catrin. She tugs at my hand and we start to run. From here it looks as if there is nothing between the sea and the three of us running down this field. If we could run and run until our feet left the ground we'd soar into the sky and down to the bay the way I do in my sleep.

Angharad trips and Catrin and I stop running and sit with her on the grass. The grass is damp and the earth cold beneath us. If I were living underground with the worms and the beetles and the grubs I wouldn't feel the cold. Mr Hughes Biology says earthworms don't feel a thing. Last term he said we had to cut a live worm in half, but I had stomach ache before I started and was sent to the sick room.

Angharad points at the hills of Llŷn that have almost disappeared behind the clouds moving towards us. 'Aunty Meg lives there, over the water,' she says, 'in Cricieth. Can you see her castle on its rock, Gwenni?'

'Not in that cloud,' I say. 'But I know it's not as big as our castle.' In my sleep I have to fly up and up and up to avoid the gatehouse and the Red Dragon on our castle before diving down again to the sands and the sea.

'We could fly across the sea to visit her.' Catrin runs down the field, flapping her arms up and down; her faint shadow looks like a long bird running ahead of her. 'We could tell her we're looking for the White Rabbit.' She wheels around and comes back, her arms like wings.

Angharad laughs. 'That's silly, Catrin. People can't fly.'

'I can,' I say.

'What, fly?' says Angharad.

'Show us, Gwenni,' says Catrin.

I fold myself into a crouch and wrap my arms around my knees. 'This is how I used to do it when I was little,' I say. Angharad and Catrin copycat me.

'We're not flying,' says Angharad.

'You have to concentrate,' I say. 'Close your eyes and try to hover above the ground.'

They close their eyes and snort and gruntle as they strain to lift themselves off the ground. Angharad falls over sideways. 'This is silly,' she says as she gets to her feet. 'Come on, Gwenni. I want to find the White Rabbit.'

Catrin takes hold of my hand and leans over and whispers, 'Can you really, really fly, Gwenni?' Her milky breath tickles my ear.

'When I'm asleep, I can,' I say. 'But I have to practise more if I want to fly when I'm awake.'

'Mami says we can do anything we want,' says Catrin. 'If we work at it.'

I stand and pull her up after me.

'She doesn't mean being naughty,' she says.

'Come on,' I say. 'Let's go and find that old White Rabbit.'

Angharad is already down by the stream, sitting on the grassy bank, pulling off a Wellington boot and her sock. The clouds' reflections make patterns in the water as the stream rushes and splashes over jagged stones on the way to the Reservoir. Does the water in the Baptism Pool come from the Reservoir? Don't think about the Reservoir, or the Pool.

'I want to paddle,' says Angharad.

'I haven't got anything to dry your feet with,' I say.

'Don't care,' she says and tugs off the second boot and sock. She dips her feet into the water and catches her breath with a shudder. 'It's cold, it's so cold,' she says. 'You put your feet in, Catrin.'

'No,' says Catrin. 'I don't like cold.'

'I'm going to have a drink,' I say. I kneel at the stream's edge and dip my cupped hand into it, pushing aside the little flurries of twigs that race past, and lift the water to my mouth to sip. It's cold as winter. Tada says the snow stays on the hills that the streams run from long after spring has arrived down here.

'Is it nice?' says Catrin. 'Mami says water is the best drink in the world. Is it nice like pop, Gwenni? Tada likes pop. He gets cross when Mami pours it away.'

Alwenna says that her mother buys a whole crate of pop from the Corona lorry every month. When I told Mam she said: Those people in the council houses spend their money like there's no tomorrow.

'It tastes like . . . like melted icicles,' I say to Catrin.

'Can I try some, Gwenni?'

'Make your hand like a cup,' I say.

Catrin cups her hand into the stream, then slurps the water from it. 'It's dripped down inside the front of my jumper, Gwenni,' she says. 'It's cold, it's so cold.' She hops up and down like a little wren on the bank.

'Rub it with your jumper,' I say. 'You won't notice it in a minute. Then we'll look down those rabbit holes.'

'D'you think the White Rabbit will be down one of them?' asks Angharad as she jumps out of the stream.

We all kneel to peer down into the rabbit holes. Angharad has rabbit droppings stuck to the wrinkled soles of her feet. 'Better put your socks and boots back on,' I say. 'Rub your feet with some of the long grass; that should be dry enough.'

'I'll dry my feet with the socks and put my Wellingtons on without them,' says Angharad. She rubs hard at her toes and then gives the bundle of damp socks to me. 'You look after them,' she says, pulling the first boot on. 'Ouch. That hurt.' She shakes the boot upside down and a piece of china falls out. It has a little forget-me-not on it. 'It was right in the toe,' she says. 'I didn't feel it when I had my sock on.'

'It must've jumped from that dropped plate,' I say, and pick up the piece and throw it into the stream. 'Lucky you didn't cut yourself on it.'

'Nobody dropped it,' says Catrin. 'Angharad threw it at the black dog to stop it making Tada cross with Mami.'

'Wasn't your mam cross with you for throwing it?' I ask Angharad.

'She's never cross with us,' says Angharad. 'And she says that Tada can't help being cross when the black dog jumps on him. So there.' She sticks out her tongue at Catrin.

'Didn't you make the dog cross?' I ask.

'Don't know,' says Angharad. She pushes the toe of her boot into a rabbit hole. 'I couldn't see it. Anyway, Catrin climbed right up on the table and hit it and hit it with the poker to get it off Tada. That's worse. Then Tada had to run out with it.' Angharad shrugs and kneels and peers into the rabbit hole. 'Gwenni, Gwenni. There's something here. I heard it, I heard it.'

'Is it the White Rabbit?' says Catrin.

'You put your hand into the hole, Gwenni. See if you can feel anything.'

Don't think about the black dog. 'I don't want to put my hand in when I don't know what's there,' I say. I pull a floating twig from the stream and push it into the mouth of the rabbit hole. The earth is dry on the inside and crumbles when I poke at it. Musty air rises from the hole, like that from the mouse nest Tada uncovered in our back-yard wall last summer. I pull my hand away. Nain says mice can give you a nasty bite any time, you don't have to be holding them by the tail. 'There's something down there,' I say. 'You can smell it.'

Catrin kneels down on the grass and sniffs hard at the rabbit hole. 'D'you think it's the White Rabbit, Gwenni?' She wrinkles her nose. 'Is that what it smells like?'

'You remember how Alice saw the White Rabbit, don't you?' I say. 'She was asleep on the grass. We could try that.'

We lay ourselves down on the grass and the dandelions, with me in the middle. Catrin holds my hand. 'Just in case we have to go after it in a hurry,' she says. 'You won't let me fall down the rabbit hole, will you, Gwenni?' I squeeze her hand.

'The first one to fall asleep, whistle,' I say. That's what Aunty Lol used to say to me and Bethan after she put us to bed when we were little. Aunty Lol is the best whistler I know. She can whistle all the tunes she plays with the Silver Band and imitate any bird. Nain always says: Like a hen crowing, Lol.

We stretch out on the grass, our feet pointing towards the sea, the watery sun trying hard to warm our heads. A chill creeps through my mackintosh from the damp earth, but I feel myself begin to drift away like one of the twigs on the stream. What if I fall asleep and fly away? I'll take Catrin with me, high into the sky, holding on tight, tight to her hand so that she doesn't fall, and let her feel the song of the Earth all around her.

The clang of the old school bell makes me leap just before I slip into sleep. Its noise starts Mot barking and the geese honking and all the lambs in the next field bleating for their mothers. Catrin and Angharad jump up; Catrin still clings to my hand. She drags me upright, even though she's so little and light.

'Time to go back,' I say.

'But we haven't seen the White Rabbit yet,' says Catrin.

'Alice saw him in England. He's probably still there,' I say. 'We didn't think about that.'

'That's far away isn't it, Gwenni?' says Catrin. 'I wish I had stories about here and not about old England.'

'I'll write one for you,' I say.

'Really, Gwenni?' Catrin swings my hand back and forth. 'Mami says you're clever at writing stories.'

'I'll begin it tonight,' I say.

The bell clangs again.

'Come on, you two,' I say. 'Last one back's a smelly rabbit.'

5

We race each other back to the cottage. I pretend to hurt my foot and hobble along so that Catrin and Angharad can overtake me. They run, shrieking, around the side of the house. I limp after them. Mot ignores me. He's busy lapping from a blue-rimmed enamel basin, slopping the water over the sides in his haste.

'You're last, Gwenni. You're the smelly rabbit,' Angharad shouts at me from the back door.

'Mami, Mami, I am so, so thirsty,' says Catrin. She hangs out her tongue the way Mot does and pants.

Mrs Evans stands on the threshold. Her mouth is still purple but not so swollen. And she's tidied her hair up into its silver combs, except for the wisps that always escape from it like little curls of smoke. She has a white handkerchief with lace around its edges in her hand that she lifts to cover her mouth before she speaks. 'You're just in time. Those clouds look as if they're bringing more snow,' she says. 'Come inside and take your Wellingtons off, then you can have some buttermilk. Gwenni, would you like some?'

I say, 'Yes, please, Mrs Evans.' Nain sometimes sends me to Penrhiw with the billycan to fetch buttermilk and gives me a glassful when I take it back to her. Nain always says: It's good for you, Gwenni; drink it quickly and try not to think about the lumps.

In the back hall Angharad and Catrin are holding on to each other to pull off their Wellington boots and push their feet into slippers. I wipe my shoes hard on the doormat. Maybe they'll be dry by the time I get home.

When we're in the kitchen Mrs Evans takes three glasses from the dresser cupboard and puts them on the table. My posy of violets is on the table, too, sitting in a cup painted with gold leaves that dance under the electric light. Mrs Evans has cleared the mess and washed the floor and the fire is leaping and crackling in the range, the flames reflected in the polished phoenix on the poker. A saucepan on the side has a whisper of steam escaping from it that smells of stew. Angharad and Catrin won't have to eat Jones the Butcher's faggots for dinner.

Mrs Evans reaches for a large jug from the larder and the buttermilk glugs from it into each glass. Angharad and Catrin and I drink the buttermilk in long swallows. It's cold and sharp and I try not to think about the lumps. When she catches me gulping down a drink Mam always says: Don't drink it on your forehead like that, Gwenni; it's common as dirt.

'Thank you, Mrs Evans,' I say, and put the empty glass on the draining board. 'Are you feeling better now?'

'I'm fine now, Gwenni,' she says.

'Mr Price will soon make you some false teeth,' I say. 'Tada says they're much better than the real thing.'

'You're a good girl, Gwenni,' says Mrs Evans. 'I've got something for you. Look.' She picks up a book from the table and gives it to me. It's fat with thin pages edged in gold. The cover is soft and green as moss and the golden letters on it curl like the ones

I imagine on the map of my town. *William Wordsworth* say the curling letters, and *Poems.*

'Look,' says Mrs Evans again. With her free hand she opens the book at a page marked by a card with a bunch of violets painted on it and points to the poem that she read to us at school. She recites, *'A violet by a mossy stone half hidden from the eye! Fair as a star when only one is shining in the sky.'* When she puts the card back it puffs a faint, powdery scent into the air.

'It's lovely,' I say.

'You can borrow it, Gwenni,' she says. 'I know how much you like reading.'

'And writing, Mami,' says Catrin. 'Gwenni's going to write me a story. A story about here. Specially for me, Mami.'

'I hope you've thanked Gwenni,' says Mrs Evans. 'D'you know, I think I've got just the thing for her to write it in.' Her voice is muffled behind the white handkerchief.

Catrin leans against me for a moment. I hardly feel her weight. 'Thank you, Gwenni,' she says.

'You two girls stay in here and lay the table for dinner,' says Mrs Evans, 'and you come with me, Gwenni.' She walks through into the parlour. 'You can borrow the book for as long as you like.'

I follow her. 'But I can't, Mrs Evans,' I say. 'Mam always says: Neither a borrower nor a lender be.'

'I tell you what, Gwenni, why don't I just give it to you? Here,' she takes the book then hands it back to me. 'It's your book now.' Mine.

The parlour is better than the town library. On each side of the inglenook tall bookshelves sag with the weight of the books they hold. And the wall opposite has shelves in rows, with books squashed together on them and more books laid flat on top of the upright books. Angharad and Catrin's *Alice in Wonderland* is on

32

the window-seat. *Alice in Wonderland* is all a dream. A falling dream. Is falling like flying?

'Come over here, Gwenni,' says Mrs Evans from behind her handkerchief. She has a table that smells of polish set out like a desk under the front window. On it are a brass holder for her fountain pens, and two bottles of ink, one black and one red, with narrow necks and fat bellies. Next to the ink bottles is a wooden rocker for her blotting paper with primroses and blue-bells painted on its sides and a knob on the top with a tiny violet on it. When I told Mam I wanted a blotter rocker like Mrs Evans's she said: I want never gets, Gwenni. I didn't tell her I wanted a desk like Mrs Evans's, too. A tower of exercise books, most of them covered in brown paper, stands on the edge of the table. The tower wobbles as Mrs Evans pulls two uncovered books from its base and gives them to me. 'I knew I had some unused ones here,' she says. 'One for your rough work and one for the finished story, Gwenni.'

I take them and tuck them under my arm with the soft green book. 'Thank you, Mrs Evans,' I say.

She turns away, and taps her fingers on her desk, as if she's playing a tune on it. She stares for a long time out through the window towards the sea and the sky. Tada always says you can see that Mrs Evans has had an education. She thinks a lot, he says, and Mam always replies: Huh, I wish I had time to think.

'So,' Mrs Evans says, 'what did you and the girls do in the field this morning?'

'We played looking for the White Rabbit,' I say. I don't mention the flying.

'And . . .' Mrs Evans pauses and turns around to look at me, but I can't see her face because she's got her back to the window. The light makes a halo of the smoky wisps of her hair, like the halo around Jesus Christ's head in the picture that hangs in our Chapel vestry. 'Did you see Mr Evans?'

'No,' I say. 'Catrin said he was out with the black dog this morning, but we didn't see him.'

Mrs Evans leaves her desk and cups my face in her hand for a moment. Her hand is cold, and I try not to shiver. 'You're a good girl, Gwenni,' she says. 'Why don't you stay in here for a while and have a look to see if there are any other books you'd like to have? As a thank-you for helping. Come through to the kitchen when you're done.' She walks through the back hall and into the kitchen, still holding her lace handkerchief to her mouth, and closes the door behind her.

I take a deep breath. The room smells of books and polish and a powdery scent like the violet card's. Where shall I begin? On the bottom shelves opposite the inglenook I see books I've borrowed from the town library. I sit on the floor to pull them out. *Heidi* has her picture on the cover with a snow-covered mountain behind her, higher than the Wyddfa. And there are pictures inside, too. And here's *Anne of Green Gables* that I made Alwenna read so that she could see how we're Kindred Spirits, and right next to it *Anne of Avonlea* that the library hasn't got. I hug it to me. Anne's hair is red and wild like mine. And, look, *Robinson Crusoe* that I borrow often, although Alwenna wouldn't play castaways with me in the back yard on Thursday because it's too childish. It wasn't too childish last week. I put them all in a pile. Here's *Little Women* and *Good Wives* in one book instead of two; I cry every time Beth dies and Mam says: Don't be silly, Gwenni. So, now I don't read that part. I'll leave *Pinocchio* where it is. When I read it I had nightmares where robbers chased me and put a sack over my head and Mam made me take the book back to the library before I finished it. She said: I must have my beauty sleep, Gwenni. That's five books in the pile, six with the green book. I won't look any more in case I see something else I want. Six books and two exercise books.

I go through the hall and knock on the kitchen door. Mrs Evans opens it and lets me in. The table is laid and Angharad and Catrin are sitting squeezed together in the chair by the range.

'I've got five more, Mrs Evans,' I say, and try to hold them for her to see. 'Is that all right?'

She glances at them. 'They're yours, Gwenni,' she says.

'I'm hungry, Mam,' says Angharad. 'When can we have dinner?'

'When your father comes home,' says Mrs Evans.

'Do we have to wait?' says Angharad.

'You know we do,' says Mrs Evans. 'Why don't you take Catrin through into the parlour and read your *Alice in Wonderland* for a while? I want to talk to Gwenni about something.'

Angharad and Catrin's slippers squeak along the flagstones in the hall as they shuffle through into the parlour.

'I think I'd better go home if it's nearly dinnertime,' I say. 'Mam will be cross if I'm late.'

'It's hard work cooking for a family,' says Mrs Evans. 'But this won't take long, Gwenni. Sit down for a minute.'

We sit down at the laid table and she says, 'You know that Mrs Williams Penrhiw looks after the girls for me sometimes after school so that I can catch up with my marking?'

I nod; my six books and two exercise books threaten to slide off my lap. I tighten my grip on them.

'Well, she's finding it a bit difficult now that they're getting older and I thought you might like to help her with looking after them. You're a kind girl, Gwenni, and Catrin and Angharad like you. It would mean going up to Penrhiw on a Tuesday and Thursday straight from school and playing with the girls until I come for them on my way home. I'd pay you, of course. It would be like having a little job. What do you think?'

If I had money I could buy my own paper and pens and comics and books and if I wanted to buy someone a present, I could. I say, 'I'd like to do it, Mrs Evans. But I'll have to ask Mam.'

'Of course you will, Gwenni,' says Mrs Evans. 'And I'm sure your mother will be glad to have you do it. Let me know when you've spoken to her. It would be good if you could start at the beginning of the new term.'

'I'll let you know at Sunday School tomorrow, Mrs Evans,' I say. 'And thank you very much for the books.'

'You won't be able to carry them like that, Gwenni, and they'll get wet if you're caught in the snow,' she says. 'Let me make them into a parcel for you.' She goes to the cupboard under the stairs to fetch brown paper and lays it on the hall floor. She wraps the six books and the two exercise books in the paper and ties the parcel round with string. 'There, Gwenni,' she says. 'I've made a little loop for you to carry it with.'

I can see Angharad and Catrin sitting on the window-seat in the parlour just the way they were when I first saw them this morning. But now they're not reading the book that's open on their laps.

'I'm going home,' I say. 'Goodbye, you two.'

Catrin slithers down from the window-seat and runs into the hall and holds me round my legs. 'Don't go, Gwenni, please don't go,' she says.

'Catrin,' says Mrs Evans. 'Let go of Gwenni. Now, Catrin.'

'I have to go, Catrin,' I say. 'Mam will be cross with me if I'm late for dinner.'

Catrin steps back. 'Is your mam always cross?' she asks. 'Tada's always cross. He was very cross this morning.'

'Catrin,' says Mrs. Evans from behind her white handkerchief. 'Come on, girls. Say goodbye.'

I hurry through the door with my parcel of books. I don't have to go past Mot or the hissing geese on the way home. I turn and wave at the girls before I round the corner to the path. 'See you tomorrow,' I shout. The string loop is already cutting into my fingers so I lift the parcel up under my arm and run as fast as I can with it across the first field and over the stile into the next one. And I don't look left or right or back again until I reach the gate into the road in case I see Ifan Evans and his big black dog.

I race down the hill past Penrhiw and don't look at the Reservoir or the Baptism Pool. Then I put down the parcel and pick Mam a bunch of primroses with leaves that are furry as John Morris's ears and try not to think about having Jones the Butcher's faggots for dinner when I get home.

6

In the living room the curtains are closed to keep us hidden from the world. They overlap where they meet so that not even the daylight can peek at us. The wind whines in the chimney and makes the fire slow to draw and we can't boil the kettle to make a pot of tea yet. Smoke gusts down into the room and swirls up past the mantelpiece and around the Toby jugs on their high shelf. They look as if they're puffing hard on their pipes as they watch Mam.

'Pull,' says Mam. 'Come on. Pull.'

Bethan holds the hooks' edge of the new pink corset wrapped around Mam and I hold the eyes' edge, and we pull and pull to make the hooks meet the eyes. But there's a big gap no matter how hard we pull. A big gap full of trembly flesh. I try not to touch it.

'It's too small, Mam,' says Bethan.

'It can't be,' says Mam. 'It's exactly the same size as my old one.'

'Can't you wear the old one?' I ask.

'Don't be silly, Gwenni,' says Mam. 'I can't get into my blue costume in the old one.'

'You don't have to wear the blue costume,' says Bethan.

38

'I always wear my blue costume on Easter Sunday,' says Mam. 'And I've got that new half hat that Siân helped me choose. She said the blue feathers are a perfect match for my eyes.' She snatches the corset from us and starts to fasten up the hooks and eyes. Her hands shake but when I try to help her she slaps my hand away. On the mantelpiece the Toby jugs narrow their eyes as Mam's blue satin dressing gown slithers open and closed around her. They puff and puff at their pipes.

'Right,' says Mam, and she steps into the corset. 'Let's try pulling it up instead of around.'

Bethan and I take hold of the top of the corset each side of Mam. The blue satin dressing gown slides over me. I hold my breath as long as I can in case Evening in Paris makes my head throb. The corset is much narrower than Mam. Bethan and I tug and tug and the corset creeps up over Mam's belly. I close my eyes so that I don't see the bulges.

'Don't pull faces, Gwenni,' says Mam. 'Keep pulling.'

'I don't know how you can breathe in it, Mam,' says Bethan.

'Never mind breathing,' says Mam. 'I have to get into that blue costume for Chapel.'

'Can we stop for a minute?' says Bethan. 'I'm getting boiling hot.'

Mam pulls her dressing gown around her. 'Gwenni,' she says, 'close the damper and put the kettle on. We'll see if the fire's hot enough to boil it now.'

I place the kettle on the logs. A flame flares up and I jerk my hand away. Bethan pulls out yesterday's *Daily Herald* from under the cushion on Tada's chair, tumbling John Morris from his sleep, and fans herself with it. John Morris curls up tighter against the breeze she makes.

'Why don't you get changed upstairs?' Bethan asks Mam.

39

'Your father's there,' says Mam. 'Stop waving the paper about. Let's try this corset again. Pass me that powder.'

Mam sprinkles the talcum powder on her skin above the corset until it mists the air. John Morris and I sneeze at the same time.

'Come on,' Mam says. 'It won't take much longer now. It'll slide easily over the talc.'

'Mam,' I say as Bethan and I heave on the corset. 'You know what I said last night about Mrs Evans wanting me to look after Angharad and Catrin after school? Can I do it? Mrs Evans said she'd pay me.'

'Teacher's pet,' says Bethan. 'Did you see all the books she gave her, Mam?'

'Can I, Mam?' I ask.

'I don't see why not,' says Mam. 'Better than sitting about here with your beak in a book.' She pants as the corset inches up, squashing her stomach upwards above it. 'And have you put all those books out of the way?'

'Yes,' I say. The cardboard box under the bed has the six books and two exercise books in it, my *School Friend* comics, the detective stories Aunty Lol lends me, the *Famous Five* books I have for Christmas every year from Aunty Siân, a list of favourite words from the dictionary at school, and my three autograph books, a blue one, a green one and a red one. Every time someone gives me a new autograph book Mam chooses a blue page and writes the same verse in it:

> *Be good, sweet maid,*
> *And let who will be clever,*
> *For after all that's said and done,*
> *The good will live forever.*

Tada always draws the family face with the family nose, the family hair done in red pencil and the family freckles done in brown. It looks like me. I used to have a diary in a red Lion exercise book in the box with PRIVATE written on the front underneath the lion's head. When she read it Mam said: There are no secrets in this house, Gwenni.

'Concentrate, Gwenni,' says Mam. 'You're not pulling hard enough.'

'I've got to stop for a minute,' says Bethan. 'Look at my fingers. They've gone all white. I can't feel them.'

She waves her hands at me and Mam. The corset is only just over Mam's belly button and the rest of her wobbles like a strawberry blancmange above it. I try not to look at the blancmange. But the Toby jugs are looking; they've stopped smoking their pipes and their fat cheeks are a fiery red.

The mantelpiece clock tick-tocks and Mam breathes along with it in little gasps. Her face is cross and crinkly underneath her yellow pincurls. She didn't have her beauty sleep last night; I had a bad dream and woke her up. For a moment we all three stand motionless. When the latch on the back door rattles it makes us all jump.

'Yoo-hoo,' calls Nain from the scullery.

'Quick,' says Mam. 'Where's my sash gone?' Her blue satin dressing gown slips around her as she catches hold of the sash and ties it round her vanished waist.

Nain comes through the scullery door and peers into the room; she hasn't got her spectacles on her family nose. 'Why is it so dark in here?' she asks. 'And what's that sickly smell?' She's in her old tartan dressing gown and her hair hangs over her shoulder in a grey plait that gets thinner and thinner on its way down.

'Magda,' she says to Mam. 'I came round straight away, as

soon as Nellie next door told me. I couldn't let you go to Chapel knowing nothing about it. Poor Guto's been flapping about all over town like an old crow, in a panic about it. Nellie says the news is spreading like spilt milk. Everyone'll have heard.'

She looks at the three of us as we stare at her. 'I saw something in the tea leaves yesterday, but I couldn't read it,' she says. 'Well, who could?' She squints at Mam. 'Are you all right?' she asks. 'What's happened to you?'

'Never mind Mam, Nain,' says Bethan. 'What did you come to tell us?'

Nain ignores Bethan. 'It's Ifan Evans, Magda,' she says. 'He's run off.'

'Run off?' says Mam, pulling her dressing gown sash tighter around her. 'What do you mean, run off?'

'Run off,' says Nain again. 'What do you think I mean? Run off and no one knows where he is. Elin won't be in Chapel this morning, that's for sure.'

Mam is still panting from the tight corset. 'But . . . who says he's run off?' she asks.

'Nellie said he didn't turn up for a meeting at the vestry with the minister yesterday evening, and when the minister went all the way to Brwyn Coch to see him, Elin said he hadn't been home since breakfast,' says Nain. 'Not for his dinner or his tea. She didn't know where he was. And he left Mot tied up all day – have you ever known him go anywhere except Chapel without that dog?'

In my bad dream Mot barked and leapt on the end of his rope as the black dog galloped towards me across the field to Brwyn Coch and Ifan Evans laughed and laughed, his face as red as the Toby jugs' cheeks. Just before the black dog reached me I screamed and woke up. That was when Mam banged on the wall and shouted: Be quiet, Gwenni; I must have my beauty sleep.

'But he's a deacon,' says Mam to Nain.

'He's a man, Magda,' says Nain. 'Don't know when they're well off, men. Look at Ifan; nice wife, educated but knows her place, a house like a pin in paper always, beautiful children. And he runs off.' She raises her eyebrows and shrugs. Her grey plait shifts off her shoulder. When it hangs straight down her back it reaches almost to her knees.

Bethan makes faces at me and mouths, 'Good riddance.'

Nain looks at us. 'What are you two doing standing there with your ears flapping?' she says. 'Go and make the tea, that kettle's boiling its lid off.'

I go into the scullery, past all the faces in the distemper. They're not watching me this morning. They've closed their eyes and grown long ears so that they can listen to Nain. I pick up the tea tray and take it through into the living room.

'I can't believe it,' says Mam. 'Not Ifan. Oh . . . oh,' she clutches her face in both hands. 'What if he's had an accident?'

I put two scoops of tea in the brown teapot and Bethan lifts the kettle from the fire and pours the boiling water onto the tea leaves. The water burbles like the stream at Brwyn Coch racing down to the Reservoir. Don't think about the Reservoir.

'They've had the men out looking,' says Nain. 'No. He's gone. Always had a roving eye, that Ifan. So they say.'

I stir the tea round and round and Bethan puts the kettle back in the grate quietly.

'I hope you didn't get soot on your clothes, Bethan,' says Nain. 'Terrible thing to get off, soot.'

Mam's face is as white as her talcum powder. 'No. No,' she says. 'Don't say that. He's a real gentleman.'

Bethan makes a throwing-up face at me.

'What?' says Nain. 'Not what I'd call him, though I've never had much to do with him, myself. I hear he can be a charmer when he isn't in one of his moods.'

'Moods?' says Mam. 'Ifan?'

'Very moody, apparently,' says Nain. 'But there, the girls would have liked that when he was young. And he was a bit of a piece when he was younger with that fair hair and those dark eyes; oh, yes, quite a good-looker. Turned many a girl's head; and not only before he married Elin, either. So I'm told.'

The wind howls in the chimney and a puff of smoke floats into the room and curls up around the Toby jugs.

'This weather,' says Nain. 'Though it hasn't snowed again, thank goodness. Dress up warmly for Chapel. You know how mean Mrs Davies Chapel House is with the heating.'

'Would you like a cup of tea, Nain?' I ask.

'No time, Gwenni,' she says. 'Have to get on before your Aunty Lol gets up. That great horse of a girl just gets in my way.' She turns for the scullery door and on her way she says, 'Let me know if you hear anything more about it this morning, Magda.' The back door slams shut behind her as the wind catches it and in the silence that follows I hear the scullery tap that Tada mended for the fourth time yesterday begin to drip-drip again.

Mam is staring into the fire, standing still the way Mrs Evans did when she stared out of the window at Brwyn Coch. Thinking.

I put milk into three of the teacups and Bethan lifts the pot to pour the tea. 'Does that mean Ifan Evans has run off with another woman?' she says.

'Don't talk rubbish,' says Mam. 'He's a married man.'

'That's what Nain said,' says Bethan.

'No, she didn't,' says Mam. 'Gwenni, do you know anything about this?'

'Me?' I say.

44

'When you were there yesterday,' says Mam, 'did you see Mr Evans?'

'No,' I say. 'I took Angharad and Catrin out to play and I helped Mrs Evans because she was in a lot of pain after Mr Price. Like you were, Mam, and she bled a lot, too. It was all over the floor.' I have that old family stomach as I remember it.

'Don't talk to anyone about it,' says Mam.

'Except me,' says Bethan.

'About what?' I ask Mam.

'Yesterday,' she says. 'Gossip is nasty.'

Mam unties her blue satin sash. 'Let's get this corset off,' she says. 'It's making me feel quite sick pressing into my stomach. I'll wear the old one. And my winter costume.'

Bethan helps her pull the corset down. It comes off more easily than it went on. The talcum powder flakes away onto the linoleum like snow.

'If you're not wearing your blue costume, can I wear your new half hat?' asks Bethan.

Mam doesn't answer.

7

We slide into our pew in Chapel just as Mrs Morris squeezes the last notes of her repertoire from the organ. That's what Mrs Morris calls it: My repertoire. The organ is old as sin and some of the notes are silent.

Mam sits in the middle between me and Bethan. She always sits in the middle. I shuffle closer to the door so that I don't have to breathe in so much Evening in Paris. Mam leans her head on her hand to pray. Whenever I ask her what she prays for she says: That's private, Gwenni. She prays for a long time this morning. There are still flakes of talcum powder on the back of her hand.

Nain was right. Mrs Evans and Angharad and Catrin are not in their pew behind the organ. And Ifan Evans is not in the Big Seat under the pulpit. All the other deacons are there in their black suits, looking like a row of old crows from the castle, and so is Alwenna's father, the song-raiser, who is allowed to sit there even though he's not a deacon.

A soft, red velvet cushion runs all along the Big Seat. But the deacons still fidget. Mr Morris turns to look at his wife, who ignores him, and Mr Pugh runs his finger around inside his collar again and again. Jones the Butcher has his arm along the back of the seat behind Young Mr Ellis and his meaty fingers tap on the polished wood. Young Mr Ellis looks at the ceiling. Alwenna's father flips through the pages of his hymn book and Twm Edwards whispers into the Voice of God's ear. The Voice of God looks up and nods at Alwenna's father.

I shift round in my seat to see if Alwenna is in her family's pew at the back of the Chapel, but Mam prods me with her elbow and I have to turn back and look to the front. Mrs Llywelyn Pugh sits two pews forward of us with her dead fox around her shoulders. I try not to look at the dead fox.

Alwenna's father clears his throat and says, 'Hymn two hundred and thirteen.'

Mrs Morris begins to wheeze the tune out of the organ and I find that I've forgotten my hymn book and have to share Mam's. But I can't read the words because Mam's hand is shaking and the print jiggles about on the page. I pretend to sing. The congregation's song rises up to the Chapel ceiling and I hear Alwenna's voice soar above everyone else's. If her voice were to carry on through the Chapel roof and up, up into the sky it would melt into the Earth's song and all the people in the whole world would think there was a choir of angels in the sky and be filled with wonder like the shepherds when Jesus Christ was born.

Everyone sits down after the hymn and the Voice of God half chants a long prayer. I listen to every word but he doesn't mention Mrs Evans or Angharad or Catrin. Or Ifan Evans. I've already forgotten what he did mention. Alwenna's father raises another hymn and as the congregation sits down again after singing, the Voice of God ascends the pulpit steps.

The whole Chapel begins to settle itself for the next half hour. The heaters stop rumbling and people cough and splutter and make themselves as comfortable as they can on the hard pew seats. Somebody passes wind and the sound echoes around the room and along the high gallery. Mam pretends not to notice but Bethan snorts as she tries not to laugh. I pull my handkerchief out of my coat pocket to hold over my nose. The three pennies for the collection that I'd wrapped in the handkerchief drop to the floor and clink past several pews. Mam clamps her hand tightly on mine. The Voice of God pauses for a second as he opens the pulpit gate and he looks down on the Big Seat and the empty space between Mr Pugh and Jones the Butcher where Ifan Evans should be. Mam's hand starts shaking again and she lets go of me and leans back in the pew and her breath flutters as if she still has her new corset on.

The Voice of God declares that his sermon is about the resurrection, the greatest miracle of all. Isn't flying a great miracle? Or falling like Alice into Wonderland? Bethan begins to cough. Mam takes a packet of Polo mints from her pocket and gives one to Bethan. The silver paper rustles like a mouse in Mam's shaky hand. A sweet mintiness mingles with the smell that's always in Chapel, of mice and must and Mrs Davies Chapel House's beeswax polish and mothballs from suit pockets and Evening in Paris.

My plait has fallen forward over my shoulder and it tickles my chin. I throw it back and the pink polka-dot ribbon I took from the middle of the bed this morning to tie around the end flies off like a butterfly into the aisle. I lean over the pew door to reach it but Mam pulls me back and holds on tight, tight to my arm. I feel her trembling but I can't move.

Jones the Butcher shouts, 'Amen. Amen,' as he agrees with part of the sermon and the Voice of God starts to build up to a fervour in the pulpit, already half singing some of his words and murmuring others so that the congregation has to lean forward to hear him. Mam is watching the Voice of God as if she's mesmerised. 'Amen,' shouts Jones the Butcher again, but Mam doesn't blink, her eyes are as wide open and still as the glass eyes on Mrs Llywelyn Pugh's dead fox.

I try not to look into the dead fox's yellow eyes. They remind me of the fox Ifan Evans flung at me when I went to look after Angharad and Catrin last Christmas holidays. I'd never been inside Brwyn Coch before and Mrs Evans showed me all those books in the parlour, the ones that Mam won't let me borrow. It was dusk when I walked home. The grass sparkled with frost in the white light of the moon and it crunched beneath my feet as I walked across the field. I looked back from the top of the stile to watch the Christmas star flicker in the sky above the cottage. When I turned round again I saw Guto'r Wern leaping down the road, wailing like the fire brigade siren, his crow black coat flapping open as he ran. I climbed down the other side of the stile and didn't notice the fox on the bottom step until I almost put my foot on it. There was a red wound in its side and I saw the fox's spirit leave the wound like a warm breath in the cold air. Then, from nowhere, Ifan Evans appeared in front of me. He picked up the fox and swung it at me, laughing all the time. He said: This would make you a fine fox-fur if you were a fine lady, Gwenni. His face was scarlet as a holly berry and his breath smelt sweet. He made as if to put the dead fox around my shoulders. I couldn't move quickly enough off the stile and I saw the fox's eyes stare at me just before I felt its warm blood on my cheek. Mot, or perhaps it wasn't Mot, perhaps it was the big black dog, leapt up and started to lick the blood from my face. I screamed and Ifan Evans laughed again. He staggered away and the dog went after him and I ran all the way across the next field to the gate and all the way down the hill and didn't stop until I got home. Mam said:

Don't make such a fuss, Gwenni; it's only a bit of blood. And she sent me into the scullery to wash my face. When I told her how piteous the fox looked she said: Don't be silly, Gwenni.

In the pulpit the Voice of God intones, 'And on the Day of Judgement, by that greatest of miracles, we shall all be resurrected, and we shall all be equal in the eyes of the Lord. The greatest and the least of us shall be . . .' He pauses, and the congregation leans forward. 'Equal,' he murmurs.

'Amen. Amen,' shouts Jones the Butcher.

Mrs Llywelyn Pugh re-arranges her dead fox around her neck. Its tail has lost its bushiness and its ears droop and its fur is dull. Its little face is between its front paws, dangling down the back of Mrs Llywelyn Pugh's pink jacket, and just on the end of its chin the fur is a creamier colour. Its glassy eyes stare at me and now I return the stare and see the sadness in those eyes. Is it sad because it didn't have a decent burial? When our old Siani Nanti died Tada wrapped her in the *Daily Herald* and buried her in the back yard. Tada said: She was a good mouser; let's give her a decent burial. Did the fox's spirit go to Heaven, like Siani Nanti's? Will it rise again? The dead fox lowers both eyelids in a slow blink at me just like John Morris does when he's being friendly. I turn my head sharply to look at Mam but she's too entranced by the Voice of God to notice that the greatest of miracles has taken place two pews in front of her.

8

The skin on the gravy ripples as I pull the slice of lamb from beneath it. I begin to cut away the fat and pack it into a neat pile at the edge of my plate.

'Don't play with your food, Gwenni,' Mam says. 'Eat it all up. You could do with a bit of fat on you.'

'I don't like the feel of it in my mouth,' I say. 'It's like eating a lump of lard.'

'I'll have it,' says Bethan. 'I like the fat.' She leans over and takes the cuttings with her fork and pushes them into her mouth. A dribble of grease shines at one corner of her lips.

Mam looks at Bethan and her tight face turns soft. 'I could eat anything I liked when I was your age, too,' she says.

'I can eat anything I like,' I say. 'I just don't like the fatty bits.'

'Eat up the lean meat, then, there's a good girl,' says Tada. 'It's good for you. Makes you strong.' He puts a forkful of meat into his mouth. 'Think of the lion. It doesn't eat anything except meat.' I try not to watch as he pulls a piece of gristle from his mouth and puts it on the side of his plate.

I slice up my meat. The sun breaks through the cloud for a moment and shines through the living room window onto the meat plate and the lump of grey lamb with its leg-bone sticking up. The fat glistens and the bone gleams white beneath the crusted blood. I push the rest of my meat to the side of my plate and eat the carrots.

'Lovely bit of lamb,' says Tada. 'Sweet as honey. Is there any more mint sauce? Pass it over, will you, Gwenni?' The scent of the vinegary mint rises from his meat and gravy as he pours the sauce over them. 'So, no news of Ifan Evans this morning in Chapel, then?'

'Nothing in Chapel,' says Mam. Her face has gone tight again, the way it's been all morning. 'Plenty after Chapel on the way home, though. You should have heard Nanw Lipstick.'

'You wouldn't let us stop to listen to her,' says Bethan. 'Mam just marched us home, Tada.'

'Alwenna's Mam always knows everything,' I say. Like Alwenna.

'Pity she doesn't keep it to herself,' says Mam.

'I heard Nanw Lipstick say it was on the cards, Tada,' says Bethan.

'Mrs Thomas to you, Bethan,' says Tada.

'I don't know how she knows these things,' says Mam. 'I think she makes up most of it.'

'What did she mean, Mam?' I ask.

'Don't talk with your mouth full,' says Mam. 'More roast potatoes, Bethan?' She proffers the plate.

'I feel very sorry for Elin Evans,' says Tada. 'Nice woman.'

'Nice is as nice does,' says Mam, and puts the plate down without offering Tada any more potatoes.

'What does that mean?' I say.

'Never you mind. Eat your dinner.' Mam's face is red as well as tight. 'I haven't slaved over that fire half the morning for you to push the food around your plate. Why can't you eat properly like everyone else?'

Bethan lifts her eyebrows at me. I shrug. We eat without speaking now. The mantelpiece clock tick-tocks in counterpoint to the click-clack of the cutlery. The Toby jugs pretend to be interested in the ceiling but every now and then I see them glance down at us. When the clock strikes one it startles us all.

'That rice pudding will be done,' says Mam, and stands up. She takes her Sunday apron from the back of the chair and puts it on before opening the oven door. A bitter smell spills into the living room as Mam pulls out the pudding dish.

'It's burnt again,' says Bethan. The dark brown skin clings to the sides of the dish and stretches over the pudding.

Mam bangs the dish down on the table. 'It wouldn't burn in an electric cooker,' she says.

'I like the skin like that,' says Tada. He smiles at Mam with his bright, white, false teeth. 'You make a beautiful rice pudding, sweetheart.'

Mam ignores him. 'Take the dinner plates into the scullery and bring in the pudding bowls,' she says to me.

I scrape the food off my plate onto Tada's bit of gristle, stack the plates and carry them into the scullery. John Morris follows me. He purrs when I put the congealed gravy and scraps of meat into his saucer. I try not to touch them. The faces in the distemper have opened their eyes again and watch everything I do.

I take the bowls to Mam and she dishes up the rice pudding.

'No skin, please, Mam,' I say when it's my turn.

'Eat what you're given,' says Mam. 'There are little yellow children starving in China who would be glad of that.'

'When I had rice pudding at Caroline's house,' says Bethan, 'it didn't taste like this and it wasn't so thick.'

'Rice pudding's got to be thick. Got to have something to get your teeth into. Lovely, this.' Tada speaks through a mouthful of pudding. He smiles at Mam.

'That Mrs Smythe was advertising for a cook,' says Mam. 'Where does she think she's going to find a cook around here?'

'Smith,' says Bethan. 'They say it Smith and spell it S-m-y-t-h-e.'

'Well,' says Tada. His voice is still stuck in the rice pudding.

'Caroline says they came down in the world when they came here,' says Bethan. 'There isn't any good help to be had. Mrs Smythe wants to move back to England.'

Tada swallows his mouthful of pudding with a gulp. 'Well,' he says.

'Caroline's father's rich,' says Bethan. 'Caroline's got her own room. You should see it. I'd like my own room.'

'I'd like my own room, too,' I say. I want my own bed so I don't have to land on top of Bethan every time I come back from flying, and a desk like Mrs Evans's to sit at and write Catrin's story with a rocker for the blotter, and a bookshelf instead of the box under the bed.

'That's enough of that,' says Mam. 'We can't all be rich. Some of us have to scrimp and save for years to afford a house with a bathroom.' She eats a spoonful of rice pudding. 'And an electric oven.'

'Caroline's brother has got a huge room of his own,' says Bethan. 'Richard.'

'You don't go into boys' rooms,' says Mam, her voice shrill.

'I only looked in, Mam,' says Bethan. 'He wasn't even there.'

'Nice-looking boy,' says Tada. 'Polite, too.'

Bethan's face turns pink.

I look at her. 'You don't like him, do you?' I say.

'None of your business who I like, Gwenni Morgan,' says Bethan. 'Tell her, Mam.'

'Now, now,' says Tada.

'Don't be silly, Gwenni,' says Mam. 'Bethan's far too young to be liking boys.'

'I'm nearly fourteen,' says Bethan.

'Thirteen and a half,' says Mam. 'Much too young.'

'You do like him,' I say. 'Yuck.'

'Be quiet, Gwenni,' says Mam.

'Shall I make a cup of tea, sweetheart?' says Tada. 'Come on, Bethan, take the pudding bowls away.'

Tada swings the kettle onto the fire and when it boils pours the water into the teapot and gives it a stir. 'Let it brew a bit,' he says and sits back in his chair.

Mam puts out the Sunday cups and saucers that I like with their pretty blue make-believe flowers and their thin golden rims that catch the light.

I watch Mam pouring the tea and I take a deep breath and I say, 'Mrs Llywelyn Pugh's dead fox blinked at me in Chapel this morning. With both its eyes. I think it was resurrected.'

The teapot shakes in Mam's hand and the bright golden tea splashes on the Sunday tablecloth and seeps into the embroidered flowers.

'Don't start,' she says. 'Emlyn, tell her not to start.'

'Listen to your mam, Gwenni,' says Tada. 'Anyway, the dead fox has got glass eyes. It can't blink at you.'

'All you do is encourage her nonsense,' says Mam. 'Flying yesterday, dead animals blinking today. What will people think if she goes around saying silly things like that? They'll think she's simple.'

'Of course they won't,' says Tada. 'Everyone knows Gwenni's a clever one.'

'Clever is as clever does,' says Mam.

'What does that mean?' says Bethan.

I know what Mam thinks of clever. She writes it in all my autograph books.

'If you're clever you'll get on in this old world,' says Tada.

'No one will think Gwenni's clever if she goes around saying she can fly and dead animals are resurrected,' says Mam.

'I think it wants me to help it,' I say. 'I think it wants a decent burial. Like we gave Siani Nanti.'

Mam stands up and leans over the table towards me. 'Be quiet,' she shouts. I can see the spittle spray from her lips and I lean right back in my chair so it misses me.

'Sit down, sweetheart, and have your cup of tea,' says Tada, and tries to take hold of Mam's hand but misses. 'Now, don't worry about what people think. It doesn't matter.'

'You wouldn't say that if you'd heard Nanw Lipstick this morning,' says Mam. 'Poor Ifan missing like this, a lovely man, a real gentleman – I don't care what Nain says – and all Nanw Lipstick can do is tittle-tattle about him.'

'But everyone was talking about him, Mam,' says Bethan. 'And about Mrs Evans.'

'Take a deep breath now, Magda, like Dr Edwards said,' says Tada. He manages to take hold of Mam's shaking hand. 'Old gossips aren't worth listening to. Ifan is bound to turn up again, large as life, you'll see. Then what will the old gossips do, eh?'

'Caroline says that Mrs Evans is pretty,' says Bethan. 'Do you think she's pretty, Tada?'

'Well, yes,' says Tada. 'Very pretty. And clever.'

Mam snatches her hand away from Tada and piles the

teacups into each other with a clatter and takes them into the scullery.

'I haven't finished drinking my tea,' says Bethan.

'We'll be late for Sunday School if we don't get cracking,' Mam says, then closes her mouth so tight her lips disappear.

9

I pull down the sleeves of my best coat to cover my hands; it's always cold in Chapel during Sunday School. Mrs Davies Chapel House turns the heaters off after the morning service to save money; Alwenna says Mrs Davies spends the saved money on silk stockings and black satin suspender belts. When I told Mam she said: That Alwenna has no shame.

I slide into the pew next to Alwenna. She turns sideways to show me the seams in her stockings. 'Look at that,' she whispers. 'Dead straight. Took me a quarter of an hour.' Aneurin and Edwin turn round to bob their quiffs at her from the pew in front of us. They're our bêtes noires; that's French for black beasts. Monsieur Jenkins says it means something you can't abide. But today Alwenna smiles at them.

Mrs Morris stops playing her repertoire on the organ and all the deacons in the Big Seat stand and turn to face the congrega- tion. Tada was wrong; Ifan Evans has not turned up. The Voice of God announces that Young Mr Ellis will look after Mrs Evans's class and welcomes the Beynon family to our Sunday School for the first time. Mam says they have a daughter my age who'll make me a nice friend instead of Alwenna.

'Why isn't Mrs Evans here?' Aneurin asks Young Mr Ellis when our class is sitting in the dark pews under the gallery overhang.

Young Mr Ellis blushes and his wire-rimmed spectacles slip down his nose. He pushes them back up with his little finger. The fingernail is dirty and Young Mr Ellis smells of the farm where he works. I try not to breathe too deeply.

'Never mind that, Aneurin,' Young Mr Ellis says. 'Now, who can tell me what important point the Reverend Roberts was making in his sermon this morning?'

Aneurin stares at Young Mr Ellis, then he starts to snigger. 'You're not as pretty as Mrs Evans,' he says. The quiff balanced on the edge of Aneurin's forehead bobs up and down and a scent of Brylcreem wafts from it.

I narrow my eyes and stare hard at Aneurin's back. He turns around; he always does. 'What are you staring at, Gwenni Morgan?' he says. 'It's true. He's not as pretty as Mrs Evans.'

'Mr Ellis,' I say. 'Mr Roberts's sermon was about our spirits, wasn't it? And the miracle of the resurrection.'

Young Mr Ellis's dirty little fingernail pushes his spectacles up his nose again. He swallows loudly so that his Adam's apple rises and falls in his throat. 'Very good, Gwenni. And what was the point he was making, can you remember?'

Aneurin makes gagging noises that Young Mr Ellis pretends he can't hear.

'Do you think Aneurin's got a spirit, Mr Ellis?' I ask.

'Every human being has a spirit, Gwenni.'

'But Aneurin is more of an animal, Mr Ellis. If he's got a spirit it would mean that animals have a spirit, wouldn't it?'

Aneurin launches himself backward out of his pew and tries to grab hold of my hair. 'You're the animal, Gwenni Morgan. You look more like a fox than a fox.'

'Vixen,' says Geraint.

'What?' says Aneurin. 'What did you say, four-eyes?'

'Vixen,' says Geraint. He takes off his spectacles and polishes them with his fair-isle pullover. 'She's a girl.'

'Are you trying to be funny?' Aneurin leans around Edwin and catches hold of a handful of Geraint's pullover and pulls it towards him.

Young Mr Ellis stands up and flaps his hands at them. 'Boys, boys,' he says.

'It's a fight, Mr Ellis.' Alwenna smiles at him and crosses her legs. Her stockings swish-swish against each other. 'You'll have to stop it.'

Young Mr Ellis pushes his spectacles back up his nose and looks at her stockings.

'Mr Ellis.' The Voice of God sounds like thunder. 'What's going on here?'

Young Mr Ellis jumps. 'Just a touch of high spirits, Mr Roberts.'

'It looks more like a fight to me. Come on out of there, man.'

Young Mr Ellis looks at the way out past Aneurin and Edwin and instead climbs over the front of the pew into the next one, then out into the aisle.

'Aneurin,' says the Voice of God. 'I shall have to speak to your mother about your behaviour.'

'Gwenni Morgan started it, Mr Roberts. It's all her fault.'

I shake my head. 'We were just talking about spirits,' I say.

'Hmm,' says the Voice of God. 'I'll swap places with Mr Ellis. He can look after my class and I'll sit here with you. Move up,

Geraint.' He sits in the pew and turns sideways to look at me.
'So, you were listening this morning, Gwenni?'

'We were talking about animal spirits,' I say. 'Can animals –
like foxes, say – be resurrected, Mr Roberts?'

The Voice of God can see Aneurin making faces at me without
even looking at him. 'Stop that, Aneurin,' he says. 'Go on, Gwenni.
What do you think?'

'They're alive, aren't they? So they must have spirits. And if
they've got spirits they can be resurrected, can't they?'

'What does everyone else think? Edwin?'

'That's daft.' Edwin has a quiff that almost matches Aneurin's,
but sometimes it collapses so he looks as if he's got a long fringe,
like Mrs Williams's old horse in the field behind Penrhiw. 'That's
just like a girl. Animals are animals, aren't they?'

'Gwenni's soft in the head,' says Aneurin.

'Aneurin,' says the Voice of God.

'But it's silly. How can animals have spirits? We wouldn't eat
them if they had spirits, would we?'

Deilwen Beynon speaks for the first time. 'Mami says it's our
spirits that make us human,' she says. Her voice is entrancing,
like a breathy whisper, and her Welsh sounds so different to ours.
I'm smiling at her, but she doesn't say any more. And now I realise
what she did say and I stop smiling.

'Does it say anything in the Bible about animals having
spirits?' I ask the Voice of God.

'Not exactly, Gwenni.' The Voice of God sighs.

'So animals could have spirits, then?'

'I suppose it's a matter of opinion,' says the Voice of God.

'My opinion is that they don't,' says Aneurin.

'Mine, too,' says Edwin. They both turn to Geraint.

'I don't know.' Geraint takes off his spectacles and rubs them against his pullover. 'But I did see our old cat's ghost. So she must have had a spirit.'

Aneurin looks at the ceiling. 'Was that when you had your specs on or off?' he says to Geraint.

'I saw her ghost, too. So there,' says Meinir to Aneurin.

'I saw my Nain's ghost,' says Eirlys. 'With Pero, her old collie.'

'I don't believe in ghosts,' says Alwenna.

I stare at her. She believed in ghosts last weekend. We went ghost-hunting around the castle. 'But you believe animals have spirits,' I say.

'No,' she says. And she smiles at Aneurin again.

'But you said your little white kitten's spirit had gone to Heaven when it got run over by Wil the Post's bike.'

'I was just a child, then,' she says.

'It was only last month,' I say.

Aneurin winks at her. She re-crosses her legs. Swish, swish.

'Well, Gwenni, I think this is a draw,' says the Voice of God. 'Now I want you all to sit here quietly until the end of Sunday School. I'm going over to see how Mr Ellis is getting on with my class.'

I pick up my Bible from beside me on the seat. Its fine, gold-edged leaves whisper as I turn them over. What are they telling me? I wonder how long it would take me to read my Bible from beginning to end, to find proof that I'm right. The Voice of God could have missed the proof. Maybe I'll find out if spirits can float on water, too. Are spirits New Testament? I'll begin with that. Tonight. The edge of the seat is digging into my legs. I shift along the pew, and see that Alwenna is leaning forward to talk to Aneurin and Edwin. Their hair is greasier than the leg of lamb. Whatever is the matter with her?

Meinir passes me a bag of sweets. 'You can take two,' she says. 'But don't give Alwenna any.'

I take one pear drop from the bag. Its sourness makes my jaw tighten. I pass the bag back to Meinir. I suck the sweet and watch a long strand of spider's web that Mrs Davies Chapel House has missed dangle down from the gallery and sway to and fro like a clock's pendulum above Aneurin's head. There must be hundreds of spider spirits in this Chapel. Tiny, scuttling ghosts. I wonder if the spirit of Mrs Llywelyn Pugh's dead fox is still here, waiting for me to rescue its body and give it a decent burial.

The Voice of God comes by with the breeze from his over-coat. 'Good, good. I knew I could count on you to behave,' he says. 'I'll let you off this time, Aneurin. Now all of you go down to the front for the hymn and the blessing.'

The classes gather back into the front pews from the musty, dusty corners of the Chapel and the youngest children are brought in from the vestry clutching drawings of Easter eggs and hopping and chirping like Easter chicks. But little Catrin isn't with them. My little wren.

'Oh, damno,' says Alwenna. 'Look, I've laddered my stocking on this silly seat.' A long white streak is travelling the length of her leg. 'Mam will kill me.'

I lean towards her. 'We made a vow,' I say, 'that we wouldn't talk to boys. And especially not to those two.'

'That was when we were children, Gwenni.'

'A vow is a vow,' I say. 'And we mixed our blood.'

'Hymn number seven hundred and sixty-five,' says the Voice of God, 'A *Pure Heart*.' Mrs Morris begins to pull at the stops on the organ, and pedals until the organ pumps out the music with only a few silent notes.

After the blessing we file out of the Chapel. The cloudy day seems bright after the dimness inside.

'I've got a really good idea,' I say to Alwenna, 'about Mrs Llywelyn Pugh's dead fox. Tell you about it on the way home.'

'I'm going straight down home today,' says Alwenna.

'But we always go for a walk after Sunday School,' I say.

'Not today,' says Alwenna.

Aneurin and Edwin stand behind her. 'Did you tell fox-face about Mrs Evans?' asks Aneurin.

'What about Mrs Evans?' I narrow my eyes at him.

'Alwenna's Mam says Ifan Evans has left her to go off with his girlfriend,' he says.

I look at Alwenna but she's examining the ladder in her stocking. 'Don't be silly,' I say. 'He can't have a girlfriend if he's married.'

Aneurin sniggers. Alwenna starts walking down the hill.

'Wait for us,' Aneurin shouts, and he and Edwin rush past me and catch up with Alwenna, one on each side of her. I watch them walking away, Alwenna's yellow skirt with its big petticoat swaying from side to side. I'll have to tell her my good idea another time. I'll go straight home for tea. This Sunday, I won't be late for it. I think of the tinned peaches and cream and thin bread and butter Tada will have made ready. But I'm not hungry, though my stomach is quite hollow.

10

I push Bethan's arm back to her own half of the bed. She snorts and mumbles and kicks her leg out so that it lies over my left ankle. Her leg is heavy and hot and it's difficult to move it back, even when I kick it with my free leg. I arrange myself flat on my back, straight out under the bedclothes. When I rescued my ribbon this morning from the Chapel floor it had two skinny dead spiders entangled in it, but they're gone now and I smooth the ribbon back in place over the feathery bumps along the length of the mattress.

Bethan put out the light before I could find anything about spirits in my New Testament, but there's a lot more of it to read yet. I only got as far as the end of the first chapter of Matthew, which is all about Jesus Christ's grandfathers, going back for forty-two generations; I counted them. He had no grandmothers at all. There's a thin moon chasing the clouds in the sky tonight but its light isn't bright enough to read by, not even if I get up and sit next to the window. When I lift my head I can just see Mari the Doll on the chair, asleep underneath her patchwork blanket. Aunty Lol gave me the red and green wool for the blanket and lent me the needles. But the needles were size eleven, and it took me weeks and weeks to knit enough squares. When I told Mam I was knitting a blanket to keep Mari the Doll warm just in case she came alive in the night and felt the cold, Mam said: Don't be silly, Gwenni; people will think you're odd. But Mari the Doll listens to everything I tell her; maybe dolls have spirits just like people and foxes and spiders. It's no good asking the Voice of God about that when he doesn't even know about foxes. I wonder if I'll find anything in my New Testament about it.

From the trees in Bron-y-graig comes the hoot of a corpse bird. Mam always says I must cover my ears if I hear it, in case it brings a death with it. I hear it every night when it's out hunting for mice and voles. Does that count as bringing a death?

This grey blanket scratches under my chin, so I fold the sheet over it and hold them both against my mouth and nose. If I breathe in the warm, aired scent of the sheet it will make me sleepy. I try not to see Buddy Holly watching from the wall at the foot of the bed, the lens of his spectacles glinting in the moonlight. I have to dress and undress under the bedclothes ever since Caroline gave Bethan the picture to pin up on the wall, but Bethan doesn't care if Buddy Holly and all three of his Crickets see her without any clothes on at all.

I leap as the back door groans on its hinges beneath the bedroom window. John Morris squawks as Mam throws him out for the night, and then yowls as soon as the door is shut on him. He likes to sleep in the chair by the fire, not out on the wall in the cold. Two doors up, Nellie Davies's bony tabby cats join in the caterwauling. I hear Nellie Davies's sash window crash open and the slosh of the water she keeps in a chamber pot by her bed as she throws it over her two cats. Nellie Davies has got good aim; the cats are quiet now.

And listen, Mam and Tada are coming upstairs; because of his limp, Tada never manages to miss all the squeaky treads. I close my eyes and keep still. The bedroom door swings open and Evening in Paris floats in on the draught. 'Fast asleep, both of them,' says Tada. He closes the door, and as I pull the sheet tighter around my nose the landing light goes out.

I feel the thump of the bed as Tada climbs into it on the other side of the wall from me, and the bedsprings twang as he settles himself down. Bethan flings her arm over my face. I pinch it and shove it back again. Alwenna has her own bed; she doesn't have any sisters to share with. But her three brothers all have to sleep in one bed. I try not to think about Alwenna.

'Don't put the light out, sweetheart,' says Tada. The light switch clicks all the same and the bedsprings twang again as Mam gets into bed.

'Don't do that, Emlyn,' says Mam. I pull the sheet and the blanket up over my ears.

'Why not, Magda? What's the matter tonight?' says Tada through the sheet and the blanket.

'Can't you see I'm worried?'

'This will stop you worrying, sweetheart.'

The bedsprings twang in a frenzy; I push the sheet into my ears.

'Don't do that,' says Mam.

Bethan grunts and turns over onto my side of the ribbon. I roll her into her own space and pinch her leg hard to make her stay there. She lies on her back and snores.

'You'll wake the girls,' says Mam.

The quiet lasts until Tada starts to breathe heavily. I slow my breathing to keep pace with Tada's and I begin to feel distant and drowsy. I close my eyes. I wonder if I'll fly in my sleep tonight;

I didn't last night, I had that bad dream instead. I want to be up in the quiet sky on my own, with only the light of the moon and the hum of the Earth for company. I wonder if I'll ever see the spirit in the Baptism Pool again.

'Emlyn,' says Mam. I jump out of sleep. 'Emlyn. Don't go to sleep.'

'Then just tell me what's worrying you, Magda.'

'What do you think's happened to Ifan?' says Mam.

'Ifan?' says Tada. 'I don't think anything's happened to him. He'll turn up. Why are you worrying about Ifan?'

'I'm . . . I used to be quite fond of him. You know that.'

'It was a long time ago, Magda,' says Tada. 'No reason for you to worry about him now.'

'Nanw Lipstick is stirring up old stories about him. And she says he's gone off with a fancy woman.'

I wriggle towards the wall and put my ear against it. The wallpaper has rubbed into a furry patch that tickles my ear.

Tada gives a spluttery laugh. 'Is that what's worrying you?' he says. 'That Nanw Lipstick will find out you once went about with Ifan?'

'I couldn't bear it. Not all the gossip,' says Mam. 'And what if she found out about . . . you know . . . Mam, as well. I couldn't bear the shame of that.'

'Oh, Magda,' says Tada. His voice is weary. 'You were hardly a fancy woman, were you? How old were you? Just a girl. And as for your mother . . . well, we've gone over and over that, haven't we? Over and over it.' The bed thumps against the wall again as Tada turns over. 'What happened to your mother is nothing for you to be ashamed about,' he says.

In the back yard John Morris has got into a fight with Nellie Davies's cats. They fizz and spit at each other. Nellie Davies complains about John Morris all the time. I don't understand why he's such a good fighter when he's so lazy. Maybe he has the spirit of a warrior in him. If foxes and spiders and dolls have spirits, a cat is sure to have a spirit too.

I press my ear back against the wall.

'Anyway, that's water long gone under the bridge,' says Tada. 'It's poor Elin Evans we should be worrying about if he doesn't turn up again, left on her own with those little girls.'

Mam doesn't make a sound.

'Nice woman like that,' says Tada. 'I can't understand the man.'

The silence stretches to the moon. I lie back and pull the sheet over my mouth again.

'Best thing all round would be if Ifan came back soon,' says Tada. 'Twm Edwards won't be able to manage without a shepherd for long and Elin could lose the cottage.'

Mrs Evans could lose Brwyn Coch! What would happen to her and Angharad and little Catrin, cast out into the cold by Twm Edwards? Catrin doesn't like the cold. Where would they live? Where would Mrs Evans put all her books?

'Well, none of our business, is it?' Tada says into the quietness. 'But someone ought to find out where Ifan's got to, fancy woman or no fancy woman. I wonder if Sergeant Jones is looking into it.'

Mam doesn't answer at all. The house sighs and grumbles around me as it settles down for the night. Bethan heaves over in the bed taking the blanket and the sheet with her. I haul them back. Bethan would like to know about Mam and Ifan Evans. Maybe Mam was only Bethan's age. Just a girl, Tada said. It's like Bethan liking Caroline's brother, Richard. Yuck. Tada begins to snore, louder and louder, in a duet with Bethan. It's difficult to think in all the noise. Now there are two things I've got to start doing tomorrow. I have to think of a plot to rescue the fox-fur from Mrs Llywelyn Pugh and give it a decent burial so its spirit will be sure to go to Heaven. And I have to find Ifan Evans. Then Mrs Evans and Angharad and Catrin won't have to leave Brwyn Coch. And they won't become homeless and nearly starve and Catrin and Angharad won't die of scarlet fever because they're living in poverty like the children in *Little Women*. Although I would help nurse them.

I pull the sheet tighter over my mouth. The corpse bird hoots again and again in Bron-y-graig and I feel the beat of its heavy wings enter the rhythm of my sleep to carry me away into the night sky.

11

I push my way through the side gate of the Police House. Beside the path the bluebells hang their heads under the weight of the morning's rain. The clouds have turned even greyer and I feel goose pimples prickling all over my arms. A breeze blows up from the sea. I raise my hand to knock on Sergeant Jones's door and it swings open in front of me. Sergeant Jones is struggling to close the window behind his desk, sneezing into a big white handkerchief at the same time.

'Martha's beating the carpets,' he says. 'That breeze blew all the dust in through the window.'

I can hear the slap of the carpet beater from the garden beyond the window drumming on the carpets. Clouds of dust rise above the clothesline and drift towards the window.

'Spring cleaning,' says the Sergeant. 'All it does is shift the dust somewhere else. If I sneeze much more I'll probably have one of my nosebleeds. Are you any good at first aid, Gwenni?'

I stand in the doorway and shift my weight from one leg to another. I don't want to think about blood; I don't want to think about Mrs Evans's poor mouth and the piteous dead fox. Sergeant

Jones waves the big handkerchief he sneezed into at me. I don't look at the handkerchief.

'Come in, come in,' he says. 'Don't stand there holding up the door frame. I haven't started that Mr Campion book you brought me last time yet, if that's what you've come about. I've been much too busy.'

'I haven't come about that,' I say. Sergeant Jones doesn't catch criminals the way Albert Campion does. He says we don't have criminals like that in our town, criminals that steal priceless jewels or kidnap people and murder them. I wonder if we have priceless jewels in our town. Maybe Mrs Llywelyn Pugh wears some under her dead fox. I want to be a detective like Albert Campion, not a detective who spends all his time digging his garden. Sergeant Jones says you have to be a policeman like him before you can be a detective. Detecting isn't a suitable job for a woman, Gwenni, he says. But he won't tell me why it isn't. Maybe he doesn't know.

Sergeant Jones pushes his handkerchief into his trouser pocket and winks at me. 'Come to confess to a crime, then, have you, Gwenni?' he says and laughs until his chins wobble.

I wait for him to stop spluttering. 'Do you find missing people?' I ask.

'Sometimes,' he says, scratching his head as if he's trying to remember when he last found a missing person. He sits in his chair, which groans as he pushes his bottom back between the arms. I sit on the wooden chair in front of his desk. The seat is cold under my legs and I shiver.

'It's a bit chilly, isn't it?' says Sergeant Jones. 'I can see snow on the Wyddfa from the bedroom window. That's April for you.' He leans back in his chair. Mrs Sergeant Jones is beating the carpets faster now. Bang-bang. Bang-bang. Maybe she thinks it's going to rain again. Or snow.

'It's about Ifan Evans,' I say.

'Thought so,' says Sergeant Jones.

'Are you trying to find him?'

'The police don't usually try to find grown men who've gone away of their own accord, Gwenni.'

'Why not? What if their wives want them back? What if their children want them back?'

Sergeant Jones sighs. His chair groans again as he leans forward over the desk. His breath is warm and smells of Mrs Sergeant Jones's famous vanilla biscuits. 'Men leave their families and homes for all sorts of complicated reasons, Gwenni. Sometimes, their families are even glad to see them go.'

'But Mrs Evans will be cast out of her house and Angharad and little Catrin will starve and become ill if Ifan Evans doesn't come back.'

Sergeant Jones laughs again, then looks at me and stops. He drums his fingers on his desk in time with Mrs Sergeant Jones's carpet-beating. 'Come on, Gwenni,' he says. 'Sometimes I think you read too many books. This is real life; I don't think things will be quite that bad. And, anyway, Ifan Evans will probably turn up again, like the bad penny.'

'What does that mean?'

'Nothing, Gwenni, it's just something people say.'

'But what if he doesn't turn up like the bad penny?'

Sergeant Jones heaves his shoulders up in a giant shrug. 'There's nothing I can do, Gwenni, not officially. I have asked one or two people who might have known something about where he might have gone, of course I have, but—'

'Have you talked to Guto?'

'I've tried, but you know what he's like, Gwenni. Anyway, no one's got any idea about where Ifan might be. So that's that.

And it's no good giving me that old-fashioned look, I've done as much as I can and I've got a lot of other work to do, you know.'

I look out at the garden through the window behind him. Mrs Sergeant Jones has finished her carpet-beating but there are still little clouds of dust hovering above the clothesline.

'I mean a lot of police work, Gwenni, not gardening work.'

It's become much warmer in the office with the window closed. I get up from my chair to undo the belt and buttons on my mackintosh. A poster on the wall next to the door has a picture of a man's face on it and the words *Have you seen this man?* printed underneath the face. 'Why can't you make a poster of Ifan Evans like this one and put it up in lots of places? Is this man missing too?'

'He's missing all right,' says Sergeant Jones, 'but he's a criminal, he escaped from custody. He's a murderer, Gwenni, that's why I've got to keep an eye out for him. Though he's not likely to come this way.'

'A murderer.' I move closer to the poster. So this is what a murderer looks like. Just like anybody else. Maybe that's why they're hard to catch.

'Have you ever caught a murderer, Sergeant Jones?' I sit down in my chair again. Maybe Mrs Sergeant Jones should make a cushion for it. A cushion with embroidered flowers all over it and dried lavender inside it like she makes for the Chapel's Sale of Work. She's almost as good as Aunty Siân at sewing. It would make Sergeant Jones's office smell summery all year.

'Not here, Gwenni. There hasn't been a murder since I've been stationed here.'

'I thought that was what the police did, catch criminals and murderers.'

'Plenty of criminals here of one sort or another. Just plain silly, most of them. And greedy.'

'Did you catch a murderer where you were stationed before, then? When I asked you, you said: Not here.'

'You're a sharp one, Gwenni.' Sergeant Jones looks at his golden watch, which has some writing etched into it, and then swings it back on its golden chain into his waistcoat pocket before I can make out what it says. He always does that. 'Well, yes, I helped to catch a murderer when I was a constable at Dinbych. Just starting out I was.' He looks hard at me. 'But it wasn't exciting, you know, like in books or the pictures. It was just trudging from door to door asking people the same questions over and over.'

'Questions like that?' I nod towards the poster.

'Something like that,' says Sergeant Jones. 'And warning people to be careful. The man had run away from the asylum and he'd killed somebody almost immediately; he wasn't responsible for his actions.'

'What happened to him?'

'We caught him and he was sent back to the asylum. He wasn't fit to stand trial.' Sergeant Jones sighs. 'He died soon after.'

'Who did he murder?'

'A farmer who was trying to help him. It was all very sad, Gwenni. And a long time ago.' He tugs the watch out of its pocket and looks at it again. 'I have to do some paperwork now, Gwenni, so you'll have to go home. Tell your mam I was asking after her.'

I scrape my chair back along the floor and stand up. 'But can't you make a poster like that for Ifan Evans?'

'No, of course I can't,' says Sergeant Jones. 'Ifan Evans isn't a criminal.'

'But he's gone away and left Mrs Evans and Angharad and Catrin and Mot and the lambs.'

'It's odd, I grant you, Gwenni. But it's not a crime. I can't chase after him for that.'

Sergeant Jones puffs and huffs as he pulls himself out of his chair and stands up. I wait by the door and put my hand up to feel the poster; the paper is smooth and thick. 'But I can,' I say. I know just what to do. I'll ask Mrs Evans for a photograph of Ifan Evans to make a poster like this one.

'No, Gwenni, you can't,' says the Sergeant. His face is purply red from the effort of getting out of his chair.

'Yes, I can,' I say. 'I can ask people if they've seen him and they'll think it's just one of my games. I'll say I'm playing detectives; I'll say I'm being Albert Campion or Gari Tryfan.'

Sergeant Jones pulls out his little black notebook from the breast pocket of his jacket that's over the back of his chair, and his pencil from behind his ear. He flips the pages of the notebook and licks the pencil. His tongue is purply red, too. I look away.

'I'll make a note of our conversation, Gwenni,' he says, 'but I don't want you asking people about Ifan Evans as if he's done something wrong. I don't think your mam would like it very much, either, do you?'

Mam wouldn't like it at all. That's why I didn't tell her I was coming to see Sergeant Jones on my way to Brwyn Coch.

He comes closer and peers at my face. 'Your mam does know you're here, doesn't she, Gwenni?'

The black telephone on his desk jangles and we both jump at the noise. Sergeant Jones lumbers back to the desk and picks up the receiver. A voice crackles at him through the earpiece. I can hear it over by the door. 'Yes, sir,' answers Sergeant Jones. 'No, sir. The holiday has held things up a bit, sir.' He pulls out his big handkerchief and mops his head. 'Certainly, sir.' He puts the phone down on its cradle and looks at me. The phone call has made even his bald head turn purple.

I look closely at the poster as I open the door. Goose pimples prickle my skin again. It's lucky there are no murderers around here.

12

'Have you seen this man?' I hold my poster high up so that Nellie Davies can see it clearly.

'Don't stand on that step if your shoes are muddy,' she says. 'It took me half an hour to scrub the smell of your old tomcat off it this morning. You tell your mam.'

I step back down and try not to breathe in the fumes of the Jeyes fluid. I hold the poster as high as I can. 'Have you seen this man?' I ask her again.

Nellie Davies pulls her spectacles down her nose and squints at the poster. 'That's an old photograph,' she says. 'Who is it?

'Ifan Evans,' I say.

'Mr Evans to you,' she says, 'and if I'd seen him I'd be telling Mrs Evans, not you.' She shuffles backwards in her big old felt slippers and bangs the door shut.

'Thank you, Mrs Davies,' I say to nobody. I take my pencil and my red Lion notebook from the pocket of my school mack-intosh and next to Mrs Davies, Number 7, I put a question mark.

I pass Nain's house and our house and climb the steps to Number 4 and hang over the railings to see if Alwenna is coming.

I waited and waited for her this morning, she always comes to fetch me in the mornings during the holidays. Mam won't let me go down to the council houses. But the only thing coming up the hill is the jangly sound of music from someone's wireless. I turn to the blue door and knock hard on it until my knuckles sting. Everyone knows that Mrs Thomas goes back to bed for a little nap after Mr Thomas has gone to work. I wait, tapping my foot to the music, and after a while the door opens a little crack and one of Mrs Thomas's bleary blue eyes appears. 'Oh, it's you, Gwenni,' she says. She opens the door wider. 'Come in and have a cup of tea with me.'

Having a cup of tea with Mrs Thomas means making it for her and I haven't got time this morning. 'No, thank you, Mrs Thomas,' I say and push the poster close to her face. 'Have you seen this man?'

Mrs Thomas gathers her dressing gown around her and looks at the photograph through narrowed eyes until my arms start quivering with the effort of holding it up. She pats her hair into place and smiles at me. 'I wouldn't mind seeing him at all, Gwenni,' she says, 'a good-looking man like that. Who is it?'

'Ifan Evans,' I say.

'Ifan Evans?' says Mrs Thomas. And she narrows her eyes at the photograph again.

'When he was young,' I say.

'Who gave you that picture?' she says.

I cross my fingers. 'Mrs Evans.'

'That poor woman' says Mrs Thomas, 'and those poor little girls left without a father.'

'I'm trying to find Ifan Evans for them,' I say.

'I wouldn't do that, Gwenni,' says Mrs Thomas. 'It's meddling.

Are you sure you don't want a cup of tea?' She licks her lips. 'I've got a big chocolate cake I made yesterday.'

I shake my head. As she shuts the door I put a question mark next to her name in my notebook. Why can't people just answer my question? I leap down all three steps into the road and land at somebody's feet; I don't know they're Alwenna's until I look up.

'I didn't see you coming up the road,' I say. 'Why are you in your Sunday clothes?'

'They're not just for Sunday,' Alwenna says. 'This is how I always dress now.'

She twirls around in front of me. Her yellow skirt flares out showing her big net petticoat and throwing out a sweet scent. It's not Evening in Paris. 'I have to be very careful not to ladder my stockings,' she says. 'You're not going through any fields, are you? Because I can't go through any fields in these.' She points at her shoes, which are narrow and pointy and have a silly bow on the front.

I shake my head. 'No fields,' I say. 'But we might have to run. Can you run in them?'

'I've given up running,' says Alwenna. 'Why are you wearing that thing?'

'What thing?' I say.

'Your school mac.'

'It might rain, or snow. And anyway, it's got good pockets. Look.' I pull out my notebook and pencil and show them to her, but she's too busy tugging her white jumper down tight over her chest to look. 'Aren't you cold without your coat?'

'Not much,' she says. 'You won't get a boyfriend looking like that.'

Boyfriend? We hate boys, she knows that. But I think of her laughing with Aneurin and Edwin after Sunday School.

'I don't want a boyfriend,' I say. 'I hate boys.'

Alwenna sighs. She pulls her jumper down again. 'Boys are all right,' she says. 'They don't come from outer space, you know. They're not aliens.'

'And I especially hate our bêtes noires,' I say.

'I think . . .' says Alwenna, then stops and pulls a square of bubblegum from her skirt pocket. She undoes the wrapping and pops the gum into her mouth and begins to chew. My mouth waters.

'What?' I say. 'You think what?'

'I think,' she says again, 'that, really, you like Aneurin. And he likes you.'

'No. Yuck,' I say. 'I hate him. He hates me. You're the one who likes Aneurin all of a sudden.'

'Aneurin's related to me,' she says. 'Didn't you know? Through Mam's second cousin in Dyffryn.'

Almost everyone is related to Alwenna's mam. She's got more relations than Jesus Christ in my New Testament. Maybe that's how she knows everything about everybody. But my family is not related to her.

'I like Edwin,' says Alwenna.

'But Edwin's stupid,' I say.

'He's quite good-looking, though,' she says.

Edwin looks like Mrs Williams Penrhiw's old horse. I just stare at Alwenna. She jigs a little dance to the jangly music still sounding in the air around us. 'Your Bethan's got a boyfriend,' she says.

'Mam won't let her have a boyfriend,' I say. 'She's too young.'

'I've just seen her with that Richard.'

'You can't have. She's gone to play with Caroline.'

'Gone to play with Caroline's brother, more like,' says

Alwenna. She twirls again so that her skirt and her petticoat flare out around her and I can see the tops of her stockings. 'I can't stay long,' she says. 'What are you doing?'

I show her the poster, which is already creased and furred after showing it to only two people. 'I'm trying to find Ifan Evans.'

'Good riddance to bad rubbish is what my mam says,' says Alwenna. 'Nobody wants him back.'

'His little children want him back.'

'I don't know why. That little Catrin's always scared of him.'

'We'll have to go round together, because I've only got one picture of him,' I say.

Alwenna studies the poster. 'No one'll know him from that,' she says. 'That must have been taken ages ago. He was good-looking when he was young, wasn't he?'

'It was the only one I could get,' I say.

'Where did you get it?'

'From Mrs Evans. Yesterday.'

'She gave it to you, just like that?'

'Not exactly,' I say. 'I sort of borrowed it.'

'You'll get into trouble,' says Alwenna.

'Come on,' I say. 'Or we'll never get round the whole town.'

I knock on the door of the next house. I can hear Miss Hughes grunt as she tries to pull the door open. Across the road the Youth Hostel echoes with voices and light glows in most of the windows. In winter the Youth Hostel is dark and silent and the twisted rhododendron trees in its garden start writhing when you glimpse them out of the corner of your eye.

At last Miss Hughes opens her door, gasping with the effort. 'It's swollen from the damp,' she says, looking swollen and damp herself. 'What do you want, girls?' A musty smell drifts out from the hallway behind her. I try not to breathe too deeply.

82

'Have you seen this man?' I show her the poster. 'It's Ifan Evans,' I say.

'What do you mean?' says Miss Hughes. 'Of course it's Mr Evans. Of course I've seen him. He's one of our deacons, Gwenni. What are you talking about?'

'I meant have you seen him since he vanished?'

'Oh, oh, who told you to ask me that?' says Miss Hughes and puts her hand over her mouth. 'Does your mam know you're doing this, Gwenni?'

'When's the baby due, Miss Hughes?' says Alwenna.

'Oh, oh,' says Miss Hughes again. 'You wash your mouth out with soap, Alwenna Thomas.'

Alwenna blows a bubble of pink gum. It has a juicy straw-berry scent. Miss Hughes stumbles around and pushes the door in our faces, pushing and pushing until it shuts.

'What baby?' I ask Alwenna.

'Her baby,' says Alwenna. 'Didn't you know about it? Everyone knows about it. Mam says no prizes for guessing who the father is. He hasn't run off with her, then.'

'She'll tell your mam,' I say.

'No point,' says Alwenna. 'But she's sure to tell yours.'

I pull out my notebook and put a question mark next to Miss Hughes's name. 'No one will answer the question,' I say.

I know that everybody's out at work at Number 2 so I'll have to come back later. That leaves Dafydd Owen at Number 1. 'Do you want to knock on Dafydd Owen's door?' I say to Alwenna.

'I'm not knocking on his old door,' she says.

'We've got to question everybody,' I say. 'Or we might miss the one person who's seen Ifan Evans.'

'Do it yourself, then,' she says. 'I'll stay here.' And she leans against the wall at the bottom of the steps.

I take a big breath and knock politely on the door.

'He won't hear that,' says Alwenna. 'Knock harder.'

I bang on the door and it swings open.

'No need to break the door down,' says Dafydd Owen's creaky voice. 'What do you want, Gwenni?' His pipe is clenched between his teeth and chugs out little clouds of smoke like a train. The tobacco doesn't smell as nice as Tada's Golden Virginia.

I thrust the poster at Dafydd Owen. 'Have you seen this man?'

Dafydd Owen takes his spectacles from where they dangle at his waistcoat pocket and pulls out a handkerchief to polish them. The handkerchief should be white and I try not to look at it. He puts his spectacles on the tip of his nose and then peers over them.

'It's young Ifan Evans,' he says. 'Where did you get this picture, Gwenni?'

Alwenna loudly pops a gum bubble. Dafydd Owen looks around me at her.

'You're Nanw Thomas's girl,' he says. 'You're just like her. Just as badly behaved.'

Alwenna blows a huge pink bubble that bursts over her nose and chin.

'Disgusting habit,' says Dafydd Owen. He looks at me. 'That picture, Gwenni. I'll have to have a word with your mam.'

The door slams shut and I walk back down the steps to Alwenna. 'I didn't do anything,' I say, 'did I?'

'You're going to be in double trouble,' says Alwenna.

'It's your fault,' I say, 'blowing bubble gum at him.'

'It isn't the bubble gum,' says Alwenna. 'It's the stockings. He's a dirty old man. Everyone knows that.'

'Where shall we go next?' I ask.

'I can't come anywhere else. I've got to go now.'

'Go where?'

Alwenna taps the side of her nose with her forefinger. I don't know what she means.

'We always play together in the holidays,' I say.

'You're hopeless, Gwenni,' says Alwenna. 'This is a stupid idea, this going around asking people if they've seen Paleface.'

'It's what detectives do,' I say and then remember to take out my notebook and put a question mark next to Dafydd Owen's name. 'I'll have to think of a different way to ask the question. No one will say whether they've seen him or not.'

Alwenna gives a strawberry-scented sigh. 'I'm going,' she says. 'And I can't come to fetch you tomorrow morning. I'm going for a walk with Edwin.'

What? I watch her walk down the hill, her yellow skirt swaying as she goes. She doesn't even look like my Alwenna any more. 'See you at the Band of Hope tomorrow night, then,' I say to her back.

I take out my red Lion notebook and write *This man is Ifan Evans. Have you seen him since he vanished?* Maybe that's the way to ask the question.

13

I haven't got any better answers after spending all morning asking the new question. Almost all the names in my Lion notebook have got a question mark next to them and my poster is falling apart. Mad Huw chased me from Tryfar Terrace because he thought I was showing everyone a picture of him, and I got a stitch in my side that has only just stopped hurting. But I think that before going home for dinner I'll just call at Number 2 in our terrace that was empty earlier; there's someone home now, I can see the light on in the living room. It may be that the last person I ask will have seen Ifan Evans.

I don't see Mam until in a rush of air she grabs my arm. 'That's enough of that,' she says, and drags me up the road towards our house. 'Get in the house. I've got a bone to pick with you.'

Mam's face is white with red blotches on her cheeks just like the Toby jugs have when they're puffing away hard at their pipes. 'Someone's been coming out of every other house on my way home to tell me about your goings on,' she says, her spit spraying onto my face. 'I've been working hard all morning and the last thing I need is to have people complaining to me about your behaviour.'

'I'm only trying to find Ifan Evans. And you're hurting my arm.'

Mam flings my arm away from her and I stumble after her into the living room. She hisses at me and I have trouble hearing what she's saying.

'I just want to help Mrs Evans,' I say.

'Quaint,' says Mam. 'That's what they're saying about you. That you're quaint. That's the next thing to odd. That's what they're really thinking.'

'But I'm not odd,' I say.

Mam drops her shopping basket on the floor and grasps me by the shoulders and shakes me. 'Odd,' she shouts. 'Odd, odd, odd. That's what they're saying.' She lets go of me and slumps into her armchair holding her face in her trembling hands. 'What have I done to deserve a child like you?' she says.

John Morris uncurls from where he's lying on Tada's chair and sniffs the air. He jumps down and starts to snuffle and scrabble at the basket, a frantic growl in his throat.

Mam draws a deep breath. 'Pull that packet on top out of there,' she says from behind her hands. 'I got some lights from Jones the Butcher. Take them into the scullery and cut them up for him.'

'I can't, Mam. You know I can't,' I say. 'All that blood makes me feel ill.'

Mam springs from her chair and snatches the packet from her basket and marches into the scullery. John Morris darts after her. I hear the soft, wet plop of the meat onto the chopping board. John Morris is hysterical. The knife thuds and thuds on the board until Mam scrapes the lights into his saucer. The fishy stink of blood wafts into the living room; I try not to think about Mrs Evans's poor mouth or the red wound in the fox's side. I glance up and see the Toby jugs turn scarlet with the effort of holding their breath.

'Nain says it will turn him wild, giving him raw meat,' I say.

The tap turns off in the scullery and there's a silence until Mam comes back into the living room and takes off her coat. Her face has come out in more red blotches. Perhaps the blood has splashed on it. I don't look at her.

'If you listened to me half as much as you listen to Nain,' she says, 'I wouldn't have the whole town telling me you're odd every time I walk home from work.'

'Only today,' I say, 'and you said it was every other house, not the whole town.'

Mam takes another deep breath. 'Just get into that scullery and start making dinner,' she says.

'What are we having?' I say. I walk past all the faces in the distemper with their wide open eyes and don't look at the saucer of lights.

'Bread and cheese,' says Mam. 'I'll have to stoke this fire up to get the kettle going.' She rattles the fire with the poker. 'I must be the last woman in this town to have to cook on the fire.'

She isn't. But I don't say so out loud.

I lift the big white loaf from the bread bin onto the table. I don't want to use the board in case Mam hasn't washed all the blood from it. The butter is too cold to spread and makes holes in the bread. I begin to slice the loaf, anyway. Nice, thin slices, only a little bit lacy. I cut the red cheese and nibble a sliver of it. It's tangy and salty and makes my hunger growl like John Morris in my stomach.

'Can't you do anything right?' Mam comes into the scullery

and takes the knife from me. 'You're not making a tea party.' She cuts thick pieces from the loaf. 'Get that jar of pickled onions down. They're going a bit soft; we may as well finish them.'

'That's because you didn't salt the onions first,' I say.

'What?'

'Nain says you have to salt the onions if you don't want them going soft.'

'Right,' says Mam. 'Sit on that stool and listen to me.'

I put a thin slice of bread and some cheese and a large pickled onion on a plate and begin to eat. The vinegar on the pickled onion is too sharp because Mam didn't put the right spices in with it. That's what Nain said, but I don't tell Mam. I wipe the vinegar off where it drips down my chin.

'I've been out all morning, working my fingers to the bone for you,' says Mam.

'And for Bethan,' I say.

'To earn money to buy a nice house with a proper kitchen and a bathroom for you.'

'I like this house,' I say. 'I like living here.' I take another thin slice of bread. The butter must have been icy when I spread it on this slice. I roll up the bread instead of folding it so I can't see the holes.

'You don't like having a bath in front of the fire and sharing a bed with Bethan, do you?'

'I suppose not. Will I have a room of my own in the new house, then?'

Mam's eyes flicker sideways. 'Yes, of course you will,' she says, then she glares at me again. 'And what thanks do I get for slaving away for you? People telling me about your antics all the way home.'

I swallow my last piece of cheese and cut some more, thinly. 'But what did I do wrong, Mam?'

'Drawing attention to yourself again, that's what. Giving people a reason to say you're odd.'

'But I can't ask questions like a detective without people noticing me. And I'm only trying to find Ifan Evans.'

Mam's hands are gnawing away at each other like mice eating cheese. Her face is tight and her voice is taut as Mr Pugh's cheese wire. 'You shouldn't be asking anyone any questions at all about him. He'll come back when he's ready. Elin Evans has only herself to blame. So prim and proper. No wonder he had to get away. Leave him be.' Mam starts picking at the loaf of bread, rolling the dough into little balls between her fingers.

'If I'm going to be a detective,' I say, 'I've got to practise.' And what if Ifan Evans is never ready to come back?

'I don't know where you get your silly ideas from,' says Mam. 'I blame Aunty Lol for giving you all those books.' She bangs the table and makes me and the bread leap. 'You're meddling in things you're too young to understand.'

'Anyway,' I say, 'you said Bethan was too young to be going out with boys but she's still got a boyfriend.'

'Don't be silly,' says Mam.

'I'm not being silly,' I say. 'Richard is her boyfriend. Caroline's brother. Alwenna says she goes to see him, not to play with Caroline.'

'That Alwenna has no shame,' says Mam. 'She ought to wash her mouth with soap.'

'That's what Miss Hughes said when Alwenna asked when the baby was due.' I don't tell her what Alwenna said about the baby's father.

Mam covers her mouth with her hand and makes a little gasping noise, just like she did when her new corset got stuck.

'And,' I say, 'she says Mr Owen Number 1 is a dirty old man. Alwenna knows a lot of things.'

Mam takes her hand from her face. It's left white marks all around her mouth. 'That poor old man tries his best. He's got no one to look after him since Mrs Owen died,' she says.

'Alwenna didn't mean that. It was something to do with her stockings.'

Mam's face blooms scarlet. Her pale pink powder stands out like dots on her skin. 'That Alwenna's a bad influence. She's just like her mother, spreading rumours like that. And she's far too old for you; she's almost Bethan's age. It's high time you made friends with some of the other girls. That new girl, Deilwen, why can't you be friends with someone like that?'

'Alwenna's always been my best friend,' I say. 'We're Kindred Spirits.'

Mam clenches her fists, then straightens her back and takes deep, steady breaths like Dr Edwards prescribed. Her face goes from red to pink. She takes some bread and cheese onto her plate, but no pickled onions, and begins to eat. Her hands hardly shake at all.

John Morris prowls beneath the table. He must have finished his lights and smelled the cheese. John Morris loves cheese, especially red, salty cheese. I drop a bit on the floor for him and he purrs as he eats it. Alwenna's little white kitten couldn't eat and purr at the same time.

'Don't,' says Mam. 'It'll give him worms. And it's a waste.'

'Where's Bethan?' I say. 'Is she coming home for her dinner?' There isn't much cheese left. And Mam has made a mess of the loaf.

Mam shakes her head. 'She's playing with Caroline. And having her lunch there, too. Lovely flat. I used to clean for old Mrs Cameron when she lived there.'

I open my mouth and Mam says, 'With Caroline. And don't think you can get me off the subject of your wrongdoing. I don't want you doing anything of the sort again, do you hear me? Cross your heart.'

I cross my heart but I cross my fingers too.

'Just look at the time,' says Mam, 'You've made me late. I've got to get some cakes made for tonight. You can give me a hand; it'll keep you out of mischief.'

'Can I come to help in the meeting, too?' I ask. There are always nice things to eat at the Sale of Work meetings.

'If Bethan doesn't want to come,' says Mam. 'Now get me that new bag of flour from my shopping basket, and be quick about it.'

Bethan never wants to help in the Sale of Work meeting. I skip to fetch the flour, then the eggs and margarine from the larder and the sugar from the cupboard. Mam snatches them from me and measures out what she needs and beats everything together in her big bowl. She's doing everything too fast. Like the clock-work mouse Aunty Lol gave John Morris; when I wound it up tight it skittered about all over the floor, crashing into chair legs and the fender and our feet. John Morris was scared of it.

'Grease those fairy-cake trays,' Mam says, and when I've done that she slaps spoonfuls of batter into them. She drops her big bowl into the sink with a crash that makes the faces in the distemper blink in fright.

'You scared the faces in the distemper, Mam,' I say.

'Don't start, Gwenni.' Mam takes an extra-deep breath. 'It's just peeling a bit.' She scrubs off tiny flakes of the paint, and more faces appear. 'Just peeling. It's time your father gave the walls a new coat.'

Will the faces open their mouths to scream out our secrets as the new distemper washes over them like a wave and drowns them?

'Right. These are ready to go in the oven,' says Mam. 'Put that kettle on. I'm going to have a cup of tea and put my feet up while they're baking. You can do the washing up with the water that's left in the kettle.'

I sit in Tada's chair to wait for the kettle to boil and pull out *The Tiger in the Smoke* from under the cushion. Mr Campion is old in this book but he's still a good detective. His wife has got red hair like me. He's solving a mystery from the war. Tada was in the war, but he doesn't talk about it. Nobody talks about it; it happened a long time ago.

The kettle boils and I make a cup of tea for Mam. I put the plug in the sink and pour in the rest of the hot water, then run some cold into it. It's not as bad as washing up after supper. There aren't any slimy bits floating in the water to tangle with my fingers. Maybe someone else will wash the dishes at the Sale of Work meeting and I can dry them. Will Mrs Evans be at the meeting tonight? If she's not there the women will gossip about Ifan Evans's disappearance. They always gossip a lot. They'll forget I'm there if I keep quiet.

There's a crash in the living room and Mam wails.

'Look what you've made me do now,' she shouts, 'upsetting my nerves with your silliness.'

When I go into the living room Mam is on her hands and knees picking up the fairy cakes and putting them back on their baking tray.

'You're lucky,' she says. 'I think they'll do.'

In the firelight Mam's face looks as if it's breaking apart like my poster. Little cracks have opened up in the face powder below her eyes and at the corners of her mouth. She pushes the hot baking tray into my hands. 'Pick off any cat hairs,' she says, 'and I'll make some icing to put on them. No one will know.' She heaves herself up from the floor. 'And don't you dare tell anyone,' she says.

14

I skip along the road beside Mam.

'Walk properly,' she says. 'You're making me feel wobbly.'

Mam holds the tin with the cakes in front of her with both hands, pulling it tight to her stomach. I had to spoon the icing on the cakes because her hands were too shaky, and then she found some cherries left over from Christmas in the larder and I cut them up so there were enough to put a little red blob on top of the icing right in the middle of each cake.

'Who's making the sandwiches tonight, Mam?' I say.

'Mrs Edwards the Bank,' says Mam.

'Good. I like her egg ones.' I begin to skip again. Mrs Edwards the Bank cuts the bread thin like Nain does and puts plenty of egg on the slices.

'You're not going to eat everything in sight again, are you?' says Mam. 'People will think I don't feed you. You can't be very hungry; you didn't eat much lobscouse for your supper. And stop skipping. Why don't you listen sometimes, Gwenni? I may as well talk to the man in the moon.'

I stop skipping. Mam knows that I don't like lobscouse. All

those bits of grey meat and white bone and potato and carrot in watery stock with globules of grease floating on top. It reminds me of washing-up water and I can't eat any of it.

'Now you're dawdling,' says Mam. 'Come on, hurry up.'

We turn up the path through the cemetery to the vestry. The vestry lights are dim. To save money, Mrs Davies Chapel House uses bulbs that don't give much light. So she can buy more and more silk stockings, Alwenna says. But I don't want to think about Alwenna.

Several people are standing in the vestry's little kitchen. There's a clatter of crockery and talk and a loud hum from the boiler as it heats the water for the tea. I listen to the hum but it's not the same note as the hum I hear in the sky. I can't see Mrs Edwards the Bank or her egg sandwiches.

'Here come some cakes,' says Mrs Sergeant Jones. She takes the tin from Mam and pulls off the lid. She hands the tin back to me. 'Here, Gwenni, put them on that plate there, and put a doily on the plate first, mind.'

There's already a plate of cakes on the table. Someone else has made cakes like Mam's and put a whole half-cherry on the icing. I look at Mam and she sniffs and says in a whisper, 'Those will be from Mrs Twm Edwards. She can afford half-cherries.' Mam's cakes would look better if they had no cherries at all on them. There's also a plate of Mrs Sergeant Jones's famous vanilla biscuits. I can smell the vanilla from here.

'I don't suppose we can expect Elin Evans this evening,' says Mrs Jones the Butcher. 'I haven't seen her once in the shop since Ifan went. She used to come in every day after school.'

'There's more to Ifan's disappearance than meets the eye,' says Mrs Morris. 'You know my cousin Morwenna from Cricieth? Well, she knows of Elin's family there. Rather a posh family but all dead now, apart from the sister of course. Anyway, Morwenna heard that . . .'

But I don't hear what Morwenna heard because Mrs Sergeant Jones coughs loudly all over Mam's cakes and nods at me and says, 'Why don't you take your mam's lovely cakes into the Meeting Room, Gwenni. There's a fire in there to sit by.' And she hands me the plate of cakes and takes hold of me by the shoulders, steers me into the room next door and closes the door on me. I place Mam's cakes on the white-clothed trestle table. I think I'll have one of Mrs Twm Edwards's cakes instead of Mam's. And a piece of Mrs Thomas next door's big chocolate cake that's here on the table. She always bakes a big chocolate cake when it's her turn. The women on the benches near the fire are too busy talking and knitting and sewing to take any notice of me, so I stay by the door.

'Little pitchers have big ears,' says someone behind the door.

'What was she up to this morning, Magda?' My stomach flutters as I hear Mrs Thomas next door's voice. 'She came to my door with an old photograph of Ifan – I didn't recognise him – and she wanted to know if I'd seen him since he disappeared. Perhaps she thought I was hiding him in the garret.'

Everyone laughs. Mam will be cross with me all over again.

'She's a character all right, your Gwenni,' says Mrs Morris. 'Now, who's going to take this tray through?'

I rush to a seat in front of the fire, far from the door, where my legs roast instantly and my back is still cold.

'You'll all have mottled legs, sitting that close to the fire,' says Mrs Davies Chapel House as she walks in with the tray of crockery. 'Come back here and lay out the cups and saucers, Gwenni.'

I put out all the saucers in a row on the trestle table and

then start to plonk a cup on each one. The egg sandwiches still haven't arrived. My stomach is hollow with hunger. Mam's cakes look small and a bit grubby. I think I got all the bits off. Mam'll be cross with me if anyone finds some of John Morris's hairs on them.

I watch Mam when she comes through into the Meeting Room behind Mrs Davies Chapel House with her big pot of tea, but she doesn't look at her cakes.

'We were just talking about Elin,' says Mrs Owen the Milk to Mam and Mrs Davies Chapel House.

'Shocking the way that Ifan's behaved,' says Nellie Davies, clicking her knitting needles faster and faster. She leans forward to whisper, 'Miss Owen Penllech was just saying that he beat her.'

'And those little children,' says Miss Owen Penllech and stabs herself with her embroidery needle and bleeds into the yellow flowers she's embroidering so that they turn orange. 'You know what happened there.'

'I don't believe it,' says Mam. 'I don't. It's just nasty gossip.' The pile of plates in her hands rattles and her face has turned pink.

'What about that little grave out there, then?' says Miss Owen Penllech and sucks a drop of blood still welling on her finger.

Ifan Evans beat Mrs Evans and the girls? And what little grave? I try to put the cups on the saucers without making so much noise.

'You'll know all about what happened there,' says Miss Owen Penllech to Mrs Dr Edwards. 'Wasn't Dr Edwards called in?'

'He was,' says Mrs Dr Edwards. 'But . . . you know . . . I'm not privy to medical matters. What goes on between Rhys and his patients is completely confidential.'

There is a flurry of movement behind me, and Mrs Edwards

the Bank comes through the door with a large square tin covered in red roses clutched to her bosom and a scent of roses blossoming from her. 'Sorry I'm late, ladies,' she says, with a little gasp in her voice. 'Oh dear, I don't like walking through that cemetery on my own, day or night. I have to stand there plucking up the courage to do it. I really do think the Roman Catholics are very lucky to be able to cross themselves, to arm themselves, so to speak, before they go into danger.'

Everyone stops knitting and sewing and looks at Mrs Edwards the Bank. Everyone in our town goes to a chapel, except for the posh people who go to church. I take the rose-covered tin from Mrs Edwards. 'What sandwiches are they, Mrs Edwards?' I ask.

'Egg, Gwenni,' she says.

Someone groans as I open the tin and the smell of the egg spreads over us like a tablecloth. But Mrs Edwards the Bank's egg sandwiches have egg right up to the edges and cress and something that tastes like salad cream but is nicer. And they never have bits of eggshell in them, or black crusts on the bread.

Everybody starts to talk and I begin to put the sandwiches on a plate so that I can hand them round. And now the room goes quiet again and I turn to the door and come eye to wide-open eye with Mrs Llywelyn Pugh's poor dead fox. I step back and Mrs Llywelyn Pugh walks past right to the front by the fire and Miss Owen Penllech and Nellie Davies move aside to make room for her. She sits there, nearest the fire, and her dead fox drapes itself sadly around her shoulders. Her legs will be more mottled than anyone else's.

'Gwenni. Pay attention.' Mam pushes the pile of plates into my hands. 'Take these and give one each to everyone. And collect their sixpences at the same time and put them in the tin.' She puts an old tobacco tin on top of the plates. 'And remember Mrs Llywelyn Pugh doesn't have to pay.'

'But she's richer than anyone else,' I say.

'Be quiet and do as you're told,' says Mam.

'I haven't got sixpence,' I say. 'Does that mean I can't have any food?' My stomach grumbles; I expect everyone can hear it.

'Don't be silly,' says Mam. 'I've put a shilling in for both of us.' She picks up the tin and rattles and rattles and rattles it under my nose.

'Magda,' says Mrs Dr Edwards. 'Sit by me. Take a deep breath now, dear, deep breath.'

I pass the plates around, and make sure everyone puts sixpence in the tin. I stop next to Mrs Llywelyn Pugh for a moment and look hard at the dead fox but it doesn't blink at me again. It looks utterly dead tonight.

'Move on, Gwenni,' says Mrs Twm Edwards, who's following me with the plate of sandwiches. I've left some in the tin, which is lucky because they've all disappeared from the plate by the time Mrs Twm Edwards gets to the end of the last row. I sit at the back next to the tin and nibble at the egg sandwiches; I close my eyes and savour the creamy egg and the peppery cress. As we all eat, Mrs Sergeant Jones talks about the arrangements for the chara-banc to take everyone to the Singing Festival in Bermo. Maybe Mrs Edwards the Bank will make the sandwiches for us all. I wonder why she's afraid of walking through the cemetery outside the vestry. Maybe she thinks there are spirits there. Nain says spirits can't hurt you. Does that mean spirits that float on water, too? I've never noticed a little grave in the cemetery, so which little grave was Miss Owen Penllech talking about? I know that my grandfather, who died when Tada was young, is there, and my Uncle Carwyn who had the family hair and used to show me how to make eggs disappear behind people's ears just like the conjurer who performed at the Memorial Hall. And Tada's sister who died of a horrible disease when she was a little girl. Probably everyone in this room has someone belonging to them in the cemetery.

It's cold here by the door; Mrs Llywelyn Pugh is taking up all the heat from the fire. She's taken off the dead fox and slung it on the back of the bench where it droops with misery.

I put my hand into the tin with the red roses but it's empty and Mam is glaring at me. Have I been eating everything in sight?

'It's very good of you, Mrs Llywelyn Pugh, to volunteer to make sandwiches for the Festival,' says Mrs Sergeant Jones. 'But are you sure it's not too much trouble to make all the sandwiches?'

I know what that means. Sardines and black crusts. Alwenna says they're minced-mouse sandwiches. If a person wears a dead fox around her neck, what is there to stop her putting dead mice in sandwiches?

'Cakes, Gwenni,' says Mrs Sergeant Jones. 'Hand the cakes round, please.'

I pick up the plate with Mrs Twm Edwards's cakes and the plate with Mam's cakes and walk round with them. Everyone takes one of the cakes with a whole half-cherry on them until there is no choice left but Mam's cakes. I'm trying so hard not to look at Mam that I knock the dead fox onto the floor as I pass behind Mrs Llywelyn Pugh's bench. Its little dead paws cling to my legs. 'No,' I squeal and I kick at the fox. Mam glares at me again but everyone else laughs.

'My father killed that, you know, young lady,' says Mrs Llywelyn Pugh in English, 'when I wasn't much older than you are now.' The dead fox has been dead longer than I've been alive. Longer than Mam's been alive, even.

'Was your father a shepherd, like Ifan Evans?' I ask her. There is a long silence. I look at Mam. She has her hand over her mouth and her eyes are closed and no one else is looking at me either.

'Dear me, no.' Mrs Llywelyn Pugh is still speaking English. 'We had a large estate. He went hunting on horseback, for pleasure. My sisters and I each had a fox-fur from him. Dear Father.'

I look down at the poor little dead thing. It's small and thin and its fur has worn away in places. Killed for pleasure? Catrin said Ifan Evans liked killing the foxes, too.

'Pick it up, Gwenni,' says Mam from behind her hand.

'I can't,' I say. 'You know I don't like touching dead things.'

'Don't be silly, Gwenni,' says Mam. 'That's not a dead thing. I told you, that's a fox-fur. Now pick it up for Mrs Llywelyn Pugh.'

I bend down and scoop up the dead fox with the empty cake plate. It slithers as if it's going to jump off but I throw it at Mrs Llywelyn Pugh and it droops over her shoulder and stares at me with its sad eyes. What is it trying to say to me? Is its spirit still there, imprisoned inside the glass eyes?

'What a quaint child you are, my dear,' says Mrs Llywelyn Pugh as she wraps the dead fox around her throat.

But I have an idea. I know what to do to give the dead fox a decent burial and save its spirit. I only have to wait for the Festival. Alwenna can help me. I look at Mam in excitement but she stares at me with that tight look on her face that means she's cross with me again about something.

15

The sky is perfect this evening. In one of my art lessons I mixed my poster paints to make a sky exactly like this; a deep, dense blue in the high curve becoming lighter and whiter towards the edge of the Earth where the hills of Llŷn look as if they've been cut out of black paper and stuck on. Mr Parry said it was too good to be true. But here it is. I want to fly up there to see the stars burst through the blue; Orion the Great Hunter with his mighty sword, and the Milky Way almost pouring its stars on my head. Last night I didn't want to look down on the town or the sea; I floated on my back, listened to the Earth's song and looked into the sky. Where does the sky end? And where's Heaven? I never see any spirits up there. I wonder if other people live where those stars shine. Aliens. In the pictures aliens are always monsters. But what if they're just like us? Would they be monsters then?

What time is it? I'd better run to the Chapel vestry in case I'm late.

I left the house ahead of Bethan and yet here she is in the cemetery before me, huddled by the vestry door with Janet Jones the Butcher from her Sunday School class. The Voice of God hasn't arrived and the vestry is still locked. Alwenna's sitting on our favourite tombstone twirling her hair and smiling at our bêtes noires.

I stride across the grass from the vestry door to the tombstone and give Aneurin and Edwin a hard stare as I pass them. I hear them snigger as I clamber onto the tombstone and sit to face Alwenna with my back to them.

'I was talking to them, Gwenni,' she says.

'Those two?' I say. 'They haven't got anything in their heads to talk about.'

'You don't give them a chance, Gwenni,' she says. 'And Edwin's my boyfriend now.'

Her boyfriend? I feel a stab of pain in my stomach as the cold from the tombstone creeps through my clothes. My bêtes noires have moved so that they can see Alwenna; they lean on a gravestone on the edge of the path. Alwenna turns so that she's facing them, and smiles and smiles.

I stroke the slate beneath me with my palm; it's been rubbed smooth and silky by all the children who've sat on it waiting for something or another to begin in the vestry. Aunty Lol told me she and her friends used to sit on this tombstone while they waited. I can trace some of the letters with my finger but too many of them are worn away for me to work out what they say. Some of the old tombstones tell a long tale of the life of the person buried in them, but I can't read this story. There must be hundreds of secrets locked away in the tombs and the graves around me.

'I have to talk to you before the Voice of God gets here,' I say to Alwenna.

She sighs. 'What about?' she says. 'It's not more daft ideas, is it? I'm getting fed up with your daft ideas.'

I shiver; the tombstone must be even colder than I thought underneath me. 'They're not daft,' I say. 'Listen—'

'Be quick, then.' Alwenna has moved so that she's half lying on the tombstone now, her arm raised to her hair. Aneurin and Edwin wolf whistle a duet at her from their gravestone. 'And I've got something to tell you,' she says.

'You two are a nuisance,' I say to the boys. 'Go away.'

'They're only messing about, Gwenni,' says Alwenna.

'No one would whistle at you, Gwenni Morgan. You've got a face like a fox.' Of the two, Edwin is my greatest bête noire.

'And hair like a fox's tail,' says Aneurin. Perhaps they are equally my bête noire.

They start to chant in unison, 'Gwenni Fo-ox, Gwenni Fo-ox.' They clutch their gravestone and double up with laughter. 'Gwenni Fo-ox.'

I turn my back on them, and ignore their noise. 'Listen, Alwenna. I've got a really good idea for getting the dead fox away from Mrs Llywelyn Pugh. I had to go and help Mam at the Sale of Work meeting last night and guess what?'

'What?' says Alwenna. 'What?'

'Mrs Llywelyn Pugh is going to be at the Singing Festival. She's helping out with the food this year.'

'So?'

'So we can get the fox then. She's not going to make sandwiches and serve jelly and do the washing up with her dead fox round her neck, is she? She'll have to take it off and put it down somewhere. That will be our chance.'

Alwenna stares at me without looking once towards Edwin and Aneurin. 'You're doolally,' she says. 'You take after your—' A loud screech makes us both jump.

The younger children have been playing tick around the

graves, flitting about like pale ghosts in the dim light. Now they all stand still as the gravestones and one of them points at the line of bats flying from the vestry's roof space.

'They'll dive at your heads and get all tangled up in your hair,' shouts Edwin.

'No they won't,' I yell. 'He's lying. Bats don't do that.'

But the children are not listening to me. As more and more bats stream from the vestry roof they race around the gravestones, taking great, gulping breaths and screeching like Guto'r Wern when he runs down the hill, their hands clasped around their heads.

The back door of Chapel House opens and a square of light shines out followed by the acrid smell of burnt potatoes, and Mrs Davies. She waves a blackened, smoking saucepan in our direction. 'Look what you've made me do,' she shouts at the children. 'Mr Davies won't be very pleased when he finds out his supper's burnt.' The screeching dies a little. 'And stop that noise.' Mrs Davies screeches louder than the children. 'You sound like a lot of old hens with the fox after them.'

Edwin and Aneurin collapse on each other and slither down the gravestone to the ground. They laugh and chant, 'Gwenni Fo-ox, Gwenni Fo-ox.'

'Come out of there,' Mrs Davies tells the children, 'or I'll send Mr Davies out here the minute he's home.' The children quieten at that and one by one come from behind the gravestones, their heads drooping.

'Now, then, sit on the vestry steps until the Reverend Roberts comes. And you two.' She looks at Alwenna and me. 'You two get down from that tomb. You know it's disrespectful to sit on it.' Mrs Davies turns her back on us and goes into Chapel House and slams the door behind her. Above the cemetery the bats swirl to the reverberations. The children clutch their hands to their heads again as they sit obediently on the steps, facing Alwenna and me on the tombstone as if they were watching the Voice of God in the pulpit.

I turn to Alwenna. 'Well?' I say. 'Don't you think it's a good chance?'

'I'm not doing it,' says Alwenna. 'It's a stupid idea. All your ideas are daft. They only ever get me into trouble with people. Anyway, I've got better things to do now.'

'Like what?' I say.

Alwenna turns and gives Edwin and Aneurin a little wave. 'Like going for walks with Edwin,' she says.

My stomach begins to ache. Mam will be cross with me for sitting on the cold slate and making myself ill. I look at Alwenna. 'And what about our investigations?' I say. 'What about finding Ifan Evans?'

Alwenna doesn't reply. She pulls a face at me and slides off the tombstone, her skirt dragging up and her stocking-tops showing. Stockings to the Band of Hope, even?

'Alwenna?' I say.

'I tried to tell you,' she says. 'They found Ifan Evans teatime. Drowned in the Reservoir. Just think, we've been drinking him for days.'

I can't speak. I feel the bile burning its way up my throat and I vomit across the tombstone and its worn-out history. A sweet sour smell steams into the air. I hear some of the children on the steps retch in sympathy.

'Gwenni, Gwenni,' the Voice of God booms from the twilight. 'Bethan, you'd better walk her home. Your mam will know best what to do for her.'

PART TWO

16

Bethan pushes me into the house, her fist hard in the small of my back. Mam and Tada sit each side of the fire. Tada reads the *Daily Herald*, his legs stretched out, his feet resting on the fender. One of his grey socks has a hole in the heel that Nain would mend if she knew about it. Mam knits the fuzzy-wuzzy bolero for Aunty Siân's little Helen that was supposed to be finished for Easter. She has her special cushion in her lap under the knitting; the pink one with the faded red roses on it. For a second, from the doorway of the living room, I see Mam and Tada as if they were a picture in a frame. Blue bits from the fuzzy-wuzzy float in the air like lazy insects. They always make me sneeze; my nose itches as I stand here.

They both turn towards me at the same time. Mam drops her knitting and half gets up from her chair. The firelight flickers on her bouncy yellow curls, and they gleam like Nain's brasses.

'It's nothing to do with me,' says Bethan, giving me another push. 'I wasn't anywhere near her. She was talking to Alwenna and then she threw up all over the tombstone they were sitting on. The Voice of God said I had to bring her home. I don't know why she couldn't bring herself home.'

'Look at the state of you,' says Mam. 'And the smell. Look at your school mackintosh. How am I going to get that in a fit state for you to wear again?'

'Are you all right, Gwenni?' says Tada. He stands up and folds his *Daily Herald* and pushes it under his seat. 'Let's get you out of that old coat.'

'Let her do it herself,' says Mam. 'Look at her, vomit all down the front of it.'

'She's disgusting,' says Bethan. 'I'm going to Nain's; I can't stand the stink.'

'Hold on,' says Tada. 'What happened exactly?'

Bethan shoves me again. 'She's a baby. She threw up because Alwenna told her Ifan Evans was found in the Reservoir.'

'Ifan?' says Mam. 'What do you mean, found in the Reservoir? Is he all right?'

'Alwenna said he'd been there since he disappeared,' says Bethan. She turns and goes out through the front door. 'I'm going next door. I bet Nain hasn't heard yet or she'd have been round to tell you.'

Mam has her hand over her mouth. Her nails dig into her face, making flares of white in her skin.

Tada puts his arm around her and pats her on the shoulder, 'Deep breath, sweetheart,' he says. 'Take a deep breath.'

'Alwenna says we've been drinking him for days,' I say. The thought makes me retch and I run through into the scullery and heave over the sink. There's nothing left to come up. I wipe my face with Tada's damp flannel; it's cold and rough and smells of his Lifebuoy soap. I'd like a drink of water but what if Ifan Evans's maggots come through the tap?

The faces in the distemper have all grown long ears to listen all the better with. I scurry past them into the living room. Mam sits shivering in her armchair. She shivers all over like Mrs Evans did when she had her teeth out. On their high shelf the Toby jugs lean over and watch Mam through narrowed eyes.

'It's the shock,' says Tada, still patting her shoulder. 'Well, it's a shock for us all.' Is that what made me throw up? I didn't like Ifan Evans, but he's the only person I know who's drowned.

'What can have happened to him?' says Mam, and I have to reach forward towards her to hear what she says. Her face is white and there are red blotches where her nails dug into her skin. The scent of Evening in Paris is strong and my head begins to throb.

'He must have fallen in somehow,' says Tada. 'Perhaps he couldn't swim.' He sighs, then turns to me. 'Gwenni, come and sit in my chair, here by the fire. The warmth will make you feel better.'

I can smell the vomit on my coat and its sour taste is still in the back of my throat. Tada takes off my coat and folds it so that the sick is all hidden. He carries it through into the scullery and opens the back door and leaves it in the lean-to. I sit in Tada's chair. I burrow into the warmth he's left behind and the scent of his soap and his tobacco. A log crackles on the fire and spits tiny flares out of the grate. Tada rushes back from the scullery and stamps out the glowing embers on the linoleum.

'Drat that wood,' he says. 'Give me coal any day. None of your spitting nonsense with coal.'

He looks at me and then at Mam. She sits with her hands over her face, making no sound at all. 'What you both need is a good cup of tea,' he says. He picks up the teapot from where it's resting on the grate and puts his hand around its belly. 'Still nice and hot,' he says, and begins to pour tea into the cups on the table. He puts two spoonfuls of sugar into each cup and stirs them round and round. He puts Mam's cup and saucer down on the floor next to her chair and hands mine to me. I take a tiny sip; the tea is stewed and too sweet. Tada looks at my face. 'Drink it down,' he says. 'Best thing for shock, sweet tea.'

'Be quiet.' Mam's shout makes me jump but I don't spill my tea. 'How can you prattle on about stupid things like that when we've just heard that Ifan is dead?'

'It's true, I suppose,' says Tada. 'Nanw Lipstick has a way of getting to know these things. I wonder if anyone is looking after Elin Evans and the little girls.'

'What about me?' says Mam. 'You think about looking after me. I'm upset too.'

Tada takes a deep breath but he doesn't tell Mam to do the same. He lifts her teacup to her hands where it shakes and splashes the tea over her lap until he takes it away again. Mam doesn't notice any of it. Tada picks up her pink cushion from the floor and tries to put it behind her shoulders but she snatches it from him and wraps her arms around it and starts to rock to and fro in her chair.

'Whatever can have happened,' she half whispers. 'Ifan can't have just fallen in the water and drowned. He can swim like a fish. Why, when you were in the army we swam every . . .' Mam stops and pulls her cushion up over her mouth.

'Well,' says Tada.

So Mam wasn't just a girl when she went about with Ifan Evans.

She closes her eyes. Tada and she are quiet and still as if time has stopped. But the brown clock on the mantelpiece tick-tocks as loud as ever.

John Morris crawls out from under Tada's chair and jumps into my lap, purring in fits and starts like the engine in Aunty Lol's Lambretta. I stroke his soft fur but I don't touch the ragged ear that was torn during one of his fights with Nellie Davies's cats. John Morris and his warrior spirit. I wonder if Ifan Evans's spirit escaped into the water of the Reservoir when he drowned. Did his spirit pass through the pipes into the Baptism Pool? Did I foretell the future, like Nain with her tea leaves, when I flew over the Pool and saw the dead Baptist?

'Well,' says Tada again. Mam doesn't open her eyes. Tada starts to roll a cigarette, tamping his Golden Virginia into the Rizla paper until the smell of it fills the living room. He licks the edge of the paper, and picks little bits of tobacco off his tongue and flicks them into the fire. He runs his thumb along the seam, then bends down to light a spill from the fire and holds it to his cigarette.

'Did Alwenna tell you anything else, Gwenni?' he says, drawing on his cigarette to light it and blowing smoke into the air.

I'm too warm now, and I push John Morris off my lap and wriggle out of Tada's armchair. 'Yes, but not about Ifan Evans,' I say. I don't want to think about him floating in the Reservoir with his eyes wide open for the moon to shine into. 'What will happen to Catrin and Angharad and Mrs Evans now, Tada? Will they be thrown out of their house?'

'No,' says Tada, sinking into his chair. 'I expect family will come and take care of them, Gwenni. I don't think they live far away.'

'But they're nearly all dead,' I say. 'I heard Mrs Morris say so in the meeting last night.'

'Surely there's someone who'll come,' says Tada. 'Well, if not, we'll do what we can for them, Gwenni.'

'Huh,' says Mam. She opens her eyes. 'What did that Alwenna tell you that wasn't about Ifan?' she says to me.

I shrug. 'She said I was doolally like my . . . but she didn't say who.'

Mam gasps as if someone has thrown cold water at her. 'That girl has no shame,' she says. 'She's got a loose mouth just like her mother. It's time you stopped seeing her.'

'But what did she mean?' I say. 'Who's doolally in our family, Mam?'

'You're a wicked girl repeating filth like that. Go and wash your mouth out with soap.' Mam springs from her chair and swings her arm back as if to hit me.

Tada takes hold of her arm. 'Go upstairs, Gwenni,' he says. 'Go upstairs and read one of your books. Your mam's had a shock. It's not your fault.'

'It is her fault. It's all her fault. I wish she'd never been born.' Mam begins to scream, then sobs.

'Try a deep breath, Magda,' says Tada. 'Come on. Deep breath.'

The living room door bangs shut behind me and I run upstairs. Mari the Doll looks at me from her chair. 'How far away d'you think I could fly before I had to come down to Earth again?' I ask her.

17

See how the moonlight shines through the trees to make the leaves dance on the white walls of Brwyn Coch. Tada straightens his jacket after knocking on the door. He says it's good manners to pay your respects the day after a death. So here we are, even though Ifan Evans drowned before yesterday; we just didn't know about it. Mam wouldn't come with us. She said: I've no respect for that woman. I pull my best coat tighter around me; the air is cold because the evening is so fine. Behind us across the bay the lights of Llŷn twinkle in the dusk. How long would it take me to fly that far? In my sleep I never fly beyond the shore on our side of the water. The eyes stop me.

Tada is still tugging at the back of his coat when Mrs Evans opens the door. He clears his throat and smiles his big white smile at her, but only for a second. 'I'm so very sorry for your loss,' he says and holds his hand out to her.

'Thank you, Mr Morgan,' Mrs Evans says and shakes his hand. 'Will you come inside? I've just made a pot of tea.' The swelling has gone down on her lip at last, but there is a smudge of a bruise left behind and I'm sure I can hear a lisp when she speaks, though

Price the Dentist has already made her new teeth. Mam had to wait weeks and weeks. Mrs Evans's hair isn't in its tidy bun tonight; it's hanging loose around her face, wavy as the stream when it tumbles over its stones.

'Well,' says Tada. He turns to me. 'Gwenni is here with me, too, Mrs Evans. She has something she needs to say to you. And yes, a cup of tea would be very welcome, thank you. Come on, Gwenni.'

Tada said I should go with him to take Ifan Evans's photograph back, but Mam didn't want me to. She didn't want Mrs Evans to know I'd borrowed it. Taken it. Stolen it. But Tada said everyone else knew by now because everyone had seen my poster, so Elin Evans would soon know if she didn't already, and anyway, she should have her property returned to her.

We walk behind Mrs Evans into the parlour with its shelves of books and its faint, powdery, violet scent. I can see the gaps on the shelves where my books used to sit, though the books next to them have keeled over to half fill the spaces. Catrin and Angharad both sit in the window-seat, in their nightdresses, ready for bed. Catrin jumps down and runs over to me and puts her arms around my legs and rubs her face in my best coat. Mam washed my school mackintosh this afternoon but she says it will be wet for days.

'I like your coat, Gwenni,' says Catrin. 'It's soft like a little lamb.'

'Sit down, Catrin,' says Mrs Evans. 'Angharad, you come to help me bring in the tea things.'

'Gwenni,' Catrin says in a whisper as soon as her mother has gone through into the kitchen. 'Have you written my story? I don't like *Alice in Wonderland*; it scares me. Don't tell Angharad.'

I sit next to her on the window-seat and take hold of her hand. It's small and cold and nestles in my palm. Tada stands in the middle of the room and turns around and around like the hands of a clock and looks at all the shelves sagging under the weight of their books and Mrs Evans's desk with the piles of exercise books still on it and the big fire in the inglenook sending a flickering light over everything.

'I've written some of it,' I say to Catrin.

She squeezes my hand and snuggles up to me. 'What's it about?' she says.

'Flying,' I say. I stroke her hand. 'You run after a white goose, like Alice ran after the White Rabbit, and fly up into the clouds with it and have lots of adventures. And you're never scared.'

'What's my story called, Gwenni?'

'*Catrin in the Clouds*,' I say.

She whispers the name and kisses my hand. 'Thank you, Gwenni,' she says.

Mrs Evans comes back with the tea tray and Catrin takes her hand from mine.

'Sit down, Mr Morgan,' says Mrs Evans. 'Do you take milk in your tea? Sugar?'

Tada sits in a chair beside the fire. The logs don't crackle and spit the way they do on our fire. 'Please,' he says. 'Plenty of milk and two spoonfuls of sugar.'

'It's good for shock,' I say to Catrin. 'Plenty of sugar.'

Mrs Evans pours my tea without needing to ask what I want in it and she makes a milky tea for Catrin and Angharad. For herself she takes a cup of black tea, which she sips though it must be hot on her bruised mouth.

No one speaks as Mrs Evans drinks her tea. Tada blows on his tea to cool it, the way he does at home. Angharad giggles, and Mrs Evans says, 'Drink up your tea, girls, and say goodnight to Mr Morgan and Gwenni.'

But the girls leave their tea and Catrin waves at me, a baby wave with her fingers. When she and Angharad have gone from the parlour and we hear their footsteps scuffling up the stairs, Mrs Evans turns to Tada. 'They've been very good,' she says, 'very good girls. Of course, they don't understand what's happened.'

'It must be hard for them,' says Tada, 'losing their father so suddenly, so—' He stops as if he's not sure what to say, but Mrs Evans doesn't seem to notice. She's thinking again, the way Tada admires, gazing into the distance beyond the parlour wall at something we can't see.

Tada lifts his cup to his mouth but before he can drink any of his tea there is a terrible howling from outside the cottage. What if the black dog has come back? Tada's cup clatters back on the saucer as he leaps to his feet and heads for the parlour door.

Mrs Evans puts her hand out to stop him and he grasps hold of it as if he's trying to protect her. 'It's poor Mot,' she says. 'He doesn't know what to do with himself without Ifan. I daren't let him off the rope.'

Mot howls again and again. What if Ifan Evans's spirit has come home from the water? I huddle into my chair and take a sip of my tea. The milk in it is on the turn. Tada sits down again and I try to signal to him before he drinks any or he'll get the old family stomach. But he frowns at me and takes a mouthful of his tea. He stays quite still for a long second then swallows it with a gulp and puts the cup back on the saucer and both of them back on the tea tray.

'Well,' he says. 'Anything I can do to help, Mrs Evans, just you let me know. I expect you've got umpteen offers. But I would be honoured to help.'

'Thank you,' says Mrs Evans. 'There haven't been that many offers, Mr Morgan, so I appreciate yours.'

'Well.' Tada's eyebrows rise into his hair.

'People don't quite understand the situation,' says Mrs Evans. 'So they prefer not to . . . become mixed up with it. Poor Guto'r Wern is the only person to call – apart from the Minister and Twm Edwards – and I could barely make out what he was saying he was wailing so much. I think he was wailing in sympathy with my . . . our situation. He frightened the girls, of course. Poor Guto.'

'Poor Guto,' agrees Tada. 'There's no harm in him. He's innocent as a child.'

There's a small silence, except for the sighing of the fire, then Tada says in a rush, 'Magda sends her condolences, of course. She wasn't too well, and asked me to apologise for her.'

I look to see if Tada has crossed his fingers. But he's lying.

'And Gwenni here has something to say, I'm afraid,' he says. He turns to me. 'Go on, Gwenni.'

I pull the poster from the pocket of my best coat. This pocket is not as good as the pockets on my school mackintosh and the poster is folded over again and become faintly green and furrier than ever where it's rubbed on my coat. I unfold the poster and smooth the creases from Ifan Evans's picture. What if Mrs Evans is cross with me? What if she's sad that I've done this to the photograph of her dead husband? I hand the poster to her. 'I'm sorry that I took the photograph without permission and I'm sorry I showed it to everybody,' I say. 'And I'm sorry about Mr Evans.' Maybe I should have crossed my fingers when I spoke the last bit.

Tada nods at me; I'm not sure what he means by it. Does he want me to say more? 'But I thought I was helping,' I say. 'I thought I could find Mr Evans for you and Angharad and Catrin so you didn't have to be thrown out of your home into the cold, and starve and become ill.'

'Well,' says Tada. 'Gwenni, Gwenni.'

Mam said I was only supposed to apologise, and not make excuses. No need to make a meal of it, she said. I forgot.

Mrs Evans smoothes the poster with her palm. The scrapes on the back of her hand have healed over into neat scabs. 'I should have been clearer when we spoke, Gwenni,' she says, 'about what I did and didn't want you to do. You did ask but I gave you no answer; I was distracted. I noticed that the picture was missing before you'd gone home but I didn't do anything about it.' She looks up at Tada. 'My fault, Mr Morgan, not doing anything about it there and then.' She smoothes and smoothes the poster as she speaks. 'My fault.'

'It's very good of you to take it like this, Mrs Evans,' says Tada. Mrs Evans sits and looks at the photograph in silence and Tada clears his throat and makes to move towards the parlour door. 'Time Gwenni and I were off. Leave you in peace.'

'I've never liked this picture of Ifan with the fox,' says Mrs Evans and she scrumples up the poster and throws it on the fire, where it catches light immediately. Tada jumps towards it as if to save it from the flames but she waves him away. 'Gwenni is a kind girl, Mr Morgan. She doesn't always do things the way other people would, but that's because she's got the intelligence to see that there are different ways of doing things. Don't be too hard on her.'

Poor Tada. He's never hard on me. I look at him. But he's grinning at Mrs Evans with his even white teeth. His family hair is flopped over his forehead with all the leaping about he's doing. He pushes it back.

'I've always said Gwenni's a clever one,' he says. 'But she upsets Magda with her . . . unusual ideas. That's the trouble, you see, Mrs Evans. Magda's worried that people will think Gwenni's . . . well . . . odd.'

'Ah,' says Mrs Evans. She takes a few more sips of her tea.

'Our families seem to do or say the wrong things sometimes, Gwenni. But they always care about us. Family is important, Gwenni. You know, my sister and I used to argue all the time.' She looks at Tada, 'But Meg would help me in an instant if I asked her.'

'That's good.' says Tada. 'And if there is anything . . . you know, just ask.'

'If Gwenni can carry on helping with the children after school, that would be a great help,' says Mrs Evans. 'To keep them occupied, and amused. She's very good with them. It would give me time to start sorting out a few things.'

'Of course,' says Tada. 'You'd like that, wouldn't you, Gwenni?'

I nod. But Mam won't like it, will she?

Tada goes on, 'Is there a day set for the funeral yet, Mrs Evans?'

'No,' she says. 'There has to be an inquest. No one knows exactly what happened to Ifan, you see.'

'Well,' says Tada. 'An inquest.'

It's lucky that Aunty Lol lends me so many detective stories. I wouldn't know what an inquest was otherwise. And I wouldn't know that you have a post mortem before an inquest. Will Ifan Evans's blood flow like water when the pathologist cuts up his body? Aunty Lol's books don't tell me that. And I won't think about it.

18

'Lol. Lol. Potato flower,' says Lloyd George in a voice that sounds like a fingernail scraping an empty tin can. He sways on the swing in his cage and pecks at his own face in his little round mirror so that the bell on the mirror tinkles.

'Does he think he's got another budgie in there with him?' I ask Nain.

'Who knows?' she says. 'But I wish that great horse of a girl would teach him something sensible to say.'

Lloyd George hasn't got much room in his cage so Nain usually lets him out to fly around the room during the evening. He always sits on my head and digs his claws into my scalp, and I have little scabs there for days afterwards. When I pick at the scabs in school Alwenna says I look as if I've got nits. When I told Mam she said: That Alwenna should wash her mouth out.

I sink and sink into the big leather armchair because the springs are worn, but it's cosy like this. I pull out my Lion notebook and a pencil. The pencil is stubby, and it's not easy to write with it. Nain rattles the fire with the poker that has a phoenix gleaming on it like Mrs Evans's and throws on some lumps of coal.

She settles herself comfortably in her rocking chair and puts her crocheted shawl over her shoulders and her spectacles on her family nose. I wonder who the very first person was to have our family nose. Nain takes out a grey sock from her sewing box. Is she darning Tada's sock with the hole in the heel?

'Where's Aunty Lol tonight?' I say. I thought Aunty Lol would help me with my research. She tells me what I want to know.

'Football,' says Nain, and clamps her lips shut. Nain doesn't like Aunty Lol playing for the women's football team, especially when it's her turn to bring home all the shirts to wash. I won't mention the football again.

'So, you want to find out about the family?' she says. 'What's brought all this on?'

'Mrs Evans Brwyn Coch said it's important to know about your family,' I say. 'So I thought I'd find out about mine. She's shown me how to make a family tree.'

Nain pokes a darning mushroom into the heel of the sock. 'You've been up there a lot these last few weeks,' she says. 'Your mam's happy about that, is she?'

'Dr Edwards gave her some tablets,' I say. 'They work a lot better than deep breaths.'

'Hmm,' says Nain. 'Well, let's do this before the light goes. Have you got your pencil ready?'

I nod.

'You have to have the names right,' she says. 'Now, my mother was Gwen Evans and my father Edward Jones. He was a small-holder but he helped other farmers tend their animals because he knew what herbs to use to treat what disease.' As she speaks Nain threads some grey wool onto a long darning needle and begins to weave around the hole in the sock, as if she's about to weave the story of our family into it. 'Am I going too fast for you?' she says.

I shake my head as my pencil scribbles across the page. Will I find out who was mad soon? Who it was Alwenna was talking about?

Nain carries on weaving. 'I was their third child, but the first girl. So, I was named for my mother. And my mother had been named for her mother. So, you see, you became part of a long line of Gwens when you were named for me.' Nain likes to tell me the story about the long line of Gwens. It was Nain's own Gwen who died of the terrible disease when she was small. Mam says I must never mention that Gwen.

'But I'm Tada and Mam's second girl,' I say. 'Who was Bethan named for?'

'She wasn't named for anybody,' says Nain. 'As far as I know. You'll have to ask your mam about that. Anyway, I married your grandfather, William Morgan, and we had seven children. Your father was the first and your Aunty Lol was the last.'

Mam says I mustn't mention Taid who died when Tada was fourteen, either, nor Idwal who died in the war and is buried far away in Greece, nor Carwyn who used to pull eggs from my ears and make pennies disappear, and then made himself disappear into the cemetery.

'So, is Tada the only one of your children with children?' I ask.

'I think you'd know if you had cousins, don't you?' says Nain. 'Your Aunty Bet in Birmingham lost her husband in the war and your Uncle Dafydd is showing no signs of settling down. As for Lol, well, who'd have that great horse of a girl?'

'Lol. Lol. Potato flower,' says Lloyd George and rattles his beak on the bars of his cage.

'Apart from the budgie,' says Nain. And she stabs her darning needle into the heel of the sock.

'What about Mam's family?' I say. Mam's family is all dead except for Aunty Siân so we don't mention them. But Nain might.

'You'll have to ask your mam,' says Nain. 'It's not my place to tell you the story of that half of your family. Ask her. You and Bethan are old enough to know now.'

'Know what?' I say.

'Whatever there is to know,' says Nain. She ties off the darning thread and cuts it with her teeth. False teeth, like Tada's. They clack as she shifts them back into place. My stomach shifts a little with them.

'Like what, though?' I say.

Nain bends her face over to examine her darning before rolling the sock into a ball with its partner and dropping it into the mending basket. 'You can take those home with you when you go,' she says.

'Potato flower,' says Lloyd George. He fluffs up his blue feathers and pecks harder at his face in the mirror. What does he see?

It's becoming colder and darker in Nain's living room. Nain doesn't like wasting coal or electricity.

'I can't see properly to write, Nain,' I say.

'First of May, today, Gwenni,' she says. 'You know I don't use the electric light in the evenings from the first of May. Anyway, I've told you all there is to know.'

I close my notebook and uncurl from the armchair. Something sharp digs into me and I pull out the book Aunty Lol is reading from under the edge of the cushion. *The Maltese Falcon*. She's almost at the end. She'll give it to me to read when she's finished it. I push it back into place.

'Nain,' I say.

'Say it,' says Nain. 'What do you want?'

'Was anyone in your family doolally?' I ask.

'Only your Aunty Lol,' says Nain. 'What made you ask that?'

'Something Alwenna half said,' I say. 'It doesn't matter.'

'She's probably got half a story from her mother about something,' says Nain. 'Nanw Lipstick's always made it her business to know other people's secrets. Trouble is, she can't see what's true and what isn't and she's not clever or sensible enough to see that everyone knows these things but most of us don't talk about them.'

'But everyone's talking about Ifan Evans,' I says. 'Not just Alwenna's mam.' Even Nain, but I don't say that.

'That's because they don't know his secrets, Gwenni. He and Elin only came to Brwyn Coch after they were married. No one knows anything much about him before that so they make it up.'

'Has our family got secrets, Nain?' Mam has secrets, hasn't she?

'Every family has, Gwenni. Big secrets, small secrets, silly secrets, bad things we want to hide. But, usually, people know what they are from the minute they happen. It's just that anyone with any sense doesn't talk about what doesn't concern them.'

'What are our family secrets about? A doolally person?'

'I suppose Nanw Lipstick could have found out about my grandfather on my father's side who died of religious mania,' says Nain. She gets up from her rocking chair and puts three pieces of coal on the fire and begins to blow under them with the brass bellows.

'But is that catching?' I ask. 'Is that what Alwenna thinks I've got? Religious mania? I don't even know what it is, Nain.'

'I'm pulling your leg, Gwenni,' says Nain. 'My grandfather died when I was a small girl. Nanw Lipstick will never have heard of him. Take no notice of what Alwenna says.'

'But he was doolally?' I say.

'Who's to say?' says Nain. 'I have to let this bird out of his cage for some exercise, Gwenni. Move to one side so I can reach.'

'Wait, Nain,' I say. 'Do you know all our family's secrets?'

'Probably not,' says Nain.

'But you'd know about anyone who could fly?' I say.

'You and your flying,' says Nain.

'What if it's something like names,' I say, 'that's passed down the family?'

'You'll have to try your mother's side for that one,' says Nain.

'It's no good asking Mam,' I say. 'But maybe Aunty Siân'll know. Maybe Mam'll let me visit her.'

'There you are,' says Nain. 'There's always a way.' She peers in the direction of the birdcage. 'My word, it has got dark suddenly,' she says. 'Maybe I'd better have the light on just for a minute to see what I'm doing here.'

She switches on the electric light. It wakes Lloyd George who has settled into a still blue bundle on his perch.

'Lol. Lol,' he mutters, still half asleep, and opens one small eye.

'I'll give you Lol, you silly bird,' says Nain.

'Mrs Evans's family is dead,' I say. 'Like Mam's. She's just got her sister, and Mam's got Aunty Siân.'

'I believe Elin Evans lost both her parents when she was young,' says Nain. 'And that's not a secret. Now let me open that cage door.'

Nain unlatches the cage door and Lloyd George shuffles along his perch to the opening. I grab my Lion notebook and Tada's socks and move towards the scullery.

'And you mind your Ps and Qs when you're up at Brwyn Coch,' says Nain. 'You can upset people by asking too many questions, you know.' She pokes at Lloyd George who doesn't want to leave his cage tonight.

'Not Mrs Evans,' I say. 'She says you have to ask if you don't understand things.'

'Isn't that just like a school teacher?' says Nain.

Lloyd George squawks and nips Nain's finger before hurtling out of his cage with his skinny black legs pointing at my head and his claws extended to land. I bolt through the scullery door, slamming it shut behind me.

19

Tada stretches in his armchair, pointing his toes at the fire with the socks that Nain mended on his feet.

'Nowhere like home,' he says, 'Nothing like Friday evening with Saturday and Sunday stretching out before you. Lovely.'

'Lovely for some,' says Mam. She knits faster. She's almost finished little Helen's bolero at last. Wisps of fuzzy-wuzzy float like thistledown from Mam's lap onto John Morris's nose and he sneezes and comes out from under her legs and crawls under Tada's chair. Pale blue filaments spiral up on the heat of the fire and stroke the faces of the Toby jugs as they pass.

'You'll be all right tomorrow, won't you?' says Tada. 'You always enjoy the Singing Festival, Magda.'

'Some people's husbands go with them,' says Mam. She heaves the knitting around on the pink cushion in her lap to begin a new row. The fuzzy-wuzzy is beginning to tickle my nose, too.

'Come on, Magda,' says Tada. 'We go through this every year. You know I'm not a chapel man.'

'It's that old football,' says Mam. Her knitting needles clack faster and faster.

'I daresay they'd have more men there if they didn't hold it on Cup Final day,' says Tada. 'But not me.'

'Are you going to see the game on Mr Williams's television?' I ask.

'Like going to the pictures, eh, Gwenni? Lovely.' Tada stretches again. 'Special match this year, too. A sad day for United. They've done well to keep going after that terrible plane crash.'

'I don't know how Robin Williams's wife can let you all into her parlour with your big feet to yell and shout,' says Mam.

'Only seven of us, Magda,' says Tada. 'Anyway, she won't know anything about it, will she? She'll be at the Singing Festival with you.'

Tada pushes himself up from his chair and takes his tobacco tin from the mantelpiece and begins to roll a cigarette. I breathe in the scent of his Golden Virginia instead of the smell of the fish we had for supper.

'When's Bethan coming home from what's-her-name's, then?' he says.

I open my mouth to answer him, but Mam glares at me and says, 'Caroline, her name's Caroline. You know that. Bethan will be back by nine.'

Mam doesn't believe what Alwenna told me about Bethan. And I was going to say Caroline, not Richard.

'Well,' says Tada. He lights his cigarette from the fire with a spill and comes round behind his chair to the table and looks at the roll of paper I've unfurled. 'That's a big sheet of paper you've got there, Gwenni,' he says. 'Where did you get that?'

'It's lots of sheets glued together to make one big one. See?' I point out the joins to him.

'Very tidy,' he says. 'What are you going to do with it?'

'Draw our family tree,' I say. I pull out my notebook from

under the sheet and open it to where Mrs Evans has shown me how to make a family tree. 'You're a leaf on it, and so is Mam. And so am I. And Bethan. But I have to find all the other leaves to go on it before us.'

'That's very clever, Gwenni. Did you do that at school?'

'No. Mrs Evans drew this tree in my notebook for me to copy. She gave me the paper and glue and helped me make this big sheet.'

Mam's needles have stopped clacking and the room is quiet apart from the hissing of the wood on the fire and the tick-tock of the mantelpiece clock. The Toby jugs yawn on the top shelf.

Tada draws on his cigarette and blows smoke rings into the air. The smell of the smoke mingles with the smell of fish. Samuel Fish's van brings fresh fish round every Friday morning but Tada says there's no telling when the fish was fresh. John Morris always eats the heads with their staring eyes. Sometimes they smell like the fish in my night-time sea. Sometimes they smell like blood. I won't think about the blood.

'Will you put down that I can blow perfect smoke rings?' Tada says, blowing some more.

'No,' I say. 'You're only supposed to put down when someone is born and when they get married and what children they have and when they . . .' I look at Mam but she's staring at the fire with her knitting needles quiet in her hands.

'Die,' says Tada.

'Yes,' I say.

But why can't a family tree record other things? Things that are passed down like noses and hair and freckles and religious mania and blowing smoke rings and whistling and being clever and flying.

'Let's have a look at what you've got so far, then,' says Tada and draws my notebook towards him. He reads out loud the names Nain told me.

'Is this what you were doing next door last night?' he says.

I nod. 'But I think Nain's missed out a lot, hasn't she?'

'I expect we can fill in the missing bits, Gwenni,' he says. He smoothes the big sheet flat on the chenille tablecloth. 'You'll have to take this cloth off if you're going to write on here or your pencil will make a hole in the paper.' He pulls the cloth out from under and drapes it on the back of his chair. 'It was very good of Mrs Evans to spend time doing this with you when she's got so many troubles.'

'She says it helps her to do something different,' I say.

'Gwenni should stop going up there,' says Mam. She drops her knitting on her pink cushion. Her fingers tap and tap on the wooden arms of her chair. 'Heaven knows what goes on up there. You should never have agreed to let her go to look after those children. I don't like her being mixed up with that woman. People will begin to talk, if they're not talking already.'

Tada takes his cigarette from between his lips and pinches the lit end and puts the rest of it behind his ear. He pushes his family hair back from his forehead. 'The poor woman can't help what's happened to her husband, Magda.'

'Poor woman. Huh,' says Mam. 'What did she do to make him leave so fast he fell in the Reservoir? Have you thought about that?'

'Well,' Tada says. He gazes at Mam. She gets up and goes to the scullery and comes back with two chunks of wood for the fire and throws them into the grate where they fizz and crackle then spit like a jumping jack.

Tada stamps the linoleum. 'Why can't we go back to coal?' he says.

'Because wood is cheap and I have to save money somehow if I'm going to have a better house than this, with an electric cooker and a bathroom,' says Mam.

Tada sighs. I begin to roll up my sheet of paper.

'Don't do that, Gwenni,' Tada says. 'Let's have a proper look.' He studies the tree Mrs Evans drew and then looks at my big sheet of paper. 'You've got plenty of room on here to make the tree much bigger. You could make it taller if Nain could remember a bit further back.' He reads the names Nain gave me again. 'I can fill in some of these gaps,' he says. 'But I'm no good with dates.' He stares at the list, lost in a place I can't see. 'The Chapel cemetery is the best place for the dates,' he says. 'Everyone's buried there. And there's that box of photographs on top of the wardrobe; I'll get it down for you. You can match the faces to some of the names.'

'That's your family,' I say. I look at Mam. She's sitting in her chair again, her knitting still on her cushion. She's watching the fire, her lips moving slightly as if she's memorising a poem for school. I whisper in Tada's ear, 'What about Mam's? Where are they all buried? Where are all their pictures?'

'Not now, Gwenni,' he murmurs. Then, in his cheerful voice, he says, 'Look, you can leave some room at the bottom, too. Here, see? After your name and Bethan's you can put the names of your husbands and your children in years to come.'

'I'm not going to get married,' I say. 'I hate boys.'

'I expect you'll change your mind when you're older, Gwenni,' he says.

But I won't.

Tada puts his hand on Mam's shoulder when he passes her to slip back into his chair by the fire but she shrugs it off. The *Daily Herald* rustles as Tada picks it up from the floor. John Morris crawls from under the chair and strolls towards the scullery, his tail flicking from side to side. He's having no peace tonight. Perhaps he'll finish his fish head before I go through, then I won't have to see its staring eyes.

I pull out my pencil case from my satchel, and my long ruler, and begin to draw a tree the way Mrs Evans showed me. Maybe I will make it look a bit more like a real tree. It will have the past, the present and the future of our family on it. But will it ever have the whole story? Will it ever have all the secrets and all the truth?

20

'I'm glad I decided to wear my old costume again,' says Mam. 'There's a chill in the air this morning.' She squints at the cloudy sky, and says in English, 'Don't cast a clout until May is out.' With both hands she pulls at the waves above her ears so that they're below her blue felt hat with its silly speckled feather. 'That's better,' she says. But it isn't.

I offer Mam the huge cake tin she made me carry from the house. The cakes for the Singing Festival have got pink icing and hundreds and thousands. The doctor's tablets haven't helped Mam to cook any better than deep breathing did. She ignores me.

'Now, Bethan,' she says. 'When the charabanc comes I want you to sit in the front seat with Gwenni and keep an eye on her.'

'What?' says Bethan. 'Why do I have to do that?' She stamps her foot. 'It's not fair. I want to sit with Janet.'

'And you,' says Mam to me. 'I don't want any of your silly nonsense. Just you mind what you say to people.'

I don't say anything. The cake tin's weight makes my arms ache; I shift it to a different position. We stand in silence at the foot of our hill. Mam smiles at nothing because she's just taken her tablet and Bethan sulks because she has to sit with me in the charabanc. I want to sit with Alwenna. Will Alwenna want to sit with me? Or will she want to sit with Edwin the horse and Aneurin on the back seat?

A rattling and screeching breaks the silence. The racket gradually grows louder until the charabanc lurches around the corner towards us. It doesn't usually make so much noise. We step back out of its way.

Mam turns to me and takes the cake tin. 'I'll be keeping my eye on you,' she says.

With a blare of its horn the charabanc stops next to us. Mam climbs the steps and then stops dead at the top. Through the windows Bethan and I can see that the charabanc is already full of people.

'Hooray,' says Bethan and she pushes past me and Mam and disappears into the smoke-filled back of the bus. I climb the steps and stand behind Mam.

'Hurry up,' says the driver to Mam.

'Who are you?' says Mam. 'Where's Wil? He always picks up here first.'

'Broke his leg,' says the driver. He pats tenderly at the quiff that vibrates on his head in time to the engine. 'I'm Ned. Doing him a favour. Doing you a favour.'

Mam looks down over the cake tin at his quiff and his boot-lace tie. 'Are you sure you know what you're doing? You look too young to be in charge of a charabanc,' she says. 'And where are we supposed to sit?'

'Magda! Magda!' Nanw Lipstick waves with her cigarette from halfway down the charabanc. 'I've kept a seat for you here, Magda.' She points at the seat next to hers. Even from here I can see the bright red stain of lipstick on her cigarette.

Mam looks round. There is no other seat except one at the very front next to Deilwen. Her mother and father sit across the aisle in the other front seat. Mam's mouth turns into a thin line when she notices Deilwen's father. He's not at home watching the football on Robin Williams's television; Mam'll be cross with Tada all over again. Deilwen's mother leans across her husband. 'Your little girl can sit next to Deilwen,' she says. 'We'll look after her.' Little girl?

'Sit here, Gwenni,' says Mam. She pulls me forward and pushes me into the seat next to Deilwen. 'Behave yourself and don't move from there,' she says. Where would I go?

Ned makes the engine grate and screech and Deilwen puts her hands over her ears. As the charabanc starts to move forward I turn and watch Mam stagger down the aisle and sit next to Nanw Lipstick. She sits right on the edge of the seat and sticks her nose into the air, holding on to the cake tin in her lap. I try to see if Alwenna is behind me somewhere but cigarette smoke is writhing around everyone in the back half of the bus and I can't find her. She must be on the charabanc if her mother's here. I turn to face the way we're going again. The fabric on the seat feels rough under my thighs; it used to be soft as the down on a baby bird.

Look at Deilwen's mother and father watching me. Deilwen's mother holds a handkerchief over her nose; it only just covers it. Deilwen smiles at me, then looks out through the window. Her nose is just like her mother's. I hadn't noticed that at Sunday School; it must be their family nose.

Guto'r Wern usually sits in the front seat where Deilwen's parents sit, with whoever is looking after him for the day. I wonder where he is; I didn't see him when I looked round, and I can't hear him. 'Did you see Guto come on the charabanc at the bottom of your hill?' I ask Deilwen.

'Oh,' she says, 'he wanted to sit next to me and I screamed and screamed and Mami said it was a disgrace to let someone like that travel with us and in the end someone took him off and said they'd both go on the train.' She shudders. 'It was horrible.'

'My father says there's no harm in him,' I say. 'He's innocent as a child.'

The charabanc rattles along the road and the road follows the sea. Guto will be following the sea, too, on the train. He likes the sea. The water reflects the grey of the clouds this morning and merges with the sky on the horizon so that you can't see where one ends and the other begins. The sea is slow, the shallow waves too lazy to carry their white frills to the shore. It isn't like this at night, the sea. I could fly far away over this sea. Last night there were more eyes than ever watching from the sea. All the family eyes were there. Would they help me to fly away? Or would they keep me here, too? I can't see any eyes in this placid sea.

'Guto can fly,' I say to Deilwen. 'And I can fly in my sleep. I fly right to the edge of the sea.'

'People can't fly,' says Deilwen. 'That's going against the laws of God.'

I haven't found anything in Matthew that says animals haven't got spirits, and I haven't read anything that says people can't fly. If it doesn't say people can't, does that mean they can?

'I don't think it is,' I say. 'Sometimes I can almost fly when I'm awake. Almost. Guto tried to teach me but it didn't work.' Mam is too far away to hear me. 'I can remember flying when I was little.'

Deilwen moves nearer the window. I don't want her to be my friend. But I don't know what Mam will say.

I turn around again to see if I can spot Alwenna and there she is in a gap in the smoke, right at the back on the long seat, laughing with Aneurin and Edwin. I need to talk to her before the charabanc reaches Bermo about my plot for rescuing the dead fox and freeing its spirit. There won't be time once we're at the Festival.

The charabanc bumps and sways as Ned fights with the levers and the steering wheel, and the smell of petrol fumes mixes with the cigarette smoke. When I was little, I used to be sick before the charabanc reached Dyffryn.

I get up and begin to walk towards the back of the bus. Alwenna sees me; she waves and then turns her face away from me as if she's made a mistake. As I pass Mam, she grabs hold of my arm. 'What did I tell you?' she says. 'Get back to your seat. Don't show me up.' I forgot I had to stay in my seat.

My arm throbs where Mam dug her fingertips into it. I sit back down next to Deilwen. I'll have to rescue the dead fox on my own. I can do that. But the only time I can do it is when we have our lunch in the vestry of Bethania Chapel in Bermo. Then I'll have to hide the fox, but where? Where?

I hear Alwenna laughing at the back of the bus. Her laugh is like her song. It peals like a bell above the noise of the engine and the chatter of the people. Deilwen's mother tightens her lips and turns to Deilwen's father and shakes her head.

Deilwen won't sit still on her seat next to me. She bumps me with her elbow. Mam would tell me off if it was me.

'Mami, Mami,' she wails. I look at her. Whatever is the matter with her?

Her mother looks at her, too. 'Stop the bus,' she shouts at Ned, rapping him on the head with her handbag and spoiling his quiff.

The charabanc screeches and squeals. It begins to slow down. But it's too late. Just as the charabanc stops, Deilwen throws up.

I watch the vomit sliding down my legs and into the tops of my socks and slithering over my sandals that Tada polished this morning until they shone like conkers. The vomit is warm and smells of porridge. I try not to breathe and close my eyes tight so I don't see it.

'Get out,' says Ned. 'You can't stay on my charabanc in that state.'

'What have you done now, Gwenni?' says Mam's voice from above me.

And Deilwen's mother says, 'Never mind, your mam can buy you a new pair of socks when we get to Bermo.'

21

We all bundle in through Bethania's vestry doors, the boys at the front and girls behind them. We're starving hungry after singing all morning. My stomach is quite hollow. Young Mr Ellis in his chapel suit is trying to keep us quiet and form us into a tidy line but no one takes any notice of him. His spectacles have slipped down to the tip of his nose and he's carried through the door and down the corridor on a tide of hungry boys as relentless as my night-time sea.

The sun came out while we were in Chapel and this vestry is hot and smells of sandwiches and cake and sweat and dust. But it's lucky it's hot; Mrs Llywelyn Pugh will have to take off her dead fox and leave it somewhere.

Mrs Sergeant Jones and Mrs Jones the Butcher left the Singing Festival early to prepare the food. Mrs Jones the Butcher stands in the doorway to the room where we eat every year. Her arms are folded underneath her huge bosom. The surge of boys stops dead and Young Mr Ellis is catapulted forward. He pushes his spectacles up his nose with his little finger but they slide down again in an instant. I'm too far away to see if his little fingernail is dirty today.

'Mr Ellis.' Mrs Jones the Butcher has a huge voice, too. 'Why are you allowing these children to run in?' She spreads her arms out to stop any of us going past. Her bosom drops to her waist and the boys begin to snigger.

Young Mr Ellis looks back at us. His face is red, and shiny with sweat. He pushes his spectacles up his nose again. He ducks under one of her outstretched arms and stands behind her and whispers something into her ear.

'We'll see about that,' she says, and she looks at us until we fall silent. 'Boys to that table, girls over there. That way we'll have no trouble,' she says, pushing the boys one after another in the right direction. We girls scuttle to our own table. I look around for Mrs Llywelyn Pugh but I can't see her. She didn't come on the charabanc like everyone else with their food plates and tins and boxes on their laps; she and her dead-mouse sandwiches were to come with Mr Pugh in his car.

The trestle table is laid with a white cloth and its stiff edges scratch my legs as I slide onto the bench.

'I hope there aren't any splinters in these to ladder my stockings,' says Alwenna as she slithers in next to me. Her new green skirt takes up enough room for two people. I try to squash it down where it billows over my leg but the net underneath it won't flatten. 'Did your mam have to get you some new socks, then?' she says.

I stick my legs out under the table for her to see. Mam will be cross for a long time about having to spend the new-house money on socks. And I can still smell porridge. I swing my legs back under the bench and try not to think about it.

'My mam says your mam should have paid for Gwenni's new socks,' says Alwenna to Deilwen at the end of the table. Deilwen takes no notice of her. 'Airs and graces,' says Alwenna, and she pushes up the tip of her nose. 'My mam's cousin down south knows her mam's cousin,' she says to me. 'She's airs and graces too. She went to work in a posh house in London, only as a maid, mind, and when she came home for the weekend six months later she'd forgotten how to speak Welsh. That's more airs and graces than your mam.'

Is Mam airs and graces? Is that what the matter is with her?

'Grace,' shouts Mrs Twm Edwards and I fold my hands together and bow my head like everyone else and Young Mr Ellis mutters something very quick and then we start on the sandwiches.

There are plates and plates of minced-mouse sandwiches with black crusts; the sight of them makes my stomach lurch and I try to hold my breath in case I breathe in a mouse spirit. There are some plates of egg sandwiches, too; if they're Mrs Edwards the Bank's egg sandwiches they won't make my old family stomach worse.

As I munch, I look around and there is Mrs Llywelyn Pugh sitting at the head of the table where the women are eating their dinner. I can't see her eating any of her minced-mouse sandwiches. But she's not wearing her dead fox. Where has she left it? I can't see it anywhere.

'What's the matter with you?' says Alwenna. 'Have you been listening to me?'

I haven't but I don't say so.

'Elin Evans,' she says. 'All that stuff about her and Paleface. D'you know about it?'

I don't know what she's talking about.

'Wake up, Gwenni,' she says. She leans towards me and breathes out the smell of minced mouse into my face. I hold my breath. 'All that stuff about him beating her. And . . .' She looks around and begins to whisper. 'Those babies' grave in our cemetery. He killed them. Everyone knows.'

If everyone knows, why is she whispering? Anyway, what babies' grave? Is this the grave Miss Owen Penllech was talking about? Is this a Nanw Lipstick half-a-story?

'You're hopeless, Gwenni,' says Alwenna. 'Don't you know anything?'

Mrs Twm Edwards comes over to our table and starts handing out the jellies. The glass dishes clatter on the tray and the red jelly shimmers inside them. If I were a criminal I would steal priceless jewels that looked like that jelly. Mrs Morris follows Mrs Twm Edwards to hand out the fluted spoons she brings with her every year. The silvery surface of the spoons has rubbed away in places and the yellow metal underneath gives the jelly a bitter tang.

How will I find the dead fox? I'm sure it's not in this room. Maybe Mrs Llywelyn Pugh took her sandwich tins into the kitchen and left the dead fox in there. I swallow some jelly, cool and slippery in my throat, and try not to notice the tang. I'll have to search for the fox.

I cross my fingers. 'I'm going to be sick,' I say to Mrs Twm Edwards.

'You'd better go and tell your mam,' she says, and backs away. 'She'll know what to do.'

'I thought you were being odder than usual,' says Alwenna. 'Can I have your jelly?'

'No,' I say, and I slip from the bench and bump my shin on its hard edge.

Alwenna shrugs. 'You won't want it,' she says and takes the glass dish with the rest of my jelly and begins to eat it.

I rub my shin and limp past the men's table, which has a pall of smoke hanging above it although there are only five of them sitting there. All the rest are at home listening to the Cup Final on the wireless or squeezed into Mrs Robin Williams's parlour to watch it in a world where it's always snowing. Guto isn't here with the men. But I saw him at the Festival, singing and laughing. Did Mrs Beynon say it's a disgrace to let him eat with us, too? Poor Guto.

The women's table is crowded and they're laughing and talking and eating all at the same time the way I'm told off for doing. I hear someone mention Mrs Evans but I don't hear what they say about her. I try to make myself invisible to walk past.

'Gwenni,' says Mam. 'Where are you off to?'

'I feel ill,' I say and rub my stomach.

'You know where the lavatory is,' says Mam. 'Make sure you clean up properly afterwards.'

'That's a bit hard, Magda,' says Nanw Lipstick. 'Shall I come with you, Gwenni?'

Mam's face turns pink and she presses her lips tight together. 'Leave her, Nanw,' she says.

I shake my head at Alwenna's mam and run towards the door. I push it shut behind me and stand to listen for a moment to make sure no one is coming. But there's no point because when I reach the kitchen Mrs Thomas next door is already there.

'Quick, Gwenni,' she says. 'Help me get these cakes on the plates. There's your mam's big tin. Put her cakes on these three plates.' She pushes the plates towards me. 'I'll take in these I've done while you're doing that.' She balances the plate holding her special chocolate cake in the crook of her arm and takes another full plate in each hand and goes out through the kitchen door. The draught from her passing swings the door shut behind her and there on the back of it, hanging on a hook with two striped tea towels, is the dead fox. See how its glassy eyes stare straight at me. They beseech me.

'Don't worry,' I say to the fox. 'I'll save you.' But how can I rescue it without touching its dead fur or its dead face?

I look along the table with all its cakes and tins and the paraphernalia from the party preparation. I tip out all the cakes from Mam's big tin and pick up a serving spoon from the table and push the dead fox off the hook with the spoon so that it drops in a slithery coil into the tin.

'Sorry, sorry,' I say to the fox as I flatten it into the tin with the spoon. And then I say it in English as well in case Mrs Llywelyn Pugh never speaks Welsh to the poor little thing. I don't look at its eyes as I struggle to put the lid on and then I push the tin under the table.

When Mrs Thomas next door comes back, I'm arranging Mam's cakes in a pyramid on each plate. The hundreds and thousands make shapes on the icing, eyes to watch me, mouths to tell tales.

22

Mrs Evans has put my school mackintosh over the back of a chair in front of the fire. She says I can't put on a wet coat to walk back home again. She's put my shoes by the fire too, and lent me her slippers. They're green with a red pom-pom each, and too big; I can wiggle my toes around in the shape of her feet in them.

Mrs Evans sits by the fire opposite my coat with her mending in her lap, drinking a cup of tea with no milk in it and watching the fire and occasionally turning her head to watch me play snakes and ladders at the table with Angharad and Catrin. The fire flares and its light licks up and down the walls. There's a paler square on the cream paint where the photograph of Ifan Evans and his dead fox used to hang under the picture of the babies.

The rain drums on the tin roof of the lavatory outside the back door and plays a higher note on the tin bath hanging on the wall next to the kitchen window. It's raining too hard to take the girls out to play. Even Mot has been allowed indoors and lies on the rag rug at Mrs Evans's feet. Now and then he lifts his head and looks around the room, then sighs and lets his head droop to his paws again. Sometimes he opens one eye to watch us play snakes and ladders.

'It's my turn, not yours.' Angharad snatches the eggcup with the dice in it from Catrin and throws a five onto the board. 'Look, Gwenni, I can go up a ladder now,' she says. 'I'm winning.'

Catrin throws the dice and moves her counter onto a snake's flickering tongue. 'The snakes keep swallowing me,' she says. 'Why do they do that, Gwenni?'

'You're just unlucky today,' I say. The snakes keep swallowing me, too. I take my turn and throw the dice and am swallowed by a snake.

'Snakes are bad,' says Catrin. 'There's a bad snake in the Bible that makes Eve eat an apple when she shouldn't have done it. Did you know that, Gwenni?'

Angharad throws the dice again and wins the game. 'I've won. I've won,' she sings. 'You're only talking about old snakes in the Bible because you're not winning.'

'I remember the story,' I say to Catrin. 'It's after the world is made and Adam and Eve are the first people in it.'

'Eating the apple made bad things happen,' says Catrin. 'Not because the apple had maggots or anything, Gwenni. It was because Eve had been told not to eat it and she did anyway.'

Could Adam and Eve hear the Earth's hum here on the ground before Eve ate the apple?

Catrin turns towards her mother. 'Isn't that right, Mami?'

Mrs Evans stares into the fire and doesn't reply. Her hand rubs her lips over and over but the swelling and the marks Price the Dentist left behind are all gone.

'You're always doing things you're not supposed to,' says Angharad.

'I'm not,' says Catrin. 'I don't, do I, Mami?' Her lips tremble and her eyes brim with tears. I squeeze her hand.

'We all do things we're not supposed to sometimes,' says Mrs Evans. What does Mrs Evans do that she's not supposed to do?

'I never do,' says Angharad. 'Do you, Gwenni?'

I think of the dead fox that I took from the vestry door on Saturday. Mrs Llywelyn Pugh had hysterics when she couldn't find it. Mrs Jones the Butcher said: It must have been one of the Bermo boys who slipped in and took it when no one was looking. Alwenna looked hard at me and then she said: Everyone knows there are bad boys in Bermo; I know some at school. Mrs Llywelyn Pugh was so upset about her dead fox she had to be helped out to Mr Pugh's car to go home. And Mrs Sergeant Jones said: That poor woman; as if she hadn't had enough troubles in her life.

'Sometimes,' I say.

'Oh, Gwenni,' says Catrin. 'Mami, Gwenni says she does bad things sometimes.' She takes hold of my hand and strokes it. 'They're not very bad, are they, Gwenni?'

I shrug and Angharad dances about chanting, 'Naughty Gwenni. Bad Gwenni. Nearly-as-bad-as-Catrin Gwenni.'

Mrs Evans puts down her mending in the basket by her chair and says, 'That's enough, Angharad. It's time you and Catrin put your game away and got washed and changed ready for bed. You can have your supper in your nightclothes. Let Gwenni drink her tea in peace before she goes home.'

'Don't go,' says Catrin as she slips down from her chair. 'Mami, why can't Gwenni live with us?'

'Because she lives with her own family,' says Mrs Evans. 'With her father and mother and sister.'

'But her mother doesn't like her as much as I do,' says Catrin.

'That's a really bad thing to say,' says Angharad. 'See? You're a bad girl. That's nearly as bad as hitting Tada's black dog with the poker. And killing it.'

'That's enough, Angharad,' says Mrs Evans.

'Well, it never came back again, did it?' says Angharad. 'Or Tada.'

Catrin's hand flutters in mine. I put my arm around her shoulders and pull her to my side. It's like hugging the breeze, as if Catrin's body is all spirit.

Mrs Evans turns her back on Angharad and to Catrin she says, 'Gwenni's family loves her. Now let go of Gwenni and go upstairs with Angharad. There's warm water on the washstand. I put some in from the kettle when I made the tea so it'll be just right for washing your hands and faces now. And don't forget behind your ears.'

Angharad grabs Catrin's hand and hauls her towards the door to the stairs. 'You don't care about Tada,' she says to her mother.

Mrs Evans stays still as the children's feet clatter and clomp on the stairs all the way to their bedroom. Then she gets up from her chair by the fire and begins to put the snakes and ladders game away in its box. I put the dice and the counters in their own little box and put it with the board.

'How are you getting on with your family tree, Gwenni?' she says.

'I've put in all the names Nain told me,' I say, 'and Tada says he can fill in some of the gaps. But I've got to find the dates from the cemetery.'

'The cemetery's a sad place, Gwenni,' Mrs Evans says. She sits in a chair by the table. 'But I'm sure you'll be respectful when you're there.'

Has someone told her that I was sick over one of the tombs? Has someone told her why?

'I like the cemetery,' I say. 'There are lots of stories written there.'

'Stories?' says Mrs Evans.

'About the lives of the people buried there.'

'Their stories live on in the minds of those who've buried them there, Gwenni.'

'But their stories are written on their gravestones for other people to know about them,' I say.

Mrs Evans sips her tea and I drink some of mine. Not from the same cups as when I was here with Tada, not from the best cups. My coat has stopped steaming in front of the fire. A cupboard door bangs shut above us and the sounds of scuffles and splashes echo through the boards.

'Nain says that even though everyone knows everyone's secret stories, no one talks about them,' I say. 'So, I have to read about them on their gravestones.'

'I don't think you'll find their secrets on their gravestones,' says Mrs Evans.

'But they're secrets until you know them. Aren't they? Mam won't let us talk about any of the dead people in our family.'

Mrs Evans doesn't say anything. She puts her cup down on its saucer.

'Mam's family is all dead, except for Aunty Siân,' I say. 'And I can't find out anything about them because we can't talk about them and I don't know where they're buried. They're not in our cemetery. So I can't find their secret stories.'

Mrs Evans runs her middle finger round and round the rim of her cup. 'Sometimes secret stories are best left alone, Gwenni,' she says.

'But it would be useful to know things about people so you don't upset other people,' I say. 'It would be useful to know things about live people, not just dead people. Mam says I upset people by saying the wrong thing or doing the wrong thing. I always upset her. But how do you know what's right or wrong to say if you don't know people's stories?'

'You're a kind girl, Gwenni,' says Mrs Evans. She sits up straight in her chair and looks at my face. 'And thoughtful. But what's happened to make you so worried about this? Is it something you think you've done to upset your mother?'

'In the Singing Festival,' I say, 'someone took Mrs Llywelyn Pugh's dead fox, her fox-fur, and she was crying and crying.' Is not saying I took it as bad as lying? I cross my fingers under the overhang of the tablecloth just in case. 'Mrs Sergeant Jones said: That poor woman. As if something terrible had once happened to her. Maybe the person who took the dead fox didn't know that Mrs Llywelyn Pugh would be so upset and if that person had known her story she – or he – wouldn't have taken the fox.'

'Why on earth would anyone want Mrs Llywelyn Pugh's old fox-fur?' says Mrs Evans.

'Maybe she – or he – thought it needed to be buried for its spirit to go to Heaven . . . or something,' I say. 'Maybe the person who took it would give it back if she knew Mrs Llywelyn Pugh's secret story. Maybe that would be more important than saving the fox's spirit. Maybe.'

'Oh, Gwenni,' says Mrs Evans. She fetches the teapot from the range and pours herself more tea. It's thick and black as treacle now. I drink the rest of mine. It's gone cold but at least the milk isn't off today. 'I can tell you about Mrs Llywelyn Pugh. It's not a secret. My family lived near hers in Cricieth; she's always taken an interest in Angharad and Catrin because of that. Her life has been sad; I expect that's what Mrs Jones was talking about. Her father and her husband were killed in the Great War; like so many.

She had two little boys, and when they grew up they fought in the next war and they were both killed. One of them is buried in the same cemetery as your Uncle Idwal in Athens, right beside Mrs Nellie Davies's husband. As your Nain says, everyone knows but no one talks about it. It's too painful.'

'But Mr Pugh is her husband,' I say.

'Mr Pugh is her second husband,' says Mrs Evans. 'They were married after the last war. He takes great care of her, but she's often very sad, Gwenni.'

'She said her father shot her fox for her,' I say.

'It's possible that's why she was upset, then,' says Mrs Evans. 'The family lost their home after her father was killed so it's possible that the fox-fur was all she had left to remind her of her girlhood; the time before all the terrible things happened to her.'

Poor, poor Mrs Llywelyn Pugh. I look at my hands below the tablecloth and I uncross my fingers. If I save the fox's soul, Mrs Llywelyn Pugh will have lost the only thing that reminds her of a time when she was happy.

'Gwenni,' says Mrs Evans. The noises above us move towards the stairs. 'Does knowing any of that help?'

Angharad and Catrin are racing each other down the stairs, screeching and laughing, their sadness forgotten for now.

'Yes,' I say. 'Thank you, Mrs Evans.' At last, I know what to do.

23

When I open our living room door heavy smoke pours out into the hallway. It surges up the stairs and it smells like when Mam singes the feathers off the goose at Christmas, only a million times worse and it gives me that old family stomach straight away. John Morris races out after the smoke with his belly low on the floor. Fumes catch in my throat and I begin to cough, and my eyes sting and water.

In the living room Mam is on her knees in front of the fire-place poking viciously at something on the fire. The flames leap out of the grate and almost catch her yellow curls as if they're playing games with her. But Mam just thrashes and thrashes the thing on the fire with the poker.

'Mam,' I say, almost choking on the words. 'What are you doing? Is Tada home?'

The fire looks as if it might set the whole house alight. It hisses and fizzles and sparks fly out from it with the smoke. I stamp on one of them. 'Are you trying to put it out?' I say. 'Shall I get Aunty Lol?' I take my handkerchief from my pocket and hold it over my nose and mouth. I don't like fire.

Mam turns to me and in the heat her face is melting like a candle. Sweat and ash and face powder run in rivulets down her forehead and cheeks and her lipstick bleeds down each side of her mouth.

'What do you think I'm doing, you silly girl.' She shrieks at me and I have trouble understanding what she's saying as well as what she's doing. She waves the poker at me and I back towards the door. The smoke swirls around her like a dirty grey dressing gown. There are bits of something sticking to the poker. I look at the fire in the grate and see two eyes staring up at me before one of them rolls into the hearth with a clunk. Mrs Llywelyn Pugh's dead fox.

'Where's Tada?' I say. Tada will know what to do with Mam. Maybe she's forgotten to take her tablets.

'Out.' Mam screams at me. 'Get out, you wicked girl. How dare you do this to me.'

'Give me the poker,' I say and I try to take hold of the handle from Mam, but she swings it around out of my reach. She begins to laugh and then to cry and cough and then she staggers around on her knees and begins to whack what is left of the dead fox down into the dying flames. Fur and ash fly up from the grate.

'I was going to give it back,' I say. I can scarcely breathe and I cough as if I've got the croup. I put my handkerchief back over my face.

Mam rocks back on her heels by the fire. 'Give it back?' She begins to laugh again. 'Are you completely stupid? How could you possibly give it back?'

'I was going to take it to Mrs Llywelyn Pugh and apologise,' I say. I wonder why Tada doesn't come.

'Why?' says Mam, her voice raspy.

'Because I should have thought about how upset she'd be when I took it,' I say.

'Did you think about how upset I would be?' says Mam. 'No, I didn't think you would.' She begins to cry again in great gulps. She rubs her eyes with the sleeve of her blue jumper. 'I didn't bring you up to lie and steal. Where do you get it from?' She rocks back and forth in front of the flames. What if she rocks right over into them?

'I just wanted to save the fox's spirit,' I say.

Mam screams until the smoke shakes hazily in the air above her. Her mouth is wide open and her head thrown back. She looks like a vixen might when it howls into the night. Then she retches as if she's going to be sick.

Where is Tada? And where is Bethan?

'Where's Bethan?' I say. 'Shall I get Bethan for you?'

'Bethan found this in my cake tin under your bed. In my cake tin.' Mam puts her head back again but when she tries to scream the breath rattles in her throat.

I say, 'I think it's all burnt now.'

Mam looks at the fire and the fur smouldering in the grate and in little heaps on the hearth tiles. The fire has died down and the smoke thinned. Flares of soot left by the flames shoot along the tiles of the grate to the mantelpiece and up the chimney breast to the high shelf. The Toby jugs have their eyes closed. They've probably never seen such smoke and so much of it coming out of the grate beneath them. Mam pokes the burnt fur and the stench pours from it again.

'What am I going to say to Mrs Llywelyn Pugh?' I say from behind my handkerchief.

Mam turns round. 'You don't have to say anything to Mrs Llywelyn Pugh,' she says, nodding the poker at me.

I step back. I don't want bits of the fox's fur to fly off and touch me.

'Mrs Evans told me such a sad story—' I say.

'Mrs Evans, Mrs Evans,' Mam says. 'You're as bad as your father with his Elin this and his Elin that. Anybody'd think the woman was a saint. She was the worst wife Ifan could have possibly had with her prim and prissy ways and her nose in the air.' Mam wallops the fire with the poker. A great puff of smoke and ash and fur billows into the air. 'That's what I'd like to do to her,' she says. 'She's a thief, if you like. Is that where you learnt to steal? Is it?'

What is it that Mrs Evans has stolen?

'But it was Mrs Evans who made me see—' I say.

Mam roars like the MGM lion.

I wonder if I ought to give Mam one of her tablets. I move to fetch them from the scullery but Mam lunges at me from where she's on her knees in front of the grate and catches my mackintosh with one hand and waves the poker at me with the other.

'Don't think you're getting away with this,' she says. She pants as she pulls herself to her feet. I stagger with her weight. Some of her yellow curls are singed at the tips and the two streams of lipstick make her look as if she's been eating some of the raw meat she gives to John Morris. Sparks from the fire have made a pattern of black holes down the front of her blue jumper. It's one of her favourite jumpers. She'll be cross about that. She lets go of my mackintosh and swivels round and pokes at the fire again.

'Nearly gone now,' she says. 'It'll soon be ashes. No one will know.'

I don't mention that Mrs Evans has guessed that I took the dead fox and will be expecting to see Mrs Llywelyn Pugh wearing it again in the winter.

Mam looks at me. 'Don't you go telling anybody about this,' she says. 'Does that Alwenna know you took it?'

I cross my fingers and shake my head.

'Everyone will think it's the Bermo bad boys,' says Mam. She gives the fire another flick with the poker. She takes a deep, shuddery breath, then coughs. 'It'll be all right. So long as no one knows, it'll be all right. So don't you go telling anyone it was you, Gwenni.' She glares at me. 'Promise. Cross your heart and hope to die. Go on.'

I can't promise, not even with my fingers crossed. I back towards the door so that I can run out and Mam follows me, waving the poker.

There's a crash as the front door opens and I move out of the way just in time for Tada to rush through into the living room. He stops still. He looks at Mam. She looks like the Guy Fawkes they put on the town bonfire. 'Magda?' he says. 'What's happened? Have we got a chimney fire?'

'Ask her,' says Mam, waving the poker at me.

Tada tries to take the poker. Mam won't let go of it; it's as if the heat from the fire has fused it to her hand. Mam begins to cry, and then cough. Tada helps her to her chair and lowers her into it. She drops the poker and covers her face with her pink cushion.

'Well?' Tada says to me.

'I took Mrs Llywelyn Pugh's dead fox,' I say. 'Not the Bermo bad boys.'

'It didn't sound the sort of thing any bad boys would want to steal,' says Tada.

'And I hid it inside Mam's big cake tin and put it under the bed. I was going to bury it and save its spirit.'

'Well,' says Tada. His mouth twitches and he looks back at Mam. She rocks back and forth in her chair like Mrs Evans did when she'd been to the dentist. Except Mam doesn't make any sound at all.

'Only I talked to Mrs Evans and I was going to give it back and say sorry. But Bethan found it and told Mam and Mam . . .' I point at the grate and its smouldering remains.

Tada bends down and begins to sweep up some of the fur with the hearth-brush. The fox's glass eyes clink on the tiles as he sweeps. He stands straight again, the brush dangling in his hand, and looks around the room. The smoke hangs in slow swathes under the ceiling and ash covers everything. Mam rocks and rocks. 'I don't know where to start,' he says.

Mam stops rocking and lowers her cushion. 'Aren't you going to tell her off?' she says. 'Am I the only one who can see how wicked she is?'

'Hush, Magda. Hush,' says Tada. 'You sit quietly there. I'll make you a cup of tea as soon as I can clear the grate.'

'Tea?' says Mam. Her voice rises. 'Tea? You stand there and listen to her telling you these stupid things and all you can think about is making a cup of tea?'

Tada puts the hearth-brush down and tries to catch hold of Mam's hand. She swats him away.

'People think she's odd enough already,' she says. 'You have to do something about it. What if she ends up like her grand-mother?' She mewls and covers her mouth with her cushion.

'Hush, hush,' says Tada. 'Gwenni, you go upstairs to read for a bit. I'll bring you a cup of tea once I get the fire sorted.'

I back out of the room and follow the ribbons of smoke up the stairs. It's going to take days and days to clean everything. Down in the living room Tada tries to soothe Mam. When I walk into my bedroom Mari the Doll looks up at me and I say to her, 'What could be so bad about ending up like Nain?'

24

The black taxi becomes smaller and smaller, then disappears into the mist on the road winding up to Brwyn Coch. Angharad and Catrin were snatched so quickly away from me by their aunty it feels as if they've been kidnapped. Maybe I've slipped into one of the stories in Aunty Lol's detective books.

I rummage about in my mackintosh pocket and find one Black Jack. The paper has stuck to it but I lick it off and spit it out. Black Jacks are my favourite sweets in the whole world. Alwenna won't eat them because they make her teeth look grimy. You can't have grimy teeth if you want boys to like you. If you can suck a Black Jack without chewing, it will last a long, long time.

Maybe Mrs Evans was just worn out after the inquest. She didn't look at me. She just sat in the back of the taxi with her hand over her eyes. Tada says inquests are not very nice things; not at all like I read about in Aunty Lol's books.

Catrin was crying for me when her aunty pulled her into the taxi. I hadn't seen her for nearly a week; Mam won't let me go to Brwyn Coch any more. But Tada said: I'm putting my foot down. And told me he'd arranged for me to have time off school today to look after Angharad and Catrin so that Mrs Evans could attend the inquest. I took them to Nain's house because our house is still a bit smoky even though Nain's been cleaning it all week. Mam's new tablets from Dr Edwards made her too sleepy to help. Nain gave us Heinz spaghetti on buttery toast and chocolate cake, and Angharad and Catrin were happy.

I lean on the railings of the Baptism Pool. The water is low in the Pool, as if the rain never falls here, and smells of decay. I don't look too closely at it. It seems long ago since I saw the spirit in the water when I was flying. Was it a premonition? Maybe I really can foretell the future, like Nain with her tea leaves. Perhaps that has been passed on to me with her name. A trickle of gory water runs from a pipe halfway down the concrete side of the Pool. Is it rust that makes it that colour, or is it blood? I try not to think where it might be coming from and move away.

My mackintosh is covered in flakes of paint and rust marks where it rubbed against the railings. I try to brush them off but they stick as if they've been glued on. Mam will be cross with me. Suddenly I am so tired that I slide down to lie in the grass. Mist swirls above me. I hear the sheep call to their lambs, though the lambs will be almost as big as their mothers by now. Nearby, a bee drones ceaselessly between the red campion stems on the bank. 'Poor thing,' I say to it as my eyes close, 'you won't find much there.' And I drift away into sleep.

A squeak jerks me awake. What is it? Then I hear another squeak. I lift my head and see Sergeant Jones wheel his bicycle out of the mist. His face is red and his white shirt has wet patches spreading from under his arms. He's slung his jacket over the bicycle's crossbar and his helmet dangles by its strap from the handlebars. I jump up from the grass.

'You startled me, Gwenni,' says Sergeant Jones. His breath

wheezes from his lungs. 'Oof, it's close today.' Waves of sweaty heat roll from him over me. I try not to breathe. 'What are you doing here?'

'I was walking up with Angharad and Catrin when Ned Hughes's black taxi came by with Mrs Evans and Miss Cadwalader and they took the girls into the taxi,' I say.

'Was Mrs Evans all right?' Sergeant Jones pulls one of his big white handkerchiefs from his trouser pocket and mops his face. But his face is just as shiny when he pushes the handkerchief back into his pocket.

'I think she was tired,' I say. 'I only spoke to Miss Cadwalader. Tada says inquests are horrible things.'

'I'm on my way up there,' says Sergeant Jones, 'just to make sure everything's all right.'

'Tada says she'll be better after the inquest. She'll be able to bury Mr Evans now.' He can lie in our cemetery with his dead babies. Will all his secrets be on his gravestone for everyone to read?

Sergeant Jones props his bicycle against the railings of the Baptism Pool and pulls his handkerchief out again to mop his face. 'This close weather doesn't agree with me,' he says. He looks at me. 'And how's your mam?' he says. 'I expect she's upset by this business, all this talk of inquests.'

'Dr Edwards gave her some new tablets,' I say. I don't mention that it's the dead fox that upset her.

'Well, I hope she's better soon. Tell her Martha missed her on Monday morning,' he says. 'She hates doing those brasses on her own.' He mops his face again and pushes the handkerchief back into his pocket. 'So, did your father tell you anything else?'

'No,' I say. 'Tell me what? Is there something else to tell? People don't tell me things because they think I'm a child.'

'You are a child, Gwenni. People don't tell children things they think will frighten them, for instance.'

'I'm never frightened,' I say.

'You should be sometimes,' says Sergeant Jones. 'It's only common sense. Now, I don't think it's safe for you to be walking out here in the back of beyond on your own.'

'Why ever not? I'm always up here. And I'm not always on my own. I often see Guto'r Wern. He's been teaching me to fly. But I think he can only fly in his sleep, like me.'

Sergeant Jones leans on the Pool railings next to his bicycle. It's too late to tell him his white shirt and his uniform trousers will be covered in old paint and rust. But maybe Mrs Sergeant Jones doesn't get cross.

He takes a deep breath. 'You know what inquests are for, I expect, Gwenni, from reading those books you lend me. For instance, this inquest today told us how Ifan died, and—'

'Everyone knows how he died. He fell in the Reservoir and drowned,' I say. 'Sergeant Jones, does this water in the Pool come from the Reservoir?'

'What? Oh, no, it's a stream, Gwenni, an underground stream. And Ifan Evans didn't die because he fell in the Reservoir and drowned. The inquest told us he was killed, Gwenni. Someone murdered him. This changes things.'

I stare at him. Murder. I thought murder only happened far away from here or in books. Who could have murdered Ifan Evans?

'Who killed him?' I say. 'Did the inquest say who killed him?'

'No. The police will have to find the killer. And while there's a murderer on the loose you'd better stop wandering about on your own like this.'

'I can help you find the murderer, Sergeant Jones. I can, really.'

'This is serious, Gwenni. It's not like finding a lost cat or even a lost person. Anyway, there are some important policemen coming from Dolgellau to investigate, policemen who are used to catching murderers.'

'Please let me help, Sergeant Jones, please. I won't get in the way of the investigation, honest. I'll investigate on my own.'

'I should think you'd know better after that last bit of investigation you did. You upset everybody, including your mam.' I open my mouth to protest and he lifts his hand, his palm towards me. 'But if you must do something, pretend it's a story in one of those detective books you give me, and work out the clues. Can you do that?'

'Oh, yes, Sergeant Jones.' He didn't tell me not to investigate, did he? 'We'll catch the murderer before the policemen from Dolgellau do.' I dance about on the grass and clamber on to the railings, balancing on the top one like I do on Tada's chair with my arms held out.

'Careful,' says Sergeant Jones.

'I can fly,' I call to him. 'I can fly and see everything.' I leap into the air. I feel a breeze whip my hair behind me into a long tail. I land at Sergeant Jones's feet.

Sergeant Jones shakes his head. 'Go straight home, Gwenni.' He takes hold of his bicycle and wheels it into the road. 'Go straight home, and be careful. This could be dangerous.'

25

Pretend it's a story, Sergeant Jones said. But this isn't like a story in a book at all. In books, the clues are laid out tidily, one at a time. I don't know where to start looking for clues, even. And now, because there's a murderer on the loose, I'm not allowed to go out walking on my own so I have no time or stillness to think about my investigation. It's more important than ever because Sergeant Jones told Tada that the special detectives from Dolgellau want to interview me on Monday. When he told Mam she started shaking and had to have an extra one of Dr Edwards's new tablets. Tada said he would go with me but Mam said he'd let me tell them all the wrong things, and anyway, they couldn't afford to lose a whole day of Tada's pay, and since Mam wouldn't be able to clean the Police House if the special detectives were there, she might as well be the one to go with me.

I fold the sheet over the scratchy blanket and pull them both up over my mouth and my nose. Tonight, John Morris isn't fighting any other cats, and I haven't heard the corpse bird at all. It's quiet and still enough now except for Tada's snores. Even Bethan is lying flat on her back without moving or snoring. I pinch her to make sure she's not dead, and she gives a giant snore and turns over, pulling the sheet and the blanket off me. I have to haul hard to get them back. My mind wanders, thinking about Mrs Evans and Angharad and Catrin, and Mrs Llywelyn Pugh and her dead fox, and poor Guto, and Mam's nerves, and secrets, secrets everywhere. 'Concentrate,' I tell myself. 'Find those clues.'

Detectives find clues at the scene of the crime. But where was the scene of the crime? Somewhere between Brwyn Coch and the Reservoir? The sheep will have eaten any clues left there. They nibble everything away. Except thistles and dandelions. Sheep don't eat the clues in books or on the wireless. Mr Campion and Gari Tryfan don't have trouble with sheep.

Bethan won't lie still now. I push her leg back to her own side of the bed. She never takes any notice of my ribbon down the middle of the mattress. I pull the sheet and the blanket around me and clamp my arms straight down my sides on top of them so she can't pull them off every time she heaves herself around.

And now, Mam's started moaning in her sleep, mumbling words I can't understand. Every night since she burnt Mrs Llywelyn Pugh's dead fox, she cries out in her sleep. Tada wakes, and I hear him without putting my ear to the wall. 'Hush, Magda,' he says. 'My sweetheart. My lovely girl.' He says the same things every time. 'I'll look after you. We'll be fine. Hush, now, hush.' When Mam is quiet, the bed twangs as Tada settles down to sleep again.

Perhaps everything will be fine once the murderer is caught. I wonder if the detectives from Dolgellau are any better than Sergeant Jones. If only I could find some clues. Maybe I'm looking at them but can't see them, like when Mam sends me to fetch something from the sideboard or the larder and I can't find it, and she says: It's right in front of your beak, Gwenni.

I feel myself begin to drift like a twig in the stream. I mustn't go to sleep. So, instead, I lift from the bed, high into the sky. Flying is magical; all the clouds disappear unless I need one to lie on, and if the moon is thin the stars give me plenty of their light. Is flying magical enough for me to find clues? I turn my back on the sea and the town, and soar up to Brwyn Coch. I hear the cottage sigh in its sleep when I fly above it. A night-light is burning in Angharad and Catrin's bedroom, but all the other windows are dark. The geese are shuffling around in their shed, and Mot is whimpering as he sleeps in his kennel.

I float down slowly towards the Reservoir. From here the fields and paths, the Reservoir and the Baptism Pool below it, the winding road, all look like a drawing on a page in an old mapbook, so that I want to lean down and write all their names on them. Instead, I search – up and down from the Reservoir to Brwyn Coch, and back again, over and over. I can't find one single clue. What if Ifan Evans's death wasn't murder? What if he fell against the stone wall at the edge of the Reservoir and hit his head on a stone and then fell into the water? I swoop lower and fly just above the wall to search for blood on the stones, but I can't see any.

I'm just about to lift into the sky again when I see a fox running away from the Reservoir, up the fields towards Brwyn Coch. I fly after it. It's running so fast that I can't catch up with it. It runs along the side of the cottage and just as it disappears around the back I hear barking below me. I look down and see the black dog racing after the fox. It barks and barks as it nears Brwyn Coch and, as if it's in a film at the picture house when the projector runs slow, the cottage begins to collapse. Its chimneys tumble down and the roof caves in. The black dog's bark grows louder, until the sky is filled with its sound. Brwyn Coch's windows fall out and the walls crumble into a heap of stones. And Mrs

Evans, and Angharad and Catrin, and Mot and the geese have all vanished.

I wake up yelling at the black dog to stop barking, and find the bedclothes twisted and damp around me. My flying turned into a bad dream tonight. And Mam is banging on the bedroom wall and shouting, 'Be quiet, Gwenni. I must have my beauty sleep.'

26

Sergeant Jones opens the door to his office. 'Come in. Come in,' he says as if he's invited us to a tea party.

Mam prods me over the threshold and whispers, 'Don't forget what I told you.' She gives me another prod with her forefinger to make sure I've heard her. But hearing doesn't mean remembering. What was it that she told me?

I give Sergeant Jones the book I've brought with me. 'The Tiger in the Smoke,' I say. 'It's really good.'

Sergeant Jones tucks the book under his arm and says, 'Just come inside, will you, Gwenni?' He mops his face and his head with his handkerchief and closes the door behind us with a bang that makes Mam jump. The office is stuffy and the smell of sweat and soap takes my breath away.

Someone else is sitting in Sergeant Jones's armchair behind the desk. The light comes through the window behind him and shades his face. His hair is dark and his suit is dark. He stands up and with his hands invites me and Mam to sit in the two wooden chairs on our side of the desk. He doesn't speak.

'This is Detective Inspector Thomas from Dolgellau,' says

Sergeant Jones to Mam and me. A real, live detective, just like I want to be. Not a policeman in a uniform.

'Pleased to meet you,' says Mam in her posh voice, and she sits on one of the chairs. The seat is narrow and her bottom spreads over the sides.

'Mrs Magda Morgan and Gwenni, her daughter, sir,' says Sergeant Jones to the real, live detective. I sit down, too, and as Sergeant Jones sits on a chair against the wall to the side of us I notice another man sitting behind us, beyond Sergeant Jones, in a corner of the office under a new have-you-seen-this-man poster, with a notepad on his knee and the sheen of perspiration on his face.

'It's hard to breathe in here with the window shut,' I say to Sergeant Jones.

'We have to keep the . . . eh . . . conversation private, Gwenni,' he says. But there's nothing outside to hear the conversation apart from the mist and the roses round the window.

The real, live detective slaps his hands down flat on the desk and says, 'I've asked Gwenni to come here today, Mrs Morgan, because she may be able to help us find out what happened to Mr Ifan Evans on April the fifth. A Saturday.' He sits back in Sergeant Jones's chair. It doesn't groan the way it does when Sergeant Jones sits in it.

'She doesn't know anything,' says Mam. 'She didn't see him at all that Saturday. She can't help you.'

I remember now. Mam told me to keep my mouth shut and let her do all the talking.

'I'd really like Gwenni herself to tell me about that Saturday, Mrs Morgan,' says the real detective. 'You can't tell what might be important in a murder inquiry.'

A murder inquiry. Mam gulps and her hands start shaking. She looks across at Sergeant Jones.

'Just let Gwenni tell it the way it happened, Magda,' he says.

'But nothing happened. Nothing happened,' says Mam, her hands clutching at her handbag.

The door from the house swings opens as Mam speaks. Mrs Sergeant Jones appears with a tea tray in her hands, humming A Pure Heart and smiling at us all. I can smell her famous vanilla biscuits from here. It's my favourite smell in the whole world. I never knew what vanilla was until Mrs Sergeant Jones showed me the pod and how she put it in a jar of sugar so that the sugar takes on its smell and taste.

Sergeant Jones takes the tray from her and puts it on top of the filing cabinet and pours tea for everyone into Mrs Sergeant Jones's best cups that her grandmother gave her. The man sitting behind us gives a funny cough, as if he's swallowed something the wrong way, except he hasn't had his tea yet. The real detective spreads his fingers wide on the desk in front of us and presses on them until the tips turn white.

Mam and I hold a cup and saucer with a vanilla biscuit each in the saucers and I begin to nibble my biscuit.

'Now that we've all got a nice cup of tea,' says the real detective, 'let's start again, shall we? Gwenni, the man sitting behind you is Detective Sergeant Lloyd, and he'll be taking notes of everything I ask you and all your answers. We'll have to speak in English, I'm afraid, in case it becomes evidence in court.'

Mam's cup chatters on its saucer. My mouth is full of scrumptious biscuit so I nod.

'Now, Gwenni,' says the real detective, in English, 'just tell me, as if you were telling a story, about your Saturday morning at Brwyn Coch; the Saturday that you went to look after the little girls because Mrs Evans had an appointment with the dentist. Can you do that?'

Does he want to know about me flying in my sleep and being common as dirt with the bread and jam, and the Baptism Pool and the Reservoir? I swallow my vanilla biscuit. 'Where shall I start?' I ask.

The real detective looks at some notes on the desk. They're too far away for me to read them upside down. He says, 'We've already spoken to Mrs Williams at Penrhiw Farm and she said she saw you on your way up to Brwyn Coch. Do you remember? Begin from just before that.'

Mam glares at me and her cup jigs on its saucer but I have to do what the real detective says, don't I? I won't mention flying. What else should I not mention?

'Take your time,' the real detective says. 'Put your thoughts in order.'

That Saturday morning seems a long time ago. The man behind me sighs. Sergeant Jones mops his face and his head again. A wasp is becoming angry in the window trying to find its way out. But it won't be able to find a way through the closed panes. We're completely sealed inside the room. My gymslip feels scratchy on my legs, and Mam's face is beginning to melt.

'Mrs Williams had just been talking to Guto'r Wern when I saw her,' I say.

The real detective holds up his hand. 'In English, Gwenni,' he says. Then he turns to Sergeant Jones. 'Guto'r Wern?' he says.

'Griffith Edwards, Wern Farm,' says Sergeant Jones.

'Carry on, Gwenni,' says the real detective.

'She said she didn't know what would become of him,' I say in English. 'And then she talked about Nain and she said I'd be late to Brwyn Coch if I didn't get on.'

'Why did she say that about Guto?' says the real detective.

'Because his mother dropped him on his head when he was

174

a baby,' I say. 'And it made him odd. Tada says there's no harm in him, though; he's innocent as a child. He's teaching me to fly.'

The man behind me chokes on his tea or his biscuit and Mam's cup gives a loud chatter. I forgot not to mention the flying.

'What was Guto doing when you saw him?' says the real detective.

'Running down to town,' I say. 'He always runs. He almost flies. But not quite.'

The real detective leans his elbows on the desk and leans his fingertips together. 'Did he come from the direction of Brwyn Coch?'

'He was probably coming from the Wern,' I say. 'That's where he lives. He hadn't had any breakfast and Mrs Williams had given him some bread and butter.'

'But could he have been coming from Brwyn Coch?'

'I suppose so,' I say. 'You have to come down the same bit of road past Penrhiw from both places. He does go to see Mrs Evans sometimes; she's kind to him. But Angharad and Catrin didn't say anything about him visiting them that morning.'

'Right, Gwenni,' says the real detective. 'Now, when you got to Brwyn Coch, what did you do?'

'I knocked on the door and said sorry I was late and gave Mrs Evans the violets.'

'Violets?' says the real detective.

'I picked Mrs Evans a bunch of violets on the way up. She likes violets.'

Mam glares at me. Her knee is jerking up and down, up and down under her tight winter skirt.

'I picked you a bunch of primroses on the way home,' I remind her.

'And after you gave Mrs Evans the violets, what did you do?' asks the real detective.

'Then I went into the house and I made her some salt water to wash her mouth with, and . . .'

'Why?' says the real detective. Maybe he isn't such a real detective after all.

'Because Price the Dentist hadn't had his whisky and made a brutal job of pulling her teeth,' I say.

'Dentist?' says the detective. 'Had Mrs Evans already been to the dentist? I thought you were going there to look after the girls while she went to the dentist.'

'Yes, but I was too late,' I say.

The detective looks at Sergeant Jones, but he's busy mopping his face.

'And she'd bled all over the kitchen floor,' I say. 'She bled worse than you, Mam, when you had your teeth taken out. And she was shaking.'

'I didn't bleed all over the floor,' says Mam. 'Don't be silly, Gwenni.'

Did I say she had?

The detective leans his elbows on the desk again and lays his forehead on the backs of his hands. He looks up at me.

'So, what were the girls doing, Gwenni, when you were doing all this? Angharad and Catrin, where were they?'

'Sitting in the parlour, reading,' I say. '*Alice in Wonderland*. I think they'd been told off for hitting the black dog.'

'Black dog? What black dog?' says the detective.

'Ifan Evans's black dog,' I say. 'Catrin said Angharad threw a plate at it and Angharad said Catrin hit it with the poker.'

'Mr Evans,' says Mam. 'Mr Evans.'

'What?' says the detective. 'Why?'

'Because the black dog was making Mr Evans cross with them all,' I say.

'But Ifan didn't have a black dog, Gwenni,' says Sergeant Jones.

'He did that day,' I say. Maybe the blood on the floor was the black dog's blood and not Mrs Evans's at all. I didn't think about that. 'The poker was like the one we've got, with a phoenix on it; Aunty Lol says that's the bird that rose from the ashes. Catrin had dropped it on the floor and I nearly tripped over it.'

I can hear the man behind us scribbling over the pages of his notebook. Am I speaking too fast?

'Yes, yes,' says the detective. 'Then what did you do?'

'Then I took the girls out to play,' I say and I don't mention the flying. 'And then we went back to the house and Mrs Evans had tidied up and washed the floor and made the fire and put a stew on for dinner. And then she let me choose some books to say thank-you and then I went home. And I picked Mam some primroses on the way. We had faggots for our dinner but I couldn't eat them.' It's becoming more stuffy and more smelly in here; the thought of the faggots makes my stomach lurch.

'Did you see Mr Evans?' asks the detective. 'In the house or when you were out with the girls?'

'No,' I say. 'He'd gone off with the black dog. Catrin said he never came home until late when he had the black dog.'

'But, Gwenni,' says Sergeant Jones. 'Ifan didn't have a black dog. He only had Mot.'

'He left Mot behind,' I say. Should I tell the detective about my bad dream? It would prove there is a black dog. But where did Ifan leave it?

'Are you certain you didn't see Mr Evans that day?' asks the detective.

'I didn't see him,' I say. 'Was that the day he fell in the Reservoir? Alwenna says it was. Maybe he'd already fallen in.' Don't think about it.

Mam's cup is leaping about on its saucer. She tries to reach over to Sergeant Jones's desk with it. She narrows her eyes at me. 'Violets,' she says. 'Violets. Huh.' And her cup spills over the edge of her saucer and falls to the concrete floor and breaks into tiny pieces that skitter to every part of the room. One of Mrs Sergeant Jones's grandmother's best cups.

The detective stands up. 'That's all . . . eh . . . thank you,' he says. 'We're trying to find out exactly what happened and when it happened on that Saturday. You've been a big help.'

I have?

27

Today, I begin my proper investigation into the killing of Ifan Evans. I didn't find any clues at the Reservoir, and the real detectives didn't tell me they had any clues, so I have to discover who the murderer is another way. Maybe if I find out as much as I can about the victim, it'll be obvious who wanted to kill him. Who knows everything about everyone? Alwenna.

It's dinner time and our class has just had double Welsh Literature with Alwenna's favourite teacher – Mr Tomos with the curly dark hair who reads poems to us in a curly dark voice. Alwenna never liked poetry until Mr Tomos came at the beginning of last term. And we had steamed ginger sponge after dinner, her favourite pudding. It tastes like washing your mouth out with soap but it'll put Alwenna in a good mood.

There she is, walking past the tennis courts, where two sixth-form boys are arguing about the score, and out towards the school field, her skirt swinging from side to side. I catch up with her a second before Aneurin and Edwin reach her. They roll their eyes at me and chant, 'Gwenni Fo-ox.' Edwin looks more like a horse than ever with the whites of his eyes showing. Has Alwenna never noticed that? They veer off in a different direction when I glare at them and go and talk to some other girl in the year below us who's giggling at them from a distance. I can't remember her name.

'What do you want?' says Alwenna. She lowers herself to sit on the grass and spreads her skirt out around her.

I sit opposite her and tug my gymslip down. It seems to be shrinking; maybe Mam's been using the wrong soap to wash it. Mam bought a blue gingham dress with a big skirt like Alwenna's for Bethan, and she says I can have it next summer when Bethan has outgrown it. She has to save all her money for buying a house with a bathroom and an electric cooker so she can't afford to buy us a dress each. 'I have to talk to you for a bit,' I say to Alwenna. We used to spend all our dinnertimes talking.

'What about?' she says.

'Our investigation,' I say. 'Will you tell me everything you know about Ifan Evans?' I lay my notebook and pencil on the grass.

Alwenna kicks them out of my reach. 'I'm not going to play any of your silly detective games,' she says. 'Or any other ones, either.'

'Wait till I tell you what happened yesterday,' I say. I lean over and retrieve my book and pencil.

'I know what happened,' she says. 'I'm not helping you to do stupid things any more.'

'But I know how to interrogate people properly now,' I say. 'And you could take notes of what they say.'

'No,' she says, shaking her head. 'No. No. No.'

'You don't have to do them in English like the real detectives,' I say.

'I'm not doing them in any language, Gwenni,' she says.

I pick some daisies from the grass and start to make a chain with them. Their petals are open wide, their yellow centres bright as the sun in the sky.

'So, why did they do them in English?' says Alwenna. She picks a daisy, too, and twirls it around by its stem.

'Because you're not allowed to speak Welsh in court, I suppose,' I say. 'And anyway, how do you know about what happened?'

'Mam's cousin's daughter who lives in Bermo is married to Dewi Lloyd,' she says.

Her mam has got relatives all over Wales, but who is Dewi Lloyd?

'Wake up, Gwenni,' she says. 'The detective that was taking the notes? Remember? He said you were a funny little thing. And your mother had the shakes. Well, everyone knows why she has the shakes, but Dewi thought she'd been drinking.'

'Drinking?' I say. I drop the daisy chain on the grass. 'She had one cup of tea. How could that give her the shakes?'

'Grow up, Gwenni,' says Alwenna, pulling the petals off her daisy one by one. 'He meant he thought she was drunk, didn't he?'

'But it's her nerves,' I say. 'You know no one has anything to make them drunk in our house. You know that, Alwenna.'

'I know. Boring,' she says. 'Mam told her cousin to tell him it was nerves. Everyone knows your mam is going doolally. It's in the family, isn't it?'

'Is it?' I say. 'What are you talking about?'

'He loves me,' she shouts, throwing the daisy stalk in the air and standing up. She brushes bits of grass off her dress, shaking it so that Aneurin and Edwin do their wolf whistling duet at her and clap.

'Who loves you?' I say.

'Edwin, of course,' she says. 'It's only a game, Gwenni.'

I pull at the skirt of her dress. 'You can't go without telling me what you're talking about,' I say. 'What do you mean about being doolally being in the family? You keep saying it.'

'No, I don't,' says Alwenna. 'And everyone knows. Ask anyone.'

'I'm asking you,' I say. 'Please, Alwenna.' I tug at her skirt again.

'Well, don't tell your mam I told you,' she says, dropping to the grass again.

'I never tell Mam the things you tell me,' I say.

'You do,' she says. 'Alwenna calls Ifan Evans Paleface. Alwenna says Dafydd Owen is a dirty old man. Alwenna asked Miss Hughes when the baby was due. She complains to my mam.'

It's true. But I didn't know the things she told me were secret. 'I won't tell her this time,' I say.

'Swear,' says Alwenna. I cross my heart. It's thudding as loudly as the tennis balls on the courts.

'Your nain went doolally,' says Alwenna. 'Not your nain next door; your mam's mother. She went right off her head when your mam was expecting Bethan and got carted off to Dinbych. So there, now you know.'

But I don't know anything. 'Dinbych?' I say. 'What, the asylum? Do you mean the asylum?'

'Well, they didn't cart her off to a hotel there, did they?' says Alwenna. 'Of course the asylum. Then she died. Now your mam's going doolally. Perhaps it's catching.'

'But I don't understand,' I say. 'Why did Mam having Bethan make my nain go doolally?'

'Did I say that?' says Alwenna. 'I didn't. But if you must know . . .'

'Tell me,' I say.

'Don't you dare tell your mam I told you,' says Alwenna.

'I said I won't,' I say.

'Yes, but this is really secret stuff. I mean, everyone knows but it's really secret. All right?'

'All right,' I say. But how can it be secret if everyone knows? Is this like the secrets Nain talked about?

'She probably had the shakes or something before that,' says Alwenna. 'Your nain. Like your mam. Then when your mam fell for Bethan she went completely doolally. Your nain, I mean.'

'But why?' I say

'God, Gwenni, you're slow sometimes,' says Alwenna. 'Your mam was married to your tada then but he was away in the war so he couldn't be Bethan's father, could he?'

Is that true? I gasp as a sharp pain pinches my stomach.

'You asked me to tell you,' says Alwenna. 'So don't blame me if it's not what you wanted to hear.'

'So, who is Bethan's father?' I say. Not Tada?

'Your mam never said. The minister talked to her about it, but she wouldn't say. Not the Voice of God; the one before him. He had to go and meet your tada off the train when he came back from the war. Your mam was big by then, so she couldn't very well pretend Bethan was your tada's baby, could she? But she never said who the father was. Mam says your tada was a saint.' She fiddles with some stalks of grass and looks up at me from under her eyelashes. 'Of course,' she says, 'everyone thinks they know who it was.'

'Who?' I say.

'You don't want to know,' she says, flicking at the grass.

'Who?' I say.

'Guess,' she says.

I can guess, can't I? But Alwenna's right, I don't want to

know. I look into her face and she smirks at me. She doesn't look like my Alwenna. 'Why haven't you told me all this before?' I say.

She stretches her arms up into the air and yawns. 'I've only just found out.'

Who else knows? Is this one of those secrets Nain talked about? A secret everyone knows but no one talks about? Bethan doesn't know. And I didn't know. Is it the reason Mam likes Bethan and doesn't like me? But Bethan's father— Don't think about that.

'Anyway,' I say, 'I don't want to talk about my family. I'm investigating a murder.'

Alwenna smirks again. She leans back on her elbows, jutting her chest in the air. 'Oh, yes. You want me to tell you about Paleface. You're lucky, then, because I've just found out all about him, too. Mam says he didn't go to the war because he was a farm worker.' She looks at me from under her eyelashes again. 'Penrhyn way, where your mam lived.'

Don't think about it; don't think about the swimming when Tada wasn't there.

Alwenna sits up and picks another daisy and starts to pull off its petals. 'Mam says when he and Elin moved here they were so religious they went to Chapel three times every Sunday. No one knew he had nasty moods and drank when they made him a deacon. Maybe being married to Elin made him like that. She's a bit prissy, isn't she?' Alwenna mimics a prissy face but it doesn't look like Mrs Evans at all. 'But he was horrible to her when he was drunk, Mam says. He hit her. You know those babies in the cemetery? Everyone says he killed them in his temper when he was drunk.'

I haven't found the babies in the cemetery yet. Are they the babies in Mrs Evans's photograph? And Ifan Evans killed them?

'But the police would have arrested him,' I say.

'What did they know?' says Alwenna. 'Mam says they couldn't prove he'd done it and Elin protected him. Silly woman. It just made him hate her worse, Mam says.'

'How do you know all these terrible things are true?' I say.

'Everyone knows about them,' she says.

'That doesn't make them true,' I say. 'And I didn't know about them.'

Alwenna gets up with a little jump. She brushes the daisy petals from her dress and hitches her belt a notch tighter and twirls round to wave at Aneurin and Edwin who are watching her. 'There's something else you don't know,' she says.

I don't say anything. Is this something else I don't want to know? Another pain in my stomach makes me catch my breath.

'I'm not your best friend any more. You'll have to find someone else,' Alwenna says.

28

Our cemetery is always cool and quiet. Tall grass laps at the edges of the graves and tombs without a sound, the way my night-time sea laps at the shore. The cemetery is the next best thing to the sky. When I lie on my tomb I almost believe that I'm flying. No one else visits the graves when I'm here, except Guto'r Wern, and yet, there are always flowers here and there on them.

The pain in my stomach gradually passes away as I rest on my tomb and leaves an empty place inside me. I watch rain clouds gather above me, hiding the sun.

How does Alwenna's mam know all these things? And how do I find out what's true and what's not? If I were a detective in a book I would know exactly how to go about finding out. Do I want to find out if it's true that Tada isn't Bethan's father?

Look at how lush the grass is and how high the hedgerows are all around. Already butterflies flit around honeysuckle that's still in bud and blossom foams like seaspray on the hawthorn. Don't take white flowers into your house or your mother will die. I once picked Mam a posy of windflowers with petals as delicate as a butterfly's wing and she snatched the flowers from me and threw them out into the road where they lay for days, dying, until the wind took them. She said I wanted her to die. That was before Dr Edwards gave her tablets to make her happy. Sometimes when I'm flying, out of the corner of my eye I see the white petals blowing across the moon or floating on the sea.

Our family graves, Tada's family graves, are here at the bottom end from the path. They're difficult to reach because the grass has grown so high. Alwenna says the grass feeds on the corpses. She says never to pick up a worm in the cemetery, it will be full of dead flesh. But I won't think about Alwenna. Or the worms.

See, here is the grave of Uncle Carwyn who died in hospital. I remember him packing his case to go away; it was laid across the arms of Nain's big leather chair. He said he would be back soon, once the doctors had mended him; he said it would give him time to practise some new conjuring tricks to show me. His last conjuring trick was to disappear so that I never saw him again.

My Uncle Idwal is buried near Athens. That's in Greece. Nain has a picture of his grave on her bedroom wall. It has a white cross, not a gravestone. There are white crosses filling the picture, with a red poppy on each one. Everyone who was killed had a special white cross. I wonder which ones in the picture belong to Mrs Llywelyn Pugh's son and Nellie Davies's husband. Tada says there are cemeteries full of white crosses all over Europe. Maybe they look like windflower petals if you look down at them from the sky.

Here is my grandfather's grave. He died a long time ago when Tada was only fourteen. And now Bethan is nearly fourteen and maybe she's lost her father but she doesn't know it. And who would tell her something so terrible? Look at the story this gravestone tells about my grandfather. I pull my roughbook from my satchel and in it I write Taid's dates and what it says on the stone. He was old when he died but his children were all young; Tada was the eldest. Taid must have been old when he married Nain. Much older than her. I didn't know that. Another secret that everybody knows except me?

There's a big stone next to Taid's grave but the brambles have reached out from the hedgerow across its face and I push them back. A thorn rips my palm and I suck the blood from the wound. There's a whoop behind me and I turn just in time to see Guto leap off my tomb with his arms spread like wings. I wave at him. He likes being here where there's no one to bother him. Nain says: The dead don't bother anyone, it's the living you have to look out for. I wave at Guto and suck my palm again and then I look at all the names on the big grave-stone. A list of names, and one squashed in at the top that says *Sarah Morgan, beloved wife of William Morgan,* my grandfather. Taid must have been married before he married Nain. And the babies, four of them. Four. All their names are here; three boys and a girl. All dead before they were even one year old. I must be related to them. But Bethan isn't, is she? Not if Tada isn't her father.

I shall have to go home soon. Mam will be cross with me. I'm not supposed to go anywhere on my own now there's a murderer on the loose. And she'll be cross when she knows I've been here finding out secrets. Don't mention the dead.

Guto is still trying to fly from my tombstone. And now that he's seen me stand up he rushes towards me and he does look as if he's flying with his ragged black coat trailing from his arms like wings. He stands in front of me and flaps his arms, grinning with all his crooked teeth showing. He's innocent as a child, Tada says.

From inside his coat somewhere he pulls out a bundle of wilting bluebells and with his free hand catches hold of my arm and runs with me half falling behind him until we reach the most secluded corner of the cemetery. I've never been down this end before where the big old yew tree overhangs the graves to make a dark cave around them. Guto pulls me forward and waves his arms about to encompass all the gravestones planted here. They are so small, they're barely visible. I kneel down and brush the long blades of grass from the stone nearest to me. And read about four-year-old *Iolo, taken to Heaven* a long time ago. Maybe his parents and all his family are dead too. Why else would there be no flowers on his grave? And here is *an angel taken home aged three years and three months.* What happens to babies when they die? Who looks after their little spirits? Maybe my New Testament will tell me if I keep reading it.

I look around to see what Guto's doing; he's kneeling in front of a gravestone shaped like an open book. I've never seen a stone like this before. I kneel beside him and watch him empty the sludge from a jam jar set in the ground in front of the open book and fill it with fresh water from a bottle he has somewhere inside his coat. Guto's coat is like the one the conjurer wore when he performed in the Memorial Hall. He puts his bunch of bluebells into the jam jar and then puts his hands together and closes his eyes as if he's saying his prayers. But he's still grinning. Each page of the open book has a name carved into it. I peer at the names in the gloom and make out *Gwion* and *Nia* and then *beloved twin children of Elin and Ifan Evans* and then:

Their story had barely begun
When the book was closed.

I copy the lines into my notebook. Mrs Evans's beautiful babies. Dead. Is that why she's melancholy? Is that why she thinks a lot? What sad and secret stories I've found today. I put my book back in my satchel and tell Guto that I have to go home but he stays on his knees, his eyes closed, praying. Innocent as a child.

29

'We had mince yesterday,' says Bethan. She wrinkles her nose. She doesn't look like Tada at all.

'This isn't mince,' says Mam. 'It's shepherd's pie.' She passes Tada a plate of grey gravy with pellets of dark meat rolling in it.

'My favourite,' says Tada, showing Mam his bright, white teeth. He takes the plate. 'Where's the potato, Magda?'

'Why do we have to have the same thing all the time?' says Bethan. 'In Caroline's house they have different meals every day.'

Mam bangs a dish of potatoes on the table and empties some flabby cabbage from a saucepan into another bowl. Some of the cabbage water dribbles over the tablecloth to mix with all the other stains. I don't look at them.

'Lovely,' says Tada. 'Nothing like spring cabbage.'

I say, 'Nain says you're not meant to boil cabbage until it's nearly pink. She says all the goodness goes out of it.'

Mam drops my plate of mince down in front of me so that it almost slops into my lap, and hands Bethan her plate. I try to push my fork into one of the dark pellets and the meat shoots across the table into Bethan's plate.

'Couldn't do that if you were trying,' says Tada. He piles cabbage onto his gravy.

'Don't encourage her,' says Mam.

'So, why have we got mince again?' says Bethan.

'Shepherd's pie,' says Mam. 'And we're having it because there was plenty of meat left over from the piece of brisket I cooked on Sunday for two more meals. I don't want to hear any more about it, Bethan. And you stop playing with your food, Gwenni, and eat it. You've no idea how hard it is to cook for you all and then listen to you complain about it.'

Have I complained?

'I'm not complaining,' says Bethan. 'I'm only saying that they don't have the same thing all the time in Caroline's house. Anyway, I like mince.'

'You've always been a good little eater,' says Mam.

'Lovely meals your mother makes,' says Tada. 'Lovely.'

I look at the mince; the pellets look like rabbit droppings and the gravy is slimy with grease. Sometimes, even John Morris won't eat Mam's mince.

'Eat it, Gwenni, or you won't get any pudding,' says Mam.

'What's for pudding?' Bethan speaks with her mouth full of potato. I don't look at her.

'Instant Whip,' says Mam. 'Strawberry.'

'Your favourite,' says Bethan to me.

But I can't eat the mince.

'I'll have her pudding,' says Bethan.

'I'll eat your mince, Gwenni,' says Tada and he takes my plate and scoops the mince off it. 'You can eat the potato and the cabbage, can't you?'

There are lumps in the potato but I try not to think about them, and the cabbage slides down my throat without me having to chew it at all so I hardly notice its bitter taste.

'And,' says Bethan, waving her fork at Mam and spraying me with globules of gravy, 'you didn't tell us that Aunty Siân's expecting another baby.'

Mam gasps. 'What?' she says. 'How do you know that? Who told you?'

The Toby jugs stir on their high shelf with a soft scuffle that I can barely hear above the tick-tock of the clock.

'Is it supposed to be a secret, then? Is that why she hasn't been here for months?' says Bethan. 'Because all the Penrhyn girls know. Gwenfair Jones told me.'

'Who's she?' says Mam.

'She lives next door but one to Aunty Siân,' says Bethan. 'You know her mother.'

Mam groans. 'Big Beti,' she says to Tada. 'Penrhyn's answer to Nanw Lipstick. Used to live in the council houses until her grandmother left her that house. You should see the state of it. Like living in a slum.'

Tada nods and chews. He swallows with a big gulp. 'Hardly the sort of thing you can keep secret, is it?' he says.

Mam's face turns red and her hands start to shake.

'And,' says Bethan, scooping more cabbage from the bowl onto her plate, 'we did human reproduction in biology today. The boys had to leave the lab so Miss Edwards could tell us about it. You never tell me things like that properly; the other girls knew it all. But now I know exactly how babies are made. Exactly. That's why Gwenfair told me; she said Aunty Siân and Uncle Wil had been doing it.'

Mam gasps again. 'She should wash her mouth out with soap,' she says from behind her hand.

'Well,' says Bethan, 'if Aunty Siân's having a baby, they have been doing it, haven't they?'

Tada's got his head bent right down over his plate as if his food has become hard to see.

'I bet you don't know how babies are made,' says Bethan to me.

I cross my fingers under the tablecloth's overhang. 'Yes, I do,' I say. We've only got as far as rabbits in our biology lessons and that's bad enough.

'How d'you know?' says Bethan.

'Alwenna,' I say. But I would never let Alwenna tell me.

'That girl has no shame,' says Mam. 'She's too old for you, Gwenni. It's time you found yourself a friend your own age.'

'Alwenna doesn't want to be my friend any more,' I say.

Everyone stops eating.

'Be thankful for small mercies,' says Mam to no one in particular.

'Why not, Gwenni?' says Tada. 'She couldn't find a better friend.'

'Don't encourage her,' says Mam, but Tada looks at her and she closes her mouth into its tight, tight line.

'Who's going to be your friend now, then?' says Bethan.

'I don't have to have a friend,' I say.

Bethan shrugs. 'Anyway,' she says, 'Miss Edwards says it's very clever, you know, this baby thing. There are these things called genes, and stuff like the colour of your baby's eyes or hair depend on your genes.' She digs her fork into her cabbage and puts some in her mouth. It must be cold by now. 'See, two people with blue eyes can't have a baby with brown eyes.' She pauses, frowning, her fork halfway to her mouth. 'I can't remember exactly how the gene thing worked, now.'

Bethan wouldn't. She peers at Mam and Tada, then at me. 'See, Gwenni's got your green eyes,' she says to Tada. 'But Mam's eyes are blue, so a blue-eyed parent and a green-eyed parent can have a brown-eyed baby like me. You see how it works? I've got to do a diagram of it for homework.'

She puts some potato into her mouth and wrinkles her nose again. 'It's got cold now,' she says.

'You're talking too much. Far too much,' says Mam. 'Just eat your food.'

'But that's not all,' says Bethan. 'Caroline and I thought we'd like to have babies, but not for a long time. There's this other thing Miss Edwards told us about. It's called contraception. She showed—'

'That's enough,' Mam shouts. Her chair skitters back as she leaps to her feet. The Toby jugs jitter on their high shelf. Their cheeks are mottled with red, their eyes small and black as bilberries. 'That's enough of that sort of talk, Bethan.'

Bethan gapes at Mam. 'Bloody hell,' she says, in English.

'And we don't swear in this house,' says Mam. 'I'm beginning to think Caroline's a bad influence on you. The sooner her mother takes them all back to England, the better.'

Bethan's knife and fork clatter onto her plate.

'Time for pudding?' says Tada, lifting his glance from his clean plate to Mam's face.

Mam takes a deep, shuddery breath. She walks to the scullery and jangles the dishes and cutlery, then brings in three pudding bowls of Instant Whip with a spoon stuck in each one. She gives one to Tada, one to Bethan and keeps one for herself. The Instant Whip fills the room with its smell of summer days, sweet and ripe. My mouth waters.

'Have you got a bowl for Gwenni?' says Tada.

'She didn't eat her mince,' says Mam.

Tada makes to get up from his chair. Mam takes another shuddery breath and narrows her eyes at him. 'There isn't any left,' she says.

Tada sits back. He pushes his bowl away from him.

'All the more for me,' Bethan sings. 'All the more for me.' And she spoons the beautiful pinkness into her greedy mouth. 'They never have Instant Whip in Caroline's house. She and Richard have never heard of it. Fancy that.' She pauses with her spoon halfway to her mouth. 'I don't like that Richard any more; he's a proper mother's boy,' she says, and eats the spoonful of Instant Whip.

Will Bethan find out from her eye colour that Tada isn't her father? I wonder how many of the people in the cemetery didn't belong to their mother or father.

'I went to the cemetery after school,' I say, 'to get some of the dates off the gravestones for my family tree.'

'I thought you were late.' says Mam. 'You've been told not wander about on your own. I may as well talk to the man in the moon.'

'You're mam's right, Gwenni,' says Tada. 'You come straight home from now on, there's a good girl.'

I nod. 'But about the family tree,' I say. 'I didn't know my taid had been married to Sarah before he married Nain. And they had all those dead babies. Should I put them all on my tree? Are they related to me?'

'Don't be silly, Gwenni,' says Mam sending a wave of strawberry scented breath over me. 'And I've told you before, it's unhealthy to hang about in that cemetery.'

'It's not silly,' says Tada. 'My tada and Sarah had five children who lived, as well, Gwenni. They were my half brothers and sisters, but they were so much older than me that I hardly knew them. All except for William who was born when Sarah died. He lived with us when I was growing up but he ran off with a circus that came passing through town one year and we never saw him again, although he sometimes sent your nain a postcard from wherever he was.'

'What rubbish,' says Mam. 'Gwenni gets all her oddness from your family, that's for sure.'

That's not what Alwenna said.

'What did he do in the circus?' asks Bethan. She's scraped her bowl of Instant Whip clean and is halfway down Tada's bowl.

'He sent us a picture postcard of himself once,' says Tada, 'hanging from a flying trapeze in a tight suit with shiny spangles all over it. Just like the song.' He begins to tra-la the song.

No one mentioned flying on a trapeze being in the family before. Nain must have forgotten. 'Maybe that's where I get my flying from,' I say.

'I don't want to hear another word of your flying nonsense,' says Mam. 'All you do is encourage her, Emlyn. Do you want her to turn out odd?'

Tada gives his head a little shake. 'You put whoever you want on your tree, Gwenni,' he says. 'They're all related to you. Nain could give you the names of all the grown-up children.'

'I don't want you going near that cemetery again,' Mam says to me.

'I wouldn't go poking about in the cemetery if you paid me,' says Bethan. 'It's creepy.' She shudders and scrapes the last of the Instant Whip from Tada's bowl. 'And,' she says, 'that Guto's always hanging about in there. I've seen him. And he's creepy too.' She shudders again.

'He was there today,' I say. 'Practising his flying from the big tombstone at the top.'

Mam's hands start to shake again as she pours the tea into the cups so that the tea splashes over the tablecloth to make more stains to give me that old family stomach when I'm eating.

'There's no harm in him, Bethan,' says Tada. 'He's innocent as a child.'

'He showed me the babies' grave,' I say. 'Mrs Evans's twins. He was putting flowers on the grave.' I take a deep breath. 'How did the babies die?'

There is a small silence. Tada glances at Mam and then he says, 'A terrible accident, Gwenni.'

'I heard . . .' I say. I cross my fingers. 'I heard at the Sale of Work meeting . . . someone said that Ifan Evans killed them.'

The silence stretches tighter and tighter until it snaps when Mam screams and slaps my face. We don't move in our seats; Bethan's mouth hangs open and my cheek burns. Then Tada stands up and catches hold of Mam's arm and says, 'I'm going to take your mother upstairs to lie down. You two clear away and wash up.'

Mam hisses. She sounds like an adder that Alwenna and I disturbed under a sheet of corrugated iron one hot day last summer. But I won't think about Alwenna.

'Not my daughter,' Mam says from between her clenched teeth. 'Not mine. I never wanted her.'

Tada pulls the door shut behind them. Bethan and I stare at the closed door then Bethan turns to me. 'Bloody hell,' she says. 'If she didn't want to have you, all she had to do was use contraception.'

30

We're too early. I can hear the men still singing in the cemetery; a choir of them, with Mr Thomas's tenor voice breaking out on its own in a lament for Ifan Evans.

I can't take Angharad and Catrin along the cemetery path to the Chapel vestry for the funeral meal so I pull them quickly in through one of the big Chapel doors. Do they understand what is happening to their father around the corner?

'The men are singing to send Tada to Heaven,' says Catrin.

'No, they're not,' says Angharad. 'They're singing to put him in the ground in a coffin where the worms will eat him. And it's your fault.'

Catrin begins to cry. 'It's not true, is it, Gwenni? The worms won't eat him, will they?'

But they will, just as they've eaten everyone else in the cemetery. 'But the spirit leaves the body and goes to Heaven,' I say to Catrin. Was Ifan Evans good enough to go to Heaven? And if his spirit is in the Reservoir, how will it get from there to Heaven, or Hell?

'See?' says Catrin to Angharad. 'Now he'll be with the babies.

Maybe he won't be cross all the time, now he's dead. Maybe he'll look after them. Who looks after babies in Heaven, Gwenni?'

So, the babies are not a secret at all. 'Angels, I suppose,' I say, though I don't know. 'The babies – is that your brother and sister?'

'They died when they were little,' says Catrin. 'They fell downstairs. We always take them flowers on a Sunday. But not since Tada fell in the water. Mami's been too . . . too . . .'

'Worried,' says Angharad.

'Sad,' says Catrin.

I help them take off their raincoats and smooth their black velvet dresses down and straighten their white collars. I lick my handkerchief and rub the mud spots off their shiny patent leather shoes. They look like two cherubs except that Angharad is a cross cherub and tries to kick my hand when I'm cleaning her shoes.

I take off my school mackintosh, which is splattered around the hem. The rain has made everywhere muddy. I tug my gymslip down; Mam said I had to put my gymslip on because it's the only dark thing I've got. It's to show respect. But I didn't have any respect for Ifan Evans.

I gather our coats up and we walk down the aisle and up the steps to go through the door into the vestry, which is full of plates of food and women dressed in black. It's as if the crows have left their nests in the castle and flown here and all started croaking at the same time. Mrs Evans said she would be in the little Meeting Room so I push my way through the women. Catrin grips my hand hard but I have to make sure I hold on to Angharad.

'Bless them.' The words float above us. 'Poor, fatherless mites.' A murmur of sympathy swells behind us. Angharad snatches her hand from mine and turns round to face the women and opens her mouth but I catch hold of her and push her through into the

Meeting Room before she can say anything. What would she have said?

Mrs Evans sits by the grate where Mrs Davies Chapel House has lit a grudging fire. Her sister is with her and some other women I don't know. And there is Mrs Llywelyn Pugh sitting in the corner with tears running down her cheeks. She would have had her dead fox on today because it has turned so damp and cold. Poor Mrs Llywelyn Pugh. Maybe I could knit her a scarf before winter, if I could do it without Mam finding out. And then I could leave it for her so that she would find an anonymous gift on her doorstep one icy winter morning which would make her warm and happy.

'Thank you, Gwenni,' says Mrs Evans and holds her arms open to her children. Catrin runs to her at once but Angharad holds back and slumps onto a bench by the door. 'Gwenni looked after Angharad and Catrin for me during the service,' says Mrs Evans to the other women and they all smile and nod at me and murmur words I can't hear.

Mrs Evans is dressed in a black darker and denser than a moonless night. There is no shine or gleam to it. Her hat with its big black veil is beside her on the bench and her hair is escaping its silver combs in smoky wisps around her face, working up to a halo again.

'You leave Angharad and Catrin here with me, Gwenni,' she says, 'and go to find your parents and have something to eat. The Chapel women have been very thoughtful and made plenty of food.'

I back out through the door and turn around to look for Mam and Tada but I can't see them in the crowd. The men have come in from the graveside now, bringing a misty steam with them from the rain, and the vestry is full of people. No one takes any notice of me, they're all too busy eating and talking, talking and eating and wondering aloud why their cups of tea are so long coming.

'She's better off without him, and that's the truth of it,' says a voice behind me. It's Miss Owen Penllech.

'It'll be hard to bring up those girls without a father. That little Angharad is a bit of a handful,' says Mrs Davies Chapel House. 'Elin would never say a word against him, you know.'

'She always put a good face on it,' says Mrs Morris. 'But everyone knew what was going on, didn't they?'

'I suppose it could be just gossip.' Mrs Beynon sounds as if she hopes it isn't. Why is she here? Ifan Evans died the day before she ever came to our Chapel.

'You haven't lived here that long, have you?' says Miss Owen Penllech. 'He's no loss, believe me.'

'Why are you standing there, Gwenni?' says Mrs Twm Edwards.

'She's keeping me company, ladies. Aren't you, Gwenni?' says Mrs Williams Penrhiw. 'Wasn't that a beautiful service the minister gave, Mrs Edwards? Quite beautiful.' She puts her arm around my shoulders, and draws me away. 'You're a good girl to help Elin with the children, Gwenni. It's difficult for her; little Angharad has taken it so badly. And there's so much to do. But there, it comes to us all sooner or later. And how's your nain? Don't tell me, I know what she'd say: Mustn't grumble, Bessie. I didn't expect to see her here, of course. She's not a one for funerals, is she? I thought Guto would be here, though. He's so fond of Elin. I was sure he'd come. You didn't see him on your way here with Angharad and Catrin, did you? No? I don't know what's to become of that boy. The police were asking him all sorts of questions, you know. And in English, too. The poor boy didn't know what they wanted from him. Well, he wouldn't, would he, being the way he is? You'd think they could see that. He's too innocent for this old world. No harm in him, just as your father says. On my word, Gwenni, there's your father by the vestry door. He'll be looking for you. Off you go.'

I spy Tada's family hair above the crowd and push through everyone towards him.

'Take a plate, Gwenni, and get some food before this lot falls on it,' he says. They've already fallen on it but I can see a plateful of egg sandwiches near us on the table. Inside my head I say: Please let them be Mrs Edwards the Bank's egg sandwiches. And I take three.

'Did Angharad and Catrin behave themselves for you?' says Tada. 'They must have been a bit upset, considering.'

'They were good girls,' I say. 'But Angharad is angry all the time, Tada. I don't know why. She's angry with her mother.'

'I'm sure she's got no cause to be angry with Elin,' says Tada. 'The woman's a saint.' I look round for Mam but she's not nearby. And then I hear her. Her voice is rising and falling like the waves of my sea at night, and someone is calling, 'Is Emlyn Morgan here? Find Emlyn; he'll take her home.'

Tada puts his half-eaten sandwich back on his plate, and the plate on the table, and the crowd parts to let him through. Mam is on her knees upon the hard wooden floor of the vestry, sobbing. Tada walks up to her and scoops her up in his arms and limps towards the door. I run after him.

'You stay here and have something to eat, Gwenni,' he says. 'I'll take your mam home to bed. It's her nerves, look. It's no good her staying here.' He heaves her over his shoulder. She seems to have fallen asleep now and her arms hang down his back like the dead fox's paws on Mrs Llywelyn Pugh's pink jacket.

As the vestry door swings shut behind them everyone starts to chatter again. Someone puts a hand on my shoulder and I spin around to see Mrs Williams Penrhiw.

'Don't worry, Gwenni, your father will take care of her,' she says. 'Now, eat your sandwiches before they curl up on the plate. Oh, look, here comes the minister. I must tell him what a lovely service he gave . . .'

Mrs Williams Penrhiw winds down as the Voice of God holds his hands in the air as if he's blessing us all. 'Dear people,' he says. 'Dear people. A terrible mistake has been made. The police have arrested Guto Edwards for killing Ifan Evans and they've taken him away to the police cells in Dolgellau. Mr Pugh is going to take me there in his car to see what we can do for Guto. But I must see Mrs Evans and the children before I set off.' He shakes his head. 'A terrible mistake.' He pushes past all the silent people, standing with cakes and sandwiches and cups of tea halfway to their open mouths, and goes into the Meeting Room and pulls the door closed behind him.

'Oh, Gwenni,' says Mrs Williams Penrhiw. 'Oh, Gwenni. That poor boy. That poor boy. Innocent as a lamb, Gwenni.'

But everyone knows what happens to lambs, don't they? That's not a secret.

31

By the time Nain and I manage to get out through the front door, Lloyd George has disappeared. Nain and I look at one another. 'You go down and I'll go up,' she says and she runs up the road, her legs kicking out sideways, screeching, 'Lloyd George. Lloyd George.' I've never seen Nain run before.

I've been in her house all evening because Tada's taken Mam to the pictures to take her mind off the funeral. Tada said not to mention Guto being arrested to her yet. Poor Guto. Nain said: Those detectives of yours must be bird-brained if they think Guto killed Ifan Evans; they won't keep him in Dolgellau long, you'll see. She was bird-brained to let Lloyd George out of his cage when the window was still open. But I didn't tell her that.

I run down the hill, then slow down. Lloyd George might be sitting on the wall outside Nain's house. How far can budgies fly? He's probably scared; he's never been outside Nain's living room before. If we don't find him, the other birds will kill him and Aunty Lol will cry. She cried when we found the baby blackbird fallen out of its nest, and that didn't even belong to her.

'Potato flower. Potato flower,' I call. I try to squawk like Lloyd George. 'Lol. Lol.'

But he's not on Nain's wall. I cross the road to lean on the Youth Hostel's garden wall where the moss is wet and squidgy, and narrow my eyes to look through the rhododendrons in the front garden. But there are no bright blue feathers lying on the ground. It's difficult to see anything in the mist and the rain. It's as if someone's spread Tada's old army blanket over the world. Lloyd George is so tiny, but his bright feathers would show up, wouldn't they?

I'm not sure which way to go now, down to the high street or along the track behind the primary school. Maybe Lloyd George made for the trees along the track. I meander along, trying to look up into all the leafy branches through the dense air. Lloyd George could be hiding anywhere. I call again in his voice, 'Potato flower. Potato Flower.'

'What are you doing?' says a voice in English from the gloom beneath the trees. A boy's voice. I don't like boys. I peer into the gloom. It's Richard, Caroline's brother.

'Looking for an escaped budgie,' I say, and carry on walking.

He catches up with me, lighting his way with a torch. 'And I'm escaping from my sister and your sister.' He smiles at me. 'Shall I help you find your budgie?' His two big front teeth have a gap between them like mine and Aunty Lol's. Aunty Lol's gap makes her a good whistler, but my gap doesn't seem to work. I wonder if Richard can whistle.

'It's not my budgie, it's my Aunty Lol's,' I say. 'You don't have to help.'

'But I'd like to,' he says. 'Was that the budgie's name you were calling?'

I have to think for a second. He has freckles over his nose, like me, too. 'No,' I say. 'That's something Aunty Lol taught him to say: blodyn tatws. It means potato flower.'

'Potato flower?' says Richard. 'What's his proper name?'

'Lloyd George,' I say. 'I can't stay here to talk, I've got to look for him.'

'My grandmother's got a grey parrot called Blind Pew,' he says. 'It swears a lot. She says it's because he used to belong to a sailor. She has to put a cover over his cage when she has visitors.'

'Lloyd George doesn't swear,' I say. 'Blind Pew from *Treasure Island*?'

Richard nods. 'Have you read it?' he says.

'Yes,' I say. 'But I like his verses better. You know: *The lights from the parlour and kitchen shone out, through the blinds and the windows and bars. And high overhead and all moving about, there were thousands of millions of stars.*'

'It's a bit babyish,' he says.

Babyish? 'I like it,' I say. 'It was in a book I borrowed from the town library ages ago with lots of verses and pictures.' The picture for that verse was exactly like my night-time sky when I'm flying.

'It's not much good, is it?' says Richard. 'The town library. We've got more books at home.'

We haven't. Tada's got a book called *Teach Yourself Bricklaying* under his chair cushion that Mam got for him so he could learn to build with bricks as well as stones and earn more money. And Mam's got a cookery book she never uses, and Mam and Bethan and I have a Bible and a hymn book each. I've got more books in the box under my bed than everyone else in our house put together. But I don't tell Richard. His family must have hundreds of books, like Mrs Evans. I wonder if their shelves sag under the weight.

From the distance comes Nain's voice, still calling. 'Lloyd George. Lloyd George.'

Richard looks at me with his eyebrows raised.

'That's Nain, my grandmother,' I say. 'She left the window open. Aunty Lol will be sad if she comes home to find Lloyd George has flown away and we haven't found him.'

Richard picks up a stick and begins to rattle the branches above us with it. Beads of water drop from them. 'We need to find him before the other birds gang up on him,' he says.

'Because he's different?' I say.

'That's right. Studying birds is one of my hobbies,' he says. 'Come on, then.'

We walk along in silence, side by side. Richard is not like my bêtes noires. He's clever; he knows things. Alwenna knows things, too, but not the same kind of things. But I won't think about Alwenna. I look into the undergrowth and up to the branches on one side of the track and Richard rattles his stick everywhere on the other side.

'What if you frighten Lloyd George with that stick?' I say.

'The fright'll make him fly out,' he says.

'It might just make him put his head in his feathers and stay where he is,' I say.

'Well, we won't be any worse off than we are now, will we?' Richard says.

We look and look. But we don't see Lloyd George anywhere. The rain falls and falls, fine and misty; it runs down inside the neck of my school mackintosh and chills me. It's hard to see anything at all. Even the lights from the houses find it difficult to spill out into this mist.

'Perhaps he flew straight down the hill,' I say. 'Perhaps he could sense the sea nearby and wanted to get back to his own country. Perhaps he still knows, deep inside his heart, where that is. Perhaps—'

'Perhaps he did,' says Richard. 'But it's a long way from here to Australia. Anyway, I expect he was bred in captivity. Shall we turn back and go down the road?' He looks up and down the track. 'I'm not sure he'd have flown into this darkness, you know.'

I can't hear Nain calling any more. I wonder how far she's gone up the hill. She didn't put a coat on before running out. What if she catches a cold and becomes ill?

'How far can a little budgie fly?' I say.

'I don't think he'd go far,' says Richard. 'I expect he's only used to flying around a room, isn't he?'

We walk back along the track towards the road. The mud will be spattered all the way up my socks and legs and Mam will be cross with me.

'You don't look like Bethan,' says Richard.

I know that. Mam's always telling me. And I wouldn't look like Bethan if I look like Tada, would I?

'You don't look like Caroline,' I say.

'I do a bit,' he says. 'Did you know we're twins?'

'Yes. Bethan said,' I say. 'Can you read each other's minds and things like that?'

'I can't read Caroline's mind at all,' he says. 'I think she and Bethan can read each other's minds. They think the same about everything. Except they don't really think much.'

We look at each other and he pulls a face at me and we both start laughing.

'You're different to other girls,' he says.

Mam's always telling me that, too. She says: People think you're odd.

'How d'you know?' I say.

'I've seen you around,' he says. I haven't seen him around, much. 'And Bethan says you're odd.'

You see? Odd, again.

He looks down at my face and smiles at me with his gappy teeth showing. 'I like odd,' he says.

My stomach jumps. Is it that old family stomach?

'Lloyd George,' I remind him.

'Indeed,' Richard says, and we stride on. He doesn't notice that he's splashing mud over my feet. From his jacket pocket he pulls two Black Jacks and gives me one. They're a bit damp.

'Thanks,' I say, and pick the sticky paper off. 'They're my favourite sweets in the whole world.'

Richard laughs. 'Perhaps Lloyd George's stayed nearer home than we think,' he says. 'Let's go back up your road first.'

'I looked along there on the way down,' I say.

'It won't take long to double check,' says Richard.

It's becoming darker and wetter all the time. Will we be able to see Lloyd George even if he's there?

We reach the road and walk past Rock Terrace and as we turn the corner to my terrace, old Dafydd Owen at Number 1 turns on his bedroom light. And there on his bedroom windowsill is a bright little blue ball. I'm sure I can see it trembling from here.

'Look,' say Richard and I at the same time.

'If we knock on the door we'll scare him away,' I say.

'But how can we get him down?' says Richard. 'I don't think I can reach from the lower windowsill. And I get vertigo, anyway.'

'I'm good at climbing,' I say. 'If you help me to climb on that side wall I can reach from there. But what shall I catch him with? He always scratches me.' I hadn't thought about that.

Richard looks through his jacket pockets and then his trouser pockets and then more pockets inside his jacket until he pulls out a wodge of paper and unfolds it into a paper bag and blows into it to open it. 'I'll hand this to you when you're up there,' he says. 'See if you can scoop him up into it. It won't hurt him. Then you can pass the bag back to me before you come down.'

Richard makes me a step with his hands and I haul myself up onto the side wall. It's wet and slithery. 'Hold on to my feet so I don't slip when I lean over,' I say to Richard and he grabs my ankles from where he's standing at the foot of the wall.

I ease myself forward bit by bit at an angle towards the windowsill. Lloyd George hasn't moved but I can see his feathers moving in and out, in and out with his breath. I aim the paper bag at him.

'Quick,' says Richard in a hoarse whisper. 'I can hear someone coming.'

I'm trying to be quick when a screech pierces the mist that swirls around me. 'Gwenni,' shouts Mam. 'What do you think you're doing standing there letting a boy look up your skirt?'

'What did she say?' says Richard, still holding my ankles. It's lucky Richard doesn't understand Welsh.

The sash window just above me crashes open and old Dafydd Owen sticks his head out and croaks, 'Murder. Murder. Help. Police.'

Lloyd George lifts his head and fluffs up his bright blue feathers and hurtles off the sill straight past my ear into the perilous darkness. Mam shrieks, and Richard lets go of my ankles and rushes away into the night too.

32

I shouldn't be here. Mam will be cross. Though she can't get any crosser than she's been since Thursday night because I won't tell her who was holding my ankles. Tada knows, but he won't tell either. My feet slow down as I near Brwyn Coch and see the front door agape.

Then Catrin comes racing along the path. 'Gwenni.' She almost screams as she tugs at my hand to pull me into the house. 'I wanted to come to see you but Mami said no we can't go down into the town, we are much too busy. But I wanted to see you again before we go away and now you've come to see me instead. Hooray.'

'Go away?' I look around the kitchen. There are faint marks on the walls where pictures and photographs once hung and crates on the floor with their tops nailed down and the dresser is in two pieces, the top leaning against the drawers, and the kitchen chairs are stacked in pairs, seat on seat, and there's no fire in the range. 'When?'

'Today,' says Catrin. She hugs my hand and puts it to her lips and kisses it.

'I didn't know,' I say. 'Where are you going?'

'To live with Aunty Meg in Cricieth,' she says. 'Mami said she didn't want anyone to know where we were. But she didn't mean you, Gwenni.'

'Yes, she did.' Angharad stands in the doorway to the hall leaning against the doorpost. 'She didn't want anyone at all to know. It's a big secret.'

'But why is it a secret?' I ask.

Angharad shrugs. The bones in her shoulders stick up like two little wings. She begins to kick her heel against the doorpost. Kick. Kick. Kick.

'Gwenni won't tell,' says Catrin. 'You won't, will you, Gwenni?'

I shake my head. 'But why are you leaving at all?'

'Mr Edwards wants the house back for a new shepherd,' says Catrin. 'And he's taken Mot to live with him. And all our geese. Even the one I followed into the sky in your story. I think he's a bad man. Don't you think he's a bad man, Gwenni?'

Angharad scowls at her. 'Mami asked Twm Edwards to have Mot and the geese,' she says. 'And he said we could stay as long as we wanted. I heard him tell Mami. And I heard Mami tell Aunty Meg that she wanted us to be able to escape from it all.'

'All what?' I say.

Angharad shrugs again and kicks at the doorpost.

'Angharad, Catrin, what are you doing down there?' Miss Cadwalader's voice makes me jump. It doesn't belong in Brwyn Coch.

'Gwenni's here, Aunty Meg,' Catrin says.

I can hear Mrs Evans's voice but it's so faint that I can't hear what she says. Catrin and I move into the hall. Mrs Evans and Miss Cadwalader come down the stairs and Mrs Evans stops halfway down.

I look up at her. 'I didn't know you were going away,' I say. 'And Catrin and Angharad.'

'It was a sudden decision, Gwenni. No time to tell anyone.' Mrs Evans brushes her hair back from her face with the back of her hand. The curly wisps wave in the draught she makes, like the seaweed under my night-time sea.

Miss Cadwalader puts her arm around my shoulders and turns me towards the door. 'You'll understand, I'm sure, Gwenni,' she says, 'how busy we are. We're expecting the big Rowlands van any minute now to move everything for us.' She pushes me towards the door and as I step over the threshold I look back and there is Catrin quivering from head to heel with tears running down her cheeks. How can I leave her? Angharad is kicking at the bottom stair now. Kick. Kick. Kick. Her face is like a sheet of paper with nothing written on it.

Out of my pocket I pull the next chapter of *Catrin in the Clouds* and the postcard I bought especially for Catrin. I push the story back in and hold the postcard out. 'Look, Catrin,' I say. 'I was bringing you this picture of the castle. See, you'd think someone was standing right up in the hills, higher than here, to take the picture and you can see the sea beyond the castle and there's Llŷn and you can just see the rock with the castle in Cricieth.' Catrin takes the card from me and looks at it, rubbing her eyes with her other hand and sniffling like a little dog. 'D'you remember thinking you could fly there?' I say. 'So, if you stand near the castle in Cricieth you can look straight back at our castle and you won't be very far away at all.'

Mrs Evans stumbles down the last of the stairs. 'Meg,' she says, 'let Gwenni take Angharad and Catrin out to play whilst we're waiting for the van.' She takes the card from Catrin. 'How kind of you, Gwenni,' she says, looking at it. 'We'll find a frame for it and Catrin and Angharad can have it on the wall in their new bedroom.'

'Just until the Rowlands van comes, then,' says Miss Cadwalader.

Catrin catches hold of my hand and we set off. The rain has stopped but everywhere is wet and the sound of water dripping from the roof and the trees follows us down the field. I look around to see where Angharad is and she's following slowly, kicking at the tussocks as she walks.

'Run, Gwenni. Run,' Catrin shouts. 'Run until we fly off the edge of the field and don't stop until we get to where we want to go.' She stops and swings round to face me. 'Can we fly far, far away, Gwenni? Can we? I don't want to live with Aunty Meg. I want to live with you.'

I squeeze her hand. 'Let's wait for Angharad,' I say, and when Angharad walks up to us I catch hold of her hand, too, and the three of us run and run until we're almost at the stream and Angharad stumbles and pulls us all down into the wet grass.

'I didn't want to run,' says Angharad.

'And I wanted to fly, Gwenni.' Catrin pants as she tries to catch her breath. 'I wanted to fly. I wanted to fly away with you.'

'People can't fly. I told you before,' says Angharad. 'It's all pretend.' She lies on the grass and closes her eyes and goes away from us.

I sit up and pull Catrin out of the dampness to sit on my lap. 'When you get to Cricieth,' I say, 'you can look at your postcard and you can pretend that you've flown all the way across that sea to get there and when you want to, you can fly all the way back to visit me.'

'But it's not real, is it?' says Angharad without opening her eyes. 'Flying.'

'How do you know?' I say. 'It can be real if you want it to be.'

'You sound like Mami used to,' says Catrin as she snuggles into my lap. Her hair under my chin is soft and smells of Mrs Evans's violet scent.

I put my arms around her and whisper, 'When you fly really high, Catrin, you can hear the Earth sing. It's like being enchanted; you never want to come down from the sky.'

'I'd like to hear that song,' says Catrin. 'Will you come to visit me, Gwenni? And teach me to fly?'

'I'd like to,' I say. 'But I don't know if Mam will let me.'

'Your mam is always cross just like Tada was, isn't she, Gwenni?' says Catrin. 'Maybe she'll go away, as well. Maybe there's a Cross Land that all the cross people go to.' She giggles. 'Maybe you'll go away, too, Angharad.'

Angharad jumps up from the grass and begins to run up the field. 'I can hear the Rowlands van coming,' she says.

'Oh, no, Gwenni,' says Catrin.

I lift Catrin to her feet and stand up myself. I hold her hand tight. 'Come on,' I say and I run up the field, pulling Catrin behind me. 'Let's see if we can fly.'

'But it's the wrong way, Gwenni,' says Catrin. 'It's the wrong way to fly away.'

And so it is.

The Rowlands van lurches and sways across the field to the house. It isn't a very big van into which to pack all their lives.

Mrs Evans is at the door watching her sister show the driver where to go. 'Catrin,' she says. 'Come here quickly. Give this to Gwenni from you and Angharad. I think she'll like it.'

Catrin lets go of my hand and runs to her mother and takes the brown paper bag from her and opens the top to peek in. 'You will like it, Gwenni,' she says.

Mrs Evans pushes Angharad towards Catrin. 'From both of you,' she says. So Catrin holds the bag and pulls Angharad along with her to bring the bag to me. I take it from her. 'Can I look now?' I ask Mrs Evans.

She smiles and nods. The bag smells of her scent when I open it, and here inside is the blotter rocker with the pretty violet painted on the knob. How did she know I wanted it so much?

'A keepsake, Gwenni,' she says. 'Don't forget us. Keep us in your heart.'

I nod. I hug Catrin hard but Angharad slips away. I turn and run past the Rowlands van as it backs up to the front door and I don't stop until I get to the road and then I huddle down on the grass verge among the damp and cottony leaves of the cornflowers and hold my stomach tight. It hurts so much I can hardly breathe.

33

Mam grabs me by the wrist and squeezes hard. 'Where have you been all afternoon?' she says.

'Walking,' I say.

'That's not what I heard,' Mam says. 'Get in that house.' She lets go of my wrist as she flings me into the hallway and I stumble against the hat-stand. Mam's gripped my wrist so tightly it has red weals all round it and I rub at them to ease the pain. This is worse than the Chinese burns Bethan used to give me when I was little. Mam pushes me through the living room door until I crash into the back of Tada's armchair.

'What's happened now?' Tada folds the *Daily Herald* and puts it under his chair cushion as he gets up. 'What's the matter, Magda?'

Mam ignores him and flounces into the scullery, her mouth a thin red line cutting into her face.

'Mam's cross because I went to Brwyn Coch,' I say.

A crash comes from the scullery as Mam drops something into the sink, then the furious noise of water running from the tap.

'She told you not to go there again,' says Bethan from Mam's armchair.

She did. But I didn't promise I wouldn't go, did I? 'I took something for Catrin and I thought Mrs Evans might need help. She always said it was a great help to have me looking after the girls,' I say to Tada. 'I wasn't there for long, and then I went for a walk.'

'You mean well, Gwenni,' says Tada. 'But you should do as your mother tells you.'

'Give us all a quiet life,' says Bethan.

'Bethan,' says Tada.

'Well, it's true,' says Bethan.

I promised I wouldn't say anything about Mrs Evans and Angharad and Catrin going to live with Miss Cadwalader. But by tomorrow everyone will know that they've gone away from Brwyn Coch. 'They were leaving,' I say. 'Going away.' I rub my thumb along the blotter rocker in my pocket. I won't tell anyone about it. Mam would probably throw it on the fire, like the dead fox. I take my mackintosh off and hang it up; later, I'll put the blotter in the box under the bed.

Mam comes in from the scullery, her face tight and red as her thin red mouth. 'About time, too,' she says. 'This place doesn't need a woman like that.' The water in the kettle she's carrying slops out of the spout. Tada takes it from her and sets it on the fire. He doesn't say anything.

The Toby jugs lean forward to watch Mam walk back to the scullery. And now that she's closed the door, Tada says to me, 'I expect Mam was worried about you, not knowing where you were. What with a murderer on the loose. It's got quite late, you know, Gwenni.'

'I thought Guto did it,' says Bethan. 'I thought he was the

murderer. Anyway, Mam wasn't worried about that. She was doolally because she knew where Gwenni was, not because she didn't. Kitty Hawk saw Gwenni going up the hill.'

'We all know Guto doesn't have it in him to do something so terrible,' says Tada.

That's what Nain said, too. But I know he has it in him. I remember the way he killed a rabbit that had been hurt and was screaming in pain. Guto picked up a stone and hit the rabbit on the head and when it was dead, he cried. Mrs Evans said he put the creature out of its misery, and it took courage to do that when your nature was as gentle as Guto's. But what if he thought he was helping Mrs Evans and Angharad and Catrin by killing Ifan Evans?

'And don't speak about your mother like that, Bethan.' Tada says. 'Now, how about laying the table. We're late with supper tonight. We'll have to listen to *Calling Gari Tryfan* when we're eating, Gwenni.'

'Why do I have to do it?' says Bethan. 'Gwenni should do it. She's the one who's misbehaved, not me. She's the one that should be punished.' She turns over a page of the *School Friend* she's holding. My *School Friend*.

'I'll do it,' I say. Tada passes me the tray from the sideboard and I put it on one of the chairs. I spread the tablecloth over the chenille cover; I put the least stained part next to where I sit so that I don't get the family stomach when I'm eating. Then the knives and forks; the special sharp knife for Tada that he had in the army and Bethan's silly spoon with the rabbit on it. A big plate each for our food. The pepper and salt pots. The bottle of brown sauce for Tada. Cups and saucers for us all. A big bowl of sugar; Tada likes two spoonfuls in his tea. The small milk jug that I like with the forget-me-nots around the rim like the china Mrs

Evans used to have on her dresser. Don't think about that. The chipped brown teapot with the tea in it, ready to be filled once the kettle has boiled. The bread board and the bread knife, the Hovis and the butter, the blue striped plate. Mam is too quiet in the scullery. Better make sure everything is set out right.

'What are we having?' I ask Tada.

'Corned beef, and cold potatoes from dinnertime,' he says. 'And an early lettuce from Lol's allotment. She likes her rabbit food, your Aunty Lol.'

Corned beef makes my stomach turn over. I couldn't eat the faggots at dinnertime either. I'll never be strong like the lion.

The kettle starts to boil over the logs and Tada leaps to take it off the fire. The water hisses along the wood in little balls, bringing a smoky smell with it. Bethan waves the smell away with my *School Friend*. She looks just like Mam as she sits there in Mam's chair; her skin is smooth and pink and her face round and her hair yellow. But her eyes are dark brown.

'I think Mam should cancel Gwenni's *School Friend* to punish her for disobeying,' she says.

'You've got punishment on the brain tonight, Bethan,' says Tada.

'You wouldn't be able to read it then, either,' I say.

'I can read Caroline's,' she says. 'She gets *Girl's Crystal* as well. And Richard gets *Hotspur*. Every week.'

I know Richard gets *Hotspur*. Yesterday, at school, he said he would lend it to me. To make up for running away the night before.

The scullery door rattles open and Mam brings in a plate with the sliced corned beef and the potatoes, and the lettuce broken up in the salad bowl she and Tada had for a wedding present that I have to be careful with when I'm washing up. Tada jumps up from his chair and takes the dishes from her and puts them on the table. Mam cuts the Hovis into thick slices, spreads butter on them and slaps them on the blue striped plate.

'You've forgotten the fork for the meat and spoons for the potatoes and lettuce,' she says to the living room and Tada and Bethan and I look at one another and Bethan shrugs and turns another page of my *School Friend*. I run into the scullery and take the fork and spoons from the cutlery holder and try not to see all the eyes in the distemper watch me. I take them into the living room and Mam snatches them from my hand and lets them clatter on the table.

'Let's get Gari Tryfan on so we don't miss him,' Tada says. I like *Calling Gari Tryfan*, too, he's a good detective. Tada fiddles with the wireless knobs. Howls and whistles come from the set and stuttering foreign voices. Tada finds the right station just in time. He grins at me, his bright teeth glittering. No one has to talk about anything if we listen to Gari Tryfan's adventures. And the Toby jugs settle back on their shelf and close their eyes.

Tonight, Gari Tryfan is rescuing a villain he was chasing who has fallen and been hurt on the Wyddfa. 'No idea, these people,' says Tada as he forks corned beef onto his plate. 'No idea how dangerous the mountains are.'

I try to choose the potatoes that haven't touched the corned beef but Mam picks up the plate and pushes some onto my plate from right next to the meat. Her mouth is still thin and red.

'I like corned beef,' says Bethan. 'I'll have Gwenni's if she doesn't want it.'

'Shush,' says Tada as Gari Tryfan climbs down a treacherous rock to arrest the injured man. How will he get him away?

Tada and I are waiting to see if Gari will reach the man without falling on the steep rock; Tada has his fork suspended halfway to his mouth with a big lump of potato on it. Gari slips and Tada gasps and there's a loud bang that I think is Gari falling but I realise it came from our back door as Nain rushes through into the living room. Gari is fighting to find a foothold as Tada stands up.

'What's the matter, Mam?' he says. 'What's wrong?'

Nain peers around the table. Her spectacles are perched on top of her head. 'Is that you, Gwenni?' she says. 'Thank goodness you're safely home.' Nain's out of breath. She looks at Mam, then at Tada. 'Haven't you heard?'

'Heard what?' says Tada. 'What's happened?'

Gari Tryfan is hanging off a ledge by one hand; his life is in the balance. The villain is taunting him but I don't know who he thinks will rescue him if Gari falls.

'Elin Evans,' says Nain. 'Eric's just been round to see Lol about some Silver Band business, we heard it from him. The news is spreading like fire through bracken. I'm surprised you haven't heard.'

Mam is on her feet now as well. 'We don't talk about that woman in this house,' she says.

Nain looks surprised. 'Well, if you really don't want to know . . .' she says, backing to the door.

'We know,' says Bethan. 'They've left Brwyn Coch. This afternoon.'

Nain shakes her head at Tada. 'Bigger news than that, Emlyn.'

'Go on, Mam,' he says. 'What is it?'

'Wil the Post saw a big black car with Sergeant Jones and those policemen from Dolgellau in it going up to Brwyn Coch and coming down again with Elin Evans in the back.' Nain pauses as if she's in a play on the stage at the Memorial Hall.

'But why?' I say. Perhaps Guto didn't kill Ifan Evans. Perhaps

Mrs Evans had to identify someone else at the police station. 'Have they found the real murderer?'

'They've found the real murderer all right, Gwenni,' says Nain. 'They've arrested Elin. Arrested her for killing her own husband.'

'Jesus Christ,' says Tada.

Mam's thin red line of a mouth becomes a red cavern as she screams and laughs until Nain goes over to her and slaps her face and she begins to cry instead.

The Toby jugs rock with the shock on their high shelf and John Morris races from under Tada's chair into the scullery.

'They've made another terrible mistake,' I say, but no one is listening to me or to Gari Tryfan.

34

'No Chapel this morning, then?' says Nain as she opens the back door to let me in.

'Mam's too ill,' I say. 'Tada said Bethan and I didn't have to go on our own.'

'So where's Bethan?' says Nain.

'Gone to see Caroline,' I say and manoeuvre my way around the ironing board in the living room. 'She doesn't go to a chapel or anywhere. Bethan says Mr Smythe's an atheist. Because of the war. He was an aeroplane pilot and he bombed people.'

'Fancy that,' says Nain.

'It means he doesn't believe in God,' I say. 'I looked it up in the dictionary at school.' I looked at S words last for my list of words from the dictionary; my favourites are *serendipity, sidereal, sonorous, stellar* . . . They move like music in my mouth.

'Bit like me, then,' says Nain. She waves the toasting fork at me. 'D'you want to make yourself some breakfast?'

'Please, Nain,' I say. 'I couldn't get to the larder because Tada's decided to distemper the scullery. In blue. To cheer Mam up.' Will the mouths be drowned by the paint before they shout out all our secrets?

'I think it'll take more than that to cheer her up after her turn last night, don't you?' says Nain. 'She's in bed, is she?'

I nod and push a thick slice of Nain's soft white bread onto the toasting fork. Nain pokes at the fire and clears a glowing cave for me to put the bread to toast. The phoenix on top of the poker dances in the firelight. Nain's brasses are always polished. Our phoenix doesn't dance at all since Mam used the poker to burn the dead fox. And Mrs Evans's phoenix has flown away for ever. I don't want to think about Mrs Evans yet.

'How's Lloyd George?' I say. He's sitting on his swing with his head on one side looking at himself in his mirror.

'He still hasn't said a thing since he came back,' Nain says. 'Lol's worried, but he seems all right to me. I quite like him quiet.'

'Maybe he had a bad scare when old Dafydd Owen opened his window and started yelling,' I say.

'He probably did,' says Nain. 'But at least it sent him straight back to his cage. And what was your mother shouting about? She was making more noise than old Dafydd. I could hear her from the top of the hill.'

'Nothing,' I say and yank the toast back from the fire as smoke spirals from it. But it's only burnt on one edge. I turn it over on the fork and hold it in the fiery cavern again.

'Hmm,' says Nain. 'I'll get the butter for you.'

She brings it from her larder under the stairs. 'Nothing like slate for keeping things cold,' she says. 'And nothing like hot toast with a slab of cold butter on it. You can toast me a slice when you've eaten yours, Gwenni.'

The toast is crunchy at the edges and hot, and the butter is yellow and salty and so cold I can see the marks my teeth make in it although it's melting by the time I'm on the last two bites and drips down my chin. I wipe my chin with my handkerchief and put a slice of bread on the fork to toast for Nain.

Nain takes her smoothing iron from the ironing board and puts it back in its holder on the range. 'I'll put this back in the fire for a bit when you've finished toasting,' she says. 'Lol's fire service jacket needs a bit of a press before tomorrow evening. I said I'd do it today for her. No time tomorrow with all the washing to do.'

'Where is Aunty Lol?' I say.

'Big football club meeting this morning,' Nain says. 'And that great horse of a girl is secretary, treasurer and goodness knows what else all rolled into one and has to be there.'

'Tada says she's a good footballer,' I say.

'It's not a woman's place though, is it, Gwenni, a football field?' says Nain.

What is a woman's place? What is my place? I turn Nain's toast on the fork. 'Is prison a woman's place, Nain?' I ask.

'I wondered when we'd get round to that,' says Nain. 'I can't tell you any more than I told you last night.'

'She didn't do it,' I say. 'Tada says he can't believe it either.'

'None of us can believe it, Gwenni,' says Nain. 'But that doesn't mean to say it isn't true. Is that smoke coming from my toast?'

I pull the toast off the fork and she takes it from me with one hand and pushes the iron in its holder onto the fire with the other hand. Then she puts a thinner slice of butter on her toast than she put on mine and sits in her rocking chair to eat it.

'What will happen to her?' I say.

Nain shrugs. 'I don't know, Gwenni,' she says. 'Nothing like this has ever happened around here before. And at least they've let Guto go.'

'Where to?' I say. 'Is he back at the Wern?'

'Dinbych,' she says. 'They've sent him to Dinbych.'

'What?' I say. 'To the asylum?'

'They'll know how to look after him there,' she says.

'How can they know?' I say. 'He won't be able to fly in there, will he? Will they let him outside so he can fly? I thought the asylum was for people who're ill. Guto isn't ill. And he can almost look after himself properly. What will they do to him?'

'Hush, Gwenni,' says Nain. 'I'm sure he's in the best place, poor boy. They're bound to have gardens he can walk round there. And he'll have all his meals. It's for the best.'

But is it for Guto's best? What if he can never fly again all the way down from the Wern to the town with his coat flapping like an old crow's wings?

'And now the detectives have made another mistake with Mrs Evans,' I say. 'I just know she didn't do it.' But how do I know that? 'And I'm going to solve the mystery and find the real murderer. They won't send Mrs Evans to Dinbych when they let her go, will they, Nain?'

Nain wipes the butter and crumbs from her fingers and puts her handkerchief back in her apron pocket. She shakes her head. 'Leave it alone, Gwenni,' she says. 'Now, talking of mysteries, Lol left another of her books for you to take. She finished it last night. It's under her cushion, that one with the birds on it.'

I shift in the armchair and pull a book out from beneath the bird cushion behind me. *The Beckoning Lady*. I open it to shake any Marie biscuit crumbs into the grate, although I never get them all out when I do that.

'The crumbs that great girl drops in her books,' says Nain. 'We could open a biscuit factory with them.'

It's true, we could. I look at what the cover says about the book. It's got Mr Campion and Amanda and Charlie Luke and Lugg in it. And murders. I'm not sure any more that murders in books are like real murders. But I want to be a detective like Mr Campion who always solves the mystery and catches the murderer, not like the detectives from Dolgellau who always get it wrong or like Sergeant Jones who worries more about his garden than about detecting.

Nain wraps a thick cloth around her hand and takes the smoothing iron from its holder. She spits on it and the spit hisses, then she shakes out her damp cloth to put over Aunty Lol's jacket and begins to press it. Steam writhes above the ironing board and a smell of damp wool snakes about the room as if Nain has lambs drying out by the fire the way Mrs Evans did at Brwyn Coch early in the spring. Don't think about Mrs Evans.

Nain hums as she presses. Her humming always makes me sleepy. I hug *The Beckoning Lady*. I won't start reading it until I've finished Matthew; I'm almost at the end. It's taking me a long time to read all my New Testament. But I did stop for a bit to read *The Maltese Falcon* instead. I still haven't found anything useful about animal spirits or flying. But Matthew tells some good stories. There aren't many women in them but there's one near the end called Magdalen, like Mam.

I jump when Nain puts the iron down in the grate. 'There,' she says. 'Isn't that smart?' She holds Aunty Lol's jacket by the shoulders to show me and then slips it onto a hanger and stands on a chair to hang it on the clothes pulley above the fire. 'It'll finish airing there.' The jacket moves in the hot air from the fire, its bright buttons glinting like stars against the sky-black fabric. Nain folds her cloth and collapses the ironing board and takes them both into the scullery.

'Let's have a cup of tea,' she says. I hear her run water into the kettle, and as she comes back from the scullery with it there's a frantic knocking at the front door.

'What on earth?' says Nain and hands me the kettle to put on the fire. When she opens the door Nellie Davies from next door stumbles into the house.

'Gwen, Gwen,' she says, clutching at Nain. 'Terrible news. Terrible news.'

'Now, Nellie, sit down,' says Nain and lowers Nellie Davies into her rocking chair that no one else is allowed to sit in. 'Gwenni, make a pot of tea as soon as that kettle boils.'

Nellie Davies leans back in the chair and her eyes stare at Nain as if they're going to pop from her head and she won't let go of Nain's hand.

'I didn't realise you knew Elin Evans so well,' says Nain, patting her free hand on Nellie Davies's knee.

'Not Elin. Not Elin,' says Nellie Davies.

'Not Elin?' says Nain.

'Not Elin.' Nellie Davies shudders until her whole body ripples. 'Ceridwen Llywelyn Pugh. The poor woman. It's all been too much for her. How shall I manage without her, Gwen?'

'What do you mean, Nellie?' says Nain. She points at the kettle and the teapot for me.

I nod, but I can't make the kettle boil any faster, can I? I put three scoops of tea into the pot and lay out three cups on three saucers. Should I use the best cups and saucers with the green pattern on them?

'Dead,' says Nellie Davies. 'Her heart broken once too often. The poor, dear woman.'

Because I stole her dead fox?

'Because of Elin?' says Nain and then answers herself. 'Of

course, Mrs Llywelyn Pugh knew her parents, didn't she? I didn't realise they were close though . . .'

Nellie Davies nods, still holding Nain's hand. 'They were close,' she says. 'She's been good to Elin. And she's been so good to me because of Bob being shot when he was trying to save her son. And both buried next to one another and so far away. And your Idwal. So far away, Gwen.' Nellie Davies sobs. 'What use was a medal when I had mouths to feed? I don't know what I'd have done without Ceridwen.'

The kettle belches steam and I pour water from it into the teapot and stir it. Three times each way.

'Oh, Gwen, I heard the birds knocking. I knew they were coming for someone. Knocking and knocking. And last night, did you hear that corpse bird in Bron-y-graig? I put my head under the pillow but that didn't stop death from coming, did it? Poor, dear Ceridwen.' Nellie Davies takes her handkerchief from her apron pocket and wipes her face.

'And poor Hywel Pugh,' says Nain. 'He won't know what to do without her, either. Was it her heart, Nellie?'

'He's beside himself,' says Nellie Davies. 'He found her this morning. Too late to do anything. He ran through the street to the Police House, covered in her blood.'

'Her blood?' says Nain. She turns to me. 'Go home to see how your father's getting on, Gwenni. Leave the tea.' I go through into the scullery and open the back door slowly, slowly.

'She cut her wrists, Gwen,' says Nellie Davies. 'Her blood had run like a river under the bathroom door.'

And as I pull hard on the back door to shut it I hear Nellie Davies wail again and again.

PART THREE

35

The cold heightens the scent of the beeswax polish on the pews. Mrs Davies Chapel House never fires the boiler in summer no matter how cold the weather. Through the narrow windows, light spills into the chill dimness of the Chapel. Here, under the gallery, I sit squashed between Alwenna and Meinir and watch the dust motes move up and down the beams of light. When I was little I thought they were angels dancing down from Heaven but Mam said: Don't be silly, Gwenni.

Alwenna pokes her elbow in my side. 'Your mam not here today, then?' she says. 'Or your Bethan?'

'No,' I say. Mam is still in bed and Tada still distempering between trips upstairs to see if Mam needs him. But she doesn't. She lies there staring at the wall and won't speak to him. He said he won't tell her about Mrs Llywelyn Pugh until she feels better. And Bethan didn't come home for lunch, which is lucky since there wasn't any. My stomach rumbles. It's hours since I had toast at Nain's.

Alwenna elbows me again. 'Why not?' she says.

'Mam's ill,' I say.

Alwenna smirks. She thinks she knows everything. But to know isn't to understand, is it?

On the other side of me Meinir is speaking to Eirlys and except for shuffling to make room on the seat and squeezing us all tighter together they both ignore Deilwen when she slips through the pew door. No one likes to sit too near her since she was sick on my socks. She bends her head to say a prayer after she sits down. Geraint turns around and nods at her from the pew in front but Aneurin and Edwin are too busy bobbing their quiffs at one another to notice her.

Young Mr Ellis strides up the aisle and into the pew in front of the boys and turns himself around on his seat to face us. Aneurin and Edwin groan and mutter but Young Mr Ellis ignores them.

'I'm having no nonsense today,' he says. 'No chattering. No speaking unless you're answering a question.' He pushes his spectacles up his nose. His little fingernail is still black. 'No—'

Alwenna interrupts him. 'What if we want to ask a question, Mr Ellis?'

'If you want to ask a question, you put your hand up,' he says.

'Like at school?' says Geraint without putting his hand up. Young Mr Ellis stares at him.

'Sorry,' says Geraint.

Aneurin and Edwin both put their hands up. Young Mr Ellis sighs and says, 'Yes, Edwin?'

'Can we ask anyone a question? Or just you?' Edwin's quiff almost collapses over his nose, but not quite. The movement wafts the scent of Brylcreem towards me. I try to not to breathe.

'Just me,' says Young Mr Ellis. 'Yes, Aneurin?'

'Is it true that when Mrs Llywelyn Pugh cut her wrists all the blood ran out of her?' says Aneurin.

Meinir squeals and hides her face in her hands.

'Not that sort of question, Aneurin,' says Young Mr Ellis. He slides along his seat away from Edwin and Aneurin and nearer to his pew door.

Edwin has his hand up again.

'What now?' says Young Mr Ellis to him.

'Did you know that the human body has got eight pints of blood in it?' says Edwin. 'I read it in my comic. So it would be like eight bottles of milk poured all round her. Only it would be red not white—'

'What did I just say, Edwin?' says Young Mr Ellis. He tugs at his tie as if he's trying to loosen it. 'No more questions. I'll talk, you listen.'

Alwenna raises her hand but Young Mr Ellis ignores her and takes a notebook from his pocket and flips the pages.

'That's not fair,' says Alwenna. 'You let Aneurin and Edwin ask silly questions and now you won't let me ask a religious question.'

Young Mr Ellis shuts his notebook. 'What do you want to know, Alwenna?' he says.

'I want to know if it's wrong to kill yourself,' says Alwenna.

'Of course it is,' says Young Mr Ellis.

'Why?' says Alwenna.

Young Mr Ellis chews his thumbnail. It's as rimmed with black as his other fingernails. 'Can one of you answer that?' he says to us. 'Sensibly.'

'Because,' says Deilwen, 'life is sacred.'

'We kill animals,' says Geraint.

'It's human life that's sacred,' says Deilwen. Her nose points up in the air as if our human life is too smelly for her.

'But if it's your life, can't you do what you like with it?' I ask.

'Do we have to talk about this, Mr Ellis?' says Meinir. 'It's making me feel sick.'

I try to move away from her, nearer to Alwenna. Mam would be beyond cross if she had to buy me another pair of socks. Alwenna shoves me back.

'Don't be a baby,' she says to Meinir.

'Your life doesn't belong to you. It belongs to God,' says Deilwen. 'It says so in the Bible.'

I haven't read as far as that bit yet. 'What if you don't believe in God?' I say. Like Richard's father. 'Then can you do what you like with your life?'

'It belongs to God even if you don't believe in Him,' says Deilwen.

'Quite right, Deilwen,' says Young Mr Ellis. 'See, everyone, killing yourself is a crime against God.'

'You go to prison if you're a criminal,' says Aneurin. 'But no one can put Mrs Llywelyn Pugh in prison, can they? Not if she's dead.'

'Not like Mrs Evans,' says Edwin.

Young Mr Ellis turns scarlet, first his neck, then his nose and cheeks and then his forehead. He tugs at his tie again and takes out a bunched-up handkerchief from inside his jacket and mops his face with it. I don't look at his handkerchief. 'Did I ask you to speak?' he says to Aneurin and Edwin. 'Now keep quiet, the pair of you, unless you can say something sensible.'

Aneurin and Edwin writhe with silent laughter and punch one another on the shoulder.

'My mam says we should feel sad for Mrs Llywelyn Pugh,' says Eirlys. 'My mam says you have to be in a very bad way to do something like that to yourself.'

'We do it all the time to animals,' says Geraint. 'We cut their throats and spill their blood.' He turns round to look at me. 'Did the Bible prove they've got spirits, Gwenni?'

'Not yet,' I say. 'But I haven't read anything that proves they don't have spirits. I think they do.'

'Me too,' says Geraint. 'I've stopped eating meat. I'm never eating meat again.' He nods at me and his spectacles catch the light and flare with fervour.

'We're allowed to kill animals,' says Deilwen. 'And eat them. It says so in the Bible.'

'Human beings are animals, too,' says Geraint. 'What's the difference between us and any other animal?'

'Doesn't that mean it's all right to kill people, Mr Ellis?' says Aneurin.

'And eat them,' says Edwin.

Meinir squeals again. 'I feel really sick now,' she says. She closes her eyes and holds her stomach and I shuffle my feet right back under the seat.

'Certainly not. Certainly not,' says Young Mr Ellis. 'You're twisting things, the pair of you. And you, too, Geraint. Now, try to be sensible.' He tugs his tie. 'Tell them, Deilwen, what it says in the Bible about killing.'

'*Thou shalt not kill.*' Deilwen puts her hands together under her chin as if she's praying. 'That's in the Old Testament. It's one of the ten commandments.'

'That means you're not supposed to kill anything,' says Geraint.

'Mr Ellis, Mr Ellis,' says Aneurin flapping his hand in the air. 'I don't understand all the commandments. What does *Thou shalt not commit adultery* mean?'

Alwenna snorts. Young Mr Ellis looks at her and she smiles at him.

Meinir sighs and lets go of her stomach and scrabbles in her cardigan pocket. She pulls out a bag of sweets and takes a pineapple chunk from it. 'This'll stop me feeling sick,' she says. She holds the bag out to me. 'You can have one, Gwenni. And Eirlys.'

I take two pineapple chunks from the bag because they've stuck together and pop them into my mouth. Young Mr Ellis is looking up at the Chapel ceiling as if he's expecting some help to arrive from Heaven. An angel, maybe. Or even God himself. The crystals of sugar on the sweets are rough on my tongue. Pineapple isn't my favourite flavour, but if the sweets stop Meinir feeling sick, maybe they'll stop my stomach rumbling.

'You're getting off the point, again, Aneurin,' says Young Mr Ellis. At least he doesn't look as if he's going to cry the way little Miss Griffiths does at school when Aneurin and Edwin ask those sorts of questions in the Scripture lessons.

'But I thought you didn't want us to talk about Mrs Llywelyn Pugh cutting her wrists and Mrs Evans going to prison,' says Aneurin.

'I don't want to talk about it, either,' says Meinir. She crunches her pineapple chunk. 'It's horrible.'

'We're talking about the sanctity of life,' says Deilwen.

'Saint Deilwen,' says Aneurin just loud enough for her to hear. But she looks pleased, not insulted, and Aneurin frowns.

'Not the sanctity of all life, though, is it?' says Geraint to no one in particular.

'Is it really just as bad to kill yourself as it is to kill someone else, then, Mr Ellis?' says Alwenna.

'Yes, it is,' says Deilwen.

'I wasn't asking you, Saint Deilwen,' says Alwenna.

'Oh, dear,' says Mr Ellis and he starts to worry his thumbnail.

'It's not so wrong, is it, Mr Ellis?' says Eirlys.

'Yes, it is,' says Deilwen. 'Mrs Llywelyn Pugh will go straight to Hell.'

Hell? We all look at her. Meinir stops crunching her sweet

and Young Mr Ellis lets his mouth hang open with his thumb halfway to it.

'And so will Mrs Evans when they hang her,' says Deilwen.

'They won't do that,' I say. 'She didn't do it. You'll see. And anyway they don't hang women any more, do they, Mr Ellis?'

'That would mean someone would have to kill her,' says Aneurin. 'And Saint Deilwen said the Bible says you shouldn't kill people, didn't she, Mr Ellis?'

Young Mr Ellis closes his mouth with a snap and jumps. Perhaps he's bitten his tongue. 'Well, uumm . . .' he says.

'The Bible says *an eye for an eye*,' says Deilwen. 'If Mrs Evans is a killer, someone should kill her.'

'But the killing would never stop, then,' I say. 'Someone would have to kill the person who killed Mrs Evans and—'

'Then someone would have to kill the person who killed the person who killed Mrs Evans,' says Aneurin. 'Gwenni's right.' He bobs his quiff at me.

What did he say? I rub both my ears. But I can hear everyone else clearly. I look at Aneurin and he winks at me. I look away. I don't want Aneurin to wink at me.

'You don't understand anything,' says Deilwen. 'Mami says she's never seen a place so full of stupid and wicked people.'

We all gasp. I'm sure even Mr Ellis gasps.

'You're so wicked, we're moving away to live,' says Deilwen.

'Good riddance,' says Alwenna.

'God and His angels,' says Deilwen, 'won't have people like you in Heaven. So you'll all go to Hell. Mami said so.'

Young Mr Ellis coughs, 'Well, now, Deilwen,' he says. 'I'm sure your mam didn't—'

'It's all in the Bible,' says Deilwen.

'Have you read it?' I say.

241

'Mami's read it,' she says. 'Three times.'

Three times? How long did that take?

'God isn't very kind, is he?' says Eirlys.

Aneurin and Edwin stand in their pew pretending to be God and his angel sending people to Hell. They send Deilwen first, and we all laugh except for Deilwen and Young Mr Ellis who flaps his hands at them as if he thinks the draught will blow them away.

Geraint polishes his spectacles on his shirt. He puts them back on and he says to Deilwen, 'I don't think you should say things like that about us. That we're wicked and we'll go to Hell. You don't know anything about this place and you don't know anything about Mrs Evans or Mrs Llywelyn Pugh.'

'That's right,' says Meinir. 'It's you and your mam that are wicked for saying things like that.'

Deilwen begins to cry. Eirlys, who is squashed tight to her side, pats her hand. 'Shall I take her to find her mam, Mr Ellis?' she says.

'She's in the vestry with Mr Roberts's class,' says Young Mr Ellis. 'I'll take you, Deilwen.' He holds out his hand but Deilwen rushes out of the pew and runs along the aisle towards the vestry door sobbing and screaming for her mother. Young Mr Ellis runs after her.

People in the other classes in the Chapel stand up or turn around in their seats to watch. I see Bethan glance from Deilwen racing up the aisle to me in my seat. She looks just like Mam. On the lightbeams the angels dance in the wake of the agitation beneath them.

The vestry door closes on Deilwen's noise. We lean back in our seats. Alwenna hooks her arm through mine without saying anything and Meinir fishes out the crumpled bag of pineapple chunks from her cardigan pocket. She pokes her finger into it and counts the sweets. 'Just enough for two each,' she says. She takes two and gives the bag to me. 'Pass it round.'

36

I don't know where I'm walking to. There's nowhere to go up this way any more. When Tada and Bethan and I had a late dinner with Nain and Aunty Lol after Sunday School, instead of tea with tinned fruit and bread and butter, Nain tried to persuade Tada to send for Dr Edwards to come to Mam. Nain said: She must be bad if she won't get out of her bed. Richard says his father saw dozens of doctors about his depression but not one of them could help him. They were special doctors, doctors of the mind. I think Dr Edwards is an everything doctor. He told Aunty Lol she'd sleep better if she put a cover over Lloyd George's cage to stop him calling her in the night. He was right. She tells everyone what a good doctor he is. But his tablets don't always help Mam. Maybe she needs a special kind of doctor, too.

The rain has stopped but the clouds hang so low I almost feel their weight on my shoulders. I've walked as far as the Baptism Pool but the road that winds up past the gates to Brwyn Coch and the Wern is as empty as those two abandoned homes. I won't go further today. But I don't want to go home yet. I lean over the Pool railings. The stream that feeds the Pool slithers down the wall and barely stirs the green and stagnant water at the bottom. The stench from the Pool is worse than the smell in Nain's house when a mouse died under the floorboards in her bedroom and started to rot. How could something so small make such a big smell? If I were a detective, I would probably have that old family stomach if I had to examine decaying corpses. And if I were a detective like Mr Campion or Gari Tryfan I would have found clues by now to help Mrs Evans. I take out the blotter she gave me from my dress pocket and smooth and smooth the tiny violet on the knob with my thumb.

Listen, there's a sheep somewhere calling for her lamb. Calling and calling. But perhaps the lamb has already been taken to market, and she'll never find it.

Now I've got bits of rust all over my Sunday dress from leaning on the railings. I always forget about the rust. It shows plainly on the grey checked cotton and won't brush off. Mam will be cross when I get home. Unless she's still in bed staring at the wallpaper.

I lean on the stone wall just beyond the Pool and slide down to sit on a big stone that sticks out at the base like a skirt with a frill around it of cornflowers with furry grey stems and thin grey leaves. The flowers are blue as the sky in the morning when I fly back to my bed. In a minute I'll see if I can fly from the Pool railings. I have to keep practising. If only I could remember exactly what I did that time I flew when I was little. I close my eyes and concentrate.

What's that? A noise I recognise but can't place. I must have fallen asleep. It's become colder and the clouds are darker. And there's that noise again. It's the squeak of Sergeant Jones's bicycle. I put the blotter back in my pocket, and stay where I am. Perhaps he won't see me in my grey dress against the grey granite.

'Did I frighten you, Gwenni?' he says. He's in his gardening clothes with his trousers held up by a piece of string. He doesn't look like a policeman who can catch murderers.

'I heard your bike,' I say. 'Where are you going? There's nothing up this way any more.'

'I wouldn't say that, Gwenni,' he says. 'But I was coming to see you. Martha just told me she saw you pass the house a while ago when I was in the glasshouse so I thought I'd try to catch up with you. Mind you, I thought you'd be almost up in Cwm Bychan by now, that's why I brought the bike.' He laughs at his joke.

But it can't be that long since I passed his house, can it? 'I didn't feel like going any further,' I say. 'And Tada's distempering the scullery so I don't want to go home yet.' What secrets are the faces in the distemper telling Tada before he drowns them?

'Your mam won't be very happy about your father doing that on a Sunday,' he says.

'She's been ill in bed since last night,' I say. 'Nain wants Tada to get Dr Edwards to see her.'

'I'm sorry to hear she's ill again,' Sergeant Jones says. 'These are upsetting times for us all. Well, Dr Edwards is a good man. He'll soon have her on her feet again.' He leans his bicycle on the Pool railings. 'I'd better watch myself on these. It took Martha a lot of effort to get all the rust off my uniform after the last time I was here.' He wrinkles his nose at the stink from the water and comes over to where I'm sitting. 'A lot of water's gone under the bridge since then, Gwenni. A lot of it as bad as the stuff in the Pool there. Mind if I sit with you for a bit?'

I move along to make room for him, plenty of room, and he lowers himself onto the stone with a loud grunt. 'Give me a chair, any day,' he says. 'Bit of an effort to get this low when you're my size, Gwenni.'

Now that I've moved I can feel my dress is damp beneath

my thighs. The stone is not as dry as it looks. But it's too late to tell Sergeant Jones that. 'What did you want?' I ask him.

'What d'you mean?' he says.

'You said you wanted to catch up with me, so you must've wanted something.'

'You're a quick one,' he says. 'Your father's right on that score.' He plucks a spiky cornflower head from the stems between his legs and twirls it between his finger and thumb. 'I just wanted to talk to you, Gwenni. A serious talk. Jokes aside. D'you think we could do that?'

He's the one who tells silly jokes instead of catching murderers, not me. But I nod.

'You've heard the news, I suppose?' he says. 'Well, silly question really.'

'Mrs Evans or Mrs Llywelyn Pugh?' I say.

'Poor Mrs Llywelyn Pugh. Poor old Hywel,' he says. 'But that's a job for the minister now, not me.' He shakes his head. 'No. The news about Elin Evans is what I mean.'

'I know she's been taken away by those stupid detectives from Dolgellau,' I say. 'I know they've made another mistake. I know I've got to find the real murderer so Mrs Evans will go free.'

'I was afraid of that, Gwenni,' he says.

'Someone has to,' I say. 'In Sunday School Deilwen said they'd hang her and she'd go to Hell. I thought they didn't hang women any more. Will they hang her, Sergeant Jones?'

'No, no, Gwenni. You're right. They don't hang women now, or men. Or only in rare circumstances. Don't even think about it.' A shudder goes through him. 'Someone walking on my grave, Gwenni. But listen to me. Seriously. Those detectives took Elin away because she confessed to killing Ifan. I probably shouldn't be telling you this, but Elin asked me if I would, and it's bound to come out anyway. You need to know it now so that you'll leave things be. Elin said you'd understand.'

But I don't understand. Mrs Evans confessed? Why would she do that? She didn't kill him. Did she?

Sergeant Jones leans towards me. 'She confessed, Gwenni,' he says. 'She said that she hit him on his head with the poker because he was drunk and abusive and she was afraid for the children. He'd already punched her in the mouth. D'you remember how you found her that Saturday morning?'

I remember her bleeding mouth; I thought she'd already been to Price the Dentist. I remember the sticky floor and tripping over the poker, but Angharad and Catrin explained that. I try to remember exactly what they told me. They never once said that their mother had hit their father, I'm certain. 'It's a mistake,' I say. 'Mrs Evans never—'

Sergeant Jones holds up his hand. 'She confessed, Gwenni. So she won't go to trial, she'll just be sentenced. And that's it. It's over, Gwenni. It's time to let it go. All good detectives know when it's time to let go.'

'Then I'll never be a good detective,' I say.

My eyes are watering and I rub them hard.

'Don't cry, Gwenni,' says Sergeant Jones.

'I'm not crying,' I say. 'It's the grass. I never cry.'

'This is how Elin wants it, Gwenni. It's important you remember that,' he says. He struggles to his feet and brushes down his gardening trousers. 'Bit damp there,' he says. 'Don't stay too long, Gwenni. Go home. It looks as if it'll rain again soon.' He wheels his bicycle into the road and heaves himself into the groaning saddle and freewheels down the hill.

The clouds have become yet darker and lower as we talked, but I sit here still. What did Angharad and Catrin tell me that

Saturday about their father? Nothing much, except that the black dog had somehow made their father angry with Mrs Evans. Was that it? That must have been when Ifan Evans punched Mrs Evans like Sergeant Jones just said. Then Catrin hit the black dog with the poker to get it away from her father so that he'd stop hurting her mother and that was why the dog's blood was on the floor. And one of the girls said that Ifan Evans ran out with the black dog. So, when did Mrs Evans have time to hit Ifan with the poker?

And why did she confess that she killed him when she didn't? Was it to save Guto?

37

Sergeant Jones said: Go home. But, just for now, I want to sit in the quiet and the stillness. And I'll have to get some of these bits of rust off my dress before I go home. I brush them with my hand again but they won't shift; so I begin to pick them off flake by flake.

If I'd found the evidence to lead me to the real murderer when I flew above Brwyn Coch looking for clues, maybe this wouldn't be happening. First Guto, and now Mrs Evans. Did I miss the clues because I was flying at night, when everything looks different? I always fly at night because I never fall asleep in the daytime long enough to fly, something always wakes me.

Perhaps I wouldn't have bad dreams if I flew in daylight. Although when Nain told us about Mrs Evans last night, I wondered if the bad dream I had about Brwyn Coch wasn't a dream at all. I wondered if it was a premonition. What if it showed me the future like the Baptist's spirit in the Baptism Pool? Brwyn Coch hasn't fallen to pieces, I know, but its family has. I expect premonitions are a bit vague; Nain's tea leaves are always vague, sometimes they're so vague she can't work out what it is they're foretelling.

A sharp flake of rust pushes under my thumbnail, and I suck it out. It tastes like the smell of blood. I spit it into my handkerchief and push the handkerchief back up my sleeve, then close my eyes and lean back against the wall. Just for a minute. Maybe Sergeant Jones was right about the rain. It's colder and damper already, and the stench from the Baptism Pool is as strong as if I was hovering right above it. On the count of three I'm going to jump up from this big stone and run home. One. Two. Two and a half. Three. I jump up and open my eyes. I am hovering above the Pool. In daylight.

I swerve around the Pool and fly up the road. This isn't as comfortable as night-time flying. The clouds are still here, massed above me, though I've climbed quite high without crashing into them. I can see my town clearly, the houses and gardens and the roads linking them all, and even a few people in their Sunday clothes. I'm too far up to recognise them. And I can see the Reservoir and Brwyn Coch below me. It looks even more like a map than it did last time. If I could fly around the whole world like this, I could become a map-maker. Miss Eames told me in our geography lesson that people who make maps are called cartographers. They use special instruments to make all kinds of measurements to draw their maps. I could become a cartographer who makes maps from what I can see. I would put in details that no instrument could possibly measure. And how do cartographers show music on their maps? I would show the shape of the Earth's song on mine, constant as the hum of bees in summer. Even under this heavy cloud I can hear it, filling me like a blessing.

But I haven't got time to stop and listen to it. I dive downwards towards Brwyn Coch, and something drops from my pocket. No! It's my blotter rocker. I race after it and scoop it up with my hand just as it's about to fall through some trees where I would never find it again. I hold it tightly in my fist. Mrs Evans told Sergeant Jones that I would understand. But I don't. I don't know how I'll ever find any clues to help her. I could fly round and round up here until I'm dizzy, and find nothing. And Sergeant Jones said: It's time to let go. I open my fist and look at my blotter rocker. I rub my thumb across the violet, and then I push the rocker deep down into my pocket.

A loud noise makes me spin as I fly. What was it? The clouds seem lower, and the air damper still. I fly as fast as I can towards the Baptism Pool and the road. Listen, there's that noise again. It sounds like a bark. Is it the black dog? The ground beneath me is turning darker by the second, and ahead of me, where there should be an open field, great trees spring up from the ground, trees shaped like the family tree that Mrs Evans showed me how to make. The black dog barks loudly, filling the sky with his noise, just as he did when Brwyn Coch fell to the ground, and a jagged flash of white light splits the largest tree in half, and each half falls to the ground with a noise like the beating of the biggest drum in the Silver Band. Is this another premonition? I don't want it. I cover my eyes with my hands so I don't see any more of it. Huge raindrops fall on me, drenching my dress, soaking through it, chilling me to the marrow of my bones. I peek out between my fingers and see that I've landed back on the exact stone by the Pool that I was sitting on earlier, and the rain is bouncing on the stones beside me.

I jump up from the stone again, and this time I'm running home. If Mam is still in bed looking at the wall, she won't see that my dress is sopping and covered with spots of rust. So she won't be cross.

38

'I didn't know we're allowed to use the library after school,' I say. I'm supposed to go straight home today. I woke with the sniffles and Nain said she had enough to do without having to look after me, so to be sure not to linger anywhere catching anything else from anyone once school was over. But Richard wanted help, and I like the library. And anyway, I got the sniffles after getting soaked yesterday; even my underwear and socks were wringing wet.

'We're not really,' says Richard. He pulls out a key from his blazer pocket and unlocks the library door with it. 'Miss Davies lets me have the key because I help her with shelving the books and writing overdue notes. She said I could use it if I wanted to work here after school.'

'D'you think she'd let me?' I say.

Richard closes the door behind us, turning the handle so it doesn't bang. It's tranquil in the library. Voices come from afar calling out the scores on the tennis courts and instructions to people on the field practising their running and jumping for sports day. The dark clouds disappeared overnight taking the rain with them but the field must be sodden. Through the library windows

I can see beyond the sports field to Eryri where the mountains seem close enough for me to reach out and touch them.

'It's going to rain again,' I say.

'Never,' says Richard. 'It's bright sunshine out there. Look how clear and close Snowdon is.'

'That's why,' I say. 'It's never the way it seems out there.'

'Oh, you.' Richard moves towards the bookshelves opposite the window.

'Really, though, d'you think Miss Davies would let me read in the library after school?' I say. 'Perhaps let me do my homework?'

'Maybe,' he says. 'She lets me come here because she knows what it's like at home when Dad's got the black dog. She says she can hear him sometimes from her flat.'

'I didn't know you had a dog,' I say. 'You never said. Does it bark a lot, then?'

He laughs. 'Haven't you heard that before?' he says. 'Having the black dog? It means being depressed. I told you about Dad being depressed after the war from all that flying and dropping bombs. Mum says he's in good company, though; even Winston Churchill has the black dog. Trouble is, it makes Dad angry. He never shouts at Mum or Caroline but he goes on and on at me. I could tell Miss Davies about your mother being cross with you all the time, if you like.'

I shake my head. 'I'll ask her,' I say

The black dog is not a real dog. I was looking at the answer all the time, and I couldn't see it. Why didn't I know that? Why didn't I guess it? So, the dog I saw with Ifan Evans last Christmas was Mot after all. And when I remembered what happened I imagined it was a bigger and fiercer dog because I was so afraid of it when it licked the fox's blood from me. And that's why Angharad, or maybe it was

Catrin, couldn't see the dog – because there wasn't a dog there, not a real one, only an invisible beast that made Ifan Evans behave like a beast himself. So, when Catrin used the poker to hit and hit the black dog that wasn't there she must have hit and hit . . . The blood on the floor can't have come from a dog that wasn't there, it must have been Ifan Evans's blood. My stomach starts to ache. Catrin, my little wren. Now I know why Mrs Evans confessed; now I understand. It wasn't just Guto she wanted to save.

'Gwenni.' Richard shakes my arm. 'Did you hear me? I have to find out about eye colour and stuff for biology. Do you want to help me with this homework or not?'

Do I? I look around the library. There are shelves and shelves weighed with books that are full of stories or ideas, or best of all, with both. Would one of these books have told me about the black dog? And there are shelves and shelves still empty. If all the shelves were filled with books, would I be able to learn everything in the world there is to know from them? Would they tell me what to do now? I put my hand into the front pocket of my satchel, and feel for my blotter rocker. Will this tell me what to do? Mrs Evans said: Keep us in your heart. Sergeant Jones said: This is how Elin wants it. And now I know why. I don't need to read anything to know what to do. I do nothing. I let it go. Like a good detective.

Richard reaches for a large book with a dust jacket so faded I can't see its title. 'Here,' he says. 'This should have something about it. Let's sit at that table by the window.'

I leave the rocker in my satchel and carry the book over to the table. The tops of the pages are covered in dust, and I blow a small cloud off them. I rub my eyes with my sleeve.

'Look at your eyes watering,' says Richard. 'You're not crying, are you?'

'It's the dust,' I say. 'And I've got a cold.'

'Don't give it to me,' Richard says. He puts two more volumes down on the table. 'I think that book you've got is probably best; I think it's one Miss Edwards gave the library from her own books.' He pulls a bag of sweets from his pocket and puts it on the table. 'D'you want a Black Jack?' He takes one and peels the paper off it. 'I thought they were your favourites. That's why I got them.'

'Thanks,' I say. 'I don't want one just now. And anyway, we're not supposed to eat in here.'

Richard tuts and puts the bag of sweets back in his pocket. 'If I look stuff up, will you write it down?' he says. 'But start with my eyes. What colour are they?'

I concentrate on his eyes. They're the colour of Catrin's eyes. Luminous as the rockpools the tide leaves behind in the summer sun. Blue, with the shadow of grey rocks and a little bit of sandiness in the depths.

'Blue,' I say.

'Your eyes are green, with chips of blue,' he says. 'Green eyes are unusual, aren't they? I've never seen any before. We'll do your family colours too. Write down mine and yours.'

It's like the family tree Mrs Evans showed me how to make, but with colours instead of names. I take my tin of coloured pencils and my roughbook from my satchel and draw two trees, then I colour a bright blue eye on one for Richard and an emerald green eye on the other for me. They look like leaves.

'My mum and my dad have got blue eyes,' says Richard. 'It's a bit boring, really. Look, it shows you here.' He points at a diagram in the book. 'Two blue-eyed parents will have a blue-eyed child. It's a bit obvious, isn't it?'

I take up my bright blue pencil and colour two more blue eyes on Richard's tree for his mother and father. 'So, Caroline's 'got blue eyes too,' I say, and when Richard nods I put a blue eye on the tree for her.

'That was too easy,' says Richard. 'Who do you get your green eyes from?'

'Tada,' I say. Mam always says Tada must have cats in the family somewhere. I colour Tada's eye in emerald green on my tree.

'What colour are your mother's eyes?' says Richard.

'Blue.' I colour Mam's eye the same blue as Richard's, though they're not the same. But I have only one blue pencil.

'See, that's a bit more interesting,' says Richard, pointing at the diagram again. 'One blue-eyed parent and one green-eyed parent can have children with blue or green eyes. Mmm . . .' He begins to leaf through the book. 'I wonder what else you can determine.'

In the hush of the library ideas and stories and information lie quietly in the books until somebody needs them. They don't clamour for attention.

'This genetic stuff is really interesting,' says Richard. He looks at my roughbook. 'Perhaps it would look more scientific if you drew a proper diagram.'

'I like drawing it this way,' I say. 'And it describes it better.'

'I'll do a proper diagram when I get home,' says Richard. 'I didn't have to spend any extra time looking up Caroline's since she's the same as me. But Caroline says she told Bethan I'd find out about hers as well. They think it's a waste of time to come to the library at lunchtime.'

'No,' I say.

'No what?' he says. 'Not find out about Bethan's? We may as well. What colour are her eyes, blue or green?'

The silence travels around the shelves, and in and out of the books until every volume holds its breath.

'Brown,' I say.

'Brown?' Richard says. 'No, that can't be right. Look . . .' He moves the book around for me to see the scientific diagrams clearly. 'A blue-eyed parent and a green-eyed parent can't have a child with brown eyes.'

'Brown,' I say and colour Bethan's eye with my only brown pencil, which makes it look as if it's a leaf that has changed colour and is about to fall from the family tree.

39

'You're a bit quiet, Gwenni,' says Nain. 'What's the matter? Is it your mam? She's been up and about today; she must be feeling better.' Nain's preparing supper in the scullery. The potatoes are peeled and in their saucepan and she's scraping baby carrots over a sheet of newspaper.

'Tada took her to see Dr Edwards this morning,' I say. 'Maybe he gave her some more new tablets. I don't know. Tada's taken her out for some fresh air.'

Nain stops scraping and looks at me. 'Cheer up. Worse things happen at sea.'

Do they? I make my mouth smile at her.

'Hmm,' she says. 'Well, don't stand there like an ornament. Help me with these.'

I pick up a baby carrot and scrape it and hand it to Nain to wash. Then I scrape another one and pop it into my mouth and crunch it. Sweet baby carrots are my second-favourite vegetable in the world. Broad beans are my first.

'Are you here for your supper?' says Nain.

I shake my head. 'We had chips from the chip shop,' I say,

'and egg. Tada fried mine hard the way I like it. I fetched the chips. Greasy Annie was asking after Mam, I think; I never know what she means. And she said not to take a dish for the chips again; she wraps them in paper now.'

'Take no notice of her,' says Nain. 'She's not a nice woman, that Annie. I'm never sure if she's not a ha'penny short of a shilling. Something went wrong when she was born. Her poor mother nearly died and Annie was ill for a long time. Just before I had Lol; that's why I remember it.'

'Is Greasy Annie the same age as Aunty Lol?' I say. 'She looks as old as you, Nain.'

Nain peers at me over her spectacles and laughs. 'She must really look old, then, Gwenni.'

Nain's skin is wrinkled like the prunes Mam used to soak for breakfast and she wears her grey plait twisted round and round her head so that she looks like the witch that tried to capture Hansel and Gretel. But I don't tell her that.

'It's hard for you to think that we were all young once, just like you, Gwenni,' says Nain.

It's true. 'What did you like to do when you were young, Nain?' I ask her. I slip another tiny carrot into my mouth.

'Oh, like,' she says. 'That didn't come into it. I left school at twelve and went into service as a maid. It was hard work, but by the time I was in my twenties I was housekeeper of a big house in London. Then I came home to the farm to look after the younger ones for Tada when Mam died.'

'And you met Taid,' I say.

'And I met Taid,' she says. 'You did what you had to do in those days, Gwenni.'

What does that mean? 'I saw Taid's gravestone in the cemetery when I was looking for dates for my family tree,' I say.

'Did you, now?' says Nain. She scrumples up the newspaper with the carrot scrapings and takes it to the compost bucket outside the back door. The lid clangs like a bell when she drops it back in place.

'And his other wife's,' I say.

'Sarah,' says Nain.

I nod. 'And all her dead babies.'

'Another thing about those days,' says Nain. 'The babies came regular as clockwork. Poor Sarah, she never got over losing so many, and the last one killed her.'

'William,' I say. 'The daring young man on the flying trapeze.'

'Your father was very fond of Wil,' says Nain. 'But Wil flew away just like Lloyd George. Saw his chance and left. Except Wil never flew back again.' She holds the pan with the carrots in it under the tap and runs water into it, then gives it a shake.

'Bethan says Miss Edwards told her class that you don't have to have babies if you don't want to. You can have contraception instead.'

'Whatever next,' says Nain. 'The things they teach you at school these days.'

'So why did Mam have me when she didn't want to have me, Nain?'

'Of course your mother wanted you,' says Nain.

'She says she didn't,' I say.

'That's just her nerves talking,' says Nain. 'Take no notice of her.'

'But she never says it to Bethan.'

Nain doesn't say anything. She concentrates on reaching for the saucepan lids from the top of the wall cupboard.

'I know about Bethan,' I say. 'About Tada not being her father.'

'Hush,' says Nain. One of the lids drops from her hand to the stone floor where it rings and rings until she puts her foot on it. 'How?'

I shrug. I promised not to tell, didn't I?

'Nanw Lipstick's girl; goes without saying,' says Nain. She bends down and picks up the lid. 'Leave it alone, Gwenni. It's up to your mother and father to tell Bethan, not you.'

'I wouldn't tell Bethan,' I say. 'But I don't understand, Nain.'

'Do you have to understand?'

I nod. 'I do,' I say.

Nain sighs and rubs her hand along her forehead. 'Let's get these pans on the fire, Gwenni. You take the small one through for me, and don't pinch any more carrots or there won't be enough for Lol's supper.'

We carry the pans into the living room and when Nain has poked the fire just right and put the pans exactly where they should be on the coals, she sits in her rocking chair and I sink down and down into the old leather armchair. Lloyd George shuffles on his perch and gives a soft sigh.

'I don't know,' says Nain. 'I suppose I'm about do the right thing here. It must be better for me to tell you than for you to hear dribs and drabs of old gossip.'

There's no book in any library that will tell me this story. 'Please, Nain,' I say. 'You've always told me how useful it is to know things so you don't go and put your foot in it.'

'Hmm,' says Nain. 'This is a bit different, Gwenni. A bit near to home. Well, listen closely, because I'm not telling you twice.' She leans back in her chair and begins to rock slowly; the chair gives a faint creak every time she rocks forwards. 'Your mother and father married when your father was on leave from the army. He only had a few days. People were marrying like that all over the country then, in haste, because of the war. Everyone was afraid that they'd never get a chance to marry their sweethearts; that they might die fighting, you know.' Nain glances up at Uncle Idwal's picture on the wall. 'Your grandmother wasn't well so your mother decided to carry on living with her until your father came back again.'

'I know about her, too,' I say. 'But not everything. Alwenna didn't know everything.'

'Well, there's a surprise,' says Nain. 'Nanw Lipstick usually manages to invent anything she doesn't know.' She stops rocking and stands up to take the lid off the carrot pan. 'Bit slow this evening, this fire.' She rattles under the pans with the poker. The phoenix poker; but I won't think about that.

'It was nerves with your grandmother, too,' she says. 'I'm not quite sure what happened to her, your mother never said anything except that your grandmother had gone to Dinbych for treatment for her nerves. I don't know how she died. She'd have been in her forties then, and that's not old enough to die, whatever you may think, Gwenni.'

'Alwenna said she went . . . she had bad nerves because Mam was having Bethan. But why, Nain?'

'Oh dear, Gwenni, you're very persistent. I suppose if I don't tell you you'll be off asking someone else.' Nain lowers herself back into her rocking chair. 'Let me think,' she says. The chair begins to rock; creak, creak, creak. 'Now, Gwenni, do you know how long a baby takes to grow in its mother's belly?'

Rabbit babies take a month. I don't know how long a human baby takes. I shake my head.

'Nine months,' says Nain. 'When your mother lived with your other Nain, I used to write to her regularly and she used to reply. I never got to see her; it was difficult then, what with one thing and another.' She glances at Uncle Idwal's picture again. 'But she just turned up on the doorstep there, almost a year to the day she and your father married, with a letter in her hand from the army saying your father was coming home because he'd been shot in the leg, and with a belly out to here.' Nain holds her hand way out in front of her own belly.

'Is that why Tada has a limp?' I say.

'What?' says Nain. 'Yes. Yes. But can't you see what I'm trying to tell you, Gwenni? It was twelve months since your mother . . . saw your father last, and if it takes only nine months . . .'

'Yes, of course I can see what you're saying, Nain. I'm good at arithmetic. But I still don't understand.'

'What is there not to understand, for goodness' sake?' says Nain.

'Why it was bad for my other nain's nerves,' I say.

'I wish I'd never started this,' says Nain. Her chair begins to rock quicker; the faint creak turns into a loud groan. 'A woman who's married to one man isn't supposed to have another man's baby, Gwenni. It's just not right. Your grandmother was a big chapel woman and I expect she would have felt the shame of it too much to bear, especially since her nerves were already bad. I expect that's how it was. I don't really know. No one does except your mother, and she didn't tell anyone. And it was none of my business. And that's that.' She rubs her forehead with her hand. 'I think I've got a headache coming on,' she says. 'It's turned so close this evening. When are your mam and tada coming home from their walk? Did they say?'

'I don't know,' I say. 'But, Nain, it is my business, isn't it? I've got bits of her as well as you in me, haven't I?'

Nain shakes her head and doesn't reply.

'And,' I say, 'Alwenna said Mam sent the minister to meet

Tada off the train. Was that because having a baby that didn't belong to him was such a shameful thing?'

'It would have been a bit of a shock for your father, wouldn't it, just to walk into the house and find your mother like that?' says Nain. 'It was a bit of a shock for him. But he worshipped the ground your mother walked on and he decided that he'd bring Bethan up as his own. And that's what he's done. Bethan never needs to know.'

'She'll work it out, Nain,' I say, 'or one of her friends will. Miss Edwards gave them homework to work out how they get their eye colour and hair colour from their parents. I helped . . . someone do some work on it in the library at school today and I don't think Bethan could have got her eye colour from Mam and Tada.'

'You leave it alone,' says Nain. 'I'll speak to your father.'

'The homework's got to be in tomorrow,' I say, 'And, Nain, Alwenna says her mother knows who Bethan's father really was.'

'Stuff and nonsense,' says Nain. 'Your mother wasn't telling anyone and your father didn't want to know. And that's really that.' She gets up from her chair. 'Just look at the time. That Lol wanted me to try to tempt Lloyd George out of his cage for a bit. She'll be back herself soon.' Nain reaches for Lloyd George's cage door.

I make for the scullery door. 'I'll wait in our house,' I say, but Nain opens the cage before I reach the door. Lloyd George doesn't fly out. He scuffles along his perch to the other side of his cage from the door.

'Look at him,' says Nain. 'The silly bird won't come out at all since he came back from his great escape. Won't fly, won't speak. That Lol wants to take him to a doctor.' She rattles her finger along the bars of the cage but Lloyd George just huddles tighter against the bars on the far side.

'Dr Edwards?' I say.

'Some special doctor for birds in Bermo,' says Nain. 'I never heard such nonsense.'

Lloyd George perches with his back to the cage door and his head in his feathers. He looks like the trembling blue ball on old Dafydd Owen's windowsill. Except his feathers don't look so bright any more.

Nain hooks the cage door shut. 'He's probably learnt where his place is,' she says. 'No good ever came of not knowing your place.'

But I don't know where my place is. And what if I don't like my place when I find it?

40

Look, Bethan is home from school before me today, sitting in Mam's armchair, looking at something on her lap. For a minute I thought she was Mam, waiting to tell me off for being late.

I didn't walk back with Richard because he had Astronomy Club after school, so I went to the cemetery on the way home. Guto's jam jar was on its side on the babies' grave. I threw away the dead bluebells and picked some stems of cow parsley from the edges of the cemetery but they were too long to stand up in the jar so I spread a lacy cream shawl of them over Gwion and Nia. Because who else will do that for them now? And then I lay on my tombstone for a while looking up at the sky, because it's almost as good as flying in daylight. I thought about my place; maybe my place is in the sky. I thought about Bethan and Mam, and me and Tada, and how we've always been two families, not one. I thought about Nain telling Tada about the eye colour. Why didn't Tada keep Bethan home from school today? Or maybe he went to the school to ask Miss Edwards not to have the lesson. But he wouldn't do that; he's nervous of teachers, except for Mrs Evans. I didn't think about Mrs

Evans, or Catrin and Angharad; I just left them in my heart. And then I walked home.

It's dark to come into the living room from the bright daylight. And there's no fire in the grate to give any light or to boil the kettle or to cook supper. Maybe we're eating at Nain's house. But I can hear Mam humming in the scullery, so she hasn't taken to her bed again. Perhaps Dr Edwards is a good doctor after all, just as Aunty Lol says.

Bethan takes no notice of me. Now that my eyes have grown used to the dimness I can see that what she has on her lap is the box of photographs Tada gave me to look through for my family tree. Bethan begins to pick the photographs out of the box, one by one, and tear them in half and drop the two pieces on the floor. Why is she doing that? I lean forward to take the box away from her but she holds on to it with both hands.

'Why. Didn't. You. Tell. Me?' she says. She lifts the box and bangs it down on her lap with each word.

Nain didn't speak to Tada about the eye colour, did she? Or Tada would have done something about it, wouldn't he?

Bethan screams and throws the box at me, and the photographs she's left inside it flutter down over us both like huge snowflakes. 'Say something, you baby.' She jumps up from Mam's chair and kicks the photograph box across the room. 'That box is full of lies.' She prods me with her forefinger, just like Mam does, and I back towards the door. 'Didn't you go with Richard to the library yesterday to do the eye thing? Didn't you tell him my eyes are brown so Tada can't be my real father? Didn't you?'

'I just said your eyes were brown,' I say. 'Anyone can see that by looking at you. I didn't say Tada wasn't your father.'

She prods me again. 'You could have told me before I went to school to sit in the lab this afternoon and listen to stupid Miss

Edwards asking everyone about their homework, couldn't you? I didn't know what to say. At least I wasn't the only one. Two of the Llanbedr boys had the wrong eye colour, too.' She begins to snatch up the photographs from the floor and tear them into small pieces that she throws into the air. 'All lies,' she says. 'All lies.' She giggles. 'Miss Edwards got in a right flap and said we were moving on to a new subject. Only she couldn't think what. Stupid woman. She said to forget all about it. But it was too late, wasn't it? Wasn't it, Gwenni?' She throws the photograph she's started tearing at me and I catch it and look at it. It's of her and me sitting on Tada's lap. I was a tiny baby so Bethan must have been about a year old. Her hair is curly and she's waving at whoever took the photograph – Mam maybe, or Aunty Lol. Tada's got his arms wrapped about us both. So, when was it we started being two families? 'You could have told me. You could have warned me,' she shouts. 'You're so stupid, Gwenni.'

I could. But I listened to Nain instead. From now on I'll listen to my own head.

'Does Mam know?' I say.

'Of course she bloody knows,' says Bethan and she picks up more photographs and throws them at me. The floor looks as if a grey blizzard has blown over it. 'Why do you think she's shut herself in the scullery humming like a bloody bee? She won't tell me who, though.'

I could tell her Alwenna said everyone knows who, but my mind tells me that Bethan wouldn't want to hear what Alwenna said.

'One good thing is, you're not my proper sister,' says Bethan. 'Maybe now people will stop thinking I must be odd just because you are. I expect you get it from Ta— your father's family. So it won't be in me. That's one good thing. I don't want to be a stupid baby like you.' She stamps her foot on the floor. 'Writing silly stories.' Stamp. 'Talking to dolls.' Stamp. 'Playing silly games.' Stamp. 'Stupid. Stupid. Stupid.' Stamp. Stamp. Stamp.

A draught bangs the living room door against the back of my legs as the front door opens.

'Nothing like coming home,' says Tada, as he does every day when he comes back from work. 'Nowhere like home.' He pushes the front door shut with his foot. 'And here are my lovely girls. But where's your mam? She hasn't gone back to her bed, has she?'

Before Tada can even take off his beret, Bethan leaps at him and begins to slam him with her fists.

'Whoa,' he says. 'That hurts, Bethan.'

'Did you know you're not my father?' she shouts at him.

Tada drops his dinner sack on the floor and manages to catch hold of Bethan's wrists. 'What are you saying, Bethan?' he says.

'You heard me,' she says. She tries to free her wrists. 'You're hurting me. You've got no right to do this. You're not my father.'

Tada lets go of her wrists. 'Of course I'm your father,' he says. He looks at the torn photographs strewn across the floor. 'Where's your mam?'

'In the scullery,' I say, and I can hear her still humming in there as if there is no noise and confusion at all going on in the living room. Tada takes his beret from his head and hands it to me. It's stiff and grey with all the dust from the stones he works with all day, and moulded into the shape of his head.

'Magda.' He calls Mam from where he stands instead of going to find her.

The humming stops and Mam opens the scullery door and walks into the living room. She looks at Bethan and smiles, then drops into her armchair.

'What have you been saying to Bethan, Magda?' says Tada.

Mam smiles and smiles but doesn't say anything. He turns to Bethan. 'You know your mam isn't well. You mustn't take any notice of what she says when she's like this. She's not herself.'

Bethan begins to labour him with her fists again and this time he doesn't try to stop her. Dust rises from his old work coat, and he pinches his nose to stop a sneeze. His hand is rough and red. Sometimes, especially in winter, his hands are dry and cracked and bleeding from working the stones, and he softens them with glycerine when he comes home.

'Mam didn't tell me. I found out at school.' Bethan screams the words at him as if he's not standing right there in front of her.

'Hush now, Bethan. Hush,' he says. He looks as if he's out for a walk and has lost his way. He turns to Mam. 'Magda, how could that happen? At school?'

Mam smiles at the living room; when she looks at Bethan her smile grows bigger. She doesn't look at me at all. I'm invisible.

'Biology,' I say. 'The biology homework, Tada. Remember? Miss Edwards gave Bethan's class homework to do about their eye colour. You can't have brown eyes unless one of your parents has.'

'You keep out of it,' says Bethan. Her brown eyes are shiny.

'Is that right?' says Tada. 'About the eyes. Is that right?'

'I don't care you're not my father,' Bethan says to him. He staggers back against the door post as if she's hit him harder than she did with her fists. 'I always knew I didn't belong to you. Gwenni's your favourite. Well, she's not anybody else's favourite. She's too peculiar. So, you can have her. I've got a proper father now. And I want you to tell me who it is. Tell me. Tell me.' She beats him again.

Tada's face is as white as his teeth and his freckles look as if they're about to jump off his face. 'I don't know, Bethan,' he says.

'Your mam never told me and I never asked. I've always – always – thought of you as my own.'

'Well, I'm bloody not,' says Bethan.

Tada's green eyes widen but Mam's smile is now so big the rest of her could disappear behind it like the Cheshire Cat.

'Elfyn Jones from Llanbedr said lots of women round here had chance babies in the war,' says Bethan. 'He said the camp in Llanbedr was full of American airmen and when they got sent back to America after the war they had to leave their girlfriends behind even if they were expecting.' She twirls away from Tada towards Mam. 'My father's an American, isn't he, Mam? Did he have to leave you to go back to America? Maybe he's a film star like . . . like Dean Martin . . . or Marlon Brando. Or a rock and roll singer. I'd like to have a famous father. Not some bloody old stone mason.'

But she wasn't born at the end of the war, she was born during it. I don't say this out loud.

And now Bethan has started to cry. Mam jumps up out of her chair and puts her arms around her. 'You're mine. Mine. Mine,' she says. 'All mine. Nobody else's.'

Bethan pushes Mam away from her. 'But I'm my father's, too,' she says. She wipes her brown eyes with the palms of her hands.

'Your father's dead,' says Mam. 'It's just you and me. You and me.'

Bethan opens her mouth wide and screams. John Morris races out from under Tada's chair towards the scullery and I put my hand into Tada's rough fist and he holds it tight.

In the silence that follows the scream, the mantelpiece clock's tick-tock is loud. I look up at the clock and see the Toby jugs almost falling off their shelf as they strain to watch and listen. They're straining so hard their faces are crimson.

Bethan steps back towards Mam and takes hold of her shoulders and begins to shake her. 'How do you know?' she says. 'Did someone write from America to tell you?'

Mam gives a moan and covers her mouth with her hands. Bethan lets go of her and she falls back into her chair and begins to rock backwards and forwards in it.

'Who was he?' Bethan shouts.

Mam shakes her head and rocks and rocks.

Tada squeezes my hand. 'Go and get your nain,' he says. 'Ask her to come to help.'

'I'm not letting her help me,' says Bethan. 'She's not my grandmother because you're not my father. My grandmother's American.'

As I run to find Nain the clock ticks louder and louder into the disturbed air as if it's a bomb that's about to explode. Like the bomb left over from the war that washed up on the beach and left a big, empty crater in the sand.

41

'So, Bethan didn't come to school today,' says Richard. 'Mind you, she's not the only one. Miss Edwards isn't here either. She looked as if she was going to collapse yesterday when she realised what she'd done setting that homework. You know those bulgy eyes she's got? And her mouth was hanging open. Just like a fish gasping for air. We never had things like this happen in my old school.'

I walk behind him because he's walking so fast I can't quite catch up and he talks to me over his shoulder. He makes it sound exciting. But it wasn't exciting for Bethan or the Llanbedr boys, was it? Or Miss Edwards. Richard reaches a patch of the school field that suits him and sits down. I drop to the grass next to him. He watches me like Kitty Hawk. 'Well?' he says.

'Tada thought it would be better if she stayed home,' I say. 'She's upset, and tired.'

She wore herself out shouting and screaming at Tada last night. And shouting in her sleep and pummelling me half the night. Every time I tried to rise from the bed and fly into the sky, she shouted at me or hit me and I fell right back again. Tada said

I could stay home, too, if I was tired. But I made up my mind to come to school.

'Caroline said Bethan went straight home yesterday,' Richard says. 'She wondered what happened. Did your mother say . . . you know . . . who Bethan's father is?'

'No,' I say.

'It's a predicament,' says Richard. I'll have to look that up in the dictionary. 'The worst thing is that Caroline upset Mum. She said she wished she had a different mother. Poor Mum couldn't stop crying.'

The worst thing? I don't think so.

There's a roar behind us and the scent of new cut grass as the school groundsman swerves his tractor towards us on his way around the field. He must be making the ground ready for sports day. Blades of cut grass and clover spatter us as he passes and we watch as he spatters several other groups sitting on the grass.

Richard stands up and brushes the bits from his blazer. 'He's doing that on purpose,' he says. 'It's typical of that sort of person.'

'That's Mr Jones, Aneurin's father,' I say. 'He comes to our Chapel.'

Richard watches the tractor, then shrugs and sits down again. 'So, what happened with Bethan?' he says.

I cross my fingers. 'Nothing,' I say.

'Oh, well,' says Richard. He stretches out on the grass and leans back on his elbows. 'It's getting darker. Look at Snowdon, it's disappeared. You don't have to have lived here for ever to guess what that means.'

'Rain, rain, rain,' says Alwenna's voice behind us. She sits next to me on the grass and picks at the clover heads.

Richard scowls at her. 'What's that in English?' he says.

I tell him. Alwenna ignores him. 'I heard, then,' she says. 'Does she know, your Bethan? Did your mam say who it was?'

'No,' I say. And because it's Alwenna, who is still my Kindred Spirit, I say, 'Bethan thinks it's an American. You know, off the camp during the war. She thinks all Americans are film stars or rock and roll singers, so she's pleased with that idea.'

'Mam says she must have had a heck of a shock,' says Alwenna. 'I know I would if I suddenly found out Tada wasn't my father.'

'She screamed and shouted at Tada a lot,' I say. 'I don't know why. It's not his fault he's not her father. And she screamed and shouted a lot in her sleep.' I don't mention trying to fly.

'But what happened in the end?' says Alwenna.

'Tada sent me to fetch Nain,' I say. 'And she tried to calm Bethan down, but all Bethan would say was that she wasn't her real grandmother so she didn't have to listen to her.'

'Then what?' says Alwenna.

'Then Bethan and I got sent to bed,' I say. 'And she hit me all night instead of Tada.'

'Will you two speak English so I know what you're on about?' says Richard.

'Time you knew some Welsh, Richard,' says Alwenna in English. 'You've lived here long enough.' Then she leaps to her feet and waves both her arms. 'Aneurin. Aneurin,' she calls.

Since Sunday Aneurin winks at me every time he sees me. I don't know why, but I do know that I don't want him to do that. I pull at Alwenna's skirt. 'Tell him to stop winking at me,' I say.

'Tell him yourself,' says Alwenna. 'He's only being friendly.'

'But why is he being friendly?' I say.

'Because he's grown up a bit? Because you both agreed about Saint Deilwen? Because he's not afraid of you any more?' says Alwenna. 'I don't know. Ask him.'

Afraid of me? I think about this, and when Aneurin comes closer and bobs his quiff at us, I say, 'Why are you being so friendly all of a sudden, Aneurin?'

He stands back for a moment, and then he grins. 'Why not?' he says. 'No special reason.' And he winks at me.

'Don't wink at me,' I say. 'I don't like it.'

'Fine,' says Aneurin, and bobs his quiff sideways at me instead. He looks so comic it makes me laugh.

'Don't wink at her,' says Richard. 'She's my girlfriend.'

What? 'I'm your friend, not your girlfriend,' I say.

Richard stands up. 'It's nearly time for the bell,' he says. 'I've got double chemistry next. I may as well go and prepare for that as sit here with you lot jabbering in Welsh. It's as bad as being in class. What's the point of having a lesson in English when everyone speaks to the teacher in Welsh?'

'Hang on, Richard,' says Aneurin. 'I wanted to ask you about Astronomy Club. How to go about joining and that . . . do I just turn up?'

'What sort of telescope have you got?' says Richard.

'Telescope? I haven't got one . . . I just thought I'd see what it was all about . . . you know . . .' Aneurin kicks at a mound of cut grass.

'It's about astronomy. Not much point in joining if you haven't got a telescope to look at the sky, is there?' Richard looks towards Mr Jones on his tractor. 'You probably can't afford one,' he says and strides away. Over his shoulder he calls, 'And it's all in English.'

'Idiot,' says Alwenna. 'Who does he think he is?'

Aneurin turns to me, scuffling his feet in the grass. 'I just wanted to say sorry about your Bethan and that.' He kicks some of the cut grass about and does his sideways nod. Behind him

Edwin bobs his head in agreement, then gives Alwenna a fluttery wave of his hand. And they both wander away.

'But what's Bethan going to do?' says Alwenna, as if our conversation had never been interrupted.

'I don't know,' I say. I watch Richard disappear into the school building.

'She's got a right to know who her father is, hasn't she? Don't you think?' says Alwenna. 'You know who I was talking about that time, don't you?'

I nod. 'How do you know it's true?' I say. 'It's only what your mam thinks. Perhaps her father is an American. Mam will never tell her, so she may as well believe what she wants.'

'Paleface didn't fight in the war like your tada and mine, remember?' says Alwenna. 'He was an essential something or other. And your mother lived right nearby him with your nain. I told you all this.'

'But that doesn't prove anything,' I say. 'There were hundreds of women nearby. Why pick my mam?'

'I don't know, do I?' says Alwenna. 'But she's the only one who's gone doolally because he died, isn't she? Even his own wife didn't . . . well, she killed him, I know . . . but d'you see what I mean?'

She didn't kill him but I won't think about that. I shake my head. 'It still doesn't prove it.'

'And he had dark brown eyes exactly like Bethan's,' says Alwenna.

I shake my head again. I don't want to tell anyone about Mam swimming with Ifan Evans, not even Alwenna. I won't tell Alwenna maybe she's right. I won't tell Bethan.

And Mam isn't so doolally; she's much better after the new tablets Dr Edwards gave her instead of the old ones. She smiles all the time.

'What's going to happen to you all?' says Alwenna.

'I don't know,' I say. 'I don't know.' I look at the storm clouds massed over the Wyddfa advancing like an army upon us. Low, dark clouds carrying rain that begins to fall in drops large as shillings, shiny and silver and hard. Alwenna and I jump up and run for the shelter of the school just as the bell jangles to tell us our time is up anyway.

42

I don't know why my feet are taking me along this road. There are plenty of other roads to walk. Maybe I need to take notice of my feet as well as listen to my own head. Maybe my feet are telling me something my head doesn't know.

The rain at dinnertime didn't clear the air much. It's almost difficult to breathe. Look, the clouds have a tinge of green, which means more rain is coming. It's dark enough to be twilight although it's only teatime.

My stomach rumbles. It feels empty. School dinner was my favourite, macaroni cheese, but although my stomach wanted it, my mouth couldn't eat any of it.

There was no one home after school except Mam. She was in her chair, with John Morris on her lap, listening to *Mrs Dale's Diary* as if none of the terrible things had happened. She said Bethan was out with Caroline and not to be late for tea. She wasn't even cross that I'd interrupted Mrs Dale. Was it Dr Edwards's strong tablets that made her so happy and stopped the shake in her hands?

Or have I dreamt everything? Maybe I'm still dreaming. Have

I gone to sleep and not woken up? People do that, it's called being in a coma. But if I'm in a coma, how did it happen? And how would I know if I'm awake or asleep? Alice in Wonderland thought she was awake when she was, in fact, asleep and dreaming. Like Catrin in her story. How will *Catrin in the Clouds* end?

See, whether I'm dreaming or not, my feet are determined to take me this way. But they're not taking me to look into the Baptism Pool today. I can smell the Pool from the road. Maybe the stench is from all the sins that have been washed away in the water. I hadn't thought of that. It must be nice to have all the bad things you've ever done simply washed away. But where does all the water go that's full of sins?

Did the water in the Reservoir wash away all Ifan Evans's sins? Have we been drinking them? My stomach lurches as well as rumbling. The big wall between the road and the Reservoir hides the water from sight and I can pretend it's not there. But my feet hurry me past all the same.

Mrs Williams is standing outside Penrhiw, leaning on her gate and looking up the road. Her head has sunk down into her shoulders since I saw her at Ifan Evans's funeral. She looks like a little gnome in a fairy story. I scuffle my feet to make a noise and she turns towards me.

'What a lonely old road this is now, Gwenni,' she says. 'A lonely old road. Where are you off to? Are you going to Brwyn Coch?'

Is that where my feet are taking me? I make an I-don't-know shrug at Mrs Williams.

'It's like the grave, that house, Gwenni. Like the grave. I don't know who Twm Edwards will ever get to live there again. I don't know what's happening to this town. We'll never be the same again, any of us, that's for sure. Your nain was saying the exact same thing to me the other day. She said: It's as if something's come along and turned us all upside down and given us a good shake before setting us on our feet again, Bessie. But you're young, Gwenni. You'll get over it.' Mrs Williams snuffles and puts her arms around me and clutches me to her large bosom. Her bosom is soft as a cloud with a powdery smell that makes me sneeze. 'Listen to me being an old misery.' She pushes me away. 'Off you go,' she says. 'Do what you have to do, Gwenni. But don't dwell on things. It's not good for you. Now, don't stay up there too long. There's more rain coming from the looks of that sky, if not something worse.' She gives me another little push to send me on my way.

My feet have brought me to the field gate for Brwyn Coch. In my head I'm not sure that this is where I want to be. Will Brwyn Coch be like the grave? I pick some of the spiky corn-flowers growing in the grass at the foot of each gatepost, though I don't know who the flowers are for.

I push through the gate and latch it behind me. The sheep gather in groups to huddle in the shelter of the stone wall. They jostle and push until they're squeezed together. Do they sense the coming rain? Maybe there is worse coming. I linger for a moment and watch the sky and the sea merge on the horizon into streamers of grey-green and violet. My feet quicken their pace, across the field and over the stone stile, but they slow again as I approach Brwyn Coch so that they're barely moving when I reach the cottage.

I peer through the front window into the parlour. The panes are clear and cold as ice under my palm. But it's dark inside and difficult to see anything. And what would there be to see? No shelves sagging with books, no fire flickering in the inglenook, no desk balancing towers of exercise books on its polished surface. I try the kitchen front window. I can see the gleam of the tap above the sink under the back window, but that's all. It is silent here; but not like the grave. The graves and the tombs in the cemetery tell me the stories of the people who lie in them, even if it's only to tell me a short, short tale like that of Gwion and Nia. This is just an empty house, not a grave I can read or talk to. It may as well be the crumbled heap of stones and slate I saw in my premonition. There's nothing left here of Mrs Evans and Angharad and Catrin. I have the only thing left; the blotter rocker in my pocket. I take it with me everywhere.

My stomach begins to hurt. I sit down on the front step and pull my knees into my stomach to ease the pain. Somewhere across the bay in the violet evening are Angharad and Catrin. But not Mrs Evans. She's a prisoner in Chester; that's all the way to England. An innocent prisoner. Who knows her secret? I do, and I think Sergeant Jones has guessed. Angharad knows, but does she understand? And did Mrs Evans tell her sister? Miss Cadwalader is stern with Angharad and Catrin. What will they do without their mother? Everyone says that Mrs Evans will go to jail for the rest of her life. Is that true? Everyone except Tada and Sergeant Jones says she deserves it. I look at the flowers in my hand; there's no reason to leave them here. I keep Mrs Evans and Angharad and Catrin in my heart, the way Mrs Evans asked me to. I'll write their story into *Catrin in the Clouds*, and maybe one day, a long, long time in the future, I'll give it to Catrin so that she'll understand. Maybe.

Another spasm shoots through my stomach and I pull my knees tight to it again and wait for the pain to pass. This is how I flew when I was young, this is the way I showed Angharad and Catrin, and poor Guto when he was trying to show me how he flew. Why won't it work?

My mind tells me I should go now. Leave Brwyn Coch and never come here again. My stomach pain has eased but when I stand up the inside of my head becomes a merry-go-round of movement and colour. I grab the doorpost and stand up still and straight and shake my head hard to clear the sensation.

I look straight down over the field to the bay. It's impossible to see where the water ends and Llŷn begins. Wraiths of mist curl low over the field. Tada says they rise from water; from bogs and streams, rivers and lakes, even from wet fields. Have these wraiths risen from the stream or from the Reservoir? Some of them float up towards the house, though there's no breeze to push them along. The biggest is shaped like a man. What if it's Ifan Evans's spirit risen from the Reservoir? Before my head can decide anything, my feet begin to run, faster than they've ever run before, across the field, over the stile, through the gate, past Penrhiw, past the Reservoir hiding behind the wall, past the Baptism Pool full of sins, down the hill, along the high street, and they don't stop until I'm standing on my own front doorstep, still holding the bunch of cornflowers. I sink down to sit on the cold slate of the step and dig my knees into my stomach to stop it hurting so much.

43

Bethan cried herself to sleep tonight. I leave her hiccupping and snoring as I rise up, up, up into the sky where the air is as soft to rest upon as Mrs Williams Penrhiw's powdery bosom. Up here, far away from everybody, the night is peaceful; there's no sound except the hum of the Earth. At school, when I sang the note to Mr Hughes Music he said it was B flat but he laughed when I said it was the note the Earth hummed. He said: You'll be hearing the music of the spheres next, Gwenni. But he doesn't know how the Earth's deep, never-ending note clothes me in rainbow colours, fills my head with all the books ever written, and feeds me with the smell of Mrs Sergeant Jones's famous vanilla biscuits and the strawberry taste of Instant Whip and the cool slipperiness of glowing red jelly. I could stay up here for ever without the need for anything else in the whole world.

I drift above the town. Now and then the clouds part to let moonbeams glance and glint on the roofs below. Almost all the house lights are out. I don't want to spend time above the town tonight, or fly up into the hills towards Brwyn Coch so I turn and swoop down to the castle, then up and over the Red Dragon waiting in its green and white cage, and out towards the sea. If I could fly across this sea, I could fly for ever. But the watchers see me; the eyes of millions, billions, trillions of shrimps, crabs, fishes, whales, mermaids, monsters are watching, watching to see if I dare to fly away. Tonight the smell of the sea is strong; a stench of fish and seaweed seems to rush towards me. Is this another premonition? Or maybe I'm too close.

My belly cramps with fear and I begin to plummet towards the water. First my feet, then my legs, touch the cold spray and I land half on top of Bethan and the bed is soaked. I scream and scream. Mam bangs on the wall and shouts, 'Be quiet, Gwenni, I need my beauty sleep.'

Then Bethan snorts and wakes and begins to shout, too. 'Mam, Mam, Gwenni's wet the bed.' She heaves herself out of it. 'You're disgusting, you stupid baby,' she says to me.

I'm lying here, cold and wet, as Mam comes through the door and switches on the light. It's so bright after the dark of the sky that I can't open my eyes. I can still smell the fish from the sea; perhaps I've brought some back with me, caught in my nightdress.

'Bethan, my own Bethan, your old things have started,' says Mam. 'I'll get you one of my cloths to put on. I'll have to buy you some proper pads tomorrow.'

'At last,' says Bethan. 'But I didn't think there'd be so much blood.'

I open my eyes into slits. There's blood everywhere. All over Bethan, all over me and all over the bed. I can feel it begin to dry and crimp on my arms. I try not to think about it.

'It just looks a lot because Gwenni's been tossing and turning in it,' says Mam. 'But we'll soon change that old sheet. Gwenni, get out of there.'

'What is it?' I say. 'What is it, Mam? Is it the fish?'

'Don't be silly, Gwenni,' says Mam. 'It's Bethan's old things started.'

'My period,' says Bethan. She begins to jig about. 'I've started, I've started,' she sings.

'I gave you that pamphlet about it, Gwenni,' says Mam. A long time ago she gave me a pamphlet from *Woman's Weekly*. I thought it was about eggs; I'm sure it didn't say anything about blood.

'Come on, Gwenni,' says Mam. 'I want to get back to my bed. You and Bethan take off those nightdresses, and you strip that sheet off. I'll have to put those in to soak in some salt right away or that blood will never come off.' She stops for a second, staring at something we can't see. 'It'll never come off,' she says. 'Never. Never.' She covers her mouth with her hands, then gives her head a little shake; she pulls her blue satin sash tight, tight around her dressing gown and goes out.

Bethan takes off her nightdress and rubs her arms and legs with it. I turn my back to Buddy Holly and try to take my nightdress off without it touching my face. Bethan's blood is all over it. I can still smell fish so I narrow my eyes and look all along the bed in case I've brought something back with me from the sea. Bethan rolls up her nightdress and throws it on the chair, right on top of Mari the Doll. I hold mine in front of me and try to rub the blood off my arms with its sleeves. Now, as well as the belly cramps I got because I was frightened, I've got that old family stomach. I try not to think about so much blood; I try not to think about the fox with the bleeding wound; I try not to think about the sticky floor at Brwyn Coch; I try not to think about Mrs Llywelyn Pugh and her blood running like a river under the bathroom door.

'Here, Bethan,' Mam says as she comes through the door. Her

hands shake as she gives Bethan a long piece of old towel and a pair of baggy knickers. 'You'll have to wear these for now. I'll get you a proper belt as well as the pads tomorrow.' Mam pushes Bethan's blood-stained nightdress and Mari the Doll off the chair and puts a fresh sheet and clean nightdresses on the seat. She wraps her arms around her middle and looks at us. 'You'll need a wet flannel, Gwenni,' she says. 'You can't get into a clean night-dress and a clean bed in that state. I suppose I'll have to get it for you.'

I stand shivering while Mam goes down to the scullery for the flannel. Bethan is trying to get the cloth folded into the knickers. 'Just wait until I tell Caroline,' she says. 'She thought she was starting last week, but she never did.'

I never, ever want to have periods.

John Morris is scrabbling at the back door but Mam shouts at him to go away. He starts yowling instead. Perhaps he can smell the fish, too. Nellie Davies will be opening her window to see what the noise is about in a minute.

The flannel, when Mam brings it up, is as cold as the seaspray. I rub hard to get the blood off where it's dried on my arms, and I dab and dab at my legs until the grey flannel turns bright red.

Bethan has stopped struggling with the knickers and is watching me. 'Mam, it isn't me,' she says. 'It's her. Look.'

She and Mam look at me. I try to cover myself with the flannel. I can feel something warm trickling down the inside of my left thigh, all the way down to my ankle and to the linoleum beneath my feet. I look down. It's blood.

'It's not fair,' says Bethan. 'Why are all the unfair things happening to me?'

'I don't want to have old things,' I say. 'You can have them.'

Mam is still watching me and watching the blood, but her

eyes are seeing something else. 'So much of it,' she says. 'It bloomed like the roses in her garden.'

'Whose garden?' says Bethan. 'What are you talking about now, Mam?' She pulls off the knickers and cloth and throws them at me. 'Here,' she says. 'It's just not fair. I should have started first. I'm older than her.' She snatches her nightdress from the chair and drags it over her head. She looks at Mari the Doll where she's tumbled on the floor and then she looks at me. 'Stupid doll,' she says and kicks Mari the Doll under the bed. 'What a baby you are, Gwenni.'

I have to stop the blood running. I pull the knickers on and arrange the cloth inside them. Then I rub my arms and legs dry with a patch of my nightdress that is clear of blood and put on my clean nightdress.

'Change the sheet, Gwenni,' says Mam. 'Take the dirty things and put them in some cold water in the sink, and put plenty of salt in with them. I'm going back to bed.' She leaves the bedroom with a swirl of her dressing gown and a gust of Evening in Paris that mingles with the smell of the fish. I hold my breath and look at Bethan. She's crying again.

'You made all the mess,' she says. 'You clear it up.' And she folds her arms and stands with her back to me looking at her picture of Buddy Holly and his Crickets, and her shoulders shake and shake.

44

I am as limp as Mari the Doll. I thought I would never walk up
the hill all the way home without having to lie down in the road.
My arms and my legs won't do what I want them to do and my
insides shake like Mam's hands. How many pints of blood did
Edwin say are in the human body? Eight? I don't think I've got
any left inside me. It's lucky Aunty Lol had plenty of pads to give
me this morning; Mam was in bed looking at the wall again.

I lean on the front door to stop my insides shaking and my
legs wobbling, but the door creaks open and I stumble backwards
into the house. Can I go upstairs out of the way without Mam or
Bethan noticing? I'm invisible to them, after all. I squeeze past
the hat-stand that takes up half the space at the bottom of the
stairs and a stinging smell smacks me in the face. I know what it
is but can't place it for a second. I sniff, not too hard. Perm lotion.
Perm lotion? Perm lotion means Aunty Siân.

The living room doorknob rattles as I turn it but no one in
the room hears me except the Toby jugs up on their high shelf
who look so bored they only just manage to swivel their eyes to
watch me in the doorway. This is like looking at a picture of a

happy family. Another picture that tells a lie. John Morris is asleep on Tada's chair with his head under the cushions, and Bethan is curled up like another cat in Mam's fireside chair, looking at a magazine. There's a pile of them on the floor by the chair leg. Aunty Siân always brings magazines with pictures in them that Mam and Bethan like to read. Mam sits on one of the hard chairs with her head covered in rows of pink curlers and Aunty Siân is carefully undoing one of them to test the curl in the hair. She has to stand sideways to do it because her baby bump is so big. She didn't have a bump at all last time I saw her.

'I think that's cooked, Magda,' Aunty Siân says. 'All we have to do now is put your head under the dryer. Stay there and I'll pull it over.' From behind the door she drags Aunty Lol's great big hairdryer that looks like a machine from outer space and stands it behind Mam's chair. 'Bethan,' she says, 'you'll have to get on the chair to plug this into the light. I'm too awkward.' And she holds both sides of her baby bump with her hands.

I push the door wide open and drop my satchel and hold my arms out to Aunty Siân.

'Gwenni. Gwenni,' she says, hugging me sideways. 'My dear little Gwenni.' Her baby bump is big and solid, though I'm sure I can feel something move in there. It must be the baby. I pull away in case I squash it. 'Look at you,' says Aunty Siân. 'How pretty you're getting, Gwenni.'

Pretty? It's not a word anyone else has ever used about me. But Aunty Siân means it even when it's not true.

'Gwenni can stick the dryer plug into the light now that she's here,' says Bethan. She picks up her magazine from where she's laid it on top of the pile.

'Fine,' says Aunty Siân. 'And you can put the kettle to boil and make us all a nice cup of tea, Bethan.' She turns her head so

Bethan can't see her and winks at me. 'I could do with a sit down and a cuppa.'

I drag a chair over under the light, click the switch off on the wall, then in the dimness climb the chair, take the bulb out and twist the plug from the hairdryer into the socket.

'Good girl, Gwenni,' says Aunty Siân. 'Now let me get this hood over your mam's head, and you clear the perm stuff away and we can all have a sit down. I expect you could do with a sit down, too, couldn't you?'

I could. But I clear the Toni home perm box and all the bits of cotton wool from the table and put them out in the dustbin. I put the dish with the smelly lotion in it into the sink to be washed and turn the tap on over it. It smells even stronger. Maybe I shouldn't have done that.

I walk to Tada's chair past Mam under the dryer. I smile at her, but she looks through me. I don't know what I've done this time. Unless it was having a period before Bethan. But what could I do about that?

I lift John Morris from Tada's chair so Aunty Siân can sit down. He doesn't want to move so he pretends to be dead and I carry him into the scullery with my hands under his fat body; his head and paws hang down one side and his tail and back legs hang down the other. He looks like poor Mrs Llywelyn Pugh's dead fox but I won't think about Mrs Llywelyn Pugh and her flowing blood or her dead fox. The scullery floor is hard and cold, and when I lay John Morris down on it he struggles to his feet and turns his back to me.

'Bring in the cake from the bottom of my bag in there, Gwenni,' calls Aunty Siân. I ease a round, upside-down cake tin from her bag and pull the bottom off. Inside the lid is a pretty doily and on the doily is a tall chocolate cake with thick white butter cream in the middle and chocolate icing on top. My favourite cake in the whole world.

I rinse my hands under the tap. Can Ifan Evans's sins get inside me through my skin? Maybe the smell from the perm lotion will drive his sins away. But I dry my hands quickly on the stripey towel, just in case, and hang the towel on its hook.

The scullery seems bigger and lighter since Tada distempered it a blue as pale as Mam's eyes. Or maybe I'm shrinking, like Alice. I wonder if all the faces drowned in the paint; there are patches here and there that could be mouths trying to bite their way through.

I pick up the tin lid with the cake on it and take it into the living room. The kettle is on the fire and Bethan is laying out cups and saucers on the table.

Aunty Siân makes a sound like a purring cat as she kicks off her shoes and stretches her legs out to rest her feet on the fender. 'This is the life,' she says. 'I could get used to this. So long as that fire doesn't start sparking like a firework again. Put Emlyn's cup out as well, Bethan. He won't be long, I'm sure.'

Bethan bangs Tada's cup on its saucer.

'Bethan,' says Aunty Siân.

'Sorry,' says Bethan.

Bethan takes notice of Aunty Siân. She likes her. Everyone likes Aunty Siân. She must have come on the train this morning; it takes a whole day to perm Mam's hair. What have Aunty Siân and Mam and Bethan been talking about all day?

Stuck under the dryer, Mam can't hear us. But she's smiling and I can just about hear her humming above the drone of the dryer. Does that mean she's all right now? I don't know. Her hands are trembling where they're clasped together in her lap.

'Cut the cake, Gwenni,' says Aunty Siân. 'A small piece for

me or I'll be the size of a house.' She wriggles her toes against the warmth of the fire. 'This is nice, isn't it? Like having a tea party. Your mam always liked a tea party. Maybe it'll cheer her up a bit.'

Tada distempered the scullery to cheer her up but it didn't work. Only Dr Edwards's tablets cheer her up. But when she is cheered up, is it on the inside as well as the outside?

With a hiss and a splutter the kettle boils, and Bethan pours the water onto the tea leaves in the teapot. We're waiting for the tea to brew when Tada comes in from work. Today, he doesn't say: There's nowhere like home. Instead, he says, 'I'll go up and get changed, Siân,' and leaves his jacket and beret and food sack on the hat-stand and goes upstairs.

Mam doesn't look as if she's heard him arrive. I watch the firelight flicker on our faces and for a moment we look like a family in one of Aunty Siân's magazines. With a machine from outer space in our midst. Maybe the aliens have captured Mam and left her empty, smiling shell behind. I don't say this out loud.

'Let's have a look at your mam,' says Aunty Siân, and she heaves herself out of Tada's chair to take the dryer hood off Mam's head. I'm sure I can see steam coming from some of the curlers and Mam's ears are scarlet. It must be hot inside that hood. Perhaps the aliens have cooked Mam's brain.

Aunty Siân undoes one of the curlers. 'Feels dry,' she says. 'Bethan, switch this thing off. And Gwenni, you get up on the chair again and unhook it. Here, I'll pass you the bulb to put back in.'

When I put the bulb back in the light comes on with a loud pop and I nearly fall off the chair. Black spots dance in front of my eyes.

'Silly me,' says Bethan. 'I switched it on too soon.'

'Don't make a fuss, Gwenni,' says Mam. I jump at the sound

of her voice. All I'm doing is rubbing my eyes so I can see to get down.

'Bethan,' says Aunty Siân, 'you be more careful. Gwenni could have been hurt. Come down, Gwenni; give me your hand. A nice piece of cake will sort you out.'

Then she carries on taking out Mam's curlers until Mam's head has yellow worms crawling all over it. The yellow has a greenish tinge, but no one else mentions it so I don't either.

'Has it taken?' says Mam.

'Definitely,' says Aunty Siân. 'We'll leave it to cool thoroughly, Magda, and comb it later. No point in risking a frizz.'

Aunty Siân's hair is a natural frizz. She always says what she needs is a perm to make it straight. Her hair is so black it has blue lights in it like a blackbird's feathers. And it curls and curls, all round her face and down to her shoulders. She ought to look like a witch but she looks more like the angel I've written into *Catrin in the Clouds*.

Tada limps down the stairs and stands in the living room doorway. He's put on his Saturday clothes and combed his family hair back with Brylcreem. He smells like Aneurin.

'Ready?' says Aunty Siân.

Tada nods and moves over to his seat at the table.

'Pour the tea, Bethan,' says Aunty Siân and Bethan begins to fill everyone's cup. I put a slice of cake on a plate for everyone, the smallest slice for Aunty Siân and the biggest for Tada.

'Let's all sit round the table for our tea and cake,' says Aunty Siân. 'Come on, Magda.' Mam laughs as Aunty Siân pulls her out of the chair and onto her feet. But she looks at Tada and stops laughing.

So, we sit around the table to eat our cake and sip our tea. I have to share a chair with Bethan and she scowls at me. Aunty

Siân chatters all the time. She tells us funny stories about her train journey and her walk up the hill with her bump. But we all seem to be waiting for something.

When we've all eaten our cake, even Mam, Aunty Siân says, 'Gwenni, at the bottom of my bag is an envelope. It was under the cake tin; did you notice it?'

I shake my head. Is this what we're waiting for?

'Well, it's there,' says Aunty Siân. 'Would you get it for me, please?'

I go into the scullery where John Morris pretends he can't see me and sits with his bottom suspended just above the floor. I dip my hand into Aunty Siân's bag and bring out a fat and furry brown envelope. I'm sure I can see a mouth gaping in the blue distemper as if it would swallow the envelope, but I don't stay to look too closely.

I give Aunty Siân the envelope. She turns it over and over in her hands.

45

Aunty Siân takes a deep breath and begins to open the envelope. 'What I have here,' she says, 'are some photographs of your grandmother to show you. Your mother's mother.'

Mam's hands begin to shake so much they drum on the table.

Aunty Siân puts her hand over Mam's hands. 'Because,' she says, 'I'm going to tell you your grandmother's story.'

Mam whimpers and the fat, yellow worms on her head writhe. 'You promised,' she says. 'You promised.'

'I did,' says Aunty Siân. She looks at Bethan and then at me. 'I'm breaking my promise to your mam by telling you about your grandmother. But I've thought for a while that the two of you should know what happened to her. So, when Emlyn came to see me yesterday . . .'

'What?' says Mam.

'I went to see Siân,' says Tada, 'and asked her to come here soon. The girls ought to know what happened to Eluned. I didn't know exactly what happened to her because you wouldn't tell me, would you, Magda? When I spoke to Siân, she told me the whole story. I don't know why you couldn't tell me.'

'I don't want anybody to know,' says Mam. She bangs the table with her fist and the cups and saucers and plates tremble. 'Not anybody. You've got no right, Siân.'

'It isn't anything to be ashamed of, Magda,' says Aunty Siân. 'It isn't, really.'

'I thought you came to give me a perm,' says Mam. She scrubs at her curls with her fingers as if she's trying to tear them out. 'Not to do the dirty on me.'

'I did come to give you the perm,' says Aunty Siân. 'And I was going to talk to you about this beforehand. But . . . well, I could see you weren't yourself, Magda, and Bethan was home, so I just decided to have a nice day with you both and wait until Emlyn came back from work.'

'Huh,' says Mam. 'Emlyn. Everyone thinks Emlyn is so wonderful.'

'I don't,' says Bethan. 'He's pretended to be my father for all this time.'

'Bethan,' says Aunty Siân. 'You're very lucky to have Emlyn for a father. But you see where all this secrecy leads?' She looks at Mam. 'It leads to sheer misery.'

Mam tries to push her cup and saucer away and they rattle against each other. Aunty Siân glances at Tada and he says, 'Go on, Siân. This has to be done.'

Aunty Siân takes a photograph out of the envelope. 'This was your grandmother,' she says. 'I was your age, Gwenni, when she . . . died. This is how I remember her. She was my father's sister but they didn't look alike at all.' The woman in the picture is standing beneath an archway of roses and she looks exactly like Mam and Bethan except that her hair is on top of her head in a big, floppy bun. 'See how much you resemble her, Bethan?' says Aunty Siân. 'She had fine fair hair like you and Magda; she had such trouble keeping it

297

up in that bun – especially when she was gardening. She loved those roses.' Bethan takes the photograph and stares and stares at it. I don't think she'll mind having that family face and that family hair.

Aunty Siân takes out all the photographs from the envelope and spreads them on the table. 'You can't tell from these photographs,' she says, 'but Aunty Eluned had an extremely hard life. Of course, I only know that from what my mother told me when I was a bit older. When you're a child you tend to accept that what happens in your family happens to everyone else's family; that it's the normal thing.'

Mam pushes her hands down on the table and tries to lift herself from her chair. 'I'm not sitting here listening to this,' she says. 'You and Emlyn have betrayed me. Betrayed me.' But she can't quite get to her feet and she slips back into her chair where she begins to sob and rock to and fro.

The Toby jugs shift themselves on their shelf and lean forward to watch.

'Has Magda had any of her tablets during the day?' says Tada to no one in particular.

'I don't think she's had anything since I've been here,' says Aunty Siân. 'Bethan?'

Bethan shrugs. 'I don't know,' she says.

'I'll get them,' says Tada. 'Dr Edwards said she ought to take them regularly.' He goes into the scullery and comes back with two white tablets and a big glass of water. 'Here you are, Magda,' he says to Mam and she takes the tablets and swallows them both with a gulp of water and then throws the rest of the glassful all over Tada. Bethan and I shunt our chair back from the table but Aunty Siân can't move so quickly and some of the water splashes over her face and she gasps with shock. Mam laughs as she watches Tada rush to the scullery and come back with the stripey towel for Aunty Siân.

'Serves you right,' she says, 'for what you're doing to me.'

'Sorry, Siân,' says Tada. 'But those tablets will work quite quickly, you'll see.'

Aunty Siân waves her hand at him as if to tell him not to worry. She finishes drying her face and dabs at some of the photographs with the towel. Aunty Siân looks at Mam, who's closed her eyes and is rocking in her chair as if she's putting herself to sleep, and she puts her hand over Mam's hands again. 'I do hate to see her like this, Emlyn,' she says to Tada.

'I can't understand it, Siân,' says Tada. He covers his eyes with his hand and shakes his head. Maybe Tada doesn't want to understand it.

'Well,' says Aunty Siân, 'me neither.' And she sighs.

'I'm going out to see Caroline soon,' says Bethan. 'So can we be quick, Aunty Siân? Please.'

Aunty Siân picks up one of the photographs of Nain Eluned. 'Your grandmother's married life was a hard one,' she says. 'She was young when she married your grandfather and they hadn't been married long when he went off to the war,' she says.

Bethan frowns and wrinkles her nose.

'The First World War,' I say to her.

'I know that,' says Bethan. 'I'm not stupid, like you.'

'Bethan,' says Aunty Siân. 'Now, your grandfather was a changed man when he came home. Whatever he'd gone through in the war made him violent a lot of the time, and unpleasant, and Eluned bore the brunt of it and became quite ill. I don't remember your grandfather, because I was only small when he caught pneumonia and died. Your mam was still at school then. Well, everyone expected Eluned to get better after that, but she didn't. My mam thought he'd made her so depressed, you know, that she didn't know how to get out of it. And you couldn't get the medicines then, like you can now, that might have helped her.' Aunty Siân stops and looks at Mam who has her eyes still closed but is smiling the way she does when she's had her tablets. Emptily. 'If help is the right word,' she says. 'Anyway, it was hard for your mam to look after Eluned, first when she was still at school and then when she was working.' She pats Mam's hands but Mam doesn't notice.

Tada interrupts. 'Then I met your mam and she was so beautiful and brave and I wanted to look after her. I'd have done anything for her. But it was wartime when we married and I had to go away. So, your mam was left on her own again to look after Eluned.' He rubs his face with his rough hands. 'So you see, Bethan, why it was your mam needed somebody to . . . Because I was away and because it was so hard for her with Eluned. She'd have gone mad without someone to . . . someone to . . .' He stops and puts his hands over his face. 'It doesn't bear thinking about. My poor Magda.'

Poor Mam?

Aunty Siân rubs his arm comfortingly. Bethan stares at Nain Eluned's photographs, one after the other. They don't tell us any of the things Aunty Siân is telling us. Like the photographs in the box that Bethan tore up. It isn't that they lie, it's that they tell a different story. How can we know which story is the true one?

'When Eluned realised your mam was having Bethan and it was obvious that Emlyn couldn't be the baby's father, she couldn't bear the shame of it.' Aunty Siân glances at Bethan. 'That already seemed a bit old-fashioned, you know; there were many other women in a similar situation. War turns things upside down, Bethan. Anyhow, Eluned became so . . . ill that my mam called the doctor to her and he had her taken off to Dinbych straight away.'

Bethan looks up from the photographs. 'Dinbych?' she says. 'To the mad house?'

'To the asylum, yes,' says Aunty Siân. 'They treated people there for those kinds of illnesses. They said Aunty Eluned responded to the treatment very quickly and they soon sent her home.'

'Are you saying Gwenni's got her madness from Mam's side of the family?' says Bethan. She picks through the photographs on the table; I look at them as she holds them up. Does Nain Eluned look mad in any of them? What does madness look like?

'What kind of thing is that to say, Bethan?' says Aunty Siân. 'Your sister isn't mad any more than you are. It was your Nain's circumstances that made her ill. It isn't catching, like measles.'

I look at Mam. I'm not so sure.

I know some of this from what Nain next door said. But I don't know how Nain Eluned died. Will Aunty Siân tell us?

'Let Siân tell us everything,' says Tada. 'Time's going on and she has to catch the train home.'

'You mean there's more?' says Bethan. 'I want to go to Caroline's, remember.'

Aunty Siân takes a deep, deep breath and she says in a rush, 'But the doctors must have made a mistake. Eluned wasn't better. When she'd been home a day she killed herself.'

'How?' I say. But somehow I know.

'No, no, no.' Mam moans and opens her eyes and tries to grab Aunty Siân's hand.

Aunty Siân looks at Tada and he nods. 'Like Mrs Llywelyn Pugh,' she says.

The Toby jugs almost tumble off their shelf.

'Bloody hell,' says Bethan, and nobody tells her off.

Aunty Siân's lips quiver. 'Your mam found her, of course. It was terrible. Terrible.' Aunty Siân's voice quivers, too. 'And she's always blamed herself.'

'For having me, d'you mean?' says Bethan. 'You're saying it's my fault? On top of not having a father, I've got to take the blame for my grandmother killing herself?'

'No, of course not, Bethan,' says Aunty Siân. 'Never think that. And remember, you do have a father who's cared for you since you were born.'

'Huh,' says Bethan. And she sounds just like Mam.

'And it wasn't your mam's fault either,' says Aunty Siân. 'Your nain was ill. If it was anyone's fault, it was your grandfather's for making her like that.'

'But the war made him ill,' I say.

'It did, Gwenni,' says Tada. 'There was no fault anywhere.'

'They shouldn't have sent her home from the madhouse, should they?' says Bethan.

'Probably not,' says Tada. 'But they did.'

'I don't think I wanted to know all this on top of everything else,' says Bethan. 'I had a really nice day with you, Aunty Siân, and now you've spoilt it.'

'It's better to have things out in the open,' says Tada. 'And it might help your mam. She doesn't have to worry about you finding out about your Nain Eluned if you already know about her.'

Mam's big empty smile disappears. She sits up straight in her chair. 'You can't tell anyone,' she says. She's trembling all over; her greeny-yellow curls wriggle in sympathy.

'It's nothing to be ashamed of, Magda,' says Tada.

'I don't want any of you to tell any one,' she says. 'Promise me. Promise. Cross your hearts and hope to die.' She bangs the table and we all jump. 'Go on, do it. Cross your hearts.'

'Magda,' says Tada.

'Be quiet,' Mam says to him. 'You weren't there. You left me. You had no right to bring Siân here to do this.' She points at Aunty Siân. 'You crossed your heart,' she says. 'You've broken your promise.'

302

'I know,' says Aunty Siân. 'And I'm truly sorry. But I was only Gwenni's age; I didn't realise what I was promising. And I didn't break my promise lightly, Magda. I agree with Emlyn about—'

'Huh,' says Mam. 'You crossed your heart and hoped to die. Maybe you'll die in childbirth. Maybe the baby'll die. You'll pay—'

A knock on the back door stops her. She covers her mouth with her shaking hand and begins to cry.

'That'll be Lol,' says Tada. He looks at Aunty Siân who is as white as Nain next door's sheets on a Monday. 'She said she'd walk down to the station with you, Siân. Are you all right to go?'

The back door opens. 'Yoo-hoo,' Nain calls. 'Lol's had to go to an emergency fire brigade meeting. And that John Morris is standing in a plate of meat in here. If that's your supper there's not much left.' There's a scuffle in the scullery and John Morris yowls. 'Off you go, you bad, lazy cat,' says Nain and the back door bangs shut.

Nain comes into the living room. 'This is nice,' she says. 'A tea party. I'll walk down to the station with you, Siân. Can't risk you falling on the hill. My goodness, look at the size of you. Have you got twins in there?'

Aunty Siân stands up and rubs her baby bump. 'It kicks enough for two,' she says, and she looks happy again. 'And how are you, Mrs Morgan?'

'Can't grumble, Siân,' says Nain. 'Can't grumble.'

'You go home, Mam,' says Tada. 'I'll walk Siân to the train.'

'D'you want me to make food for you all now that the cat's had your supper?' says Nain.

'We'll get some chips,' says Tada. 'It'll make a change.' He hustles Nain back through the scullery door before she has a chance to notice Mam crying and rocking and muttering to herself at the table.

46

The back door slams behind Nain on her way home and the front door slams behind Aunty Siân and Tada on their way to the station.

'I'm going to see Caroline,' says Bethan. Mam sits up and stretches her hand out towards her. Bethan ignores her and vanishes like Tada and Aunty Siân through the front door, and I'm left here with Mam.

'Sharper than a serpent's tooth,' says Mam.

'What?' I say.

Mam doesn't reply. Instead, she rocks back and forth on the seat of her armchair. Maybe all this rocking she does is working something loose in her head. Maybe it's nothing to do with the space machine cooking her brain.

'I'm going to Nain's for a minute,' I say.

'No, you're not,' says Mam, snapping to attention as if one of the loose pieces has rolled back into place. 'Who do you think is going to get the chips if you go off to Nain's?'

I don't mind fetching the chips. It's better than staying here and it's better than having to tell Nain everything that happened before she came round. Because she'll be wanting to know.

'Shall I take the money from your purse?' I say. Mam doesn't answer again but I take her purse from the left-hand drawer in the sideboard. 'Shall I get Tada a fish?' Tada likes fish.

'I'm not wasting money on fish for him,' says Mam. 'He can have a fried egg like everyone else. Get a shilling's worth of chips.'

I take a shilling from her purse. It's smooth and thin. Hundreds of fingers must have earned it and spent it. I put it in my gymslip pocket and head for the door.

'Take a dish,' says Mam.

'Greasy Annie said not to bother with a dish last time,' I say. 'She said to have it wrapped like everyone else.'

'Greasy Annie is common as dirt,' says Mam. 'Wrapping the food in filthy old newspaper. Her poor mother would turn in her grave. Take a dish. Take that glass one with the lid. That'll show her.'

What will it show her? Greasy Annie wouldn't think Mam could show her anything. Greasy Annie thinks she could show Mam a thing or two; she said so last time. I didn't know what she meant but it made everyone in the chip shop laugh. But I don't tell Mam that.

'I can't take a dish when she said not to,' I say.

'Take. The. Dish,' says Mam. She bangs her hand on the arm of the chair with each word.

'No,' I say. 'Don't make me take it, Mam.'

Before I realise what's happening Mam jumps up from her chair and smacks me across my face with the palm of her hand. The sting in my cheek makes my eyes water.

'Satan. Satan.' Mam hisses the words at me. Her spit sprays my stinging cheek. I try not to think about the spit. What did she call me? Are her brain pieces coming loose again? I back into the door but she comes after me, her arm raised to slap me once more. I must get Nain.

The door slams into my back as someone opens it.

'Get out of the way,' says Bethan. 'What a stupid place to stand.' Tears run down her face and she's out of breath.

'Bethan, my Bethan,' Mam says. She closes her eyes and holds her hands out to Bethan, her palms upwards, like a saint in a picture. Bethan takes no notice of her but there's no room to move so I take hold of Mam's shoulders and shuffle her back towards her armchair. Maybe she thinks Bethan's helping her because she smiles her empty smile and lets me push her onto the seat.

Bethan holds out a scrumpled piece of paper to me.

I take it; it weighs more than paper. 'What is it?' I say. 'What's the matter?'

'The matter,' says Bethan as she scrubs the tears from her cheeks with her fists, 'is that stupid Mrs Smythe won't let Caroline speak to me.'

'What?' I say.

'What? What?' Bethan mimics me. 'It's all your fault. Making friends with that Richard. I told you he's a mother's boy. He tells his mother everything. Look at that note.'

I try to unscrumple the paper and a stone falls out and drops on Bethan's foot. She kicks me on my ankle in return. 'You're so stupid, Gwenni,' she says. How was I to know the paper was wrapped round a stone? Things like that happen in *School Friend* and to the Famous Five. Not to me.

The paper is a sheet from a school roughbook and it's difficult to smooth out well enough to read the pencilled writing. Bethan snatches it from me and waves it in my face as she says, 'Caroline says that Richard told his mother all about Tada not being my father, and all about Mam being doolally. She says her mother's sending them to stay with their grandmother in England until they can find somewhere else to live where we won't be a bad influence on them.'

'A bad influence?' I say.

Bethan throws the note on the fire where it flares up, then settles into a thin sheet of ash that breaks into pieces and disappears up the chimney.

'Are you sure that's what it says?' I say. Though there's no way of checking now. 'Because Richard told me ages ago his mother wanted to move away.'

Bethan stamps her foot. 'It's all your fault, stupid. All your fault.'

'Gwenni's bad. Gwenni's bad.' Bethan's shouting has started Mam off again. She's pulled her pink cushion with the red roses from behind her and is hugging it as she rocks in her chair. To and fro, to and fro. She rocks in time with the tick-tock of the brown clock. 'Bad-bad. Bad-bad.'

Am I?

'I only wanted you, Bethan. You and your father. And now there's only you. Only you.' Mam hugs her pink cushion harder. Then her hand darts out and she catches Bethan's wrist and tries to pull her down beside the chair.

'Stop it.' Bethan shouts and Mam lets go so that Bethan staggers back from her. She turns to me. 'D'you think Aunty Siân was wrong?' she says. 'D'you think what Nain Eluned had was catching after all?'

We look at Mam. She's shaking as she rocks and her uncombed yellow curls seethe on her head as if they're alive. Her face has started to melt the way it did when she burnt Mrs Llywelyn Pugh's dead fox. Sweat runs down from her forehead and along the sides of her nose and along her top lip where it takes her lipstick with it to run in bloody streaks down each side of her mouth. Is this what madness looks like? What must it feel like?

'She's absolutely bloody bonkers,' says Bethan. 'I expect that's how you'll be when you're older. I expect you've already caught Nain Eluned's illness from Mam; that's why you're so odd.'

'Satan.' Mam points at me. Her arm shakes, her hand shakes, her finger shakes, but there is no mistaking where she's pointing. My stomach starts to hurt. Why is she calling me that?

'What's she on about?' says Bethan.

'Your father is the Devil,' says Mam, her finger still pointed at me. 'The devil forced himself upon me and begat another devil. You are no child of mine.' She sounds like someone reading the Bible. Is she talking about Tada?

'What about my father?' Bethan shakes Mam's pointing arm. 'Who's my father?'

'An angel,' says Mam.

'Bloody hell,' says Bethan.

'An angel who came in my hour of need,' says Mam. She smoothes her pink cushion and frowns. The red petals on the cushion look rusty in the firelight. 'Is this his blood?'

'Now what's she on about?' says Bethan.

Blood. Eight pints of blood in every human body. It shows where people belong and where they don't. It spills on floors; it trickles into Reservoirs; it runs under bathroom doors. It will pour out of me every month.

'No. Not his blood,' says Mam. She strokes her cushion. 'Her blood. See how it blooms like the roses in her garden.'

'She said that last night,' says Bethan. 'That was your fault, too.' She peers at Mam's pink cushion without getting too close. 'Are those funny petals really blood? That's disgusting. I've been sitting on that cushion.'

Mam begins to rock again. She holds the cushion as if it's a child she's nursing. She speaks to it. 'You came from Mam's house, the only thing. Mam said you devil Magdalen you'll send me to an early grave the way you carry on is enough to drive me to despair. What did I do to deserve such a devil for a husband such a devil for a daughter? You'll pay when that child is born. Sharper than a serpent's tooth. Sharp, sharp.'

Bethan's hand creeps into mine and I hold it tight, tight. When will Tada be home?

Mam rocks and rocks. 'Mam said this cushion is my only comfort in this life. You are to have this cushion when I'm gone Magdalen never to forget me. The cushion will be your penance Magdalen. You must never forget me you must never forget that you have pushed me into this madness made me commit this sin she said. Don't do it Mam I said. But it was done. Her blood bloomed like the roses in her garden. Her wrists like mouths but not talking. Don't talk, don't tell. Hush.' Mam lets go of the cushion and puts both her hands over her mouth.

Bethan pulls her hand away from mine. 'Bloody hell,' she says. 'I'm going to get Nain.'

47

Nain takes one look at Mam hugging her cushion and watching things we can't see in the fire and says, 'I'm fetching Dr Edwards. You two sit here quietly and don't upset her any more. Gwenni, make some tea.'

I don't think Mam wants tea. I don't think Mam would know a cup of tea if I held one in front of her. But I nod at Nain anyway.

She leaves through the front door and the draught rushes through the house and slams the back door that she left open on her way in. Bethan and I both jump at the noise but Mam doesn't notice it. She stares at the fire, which flares and flickers with the draught. Smoke puffs out from it and misses the chimney, swirling its way up past the mantelpiece and around the Toby jugs instead. They're looking scared; their cheeks have paled as if this amount of excitement is too much for them. They're looking at the ceiling instead of leering at the woman on the sideboard or watching Mam; the cracks in the plaster up there must be the most interesting things in the world. Maybe even the Toby jugs are afraid that madness is catching. The smoke threads between them and along the ceiling and hovers around the pale electric light in its glass shade.

'Pooh,' says Bethan, fanning the smell of the smoke away with her hand.

The smoke against the light looks like wisps of cloud across the moon. But there's no peace here like that of my night sky, and no music. If Mam could hear the Earth's music, maybe she would be filled with so much wonder there wouldn't be room inside her for illness.

'Tada should be back soon,' I say. I look at the clock; Aunty Siân's train must have been late arriving or Tada would be home by now.

'Your tada,' says Bethan. 'Not mine.' She chews her thumbnail. I can see that it's already bleeding around the edges. 'I'm never going to know who mine is, am I?' She kicks back at the leg of her chair. 'An angel. Huh.'

Mam moans softly. It's hardly a noise at all. She sounds like a newborn kitten John Morris once stole and carried home that mewled like this for its mother. We never knew why he stole the kitten. Perhaps he was its father; I didn't think of that. The kitten's mother gave him two deep scratches on his nose when she fetched the kitten back. They took weeks to heal.

Bethan and I don't speak; a silent agreement not to disturb Mam any more. What is Bethan thinking? She has too much to think about. When she notices me looking at her she turns sideways in her chair so that I can't see her face. I sit here resting my elbows on the table, watching Mam out of the corner of my eye. Has her life become as unbearable as Nain Eluned's? What if she tries to do something that Bethan and I can't stop her doing?

I hear voices outside the window and when the door opens Tada comes in with Dr Edwards close behind him. Nain follows them, standing on tiptoe and trying to look over their shoulders.

Dr Edwards stands and watches Mam, then he gives a sigh

and brings his black bag over to the table and takes out a syringe. Bethan sucks in her breath when she sees it. Dr Edwards smiles at her and draws some liquid into the syringe from a vial; he squirts some of it into the air. He holds the syringe behind his back and walks over to Mam and crouches down beside her chair.

Dr Edwards glances first at Tada, who is still in the doorway, then he says, 'This will be just a little prick, Magda. Nothing to worry about. You'll hardly feel it and it'll make you nice and sleepy.'

He balances the syringe on his thigh and takes hold of Mam's arm and pushes up her sleeve. It must be difficult because Mam won't let go of her pink cushion. She behaves as if Dr Edwards is not there. Perhaps he's as invisible to her as I am. Perhaps she thinks that if she can't see us we won't exist. Maybe no one real exists for her at this moment. Except Bethan.

Dr Edwards plunges the needle into her arm. He looks up at Tada and says, 'This will be very quick, Emlyn. She'll sleep until the ambulance comes. It's the best thing.'

'Ambulance?' says Bethan.

'Your mam's ill, Bethan,' says Dr Edwards. 'She needs to be somewhere she can be taken care of. Now,' he walks to his bag and packs away the syringe and the empty vial, 'if you walk down to the surgery with me, Emlyn, we can have a chat about this. We'll hear the ambulance when it passes and be back here by the time it's parked up.'

Mam is already asleep and before he and Tada leave Dr Edwards lifts her eyelid and peers at her eye and checks her pulse against his big pocket watch. 'Cover her with a blanket,' he says to Nain. 'And she'll be fine where she is.'

I fetch a blanket from our bed. Nain tries to take the pink cushion from Mam, but she's clutching it too tightly even in her sleep, so Nain lays the blanket over Mam and the cushion, and tucks the frayed edges in around Mam's legs.

'I'll just pop home for a minute in case Lol's back. Just so she knows what's happening,' says Nain. 'Your mam will sleep now, so don't worry.'

Don't worry?

'What about the ambulance?' says Bethan.

'I'll be back before that comes,' says Nain.

'I don't mean that. I mean where's it taking her?' says Bethan.

'Ah, well . . .' says Nain.

'Dinbych,' I say. 'The asylum. Like Nain Eluned.'

'The bloody madhouse,' says Bethan.

'Bethan,' says Nain. 'They don't call it that. It's a hospital now. A special hospital for . . . well, for . . .'

'Nutcases,' says Bethan. 'Like Guto'r Wern and Mam. D'you think they'll recognise each other? Mam'll have a fit.'

'They'll mend your mam, you'll see,' says Nain. 'They've got all sorts of treatments nowadays. Mend anybody. She'll be home in no time.'

'Huh,' says Bethan, slumping into Tada's chair.

'I won't be long,' says Nain. 'Fetch me if you need me.'

As she walks out through the door, John Morris sneaks back in. He stands and looks from Mam to Bethan, from Bethan to Mam, then jumps onto Mam's lap and treads round and round on the blanket before he curls up on it and closes his eyes.

It must be nice to be a cat, coming and going as you please. Some people in faraway countries believe that instead of going to Heaven when you die, you're born again. You could be a boy or a girl, a worm or a bird, a horse or a sheep. I'd like to come back as a cat. Maybe once I was a cat and came back as a girl. Or a fox, maybe I was a fox and that's the part of me Aneurin sees. Or perhaps I was a bird, soaring up into the sky, floating on the thermals; that would explain why I can fly. But doesn't that prove that animals have spirits just like humans? Spirits that they pass along from life to life.

In her sleep Mam gives a shuddering sigh. John Morris opens one eye and purrs and closes it again. The blanket will be covered in his cat hairs. That will probably make it thicker and warmer, which is lucky because it's an old blanket from the jumble sale and has worn too thin to be warm in winter. Mam insisted it was brand new from a shop in Llandudno. Maybe when you have something loose in your brain you can't tell the difference between truth and lies.

Bethan is chewing her fingernails again. She and Caroline had a competition to see who could grow her fingernails first and Bethan won. But her nails will be all gone again now; I can see from here that both her thumbnails are bleeding.

Where will Caroline and Richard go? Poor Richard. Maybe we will become pen-pals. Monsieur Jenkins made a special announcement in assembly that he wanted lots of us to become pen-pals with children in a school in France. But we had to write in English and be written to in French. He said no one in France wanted letters in Welsh. Richard won't want letters in Welsh.

Bethan will miss Caroline more than I will miss Richard. Will Janet Jones the Butcher want to be best friends with her again? She's leaning against the cushions on Tada's chair and her thumb has crept into her mouth. I fold my arms on the table and lay my head on them. If I fall asleep maybe I can leave all this behind and fly into my night sky.

A bright blue light and a loud noise pulsing through the window startle me awake. Mam stirs and mumbles. John Morris slides off her lap without waking, taking the blanket with him and landing in a heap on the linoleum. Mam clutches her pink cushion. Even in her sleep she looks frightened at the commotion. I get up from the table and go over to her and stroke her hands as they grip the cushion. 'You'll soon be back home, Mam,' I say. 'Don't worry. I won't leave you. I'll look after you until you've mended.' Then I turn round and shake Bethan by the shoulder. 'Wake up,' I say. 'The ambulance has come.'

48

The ambulance has gone quietly into the night, and Mam with it, still asleep, a smile on her face. Will she know where she is when she wakes?

Dr Edwards said he would take Tada in his car after the ambulance, so he could see Mam settled in. Nain gathered some clothes together for her and said that she would look after Bethan and me until Dr Edwards brought Tada back home. So Tada has gone, too. Will Mam care that he's there?

Was Alwenna right? Was it Ifan Evans's death that pushed Mam into being ill? Was he Bethan's father? Look at the clues. Bethan has the same colour eyes as Ifan Evans. He was Mam's boyfriend for a while before she met Tada, and maybe afterwards – remember the swimming? Mam always stood up for him. And her nerves did get worse from the minute Nain came to tell us he was missing; before that she was her usual cross self. But this is what detective stories call circumstantial evidence, not proof. I suppose the eye colour could be proof, but lots of people have dark brown eyes. Against all this circumstantial evidence is what Mam said about Bethan's father; she said he was an angel. Ifan Evans was not an angel.

'Move your feet, Gwenni,' says Nain. She's still puttering about, picking up invisible bits, straightening the furniture, throwing wood on the fire, folding the grey blanket, plumping up the cushions on the armchairs. But Mam's pink cushion isn't here for Nain to plump up. I tried to tell Tada what Mam said about the cushion, but he didn't understand me. He said it was the only thing Mam brought with her from her mother's house and if it made her happy it was best for her to take it with her.

But the pink cushion didn't make her happy, did it? I should have burnt it like Mam burnt Mrs Llywelyn Pugh's dead fox. The cushion made Mam miserable; it reminded her every day of terrible things that should have faded in her memory. Nain Eluned wanted it to remind Mam. Because she was mad, too. When people are mad, do they become different people, or are they versions of themselves with all the horrible things about them magnified? Mam was always cross with me but after Ifan Evans disappeared she became worse and worse. I didn't tell Tada she called me Satan.

'Where's that nuisance of a cat gone?' says Nain. 'Did he run upstairs?'

'He went out,' I say. 'The noise from the ambulance scared him and he went out when you came in.'

'Are you sure?' she says. 'We don't want him making a mess of the beds.'

I nod. I saw John Morris run out. He doesn't run much, so he must have been frightened.

'Right,' says Nain, standing over me, her hands on her hips. 'Don't sit there brooding, Gwenni. That's no use to man nor beast.'

'I'm just trying to work out how it all makes sense, Nain,' I say.

'It doesn't,' says Nain. 'It's life, Gwenni. Just kicks you in the teeth sometimes. You may as well get used to the idea.'

317

'I won't have any teeth left if it kicks me any more,' says Bethan.

'No good feeling sorry for yourself, Bethan,' says Nain. 'Worse things happen at sea.'

Bethan's mouth drops open. After a second she says, 'You're not my real grandmother so you've got no right to tell me what to do.'

Nain's face flames like the fire. 'Your father left you in my care, young lady.'

'He's not my real father either,' says Bethan.

'He's as real a father as you'll ever have,' says Nain.

'My father was an angel,' says Bethan. 'Mam said so.' She wasn't so pleased with the idea when Mam told her.

'Stuff and nonsense,' says Nain. 'I've heard everything now.'

Bethan jumps up from Tada's chair. 'I'm not staying here another minute,' she says.

I hear Nain's false teeth grind together. She takes a deep breath. 'Go to bed, then, Bethan. You, too, Gwenni. Unless you want something to eat first. Best thing for you both would be a good night's sleep.'

My queasy stomach is back; I can feel it all the way up my throat. So I just shake my head at Nain.

Bethan stamps her foot. 'You're so timid and stupid, Gwenni,' she says. 'And I said I wasn't staying here and I'm not.' And she opens the living room door and then the front door and runs out into the dark.

'For goodness' sake,' says Nain. 'You stay here, Gwenni. I'll go and get Lol to go after the silly girl with me.' And she, too, disappears into the night.

As she vanishes, John Morris sidles in through the open door. He stops and looks all around the living room before coming in.

What does he think is going on in this house? Maybe he thinks he lives in an asylum. He jumps onto Tada's chair but I don't want to sit in Mam's chair so I move John Morris there. Now I'll be able to curl up on Tada's big cushion with the smell of his Golden Virginia and his Lifebuoy soap. John Morris treads and treads in a circle on Mam's seat before he settles down. Has the rose-petal blood on her cushion rubbed off on the other cushions and the covers? It's lucky I always sit in Tada's chair.

The wood Nain put on the fire has almost burnt through, so I throw two thin pine logs on quick so no flames can catch my hand and the logs spit at me. I stamp the tiny red embers that land on the linoleum. If I was really Satan, or any devil, I would like fire, not be afraid of it, wouldn't I?

Maybe a cup of tea will push the queasiness away. I take the kettle into the scullery and fill it under the tap. The electric light is poor in here, but I can see that the walls are blue and clear as a cloudless sky. I rub the wall by the sink with my hand. There was a mouth just here that was huge with the secrets it had swallowed. But there's nothing here now. Maybe Tada did drown them all with his blue distemper. Maybe I just imagined they were returning. Or maybe they ate and swallowed so many secrets today that they got our old family stomach and lost the taste for them.

I take the kettle to the grate. The pine has made a red-hot bed for it. The water on the sides of the kettle fizzles in the heat as I lower it onto the fire. I sit in Tada's chair to wait for the kettle to boil and snuggle into his cushions and take a deep breath of his scent from them. But there's something more than his tobacco and soap; there's whiff of something that burns my nostrils. If fear had a stink this would be it. Poor Tada.

Will anything ever be the same again? Where did all of this start? Long before I was born, long before Mam was born. Here is the evidence. First there was the Great War, a terrible war. Maybe it began even further back, but I have no evidence of that. The war made my grandfather violent; my grandfather in his violence drove my grandmother to madness; my grandmother's madness made my mother ill. My mother's illness made her behave in a strange way; though it wasn't strange to her. Here, Ifan Evans comes in, before, and maybe after, my mother married my father; Tada who never wanted to leave her to go to another old war. Then come Elin Evans and the lost babies and Angharad and little Catrin. I don't have any evidence that Ifan Evans killed the babies; what Nanw Lipstick says doesn't count. Where did Ifan Evans's black dog come from? Maybe the war made someone in his family ill, too. And Mrs Llywelyn Pugh's husband had died in the war and her boys in the next war and then I made everything worse by stealing the dead fox, which Mam burnt before I could give it back. Then Elin confessed to killing Ifan because the detectives arrested Guto. She didn't want them to find out who really killed Ifan. Don't think about that. I have no evidence that any war was to blame for Guto's mam dropping him on his head. And Elin's arrest was more than poor Mrs Llywelyn Pugh could bear. When will it ever end? Mrs Williams Penrhiw said: We'll never be the same again, any of us. Is that true? Is this what Nain means when she says life gives you a kick in the teeth? It seems more like battering and bruising and breaking your whole body and maybe even killing you.

The kettle's boiling water out of its spout. I take it off the fire before it quenches the flames. I don't really want a cup of tea any more. My stomach is hurting and I want to stay here in Tada's chair and go to sleep. Maybe then I'll fly into the night sky and all this will be far away. Look at the steam rising right up to the ceiling from the kettle spout, as if it's a genie. Those Toby jugs are peering over the edge of their shelf again. I'm going to sweep them off so they'll smash into tiny pieces in the grate. Who is left to notice that they've gone?

If I stand on the arm of Tada's chair I might just be able to reach. I climb up on the knobbly cushion and then onto the arm and try to get my balance. It's difficult because there's nothing to hold on to. I can hear the brown clock; the clock that never stops. Tick-tock, tick-tock. I close my eyes and reach my arms out to stop wobbling. When I'm perfectly still I open my eyes and stretch up on my tiptoes to reach the nearest Toby jug and my feet lift off the arm of the chair and I float upwards. I bump my head on the ceiling and drop until I'm level with the mirror. My hair streams out like a fiery comet's tail beyond the mirror's frame, like the photograph of the comet's tail streaming beyond the edge of the page that Richard once showed me in a library book. I rise to the ceiling again. How strange the living room looks from here, like a room in a doll's house. I twist and curve towards the three Toby jugs. They look different, too. The handle on one of them has been broken and glued back again. Their glaze is crazed with tiny cracks and their eyes are dead specks of paint. Cobwebs weave them together on their shelf and my breath makes a panicky little spider dive into the middle jug. Their scarlet cheeks are powdered grey with dust. Why was I ever afraid of these? I leave them and fall and rise like a bird on the wing.

Look at me. I'm flying.

49

Outside, the sun is hot in a clear sky, and when I walked home from Sunday School with Alwenna the smell of rose petals was strong in the air. In the living room it's much darker because the sun has moved to the west now, and it's cooler, too, so Tada has lit a small fire. John Morris is stretched out on the hearth, as close as he can get to the grate. We don't need a big fire because we don't have to cook; we're going to Nain's house for supper.

Tada's folded the chenille cloth and hung it over the back of his chair and I've spread a big sheet of drawing paper on the table. It's really six sheets that I glued together to make one big one and it's crinkled a bit along the edge of one piece where my cardigan sleeve got stuck to the glue, but Tada says we won't notice that once he's drawn the map on it. He's drawing a map to show me where Mam is, and the roads to reach her, so that I can see that she's not so very far away. I've put out all my colouring pencils and my fountain pen for him, and my blotter rocker with a clean square of blotting paper in it that Aunty Lol gave me. The old blotting paper is covered with Mrs Evans's back-to-front writing and is in my box.

Every Saturday, after breakfast, Tada borrows Aunty Lol's Lambretta and travels to visit Mam along the map he's drawing. Her treatment isn't working yet and she doesn't speak to him. He sits all afternoon and holds her hand and tells her about his plan to buy a house with an electric stove and a bathroom for her. And then he arrives home after supper and goes to bed and cries. I hear him through the bedroom wall. But he doesn't cry on any other day of the week.

Today, he went to visit Bethan at Aunty Siân's house. He says she likes living with Aunty Siân and Uncle Wil and little Helen. And she likes helping with the baby. Is that true? I see her every day at school and she pretends she doesn't see me. But she always did that. Alwenna asked me if Bethan is ever going to come home. I don't know. Can you glue together two halves of a split tree like two pieces of paper?

'Will you put Penrhyn on the map?' I say. I pull my chair closer to Tada's. 'With Aunty Siân's house?'

'I'll put all the places you want on it, Gwenni,' says Tada. 'And you can write their names on them.'

I haven't got a pen with golden ink but my fountain pen has a good nib in it for map-writing.

Tada has drawn the shape of the land. He's got the arm of Llŷn almost to its hand, although we don't know anybody there. He's drawn the coast down to Bermo where he's put a little chapel, and where our town stands he's made a castle with the Red Dragon flying on it. Tada would make a good cartographer. Miss Eames says cartographers have to be neat and accurate. He draws Aunty Siân's house in the armpit of the map, and then begins to put in mountains of all shapes and sizes, and winding roads.

'You can colour the mountains, if you like,' he says.

'Does Aunty Lol's Lambretta go up and down all those mountains?' I ask.

'The roads go round, mostly,' he says. 'But it takes a while. It's all right now, but I wouldn't want to ride the Lambretta in snow and ice. Or strong winds. Still, your mam will be home long before winter.'

'Guto's never coming home to the Wern, though, is he?' I say.

'Poor Guto,' says Tada. 'Innocent as a child. But he's not ill in the same way as your mam, Gwenni. I've seen him a few times. He's quite happy there, you know. Quite happy.'

But he can't ever fly away, can he? It's like being in prison, like Mrs Evans. She can't get away. Or in a cage, like Lloyd George. Though he never wants to leave it now, Nain has to prod him out.

The fire hisses and a blue flame shoots up from the coals. John Morris twitches in his sleep. Nain will have a bigger fire going to cook supper for us all.

'I wonder what Nain will make for supper,' I say.

'I don't think it matters, does it, Gwenni?' says Tada. 'You always seem to enjoy it.'

I do. My cardigan is getting a bit tight, and my gymslip is really short now. Nain says she'll try letting the hem down. She says I'm all legs, like Aunty Lol. Or like a horse.

I watch Tada's pencil skimming the paper. He's making a beautiful building that looks like a palace of golden stone.

'What's that?' I say.

'That's where your mam is,' he says.

I didn't know asylums were so beautiful. Maybe Mam likes it, just like Guto. Maybe she really will get better there. Dr Edwards said her illness is one he's very interested in, and explained it to

Tada and me. Bethan wouldn't stay to hear him. He said Mam was in the best place to have the best treatment for her condition, and once the treatment works she can come home. But there's no cure for her illness, and she'll have to keep taking special drugs for ever, and will need Tada's help to stay well. Tada said: I'll do anything for her, doctor, anything.

Dr Edwards said that Nain Eluned probably had the same illness as Mam, because it can be passed to your children. When I told Alwenna, she cried and said: I didn't mean it when I said you were doolally like your Nain. I told her Dr Edwards says it's not all bad anyway. He says lots of people with the illness are creative. That means having a good imagination so you can be an artist or writer or a clever detective or cartographer or doctor. I'd like that.

'Are you all right doing this?' says Tada. 'Have you got homework to do for tomorrow?'

I shake my head. 'Alwenna and I did our homework yesterday. She came up here.'

'I'm glad you two are pals again,' says Tada.

He lays down the blue pencil he's using to draw the rivers, and stands up to look at the map. 'You can see the whole thing better like this,' he says.

'It's like when I'm flying,' I say.

'It is,' he says. How does he know that? He reaches to the mantelpiece for his tin of Golden Virginia and his Rizla papers, and begins to roll a cigarette. Then he lights it with a spill from the fire, and stands there smoking it. 'You're still doing it, then?' he says.

'Flying?' I say.

He nods, sucking on his cigarette, narrowing his eyes against the smoke so that I can't see what he's thinking.

'Yes,' I say.

'Well,' he says. He sits down again and carries on drawing the rivers. I never knew we have so many rivers where we live. Tada'll have to tell me the names to write on them.

'And are those Toby jugs still keeping an eye on us?' he says.

I dusted the Toby jugs just yesterday. They gleam in the light from the window. 'No, Tada,' I say. 'That was just my imagination – you know that.'

'Right, then,' he says. 'Now, anything more for the map?'

'Catrin,' I say. 'And Angharad.' They're in my heart, but they're in Cricieth too. 'Can you draw their castle?'

'Cricieth is just here,' says Tada, making a neat grey rock and small grey tower. 'See, it's directly across the bay. That's why we see it so clearly.'

One day I'll fly over the bay to find Catrin, my little wren, and I'll take her up into the sky, holding her tight, tight by the hand so that she doesn't fall. We'll fill ourselves with the Earth's song and trail it behind us like a comet's tail across the sky, high above all the faraway countries and all the seas of the world, and everyone and everything will hear its sonorous hum, even Mam, and be filled with wonder. And then I'll make a map of it all.

'How would you draw music on there?' I ask. 'So people can hear it when they look at the map?'

'Music people can hear,' says Tada. 'I'll have to think about that one, Gwenni. Anything else?'

'Mrs Evans,' I say.

Tada looks up from the map. 'You know more than you're saying about all that business, Gwenni.'

I do. Is Tada asking me to tell him? I can't tell anyone. Not even him.

'Well,' says Tada. He finishes his cigarette and flicks the stub into the fire. 'The place where Mrs Evans . . . lives is too far away to be on the map, Gwenni. But if we both remember her when we look at the map it'll be just the same as if she was on it.'

The place where Mrs Evans lives is a prison. Does it look like a castle with high walls and small windows?

'Pull your chair nearer,' says Tada. 'We'll both do this colouring or we won't finish in time for supper.'

We sit side by side, shading the mountains and the lowlands, the rivers and the seas, and the winding roads that lead anywhere you want to go. And I write the names of the places and the people where Tada has drawn them and blot the ink tidily with my rocker.

We both start when the back door rattles and Nain shouts, 'Yoo-hoo. Supper's ready.' And as she races into the living room, John Morris races out; he's afraid of Nain. She looks at what Tada and I are doing and says, 'How long did that take you? You should have asked Lol for her mapbook, Emlyn. You know she's got one. And she never uses it.' And she rushes out again, calling, 'Come for your food,' just before the back door bangs shut after her.

Tada and I look at our map. Aunty Lol's maps are nothing like this one. This map is beautiful, and when Tada works out how to write the Earth's hum into it, it will be perfect.

'Are you sure you don't fly, Tada?' I say.

'Only in my dreams, Gwenni,' he says.

But I'm not so sure.

ACKNOWLEDGEMENTS

Thank you, above all, to Glenn Strachan, and, for help ranging from expert advice to bad jokes, to: Lindsay Ashford, Heather Beck, Llio Evans, Richard Hollins, Adam Ifans, Rachel Ifans, David Llewelyn, Beverley Naidoo, Gladys Roberts, Orion Roberts, Anya Serota and all the lovely people at Canongate, Cai Strachan, Kate Strachan, Lavinia Trevor, and Barry Williams.

$\frac{7}{09}$